her perfect life

SAM HEPBURN

HARPER

Harper
An imprint of HarperCollins*Publishers*
1 London Bridge Street
London SE1 9GF

www.harpercollins.co.uk

Published by HarperCollins*Publishers* 2017
2

A catalogue record for this book
is available from the British Library

ISBN: 978-0-00-820958-2

This novel is entirely a work of fiction.
The names, characters and incidents portrayed in it are
the work of the author's imagination. Any resemblance to
actual persons, living or dead, events or localities is
entirely coincidental.

Typeset in Sabon by Palimpsest Book Production Ltd,
Falkirk, Stirlingshire

Printed and bound in Great Britain by
Clays Ltd, St Ives plc

MIX
Paper from
responsible sources
FSC™ C007454

FSC™ is a non-profit international organisation established to promote
the responsible management of the world's forests. Products carrying the
FSC label are independently certified to assure consumers that they come
from forests that are managed to meet the social, economic and
ecological needs of present and future generations,
and other controlled sources.

Find out more about HarperCollins and the environment at
www.harpercollins.co.uk/green

To James, Charlotte, Murdo and Lily

1

Hard heels clack across the floor above Juliet's head. One way across the sitting room to the window. Then back the other – clackety bloody clack – to the door. Juliet slides her legs off the sofa, blinking groggily into the gloom as she gazes from the pale flicker of the television to the timer on the cooker – 02.13.

She stretches to ease the crick in her neck and feels the first throb of a hangover behind her eyes. She checks the bottle on the floor beside her. It's empty. She searches the fridge and the cupboards, wincing at every stab of sound from upstairs – the judder of water into a kettle, the yank of a drawer and the endless clack of those bloody heels. She grabs hold of the broom, about to thump the handle on the ceiling. Then she laughs – not much of a laugh – and lets the broom drop. It's been a bad day but not bad enough to turn her into the mad old woman in the downstairs flat. At the back of the cupboard under the sink she finds a half-bottle of whisky. She doesn't usually drink spirits, just on nights like tonight, when it all gets too much. She pours half a glassful, fills it up with orange squash and takes it back to the sofa, lighting a cigarette as she goes. She reaches for the remote and flicks through the channels. An impossibly shaped blonde in silver lamé spins a roulette wheel – 'be lucky, lucky, luckeee . . .' – a cheese-ball preacher begs her to find a place in her heart for Jesus, a lizard darts its tongue to catch a fly and – fuck – there she is. Our perfect pocket-sized Gracie Dwyer. Clean, clean, clean in her perfect kitchen. She's leaning ever so slightly towards the camera, a *come-on-we-can-do-this together* smile on her lips while her nimble little fingers beat flour into a pan of yellow gloop on a spotless stone worktop. 'The trick to perfect choux pastry,' she is saying, 'is to keep beating until every fleck of white has gone from the mixture.'

Juliet tries for the off button but her clumsy fingers hit the pause. Gracie freezes on screen. She stares at the face. Always if you look long enough at a frozen frame you can find something – some imperfection: a spot, a patch of caked makeup at the hairline, a drag in the skin at the throat. If not that, then something gormless and off-guard in the eyes or in the halted movement of the mouth. Something.

But there's nothing. Nothing at all. Gracie Dwyer is perpetually perfect. Even frozen.

This time Juliet finds the off button. She stubs out her cigarette, lurching a little as she totters to her bedroom.

2

Gracie keeps count. She can't help it. She's doing it now. While the passengers around her sip their drinks and flick through the in-flight entertainment she's skimming the dates in her diary. It's been nearly five months – one hundred and forty-three days to be exact – since she's received an anonymous package, a taunting message or a silent phone call. She's hurrying on through the pages, adding to the 'to-dos' on her list and scoring through the tasks she's completed when a jolt of excitement puckers her cheeks into a smile, her first real smile for days. She's going home. No more dawn risings to go over her filming notes. No more missed calls from Tom. No more juggling shooting schedules and time zones to Skype Elsie at bedtime, only to wave at her and tell her silly jokes, when all she wants is to fill her lungs with the after-bath smell of her skin. She snaps the elastic around the diary, lays down her pen and gazes at the syrupy oval of sky framed by the cabin window, almost breathless at the thought of that small damp body pressed against hers.

But there is guilt there too, at how good it had felt to be in New York. To walk from her mid-town hotel to the TV studios, join a queue for coffee or test out a lipstick

3

untroubled by the glances of strangers or the scuff of a footfall catching up with her own. If the Americans buy her show is she crazy to think that at least in the States life could go back to the way it was before the threats began? When she enjoyed being recognised in the street, and jokey requests from passers-by to sign crisp packets, plaster casts and body parts made her laugh and reach for a Sharpie?

She folds forward rubbing her arms. Two weeks in New York have softened her, weakened her guard, but she feels it now, the wariness seeping back into her bones, stiffening her spine, vertebra by vertebra. How quickly it comes, she thinks, and a part of her accepts its return, welcomes it even; the part that still clings to the childhood belief that she can pay with pain to keep the precious things safe.

She glances up, drawn by the hiccupping wails of the baby across the aisle. He's a square-faced little boy in a tiny checked shirt and denim dungarees, writhing in his mother's arms and batting away the bottle she dabs at his mouth, just like Elsie did, all the way home from St Lucia that first summer she and Tom took her on holiday. Gracie remembers their helpless attempts to comfort her, the irritation of the other passengers and her own mounting fear that her mothering would never be good enough. The woman thrusts the baby and the bottle at her husband and stands up, smoothing her milk-stained T-shirt and wrinkled skirt. Gracie darts her a sympathetic smile. The woman is pregnant again, two, three months maybe; barely enough to show, but enough to draw her hands to the curve of her belly. The sight of those cupped, protective fingers loosens other memories. Gracie's thoughts skid and slide away to seek calm among her plans for the weekend: the park with Elsie, bed with Tom.

Her heart beats hard as she returns the glazed goodbyes of the cabin crew and passes from the warmth of the plane into the cool of the covered walkway. Not long now. Tom will be standing in the arrivals hall, holding Elsie's hand and pointing at the flashing 'landed' sign beside her flight number.

The baggage hall is busy, even for a Friday night. Fretful children traipse after ratty parents and hollow-eyed tourists grip their trollies and twist around looking lost. Gracie stands beside the carousel, head down, pretending to rummage in her handbag. The moment her suitcases bump into sight she sweeps them onto her trolley and runs.

'Gracie! Gracie Dwyer! Would you mind?'

Damn! Heads crane. She feels them. Taking a breath she stops and turns. A middle-aged woman is fluttering towards her in a pale blue mac, phone held high, while her tall, balding husband stands by, clenching apologetic hands. 'I love your show,' the woman says, breathy with delight. She tilts the handset and presses her powdered cheek to Gracie's as she clicks. 'Your lemon and walnut tart is the only way I can get my son to come home.'

'There'll be lots more puddings in the new series, so make sure you catch it.' Gracie's smile is warm.

The woman glows and says coyly, 'You know, you're even prettier in the flesh than on TV.'

'That's very sweet of you, but after six hours in the air I feel like a total wreck.'

With another smile Gracie breaks away and hurries through 'Nothing to Declare'.

The glass doors slide back. Her eyes flit across the waiting faces. A swell of joy as she spots them behind the barrier, jammed between a collection of bored drivers bearing name cards; Tom's dark head, bent to check something on his phone, and Elsie, her gorgeous girl, reaching out shouting, 'Mummy, Mummy!'

Gracie runs faster, letting her trolley roll away as she scoops Elsie into her arms and presses her nose into her hair. She lifts her face to Tom's, eager for the greedy pressure

5

of his lips. He's bending down, snatching Brown Bear from the floor, returning him to Elsie's outstretched hand and his kiss, when it comes, is almost lost in their exchange of eye-rolling relief at disaster averted.

Tom picks up her bags. She follows him to the car park, hand in hand with Elsie who jumps and skips, bursting with stories about school and sleepovers and other people's dogs. When the fuss with luggage and seat belts is over Tom sits and holds the wheel for a moment before he turns the ignition. She sees a tiny patch of stubble he's missed with the razor, six or seven coarse dark hairs standing upright and defiant on the curve of his jaw.

'You OK?' she murmurs.

'Yeah, fine.'

'You seem . . . tired.'

'Oh, you know.' He tilts the mirror and backs out of the space. 'So, how did it go?'

'The execs seemed happy enough. But in the end it's all down to the focus groups.'

'When will you hear?'

'Could be weeks, could be months. But if they *do* go for it why don't you bring Elsie over for the last week of the shoot? We could stay on for a few days, have a holiday.'

'Depends what I've got on.' He shoves the ticket into the machine. 'Things at work are a bit . . . up in the air.'

The car gives a little jerk as he accelerates up the ramp and out into the grey Heathrow dusk, blustery gusts of rain buffeting the car. She lays her hand on his shoulder. 'Pain about Bristow's.'

He rams the gearstick and pulls out into the traffic. 'If they want crap they've gone to the right place to get it.'

She twists round to catch Elsie's sleepy story about the *real* witch's cat she saw when she went trick or treating. 'He had a little pointy hat *and everything*.' Gracie looks back, seeking Tom's smile. The wet road holds all his attention. The raindrops on the windows glitter blue and green and red, brightening the darkness as he pulls off the M40 onto the rain-slicked streets of Hammersmith. The wipers thump and swipe across the windscreen. She murmurs softly, 'Was there anything . . . in the post?'

He shakes his head without looking at her. 'God, no.'

Gracie waits for him to acknowledge her relief, slide his hand through her hair and tell her how glad he is to have her home. But he's flicking on the news – Syria, Iraq, the economy. She tries not to mind. Losing the Bristow's tender will have hit him hard. All that work. All that build up. All that disappointment. Best to say nothing. They'll talk about it later. When they are alone and she can comfort him properly. A flicker of warmth curls between her thighs.

As Deptford gives way to Greenwich she stares out at the ghostly domes of the old admiralty buildings, the winking blur of pubs and cafés, the narrowing streets and the stretches of river glimpsed between blocks of newly built flats. He pulls off the road onto a cinder track that winds past shadowy building sites caged by wire fences, lit here and there by the jaundiced flare of security lights. The tyres splash and bump through puddles of oily water until they find tarmac again. Tom clicks the fob, the security gates slide open and the pale glow of their house of glass rises through the darkness.

Gracie swings her legs out of the car. Blinking into the rain she turns to gaze across the vast black shimmer of the river to the glitter of lights on the Isle of Dogs. There is a taint in the air, a reek of rot pouring in from the sewers of the city and seeping up through the silt. A squat river barge chugs downstream, its bow lights casting a gauzy glow across the water. As the slide of the electric gates cuts off the view she turns back to the Wharf House. Even after three years she still has moments like this when she can't quite believe that this minimalist expanse of glass and sunken spaces is her home. It took years to complete and won Tom a prize: a moment of glory and a shard of bronze sprouting through a block of granite. She remembers the first time he brought her to see the site; how she'd picked her way across the pipes and coils of cable lying idly in the mud, and nodded and smiled as he'd turned his back to the wind to steady the flapping plans, wishing she could lift her eyes to the skeleton of ribs and struts and see what he could see.

'Look, Mummy, look what I made!' Elsie is hopping from foot to foot, pointing to the 'Welcome home' banner strung across the door.

'Wow, darling! That's amazing!'

Tom lugs her bags across the hall and dumps them down while Elsie hovers close, pulling at the catches. 'What did you get me, Mummy?'

'Oh, no!' Gracie claps her hand to her mouth. 'I forgot to buy presents.'

Elsie howls with laughter and swings back on Gracie's free hand, pivoting on one foot. 'No you didn't!'

Gracie unzips one of the suitcases and pulls out a pair of pink sequined trainers. 'Ta – daa!' She smiles at the joy on Elsie's face, delves again and brings out a grey cashmere beanie hat for Tom that took her a stupid amount of time to choose. He pulls it on and wears it as they put Elsie to bed. They stretch out, one either side of her, while she hugs the trainers to her chest and Gracie opens *The Worst Witch*, picking up the story where she left off the night she left for New York. After a couple of pages Tom kisses his daughter and slips away, murmuring about supper. Hungry for one of his blackened, bloody steaks and some good red wine, Gracie smiles and glances up to watch him go.

She reads on until Elsie's eyes flutter shut and her breath

grows deep and steady, then she sits for a moment, drinking her in; the dark curls coiling across the pillow, the golden skin, the snubby little nose and chin – softened versions of Tom's – before she kisses her forehead and runs down to the kitchen.

The absence hits her.

No clinking plates. No hissing pans.

So it's a takeaway then. Their favourite Thai, or the new Burmese she's been dying to try. Tom fills a glass and passes it to her. She sets it down beside the discarded beanie hat and moves closer, hips swaying, arms held high to slip around his neck. He stiffens, sweaty and grey, his pupils fixed, unwilling to focus even as he looks at her.

'Tom?'

He pulls away and picks up a paper tub, still icy from the freezer. She moves forward, her eyes seeking the label on the lid. A little laugh erupts from her throat. *Laugh with me, Tom. Tell me you love my fish pie. Tell me you didn't want to waste time cooking on my first night back.*

He clicks open the microwave and in it goes. Her homecoming supper.

'I'll make a salad.' She bends into the fridge, little detonations of panic exploding down her spine.

Behind her he's opening drawers, rattling cutlery, making noises that float in the silence. Thoughts stream across her mind like a band of breaking news: robberies, accidents, death, disaster. But how bad can it be? Elsie is tucked up in bed and the two of them are here, safe, together. Refusing to acknowledge the darker possibilities unfurling in her brain she tears at leaves, makes a dressing, picks up the servers.

The microwave pings.

'It'll need a few minutes in the oven to get crispy,' she says.

He doesn't move. She gives it a beat and says quietly, 'Are you going to tell me what's wrong?'

9

He stands looking at the floor, gesturing helplessly with his hands. 'You have to believe me, Gracie. I never meant it to happen.'

She pushes at the rising dread. 'Just tell me. Whatever it is we'll deal with it.'

He drops into one of the narrow steel-backed chairs he designed himself, his head down, his fingers pressing into his scalp; long, sensitive, blunt-nailed fingers that wear the slim platinum band that matches hers. She reaches for the moment when she slipped it over his knuckle, the pride and nervousness she'd felt as everyone they cared about looked on. *Please, God, let it be a problem with money or work. Something that can be borne, or fixed, or forgotten.*

'I swear I didn't plan it. I hardly know her.'

'*Her?*' The word spurts like vomit through her teeth. She knows then that this is beyond fixing or forgetting.

'We'd just lost the tender. I was drunk. We all were.'

She pictures the women she meets at ACP functions: attractive, smartly dressed women who smile at her and remember her name when she struggles to remember theirs, an eternity passing before she manages to whisper, 'Who?'

'One of the interns.' Tom clenches his fists. 'Oh God, I'm so sorry. I was in a bad way. You know how much I had riding on that job.'

All that fear, Gracie thinks. All that pain. It wasn't enough to keep the precious things safe.

'So you thought, oh, I know, I'll fuck a twenty year old. That'll cheer me up.'

'No!' His head hangs on his chest. 'I lost it. I wanted to pass out, forget everything. Then someone called me a cab and suddenly there she was, telling me she'd always wanted to see the house.'

She backs away, her head shaking slowly. 'Not here, Tom. Please don't tell me you slept with her here.'

10

His hunched silence rips something inside her and all the quiet confidence she has built up over the years of her marriage comes spilling through the tear. She slithers down the wall, crushed by the realisation, stark and sudden, that the barrier between having everything and having nothing is as flimsy as a rejected blueprint.

'Where was Elsie?'

'Issy's sleepover.'

That pinpoints the night. Gracie sees herself finishing up at the studios and rushing off to eat sushi with the crew. Sipping sake, discussing the next day's running order, catching a cab back to her hotel room. Sleeping alone. She raises her head. 'Is she beautiful?'

'What?'

'I said, is she beautiful?'

'No! God, no.' He says it vehemently, as if somehow this will exonerate him. 'It wasn't about that.'

She looks around her at her home, her life, her husband. All she sees is a tumble of rubble. 'So what *was* it about, Tom?'

'I don't know.' He presses his palms against the bevelled edge of the table and sinks his head towards the green of the glass. 'I felt empty, angry. I couldn't face being on my own.'

'Don't you dare put this on me. Don't you dare!'

'I'm not . . .' He throws back his head and drags in air. 'When I sobered up I couldn't believe what I'd done. I told her it was a mistake and she went crazy. She . . . threatened me. She said she'd tell you and the board if I didn't let her work on one of my projects.'

'So did you?'

He swallows. 'The Copenhagen clinic. But I won't have to see her. I put her with the team working on the atrium and I've handed that side of things over to Geoff.'

11

As if this is penance enough, he kneels down and reaches for her. Her hands fly out, pushing him away, startling them both with her strength. 'You'd never have done this to Louise!'

He jolts at the accusation, a shock response as if he's been struck. She can see he's steeled himself for fury, tears, distress. But not for this. She doesn't care. He searches for words to deny it but the effort breaks him down into sobs. 'It's not about Louise.'

'I've never been enough for you.' She shunts away from him, pushing her heels against the slate floor. 'I was always second best.'

He crawls towards her, appalled, dumbfounded. 'No! You're you and Louise . . . was Louise.'

She turns her head away, trying to hide her tears, but her fingers clutch her top, clawing the thin fabric in an effort to gain control. 'And what about this bloody intern?'

'She's nothing.'

'So you were willing to risk everything we have for some scheming little nothing?'

'Christ, Gracie, what do you want me to say? I was drunk . . . I feel like shit . . .'

'So that's it? You got laid and she got a plus point on her CV?'

He drops his head and scrapes his hand down his face. 'It wasn't just about getting on a project. She'd got it into her head that she and I had . . . some kind of future . . . and now she's lashing out.'

'What do you mean?'

'She's threatening to make a formal complaint.' He closes his eyes. 'To tell the board and the press a pack of lies about me offering her work, pretending I was going to leave you . . . getting her drunk and fuck knows what else.'

Gracie waits until he looks at her. She stares into his

eyes. Dark brown eyes, that shift and dither. There's a screeching in her head, a feeling of weightlessness.

'That's what this confession is about, isn't it? Damage limitation!'

'No!'

She throws back her head. 'If you'd managed to buy her silence, you'd never have told me.'

'Gracie—'

She glares at him, daring him to lie.

'I'll do anything to make it up to you.'

At least he hasn't denied his cowardice. But the angle of his head and the tilt of his shoulders trigger a creep of suspicion. 'How many others, Tom?'

'Christ!' He turns away, furious. 'How can you even ask?'

In that moment she sees a stranger. A lean-faced, dark-haired stranger in a black T-shirt and expensive jeans who has no idea that he has broken something he can't mend; something precious that was hers and Elsie's, as well as his. Can't he see that this drunken fuck with a pushy intern nearly half his age has made a rupture in their lives – clean, complete and total – with everything that has gone before?

'What's her name?'

'Does it matter?'

'Yes.'

'Alicia.'

'Alicia what?'

'Sandelson.'

She struggles to her feet. He moves towards her.

'Don't come near me!'

He lifts his hands and watches her leave.

3

That night Tom sleeps in the spare room and Gracie lies awake, listening to the drum of the rain and picturing Alicia touching her things, lying between her sheets, pushing her face into her pillow and she wonders how she will survive. Yet when she tries to imagine a life other than this one she has built with Tom all she sees is a vast emptiness devoid of joy or comfort or hope. This is the way she had felt in the bleak, lonely months before she met him, the way she'd thought she would never have to feel again. She reaches for her mobile then lets it drop. Daphne is in Milan, probably in bed with her latest lover, and even if she picked up what would Gracie say? What's happening inside her is too frightening, too visceral to explain, even to her closest friend.

She slips out of bed and tiptoes downstairs, past the photographs that hang on the open brickwork. Stark looming images, shot by Louise, charting the first stages of the creation of the house. Gracie thought she knew them, every line and shadow; the demolition of the old wharf, the bulldozers arriving in a scarred expanse of moss-grown debris, spindly saplings thrust into the wind, the writhing tree root washed up by the tide, dead but for one determined shoot of green. But tonight, in the dim light of the lamp left on for Elsie, they seem alive, taunting her with renewed power and vigour; her own face, puffy with crying, a wavery distraction in the glass. Her eyes fasten on the photo of the tree root. Taken the day Louise found the plot of land, the shot has been reprinted on a thousand posters and postcards, variously interpreted as an image of hope, regeneration and a dogged refusal to die. The *Observer* magazine used it in their memorial tribute to Louise's work, along with the most haunting of the worn faces and desolate landscapes she'd taken for them in Bosnia, Albania and Darfur. Gracie's legs buckle. She reaches for the wall, imagining Alicia pausing here on her way to the bedroom, halted by this picture. Did Tom stand behind her, holding her shoulders, kissing her neck as he'd once kissed Gracie's when she'd stopped, drawn by this same photograph, in the hallway of his flat in Holloway?

She pulls away and stumbles down to the kitchen. She feels the cool slate beneath her feet, sees the pearly shadows of the raindrops speckling the white of the walls and the square of sky above the light well, all realised exactly as Louise had envisaged them, the DNA of her vision imprinted not just in the design and structure of this house but in the subtle ageing of the wood, the ever changing reflections in the angled glass and the long slow weathering of the stone.

Gracie sits in the dark for nearly an hour before she drags herself back to bed. She closes her eyes, too tired to fight it now. Cogs uncouple in her head, dismantling her defences, and she sleeps. For a while she hovers in a restless dark. And then it begins. The dreadful pitch into a ruined landscape where she runs and runs from someone she can't see until the way is blocked by an iron gate fastened by a padlock and chain. Forced on by a brush of breath on her neck she swerves away, stumbling through the doors of a blackened warehouse and spiralling down a stone staircase until she senses a flutter of movement in the shadows and trips and falls like dreamers do, to wake with a buck of panic, struggling to scream. She reaches for Tom. Her bed is empty. He is not there to turn in his sleep, pull her to him and murmur that she is safe.

She rises and moves around the house, tormented by reminders of the contentment she has lost – a snapshot of the three of them stuck on the fridge, their joint names on a school permission form, their shirts and socks entangled in the dryer, all cruelly untouched by the savage unravelling of her grief. She takes down the snapshot and gazes at the faces – hers, Tom's and Elsie's – trying to envision a future untainted by the fear of losing everything she loves.

Over the next few days Tom gives her time, something he's been careless about for a while. He talks animatedly about the layout of her next cookery book and her plans to open a second branch of her café bakery, sending her details of properties he's found on the internet. She feels his helplessness – the tightened lips and weary exhalations signalling his irritation. He wants things back the way they were, yet he has no idea how to make it happen. She is the one who always smooths out the problems, the one who mends the broken things. But she can't mend this. Right now she can't even think straight. Using the search for new premises as an excuse to detach herself from the rhythms and demands of her own life, she spends hour after hour driving through the streets of London, losing herself in the everyday comings and goings of others. Somehow, catching the swish of a curtain or the slam of a front door, slowing her car in an unfamiliar side road to accommodate someone else's drop-off or pick-up or hurried trip to the corner shop, helps to soothe the turmoil in her head and dilute the fear and anger corroding every cell of her being.

In the evenings she and Tom avoid all mention of Alicia and her threats, although once when Tom thinks she's downstairs, she hears him on the phone.

'It's the powerlessness, Geoff, not knowing if the little bitch is bluffing . . . Christ, I don't know how much longer I can take it . . .'

There he is, the father of her child, contrite and attentive as they arrive at the launch of her new cookbook, smiling as she mentions him in the speech she wrote before she went to New York and hasn't had the heart to change. She even reads out the line where she thanks him for just being there because she couldn't do any of the things she does without his love and support. His smile doesn't falter when every face in the room swings round to see the husband of 'adorable queen of the kitchen', Gracie Dwyer; a hundred pairs of eyes taking in his appealing long-limbed slouch, the rumpled hair, the open-necked shirt gleaming white against skin the colour of perfect toast. She can almost hear the sighs of approval. Afterwards she bears it stiffly as they pose for the photographers – the beautiful couple with the happy wholesome life – he with one hand pulling her close, the other holding up a copy of her book. *This is the shot they'll use*, she thinks as the lights flash. *If the intern goes to the papers, this is the picture they'll plaster all over the tabloids.*

In the taxi home she sits forward, hanging onto the strap to stop anything of her body brushing Tom's, but there's hope in his eyes as they walk into the house, as if the pretence of tonight has become reality. She stops the hand he lifts to caress her cheek, moves it aside and hurries to the kitchen to fill the kettle. 'Tea?'

'No thanks.' Tom pours himself a whisky and sprawls in

a chair a little drunk, grunting as he picks up the papers on the table. He takes a moment to register that they're property brochures: pubs, restaurants, shops. He flips through them. 'Christ, have you seen the rents on these places?'

'You can throw them away. I've found somewhere.'

He looks up, hurt. 'You never said.'

She stirs the teapot, staring into the steam.

'Are you going to show me?'

She doesn't respond.

'Come on, Gracie.'

She opens her handbag. Hesitates for a moment then hands him a folded sheet. He shakes open the details of a seventies pub in Battersea – stained red brick, peeling green paintwork and tinted glass. 'You're kidding. It's ugly, over-priced and way too big.'

'I need space.'

'Not this much.'

Gracie eyes him uneasily. 'It's going to be more than a café bakery. I'm going to have a cook shop, serve a bistro menu in the evenings and run cookery workshops upstairs. Kelvin's developing a spin-off series built around the courses.'

'When did you come up with all this?' That hurt face again.

'I've been doing a lot of thinking since I've been back from the States.'

'And what? You weren't even going to consult me?' He flings the brochure across the table. 'This is what I do, Gracie! What I know about!' He swallows and softens his voice. 'You need a building with character, something distinctive that will reflect *you* as well as your food, like the amazing old chapel this new French client wants me to convert into a restaurant. Why don't you come and have a look at it, get some inspiration?'

Her eyes dart away from him.

'Don't do this, Gracie. Don't shut me out.'

A silence grows between them, barely dented by her agonised whisper. 'How can I make any plans that depend on you?'

'Fuck!' He mouths the word, and claws back his hair. 'So what are you saying? That I'm not part of your future?'

'I don't know, Tom. Sometimes I look at you and I catch myself seeing the man I love, then I realise he doesn't exist.'

'What can I do? Just tell me what I can do.'

'Why are you asking *me*? I didn't make this mess.' She puts down her mug and moves to the door. 'I'm going to bed.'

'Gracie, please—' He lurches after her.

She turns on the landing. 'Shh. You'll wake Elsie.'

He lowers his voice. 'The new café is something we can build together. You and me.'

'You destroyed what we built together, Tom. Have you even thought what it will do to Elsie when that girl's tacky revelations are splashed all over the papers? She's five years old for God's sake! And what about me? I can cope with the sniggering and the pity but every single penny I put into paying off the crippling mortgage on this house depends on the way people see me – happy, wholesome Gracie. How's that going to work when they find out my husband can't keep his dick in his pants?' She closes the bedroom door and leans against the wall, biting back her tears as his footsteps fade away down the landing.

4

'OK, Gracie. Let's go again. Just hold the bowl a bit higher when you show us the chillies.'

She pouts for Emma's waving wand of lip-gloss and swings into action. *This is how I get through this*, Gracie thinks while her hands move deftly over the bowls and pans on the countertop. *I chop and dice and stir for the cameras and pretend that everything is fine, that I sleep at night, that this suffocating sense of loss is something I can bear.*

The running order is full – black noodles with prawns, then her super quick fig and blueberry tarts, a chat on the sofa with specialist herb grower Akshay Kumar, tips for healthy packed lunches that kids will actually eat and, for the leftovers slot, her new garden pie, adapted from a family recipe sent in by a viewer. She spears a prawn, bites through the spicy pink flesh and smiles at the camera.

'Cut!' The floor manager gives her a thumbs-up, calls a ten-minute break and stands back to let a flurry of assistants swoop in to reset the counter. Emma hands her a mug of coffee. 'You all right?'

'Bit tired.' Gracie slips off to the loo and locks herself in a cubicle. She presses her forehead against the tiles and spends the first five minutes of the break sobbing quietly, imagining the worst, the second five patching up her makeup and assuring herself that the worst can't happen. She won't let it. She twists a strand of hair back into the soft knot on top of her head, flicks her fingers through her fringe and gives her cheeks a savage prod. She's nearly thirty-six for heaven's sake and her face still has an open, almost childlike quality which she tempers for the cameras with sweeps of black eyeliner and slashes of crimson lipstick. Her height doesn't help. At five foot four she's used to people blinking when they meet her. 'Gosh, you look so much taller on TV.'

So different from Louise's fair, willowy elegance and the pert freckled features of that scheming little cow Alicia Sandelson. She rocks forward, closing her eyes. Like a fool she'd looked Alicia up on Facebook and now that hiss of a girl has a face – a milk-skinned, pink-lipped, heart-shaped face with a halo of pale curls. She's smart too – Oxford and an internship at ACP. But it's not the endless posts charting her glittering time at university or the photos of her partying in skinny jeans and halter tops that flicker through Gracie's head on an unstoppable loop, it's the shot of her lying on a beach in a white bikini. Not because Alicia looks particularly pretty in it. She doesn't. And not because her body is anything special, it's angular and streaked with sunburn across the chest and shoulders. It's the unshakeable self-confidence in her eyes that spreads hurt through Gracie's body. This is a girl who has no fear of failure, a twenty-two year old who functions without doubt.

She pictures Alicia sitting up pale and freckled against her own freshly laundered pillows, those small nubby breasts flushing pink with indignation as she threatens to tell the world that Gracie Dwyer's husband lured her into bed with promises of future employment and long-term emotional commitment.

21

She appears back on set, moving stiffly across the studio floor as if she's carrying a brimming pan. She reaches the safety of the counter and focuses on the flour drifting through her fingers, ghosting the sides of the glass bowl. *This is how I survive.* She pricks and peels and slices and sprinkles and listens to the light-hearted voice that flows from her lips extolling the virtues of unsalted butter and unbleached flour. But her heart is not light. Not light at all and her mind is spinning and spinning and spinning.

She smiles for Akshay Kumar, rattles off the link to her filmed discussion with a class of face-pulling six year olds about the yuckiness of squidgy bananas and soggy sandwiches, keeps her voice upbeat as she guides the viewers through a selection of stuffed pitas, cold pastas and gaily filled wraps, and gets serious about waste as she slices cold carrots for the garden pie. When the floor manager signals that the gallery is happy she calls a hurried thank you to the crew and leaves without stopping to check in with the production team or even to wipe off her makeup.

5

Juliet needs this job. God, how she needs it. A fledgling brand with a sure fire future doesn't come her way very often. But get this meeting right and the marketing contract for Shoesmith and Hayman's artisan gin could turn her life around.

'In the end, it all comes down to the botanicals.' Don Shoesmith – bland and fortyish – gazes at the bottle in his hands as if it's some kind of holy relic. 'What the judges went for was our unique blend of natural flavourings.'

Juliet, who has spent the previous night mugging up on the terminology, nods knowledgably. Don's on side, eager to sign her up and get back to sourcing his orris root and organic Sicilian lemons. It's Matt Hayman, his partner, who's not so sure. He's rocking back in his chair, assessing her. He's younger than Don, but not by much. Two middle-aged engineers in badly designed promotional sweatshirts, swept way out their depth by the rip tide success of their backyard distillery. Their 'office', a hastily assembled table and chairs at the end of Don's garage, is proof of that – boxes of papers and cases of bottles vying for space among tins of paint, coiled extension leads and a dusty deflated paddling pool.

Juliet turns her head and aims unblinking eyes at Matt. He's a worrier, so terrified about paying the mortgage now that he's jacked in the nine to five he daren't make a decision. She stokes up his insecurities. 'There's no point having a great product and winning awards if you don't get the marketing right. When are they making the announcement?'

'Friday.'

She sucks her breath. 'Four days to create a social media campaign to capitalise on the publicity *and* get a strategy in place to keep up the momentum. It's going to be tight. Do-able but tight.'

He's visibly twitching, desperate for reassurance. Time to throw him a lifeline. 'The first thing I'd have to do is fix your website. Sorry, but it's sending out totally the wrong message.' Brisk professional smile. 'From now on everything associated with your brand has to be as crisp and distinctive as your product.' Juliet taps her computer and brings up the home page she's mocked up for them. 'I could have this online for you by Wednesday night.'

Matt thumps forward on his chair and runs an eye across the screen, obviously impressed but still hesitant. What's his problem?

'My wife's got a friend at one of the big agencies. She says they can offer us a complete PR and marketing package.'

So that's it. *Well fuck you Mrs Hayman.* A sympathetic shake of her head. 'We both know the big agencies are all about processes, systems and top-heavy teams. Fine for big corporate clients but totally wrong for a niche start-up like yours. What you need is the personal touch. Someone who's always going to be available when you pick up the phone. Someone flexible who can move swiftly to deal with the tiny problems that crop up day to day leaving *you*,' she flicks a finger at Matt's peeking polo shirt collar, 'to concentrate on the product. All for a fraction of the price the big boys charge.'

Matt knocks his knuckles against his chin, almost hooked. She pictures him relaying these lines to his pushy wife, asserting himself as the thrusting entrepreneur who knows what's right for his business and his brand.

'And with me you get a single vision developing the strategic and creative solutions as well as planning and executing the campaign.'

'And you could handle all that?'

'Absolutely.' He's nodding now, clinging to every word. 'Obviously as I helped your business to grow I'd expand my team but it would always be me overseeing the decisions. Now, let me show you the thoughts I've had about product placement.'

Her phone buzzes in her pocket. 'Excuse me.' She pulls it out. Thumb poised to decline the call she glances at the ID.

Nononono. Not now.

A flare of resentment burns hot and bright, dipping to a flicker in the sudden rush of panic.

She looks at Matt. He's twitching again. 'Sorry.' She presses the phone to her ear, rising on wobbly legs as the words *Freya, climbing frame, fall,* pulse to the frantic beat of her heart. 'She got a nasty bump on the head,' the school nurse is saying, 'the ambulance is on its way.'

Face numb, fingers cold, she's throwing her laptop into her bag, barely able to breathe. 'My daughter . . . I have to go.' She turns at the door and says desperately, 'Could we pick this up tonight? Maybe on Skype? I promise . . . this won't happen again.'

It's a lost cause. The look of abandonment on Matt's face and the bitter taste of defeat at the back of her throat tell her that.

6

Gracie steps out of the shower and emerges from the bathroom to find Tom in their bedroom rooting through his sock drawer.

'Tea,' he says, pointing to the tray beside the bed.

'Thanks.'

He watches as she lifts first one foot then the other onto the bed to smooth cream onto her legs. 'Here.' He tosses a brochure across the duvet.

She glances down at the photo of a slate-roofed chapel, its scarred walls defaced with graffiti and peeling posters.

'What's this?'

'The place I was telling you about. That French guy, Mersaud, he's pulled out. It could be ours, Gracie.' His eyes come back to hers, narrowed and hopeful. 'It's ideal for the new café and there's masses of space for a cook shop *and* your cookery school.'

She tightens her towel across her chest. 'It's a ruin.'

'Which is why the agent thinks we could get the price right down. I could do something really interesting with it – look at those fantastic windows. It's exactly the kind of place you should go for.'

'You mean it's exactly the kind of conversion you like working on.'

'That's not fair.' His voice is scratchy with hurt.

She wipes her fingers on the towel and turns the page. 'E5? That's—'

'Clapton.'

'*Clapton?* That's miles from anywhere.'

'Twenty minutes from our old flat. In five years' time it will be on a par with Hoxton.'

'I'm tired of schlepping across London every day, wasting time I could be spending with Elsie.'

'This has got to be a business decision. I've sent you the stats Mersaud had done. That whole area is perfect territory for an upmarket food retailer.'

'So why did he pull out?'

'I don't know. And now he's stopped returning my emails. God knows what he's playing at.'

'That's odd.'

'Yep. He hadn't actually signed anything, but he was messaging me all last week telling me how excited he was about meeting me and how my vision was exactly what he was looking for.'

'Maybe he realised how much it was going to cost.'

'It's an investment, Gracie. I've sent you a couple of the preliminary sketches I did for him.'

She sighs. 'I'll look at them later.'

He pulls open the wardrobe and fingers a row of ties. 'Blue or pink with this shirt?'

She can't bring herself to answer. Aware of his eyes on her, she sifts through the letters he's brought up on the tray and rips open a plain white envelope. She tips the contents into her hand. 'Oh, no . . . please God, no.'

A coral earring lies in her palm. A single teardrop of

polished rust-coloured stone. Beside it a slip of paper printed with two words:

```
Hello Gracie.
```

She recoils as if she's been burned and hurls the earring, the note and the envelope onto the floor. 'The bastard,' she sobs. 'The bastard!'

Pauline Bryce Diary
January 1st

It's the same every morning, I open my eyes, see the zig-zag crack in the ceiling and the brown stain round the window and I feel sick inside. But today it's like I'm suffocating. I roll over, see the date on my alarm clock and realise why. I can't take another year of this. I just can't. So I go downstairs and ask Mum for a loan, not much, just a few hundred pounds to get me to London and keep me going till I find a job. She won't even listen, keeps saying she doesn't have that kind of money – which is a lie. Then Ron piles in with his 'stick with college, young lady, get your qualifications', blah blah. No point telling him there's another world out there. If I get a job in London – property, advertising, something like that – I won't need qualifications. I can work my way up. And when I start my own business I won't have to put up with Ron Bryce or anyone else telling me what to do. Robson's as bad. All that fuss about a few packs of Silk Cut and a copy of OK!. I'd go mad without my mags. So now I just run a razor blade down the pages I want and shove them down the lining of my coat. It's not enough though. I need the real thing. Sitting up here in this shitty little room, reading about other people's houses, cars and lives – it's killing me. Screwing me up so tight I'm just about ready to snap.

7

Gracie stares down at the torn envelope as Tom pokes it with his socked toe. It's half the size of the stalker's usual brown jiffy bags. The typeface on the note and the address is different too. 'It's been nearly six months,' she says, her voice small and bitter. 'I was actually beginning to convince myself he'd stopped.'

'When did you last see those earrings?' He's gone into calm mode, taking control.

She lifts her head. 'The day before I went to the States. I wore them for *The Times* photo shoot.' She runs to the wardrobe and digs wildly through her jewellery box. 'The other one's gone too.'

'You probably left them at the studio.'

'They're the ones you got me in Florence.' She pulls at her earlobe, frowning, uncertainly. 'I'm sure I'd have noticed if I'd left without them.'

'Anything else missing?'

'I . . . I don't think so.'

'Do you want me to call Reeves?'

'I'll do it.'

They both know the drill. He runs downstairs to fetch

a freezer bag from the kitchen and Gracie uses her eyebrow tweezers to drop the envelope, the note and the earring inside. She's closing the zip seal – a trembling pinch and slide of her fingers – when her head begins to shake. 'I don't understand . . . why the change of packaging? It's like . . . like it's not him.'

His gaze sharpens though his words come slowly. 'Maybe it's a copycat. Someone playing a sick joke.'

'Oh, great! So now there's two crazies out there who hate me. And why now?' Gracie's eyes slide away, her hand rising to her mouth. 'Oh, God . . . that *girl*!'

'No. No way.' He's shaking his head, but the movement seems strained, mechanical.

'She had a motive.' Gracie grimaces. '*And* an opportunity.'

'She wouldn't. Not something like this, it's . . . it's not her style. It'll be someone at that shoot. Or one of the nannies Heather's had round.'

'If there's even a chance it was her we *have* to tell the police.' Her face crumples. 'And we'll just have to pray they don't leak it to the papers.'

'But they will. They always do.' His hands chop air. 'We can't risk it, not when I'm certain she didn't do it and when there's still a chance she'll keep quiet. It'll just mean having our private lives dragged through the press for nothing.'

'So what do we do, Tom?'

'I'll talk to her. Geoff sent her off on a course but I'll do it as soon as she's back in the office.'

He's taking care not to look at her. She's taking equal care not to raise her voice.

'What do I say to Reeves?'

He moves to the window. Outside a seagull hovers on the wind, beak parted, wings outspread before it dives for a scrap of flotsam bobbing on the tide. 'Just tell him she came round to look at the house. At least until I've spoken to her.' He swings round. 'If I think there's the slightest possibility she was involved I swear I'll tell him everything.'

She sees the face she once trusted through a blur of tears, unsure if he's trying to protect her, himself or that scheming little intern.

'Don't cry, Mummy!'

Elsie scampers across the room in a ladybird onesie and catapults herself onto their bed. Gracie hurries to dab her eyes with the corner of the towel. Elsie wriggles between them and inspects their faces with disapproval. Pursing her lips she taps each of them with a finger and says in her small husky voice, 'Mummy, Daddy, one two,' ticking off the immutable constants in her life, the load-bearing struts that can never be allowed to weaken or give way. Gracie squeezes her eyes tight shut but the tears keep coming. Tom tries to enfold them in his arms, his wife and his child. Gracie flinches away, his attempt at a moment of healing marred for her by the fleecy touch of Elsie's onesie, bought for the bug-themed sleepover that left their home clear for his betrayal.

Gracie doesn't want to look at the bulging Ziploc bag on the duvet. She stares instead at her mobile and inhales the smell of coffee. Music from the radio drifts up the stairs. Tom opening a door, calling to Elsie, *Do you want a boiled egg?* Knowing she has to do this, she makes the call.

'Inspector Reeves, please.'

'Inspector Reeves is on secondment.'

She bites her lip, overwhelmed by a shiver of abandonment. 'How . . . how long for?'

'Eighteen months. What is the nature of your call?'

'It's about . . . an existing case.'

'Name?'

Gracie hesitates. 'Dwyer. Grace.'

The familiar pause. Just a fraction of a second as the operator registers who she is. 'Putting you through to Inspector Jamieson. One moment, please.'

8

Mark Jamieson has a look of a bull terrier – prematurely white-haired, hard-muscled and pinkish around the eyes. He gives the kitchen an openly curious glance as he sits down, appraising Gracie's pans and knives and the layout of her workspace. She thinks fondly of Reeves's paunchy bulk and good-natured contempt for what she does. *Cooking? I leave all that to the wife.*

Jamieson accepts a cup of coffee, asks awkwardly about the blend of beans and lines up a biro beside the folder he's taken from his briefcase. 'I had a look at the case file before I came out, Ms Dwyer, and I'd like to apologise for the press leaks.' He hands her his card. 'I'll do my best to see it doesn't happen on my watch. But unless it's an absolute emergency it might be best if you contact me direct on my mobile.'

She nods and pushes a jar of cookies across the table. Jamieson selects a square of pecan shortbread. 'Thank you.' He takes a bite, unable to disguise the kick he's getting out of eating biscuits baked by Gracie Dwyer. Gracie doesn't let on that these were made by Elsie's nanny.

'Is that the package?'

She slides the Ziploc bag towards him. 'The font and the envelope are different,' Gracie says. Her eyelids flutter shut. 'My husband thinks it might be a copycat.'

'It does happen. Idiots after a taste of publicity.' Jamieson scans his notes, his fingers beating a rhythm on the side of his coffee mug. 'Is there anything to link this earring to any of the other items that were sent to you?'

She flinches as he names them one by one: the lipstick she'd mislaid, the scrap of silk from a favourite scarf she'd hung briefly in a restaurant cloakroom, the clasp from one of her handbags, the lid of the fountain pen she'd had since she was at school. Fragments of her life transformed into threats: *If I can get close enough to steal this, I can get close enough to touch you, to punish you, to kill you.*

'Only that it was mine.'

'You last wore these earrings at a photo shoot on the tenth?'

'Yes.'

'And you're sure you had them on when you walked through that door?' He points his biro towards the hall.

'Not *one hundred* per cent, but I'm usually pretty good about not leaving things behind.'

'Did you go out that evening?'

'No. I was packing for New York.'

'Any more notes, phone calls or unwelcome cyber contact since you last spoke to Reeves?'

She shakes her head. He fixes her with his pale probing eyes. 'I'm sure you know that this type of harassment is typical of someone who thinks you've humiliated them in some way or treated them unfairly. The trigger can be the smallest of slights or even something imagined, but it's very real to them.'

'Yes,' she says. *Why is he talking to me as if he's reading from a charge sheet?*

'Can you think of anyone who might bear you a grudge? Someone from your past who might resent your success?'

Gracie wants to scream. She's been over this a hundred times with Reeves, starting the morning she got the first note. Four words, printed on pristine white paper in the typeface she's come to loathe.

You deserve to die.

How could anyone read a message like that and not search their past for an unpunished crime: a casual cruelty inflicted in a long-forgotten playground, the spurning of a lover, the blunt rejection of a grating, over-eager job applicant? She is guilty, she knows, of all these sins and more. Which is why the word *deserve* stays with her. Not you *will* die or you *must* die but you *deserve* to die as if, as those latex-gloved fingers typed the words and folded the note into the envelope, they were acting as agents of justice, disclosing a truth which Gracie's own conscience was refusing to accept.

'I can't think of anyone I've hurt deliberately but there's obviously someone out there who thinks otherwise.'

'Anyone you've had problems with recently?'

I could shout it out, she thinks. Tell him everything: *Yes, Inspector, there's a girl my husband slept with who wants to destroy my marriage.* But that's not the line that she and Tom have agreed. She hunches forward, sliding her hands between her knees like a nervous child. 'No.'

That look again, as if she is a specimen in a jar. 'Anyone who's come back into your life after a prolonged absence?'

'Not that I can think of.'

He studies the file. 'I see from the notes that these packages began soon after you moved into this house, then suddenly stopped about six months ago.'

'Yes.'

'Reeves thought the lull could be due to the culprit going to prison for another crime.'

He doesn't volunteer what kind of crime Reeves thought that might be and Gracie, probably sensibly, doesn't ask. He says hurriedly, 'Personally, I think he's wrong. Apart from this fixation with you I think your stalker probably behaves like a normal, law-abiding citizen.'

'Why do you think that?'

'Just a gut feeling, Ms Dwyer.'

Gracie's fingers pull at the edge of her shirt. 'What else does your gut tell you?'

'Given the objects they pick, I think it could well be a woman, or a man and a woman working together.'

'So why would they suddenly stop?'

'Maybe they didn't.'

'What do you mean?'

'Not making contact for a while might be part of the power game. A ploy to keep you on edge, not knowing when, or if, it's all going to start up again. Likewise the switch in packaging – trying to keep you guessing. I've seen this kind of thing before, stalkers who suddenly change their tactics to deny their target any sort of certainty. Now, have you got those names for me?'

Gracie fetches a printout from the countertop. She points to the two neatly typed lists and says in a small voice, 'These are the people who were at the shoot and these are the ones who came to the house. I've marked everybody who's been interviewed before.'

He raises an eyebrow, impressed by her efficiency. Gracie carries her mug to the sink and looks out across the river as she rinses away the coffee dregs. 'They're mostly other nannies that Heather's had round after school.'

'Heather . . . that's your nanny, Heather Patterson?'

'She's been with us for three years. She's totally trust-worthy.'

'And your husband?'

'My husband?' *No, Inspector. My husband is not trust-worthy.*

'Did he have people round while you were away?'

'A few from his work.' Gracie's chest tightens as she bends to stack the mug in the dishwasher. 'He's an architect.'

'Alicia Sandelson, is she a nanny?'

'No. She's one of Tom's interns.' The pressure on her chest grows unbearable, as if a giant hand is trying to flatten her. 'She came to photograph the house. People do, especially students.'

'All right, we'll contact everyone on this list and I'll get the earring and the envelope analysed but if they're as clean as the other packages I can't see us getting very far.' He lifts the makeshift evidence bag between his thumb and forefinger and lets it sway. 'It's important that you stay vigilant. As I say, the culprit is probably the last person you'd expect to be capable of doing something like this.'

Gracie gazes out at the rain-puddled terrace, with its stone planters and tidy islands of paving and pebbles, her eyes drawn to an ugly little figurine that Louise brought back from a trip to Borneo. Its head is far too big for its clumsily dancing body, its eroded mouth is stretched wide in an eternal leer and its hollow eyes stare back steadily, mockingly, into hers.

9

Gracie pushes open the door of the steamy little trattoria in Meard Street and feels a choke of relief as she sees Daphne Dawes, lifestyle journalist, regular pundit on the daytime TV circuit and Elsie's sporadically enthusiastic godmother, sitting in a dimly lit booth at the back, her face partially hidden by a fall of dyed red hair. Wine glass in one hand, phone in the other, she taps the toe of a shiny ankle boot against the table leg; an exotic oddity in this world of vinyl-covered banquettes, oversized pepper mills and autographed portraits fading in their frames. But Stefano's is where she and Gracie come to thrash out their problems, attracted by the comforts of the unreconstructed menu and the certainty that they will never bump into anyone they know.

Gracie feels steadier as she squeezes towards her through the closely packed tables. Oddly, Daphne has had this effect on her since the day she teetered past Gracie's cake stall in Broadway market, caught a kitten heel in a rise in the road and fell over. Despite her smudged makeup and mussy beehive there was a wobbly dignity about the way she ignored her bloodied knee, pulled herself into Gracie's chair and lit a cigarette; and something brave and heartening about her snappy response when Gracie asked her if she was OK. 'No. I'm bloody not. I'm hungover, I've just been dumped and my editor wants eight hundred words on the latest leisure trend by tomorrow. Oh yes, and it's got to be sharp and funny.'

They agree that it was one of those moments when fate snaps her fingers and everything changes, though ten years on they still argue about whose idea it was for Daphne to devote her column to the joys of baking. Either way, Gracie couldn't believe it when Daphne rang the next day to set up a photo shoot and asked for the address of her website. Still in her pyjamas, she managed to race to her laptop and pull the name *Gracie's Kitchen.com* off the top of her head, twenty seconds before she clicked 'confirm' to buy the domain name. She's still got that article, along with the letter it prompted, asking her to audition for an occasional baking slot on a daytime TV chat show.

'Sorry I missed the launch,' Daphne says, eyes still on her phone. 'How'd it go?'

Gracie slides into the seat opposite. 'All right.'

'We're running the first extract on Sunday. They've agreed to a sidebar plugging the series.'

'OK.'

'You could sound a bit more enthusiastic.'

'It's started again,' Gracie says shakily. 'One of my coral earrings and a note saying, "Hello Gracie."' Daphne's thumb pauses. 'Only this time the packaging was different, so I didn't realise what it was till I'd opened it.'

'Have you told Reeves?'

'He's gone off on secondment. They sent this other guy, Jamieson.'

'Cute?'

'Kind of creepy.' Gracie picks up the menu, the red plastic

cover slightly sticky beneath her fingers. 'Tom thinks it's a copycat. Jamieson thinks it's the old stalker back to his,' she takes a breath, 'or her, old tricks.'

'What do you think?'

Gracie keeps her gaze on the blurring selection of pizzas. 'I think it might be a new her,' she says. 'And new tricks.'

'Really?' Daphne presses send. 'Why?'

'Tom slept with one of the interns in his office.' Saying the words out loud is like kicking off a crippling pair of shoes and pressing her aching feet against a slab of marble. She looks up slowly, a pained expression on her face. Daphne is Tom's friend too, her rackety affairs and caustic observations part of the fabric of their lives.

'You're kidding.' Daphne drags her eyes from her phone. 'When?'

'While I was in New York.'

'Christ! What a shit.' Daphne fills Gracie's wine glass and lowers her voice. 'You think it's *her* who sent the earring?'

Gracie nods. 'Tom told her it was a mistake and she went off on a crazed power trip, threatening to tell me and the board if he didn't let her work on one of his projects.'

'Good for her.'

'Daph!'

'Well honestly, it serves him bloody well right. It's not 1972.'

'And she's not some poor little innocent. She practically jumped him when he was drunk.'

'Oh, for God's sake. No one forced him to screw her.'

Gracie grows still. Imagining Alicia. Imagining Tom.

'How did she get hold of your earring?' Daphne's voice is sharp, wrenching Gracie back from the vision of her husband and his lover.

'He . . . he slept with her in our house.' Gracie drops

41

her head as if she is the one who should feel ashamed. 'In our bed.'

Daphne sucks her breath. An elderly red-faced waiter arrives. Daphne orders two plates of rigatoni with ragu and pushes him away with the menu. 'Do you really think it was her?' she says when he's gone.

'Oh, I don't know. Tom says it's not her style. We're not telling the police *why* she was in the house but she's on the list of "visitors" they're going to interview.' She lifts her fork and stares bleakly at the prongs. 'If I'm honest, I think I'd rather it *was* her than the faceless weirdo.'

'Sure. And why would he stop for months on end then suddenly start up again?'

'Jamieson thinks it's to keep me on edge.'

'Bollocks.' Daphne dips a breadstick into her wine. 'It's obviously this intern trying to get back at Tom. How did you find out about her?'

'He confessed. The night I got back.'

'Why?'

'How about because he loves me and he can't bear keeping secrets from me?'

Daphne watches her and waits, her head tilted a little on her neck. Gracie keeps her eyes fixed on the fork in her fingers. 'Apparently it wasn't just about enhancing her CV. She thought she and Tom had a "future" and now she's threatening to go to the press.'

'Have you talked to Daley?'

'No.'

'You need to. Maybe he can keep a lid on it.'

'He does PR, not miracles. See it from her point of view. She's angry, she wants revenge.'

'At least it proves it's over.'

'Oh, yes. It's over for her and Tom. Not for me. It's never going to be over for me.'

'Oh, come on.'

'He says he hates himself, that she meant nothing and I believe him. But—' Gracie's hand moves to her lips but the words come spewing out. 'It feels as if Louise has done this to punish me.'

It's a shocking moment. Daphne stares at her. And goes on staring, as if she's seen something disturbing and can't tear her eyes away. '*Punish* you?'

'For being alive. For daring to marry her husband.'

'Fuck's sake, what's the matter with you? Tom screwed up. That's what men do.'

'He'd never have cheated on *her*.'

'Stop this.' Daphne moves aside and points to the speckled Campari mirror on the wall behind her. 'Look at yourself. You're gorgeous, funny, smart and you've got more sex appeal in one toenail than that po-faced ice queen had in her whole body.'

Gracie catches her reflection in the mirror and looks away. 'She was the love of his life.'

Daphne bites on the breadstick and points the broken end at Gracie. 'He was a wreck when you met him, still would be if you hadn't married him. He knows that.'

'I just happened to be there – good old Gracie picking up the pieces.'

'Paying for his sodding house.'

'Not all of it.'

'Oh, come on. If it wasn't for *Cooking with Gracie* it'd still be a building site.'

'I never cared about the money. I just wanted him to be happy.' She twists away, struggling to breathe.

Daphne grabs her wrist. 'You've got to let this go.'

'I can't.'

'Because you want the impossible.'

'I don't.'

43

'You do. You convince yourself that men are something they're not and when it turns out they're pathetic and human you fall apart. Look at the state you were in after that tosser Harry Flynn. All over the place for months. Right up until you started seeing Tom.'

Gracie presses her lips together, this talk of Harry loosening more pain than she can bear.

Daphne's voice softens. 'Tom loves you, Gracie. Anyone can see that.'

'Not the way he loved Louise. Oh sure, he wants things back the way they were and he thinks if I let him convert some crappy old church into my new café everything's going to be fine. But I can't trust him. Not any more.'

'It's over, Gracie. You said so yourself.'

'Over with *Alicia*. But it wasn't just a fuck. If it had been then maybe, eventually, I could have dealt with it. But Alicia's like Louise. She understands his world. She can talk to him about architraves and bloody elevations and when she told him he was a genius and the Bristow's client was an idiot, it actually meant something.'

'Is that what he said?'

'No. But think about it. It happened the night he lost the tender. He brought her home so she could rave about his prizewinning masterpiece and bolster his ego in ways I never could. You know what he's like about his work. He needs constant validation. Sooner or later he's going to leave me for someone who can give it to him.'

The waiter appears with their food. Gracie blots her eyes with a napkin while he spoons parmesan from a steel pot and waves his ridiculous pepper mill. Daphne glares at him. He retreats. 'Eat.' She forks up a mound of pasta. 'You two are the perfect couple. It's never going to happen.'

'Like Tom screwing an intern was never going to happen?'

There's a fevered desperation in her voice, a shudder when she breathes.

Daphne looks her in the eye. 'You're not going to leave him?'

For a moment Gracie is hyper-aware of everything: the fragility of the glass in her hand, the murmur of voices, the crash of plates in the kitchen. 'Think what it would do to Elsie.'

'Is that the only reason you're staying?'

Gracie blinks at her. 'I love him. I loved our life together but now, every time I see another woman, I hate her because she could be the one who takes him away and then I go home and it's . . . like I don't belong there, like I've got no right to . . .'

Daphne's eyes drill into hers. 'No right to what?'

'Live in Louise's house.'

'Yeah, well you know my feelings about that.'

'I swear it didn't bother me before. Not really. Not when everything was OK. But now—'

Daphne throws aside her napkin. 'Tell him to sell it.'

'I can't. You know I can't.'

'After what he's done?'

Gracie's face sags with wretchedness. 'That house is a part of who he is. I can't ask him to give it up. Specially not now.'

'Why not?'

'Losing the Bristow's tender has totally crushed his confidence. The house is his reminder that he's got what it takes.'

'What's more important to him – that bloody house or his marriage?'

'If I made him leave it he'd end up hating me.'

'What about *you*? What do *you* want?'

Gracie grows still. 'Certainty, I s'pose.' She stares across the restaurant. 'Certainty that I'm not building my life on

45

something Tom can snatch away next time some intern bats her eyes at him.'

'Well dream on. No one gets that. Why do you think I'm still single?' Daphne pours herself more wine. 'You look like shit.'

'Thanks.'

'Are you sleeping?'

'Not really. I lie there for a couple of hours then I get up and wander round and . . .' her face crumples '. . . I see Alicia in every room. It's like I can smell her, like she's laughing at me, mocking me for thinking I could ever take the place of a woman like Louise.'

No longer brash or hectoring, Daphne says, 'You can't go on like this.'

Gracie's eyes are closed, her voice a rasp. 'I know.'

'So what are you going to do?'

'I don't know, Daph. I just don't know.'

Pauline Bryce Diary
January 12th

I'm in the shop this morning flicking through the magazines and I see this feature:

Use What You've Got to Get What You Want – Your Six-Point Guide to a New Life

1 – Fix your 'Big Picture Goal'.
2 – Break it down into small targets – the pathway to your dream.
3 – Plan small steps to reach each target.
4 – Use what you've got to take the first step. (If that doesn't work, take a smaller step.)
5 – Plan A might fail. Always have a Plan B standing by.
6 – Keep a record of what you're doing. (Use it to keep your plans on track and to remind yourself how far you've come.)

And remember: You can turn the things you hate about your life into the tools to change it.

It's been on my mind all day.

10

'The traffic was a nightmare. Two hours it took me to get to the school.' Gracie pulls a bruised apple out of Elsie's school bag and tosses it into the compost bin. 'The boy's mum was very nice about it but he had a hell of a mark on his arm.'

Tom bounces a pen nervously between his palms. 'All kids scrap in the playground. How do they know it wasn't him who started it?'

'Her teacher says she's been acting up for a couple of weeks.'

'Why?'

'Kids pick up on stuff. Elsie knows things aren't right between us. It's making her feel insecure.'

'What's she been doing?'

'Getting moody, refusing to share. Let's face it, she's never found that very easy.'

'You're saying we spoil her.'

'A bit.'

'It's you as much as me.'

'Yes!' She strains for calm. 'It's something we both need to work on but that's not what we're discussing right now.'

'OK. OK. So what do we do?'

'Whatever happens between us,' she sees him flinch, 'we

have to reassure her that being parents comes first. That we can still function as a proper family.'

'A *proper* family.' He says the words slowly, as if he's weighing their meaning.

Outside the wind picks up, hurling rain against the glass wall. He gets up very deliberately and closes the blinds.

'Yes,' Grace says. 'And that's going to take more than putting on a front when she's around and sniping at each other when she isn't.'

'All right then!' He pivots round, red-faced and angry. 'Let's have another child. That's what *proper* families are about.'

His words pinch an old bruise, an injury inflamed by weeks and months of persistent arguments from him and tearful insistence from her that she doesn't need another child, she has Elsie. But this time she doesn't cry. Instead she meets his anger with a flinty fury of her own. 'Are you insane? We can't use a child to mend our marriage.'

'People do.'

'Not me, Tom. I can't believe you're using this as an excuse to bring it up.'

'For Christ's sake. I shouldn't need an excuse.'

She turns away, tears welling. 'This isn't about you. It's about Elsie. About making her feel secure enough to cope if that girl's story hits the papers.'

His hands flail helplessly. 'Sorry. I'm sorry. You're right.' He gazes at her, lost, boyish, bewildered. 'I just want things to be right again, to put this behind us and move on.'

'It would help if you weren't away so much. Right now Elsie needs to see more of both of us.'

'It's difficult. After the Bristow's fiasco I'm not exactly man of the moment at work and if—' He exhales softly, unable to go on.

She looks away and says briskly, 'We need to make it a priority. I'm going to try and pick her up from school at

49

least twice a week. But it's impossible on filming days and when I'm at the bakery I practically have to leave after lunch to get there in time.'

'All right. I'll do it when I can. But it'll mean going back to the office in the evening.' He gets up. 'I've got emails to catch up on.'

She watches him go and releases her tension by ripping parsley for a seafood broth that she knows neither of them will have the heart to eat.

When Tom comes home the next evening there's something different about the way he moves to the fridge to get himself a beer, a lightness that Gracie hasn't seen since she's been back from New York. He holds up the can. 'Want one?'

She shakes her head, wrists rocking the dough in front of her, pushing and pummelling. He leans back against the worktop, snaps open the can and takes a gulp of beer. 'I talked to Alicia.'

'Oh.' *I can do this. I can have this conversation.*

'I told her you know everything and that we're putting our marriage back together.'

A lump turns in Gracie's throat.

'Then I told her about the earring. I said the police wanted to interview everyone who'd visited the house as part of their on-going investigation into the stalking and that we'd given them her name.'

Gracie wipes her hands and pulls on the oven gloves. 'And?'

'She was shocked. Genuinely so. She didn't even know you'd been stalked.'

'Mind out.' She shunts him aside and opens the oven. The heat hits her face and she feels an overwhelming urge to crawl inside and curl up with the sizzling beef.

He looks down at his beer. A silence grows. He's gearing

up for something. She can tell. She slams the oven door. 'No more confessions, Tom. I can't take it.'

'No, no. Nothing like that. It's just, well, I'm not proud of this, but I told her if she went to the press with her allegations it would make her the only person on the police's list who had a motive for harassing you.' He takes another swig of beer and wipes his mouth.

Gracie looks away, shaken by an unexpected pang of sympathy for this girl her husband slept with and spurned. In his selfish, thoughtless way he's hurt them both. 'What did she say to that?'

'She got angry. She said she didn't do it and that a motive wasn't evidence. So I told her the media didn't care about evidence. One sniff of a rumour like this and there'd be *Celebrity cook stalked by husband's crazy ex lover* stories all over the internet and I couldn't see future employers counting that kind of publicity as much of a plus on her CV.'

'And then?'

'She walked out. But she knows I'm right, Gracie. She's off our backs, I promise.'

Gracie wedges a clove of garlic into the crusher and squeezes hard. 'Oh, great, so that makes everything all right. It's like you never slept with her.'

He puts down the beer and takes her by the shoulders. 'I'm not saying that. But you're right about what the publicity would do to you. To Elsie. To us. We need privacy to work this out.'

She twists away and throws the crusher into the sink. Steel on steel it clangs like a fractured bell. She stabs two fingers into her brow, her breath coming fast and erratic. 'What about what's in here, Tom? Inside me? Shutting Alicia up won't wipe that away.'

'So what will?'

'I don't know.' She's sobbing now.

'I love you, Gracie. I want to make this right.'

'Can't you see that makes it worse? I can't leave, I can't stay. Half the time I can't even breathe.'

He moves towards her. She turns her back and he walks away, the thud of his shoes on the stairs sounding his retreat.

Her legs feel weak. She reaches for her phone and collapses into a chair, stumbling on the words as she tells Daphne what Tom has done. Daphne responds with a gutsy honk of laughter, almost choking she's so amused.

'What's so funny?'

'Tom. I never thought he had it in him.'

'What do you mean?'

'It's pretty damn convenient.'

'What is?'

'Your earring turning up just in time to get him off the hook.'

Gracie makes an odd choking noise. 'You think *Tom* sent it?'

'He's the one with access to your things. He's the one who started talking about copycats, and then – surprise, surprise – he's suddenly got this girl right where he wants her.'

'He would never do anything so horrible. He knows how much those packages upset me.'

'Seeing his affair splashed all over the papers would upset you more.'

'Oh God. He screwed that girl and the ripples just go on and on. I can't take it, Daph. I can't do this.' She cuts the call, and clutches the phone to her chest, ignoring the frantic buzzing as Daphne tries to call her back.

The following night it's nearly one o'clock when Gracie hears Tom come home. He hovers at her door, then moves on down the landing unsteady on his feet. Just after dawn she hears him go out again.

At dusk when the jagged geometry of Canary Wharf begins

to wink and glitter in the distance she stands at the bedroom window and sees him leaning on the iron railing by the river path, staring out across the water. He lifts his head, as he always does, to catch the crimson flare of the sunset reflected on the glasswork of the house, but now, as he approaches the gate, he moves with the limping strut of a guilty man taking his last breath of freedom. The front door slams.

'Gracie!'

She hurries downstairs, pushing her hair behind her ears. He is at the sink filling a glass with water. He turns to her as he drinks. 'I saw Daphne last night.'

'You don't have to explain yourself to me.'

'She's worried about you. About us.'

'I had to talk to someone.'

'I'm not blaming you . . . in fact I'm glad.' He sets the glass down and stares into the sink. 'I'm going to sell the house. It'll be a fresh start. For both of us. Away from . . . the memories.'

She stands rigid. Selling the Wharf House will rip a hole in his heart almost as big as the one he has ripped in hers. He pulls her close and wraps his arms around her. 'But you'll have to deal with the sale, I can't—'

'Tom—' she struggles to free herself. He holds her tighter. 'You need time to think about this. Leaving this house wouldn't be a cure-all, just a chance to start the real work we need to do. There'd be no going back and no guarantees.'

'I know and I want to do this, Gracie. I want to make things right.' She feels the pressure of his chin on her skull, the ripple of his Adam's apple as he swallows. 'We'll move somewhere in easy reach of the bakery and the studios, put Elsie into a school nearby and start afresh.'

Gracie closes her eyes, grateful, relieved and at the same time terrified that this new life they're embarking on might fail to give her the security she craves.

Pauline Bryce Diary
Jan 14th

Two more of the creeps come in the shop today. These ones don't even bother buying anything, they just hang around waiting for Robson, smoking those shitty little cigars and jangling the change in the pockets of their macs. In the end he turns up and takes them down to the cellar and a bit later they all come up together and go out. The creeps are looking shifty but Robson's shoving a bundle of twenties into his pocket and he's laughing and joking and saying he'll get them a drink down the road. I wait a bit to make sure he's not coming back then I take his keys and go down and have a look around. It's disgusting. His 'special stock'. I can't believe some of the stuff. Kids, animals, you name it. It makes me feel sick. All the way home I'm thinking about threatening him – the money for London or I tell the police. But I've seen his nasty side, so for now that's Plan B. I can't see me needing it, though. Not with the Plan A I've come up with. Like that feature says – use what you've got.

11

Gracie jumps at the invitation to spend Christmas and New Year at Tom's sister's rambling house outside Bristol. It's a chance for the two of them to lose themselves and each other in the chaotic jollity of squeezing ten around the kitchen table, hunting down missing wellingtons, dashing out to pick up more wine and sharing the guest bed with Elsie and a wheezing, overweight Labrador.

As soon as they get back to London they take a couple of days off to begin their hunt for a new house. It comes as a shock to find themselves alone, facing up to the fallout from Tom's betrayal. But somewhere, in setting the sat nav, laughing at the overblown language in the brochures, and traipsing through other people's dreams and dirt, a little of the strain dissolves.

Gracie sifts through the pile of 'possibles' in her lap and takes a sip of her coffee. 'My favourite's still the warehouse in King's Cross.'

Tom grunts, chewing down the last of his baguette as he swings off a roundabout. She looks up. 'Where are we?'

'Making a little detour.' He pulls up on a litter-blown forecourt. With a pang she recognises the building in front of them. It's the chapel he told her about. Without a word he gets out and stands with his feet apart, gazing at the building. Gracie stays back, her hand on the roof of the car, taking in the boarded-up windows, the angry neon tags, the bowed roof. Her eyes dart away to rest on Tom. From the tilt of his head she knows that he's seeing beyond the graffiti, flapping posters and bubbling paintwork to the fabric of the structure, imagining light flowing in through those boarded-up windows, the stone walls scrubbed clean and those big wooden doors flung wide.

'You've got to be kidding. It's miles from anywhere *and* it's falling apart. Look at it.'

'Where else are we going to find a space with this much character and potential?' She notes the *we*. The way he's wedding himself to her new project.

'There's loads of parking space at the back, which leaves all this free for an outside eating area.'

'What about the road?'

'We'll cut off the noise with glass panels. Come and see inside.' He grins and holds up the keys.

He pulls her through the high double doors into a cool darkness that smells of piss and damp. The room is a long rectangle – crumbling pink walls embossed with graceful white moulding, a scarred marble floor heaped with rags and newspapers and a dark wooden balcony running beneath the domed ceiling.

'A false floor up there would give you plenty of room for your workshops and we'd soundproof the whole thing so there'd be no problem with filming.'

'It'd cost a fortune.'

Tom's not listening. He's skimming through a set of sketches on his tablet, making excited sweeps with his arm as he talks. 'Can't you see it, Gracie? Kitchens back there, a big counter on this side for the bakery, seating all across here and the cook shop at the end with its own entrance.'

His enthusiasm brings the damp echoey space alive. For a moment she really does see what he sees.

'Think about it at least,' he says.

Conscious of the wild thudding of her heart she paces slowly, imagining what she could do with this place. 'I'd have to have a proper look at the stats for the area, and put a business case to my backers,' she says.

'Of course. It's all in that research the French guy had done.'

She gazes up at the ragged holes in the plaster. 'To get this place the way I'd want, I'd need to be totally hands on.'

'I'd be the one managing the build.'

'No, Tom. I'd have to be involved in every decision, and if the company goes ahead with this out-of-town thing—'

He looks up, bewildered. She gives an impatient shake of her head. 'I *told* you about it. The bit of land one of the backers has bought in Oxfordshire. He'll build on it eventually but for the next couple of years he wants Gracie's Kitchen to put up a semi-permanent marquee and use it for weddings and events. I'd get a manager in to run it but I'd still need to be across the planning.'

'OK.'

'It's not OK. How could I juggle all my other commitments if we buy a house in Primrose Hill or the other side of Highbury and I'm dashing over here every day? It's Elsie who'd lose out. I'm not having that. Half the point of moving is so that I can spend more time with her.'

'So . . .' a nervous half smile, 'do you want to check out houses in Clapton?'

'All I'm saying is that if we did go for this place, and it's a *massive* if, living nearby is the only way it could work. But we wouldn't find anything you'd want to live in round here.'

He shrugs and taps his tablet. 'We might as well see what there is.'

She watches him type in the postcode and swipe through nearby properties on Zoopla. Slowly she brings out her phone and does the same. She's still searching as they get back into the car, looking up only to shake her head at a loft conversion he'd wondered about, that turns out to be above a noisy engineering plant. At the traffic lights she clutches his arm and leans over to show him the photo on her screen. 'Look at this one. It's a little bit further out than I was hoping, but worth taking a look.'

He rubs his hand across his chin as she flicks through the photos of the interior. 'Nice.' He punches *Falcon Square* into the sat nav.

She gazes out of the window, taking in the old-school betting shops, the cheap takeaways still hung with winking Santa lights and a redbrick Victorian school. He hesitates at a noisy junction, cuts past a bow-fronted church and turns into a square of shabbily grand Georgian villas.

He slows the car, twisting in his seat to look up at the long sash windows glinting in the wintery sunlight. 'God, I love London,' he says. 'Where else could you turn off a shitty high street and find a place like this?'

As he pulls up outside number 17, Gracie looks around and finds herself imagining the life she might lead if she lived here, the people she might bump into in the park or the supermarket. She glances at Tom. His smile is smug. She forgives him that. It's a small price to pay for this glimpse of a future that doesn't leave her feeling hollow inside.

Six months on from Tom's confession Gracie wakes shivering and afraid from the running dream. It's their last night in

Greenwich and she paces the landing, gazing at the construction lights on the cranes across the water, the dabs of brightness moving with the ripples of the blackened tide. It's windy outside, spatters of rain mist the panes as she presses her palms to the glass and silently hands the Wharf House back to Louise.

There's movement behind her. She swings round.

'I couldn't sleep either,' Tom whispers.

'How are you feeling?'

'Numb. Angry with myself. Sad about leaving the river.'

'I'll miss it too.'

'But I'm taking everything that matters with me.' He slips his arms around her.

Hesitantly, she leans into him, her throat almost too tight to speak. 'We still have to go on working on us.'

'I know.'

'But once we're settled,' she says – barely a whisper, 'let's think about giving Elsie a brother or sister. Take a proper look at the options.'

There's a slight shocked pause as he takes this in. 'Why the change of heart?'

Her arms tighten around his waist. 'I never stopped wanting another baby, I just put the feelings on hold when . . . it didn't happen. Scared of the disappointment I suppose. But you're giving up this house for me and I want to do this for you, for us, for Elsie.' Taking his hand, she leads him back to their room and they make love. Gentle tentative love that makes her want to cry.

12

Juliet ignores the screeching horn of the van bearing down behind her, swerves back into the stream of traffic and completes a second circuit of the roundabout, transfixed by the words *Gracie's Kitchen Coming Soon* printed in red across the white tarpaulin flapping from the roof of the old meeting house. Wincing at the shriek of her brake pads she pulls onto the forecourt, lights a cigarette and brings up the local business forum on her phone. There's already a whole raft of comments. All positive. Of course they are. Who wouldn't want a celebrity setting up shop in a rundown part of town? She closes her eyes, sick at the thought of Gracie Dwyer's latest venture taking root and blossoming right under her nose. It takes a few minutes of slow breathing before she can bring herself to click the link to the piece in the local paper. There's a photo of Gracie. She's standing in front of the tall panelled doors, feet away from where Juliet is parked, one hand resting on the brass doorknob, her head turned towards the camera, her lips parted in that signature smile of entitlement. Juliet's focus slides to the article, her thumbnail worrying the filter of her cigarette as she reads the pull-together of predictable quotes lifted from a press release. It's only as her gaze returns to Gracie's serenely confident face that her thumb grows still and a quiver of possibility passes through her body, filling a place inside her that has been empty for a long, long time.

She steps out of the car and walks around the building, kicking aside the broken bottles and standing on tiptoe to squint through a crack in the shuttered windows. It's a mess inside, but the Quakers or Shakers or whoever it was built this place had certainly known what they were doing. She's grinding the butt of her cigarette into the blistered tarmac when her phone buzzes in her pocket. It's Ian. Again. She presses cancel and leans back against the wall, letting the chill creep through her flimsy jacket into her skin.

The phone vibrates again. It's been bliss while he's been in Australia but she can't stall him any longer. She lights another cigarette and lifts the handset to her ear. Silence, then that slow intake of breath before he speaks. 'You've been ignoring my calls.'

She bites her lip, annoyed at the effect his voice still has on her.

'I've been busy.'

'I want to see Freya.'

'When?'

'Sunday. I'll come over and pick her up. It'll give you and me a chance to talk.'

'No!' She steadies her voice. 'No, it's all right. I'll bring her to you. Pick a time and a place.'

'Two o'clock. My flat.'

'Somewhere public.'

'For Christ's sake.'

'I mean it, Ian.'

'Clissold Park then. By the café. I've got rights, Juliet.'

'I've never stopped you seeing her.'

'No.' She can hear the smile. 'But you'd like to.'

'Let's not do this.' She's getting back in her car, drawing on the cigarette, raw and on edge.

'There's something you need to know.' He pauses, the way he always does before he jabs a knife between her ribs. 'Merion's pregnant. An accident but we're thrilled.'

Seven words, seven stabs in the heart that leave her bleeding out the agony of three rounds of IVF and four years of wanting, waiting, hoping, praying before she finally got to hold Freya in her arms. She's conscious of the burn as her lungs take in the smoke and the breathy tremor in her voice. 'What do you want? Congratulations?'

'We thought you should tell Freya. It'll make it easier for her.'

We? That doormat Merion with her lispy voice and floppy fringe hasn't had any say in this. It's Ian, out to inflict maximum pain. Enjoying it too. She wants to refuse, but at least if she's the one who tells Freya, she can do it gently, soften the blow.

'After the baby's born I'll take Freya out to Sydney so she can get to know her new family.'

Juliet doesn't reply, won't give him the satisfaction.

'Are you managing all right?'

'Don't patronise me.'

'I'm not. The bank's been having computer problems. I wanted to check you'd had your money this month.'

Like hell. She's sure it's him who's held back the payment. Like he does every now and then just to remind her that he can.

'Not yet.' She's pleased with the way that came out. Off hand. As if his stingy maintenance is neither here nor there.

'You should have called me.'

'I'm managing.'

He laughs. The bastard actually laughs. 'What are you doing? Rationing the wine and fags?'

Fuck you.

She cuts the call. If her life were a movie her best friend would have had doubts about Ian from the start. But she'd never had a best friend. There'd been a couple of girls at school, the kind who were all over you one minute and turned on you the next, tittering behind their hands like you were some kind of freak, and the last flat share, the one with Sandra, had been OK until Sandra started seeing that creep Alex. What was Juliet supposed to do? Keep quiet about him turning up in her room, all morning breath and sweat as soon as Sandra left for work? And what kind of idiot was Sandra to believe his crap about Juliet coming on to him? Christ, the thought of his pale spotty face and sticky hands made her feel sick. She checks Sandra and Alex out sometimes – two kids, a semi and camping trips to Cornwall. Juliet never wanted any of that. She'd wanted Ian, with his extravagant lifestyle and his hunger to get rich, even though there were times when the sex tipped from passion into pain, days when his moods darkened the flat like squid ink and nights when she'd yearned to go out, get pissed and wake up with someone she'd never see again. She should have bailed out as soon as she caught him reading her emails, but she'd been checking his for a while and there'd been a time when their mutual jealousy had excited her, when she'd enjoyed the envy of the other women when he turned up half way through her hair appointments and waited in the salon, relaxed and smiling until she was done.

She's late now. She's always late and Freya, bless her, never complains. She's such a sweet-natured little thing, happy in her own world. God knows where she gets it from. Not from her father, that's for sure.

That girlfriend of his, Merion, she can't be more than twenty-five. Who'd want a baby at that age? It's Ian. Another bid for a boy. This time with someone he can control. She slams her foot on the accelerator and shoots out into the traffic, telling herself it'll be all right, that no exhausted young mother wants to be lumbered with a step-kid. The thought calms her, though she isn't looking forward to telling Freya that her darling daddy is having another baby. She checks the time. She'll have to hurry if she's going to make her deadline – ad copy for another crappy weight loss product. Useless probably but she's been lying for a living for so long it won't be difficult to knock something out. With these kind of jobs it's just a question of getting into the mind-set of the target market and feeding them what they want to hear. In this case fat lazy cows who want to lose weight without giving up chips and chocolate.

She swears softly as she hurries through the school gates and sees Freya sitting on the steps with her chin on her knees, Miss Cahill hovering beside her, mouth pursed, ready to '*have a little word about time-keeping*'. Juliet stalks past her and grabs Freya's arm. 'Come on, quick, I'm parked on a double yellow.'

13

'Hey, what's happening?' Gracie drops her keys into her bag and opens her arms to Elsie, who comes hurtling down the stairs in a floppy straw hat and wrinkled grey tights jammed into pink satin ballet slippers. Gracie bends to kiss her. 'What's with the outfit?'

'I'm going to be a mushroom in Lynda's show and you have to make me a costume. The tickets cost three pounds fifty. Daphne can come if she wants. She can write about it in the paper.' Elsie twirls away and runs back upstairs, passing Heather on her way down with a basket of washing.

'Sounds like it was a success,' Gracie says.

'Not bad. The place is a bit grotty but she seemed to enjoy it.'

'Did she make any friends?'

'She got talking to a girl called Amber. Her mum teaches round the corner at Dunsmore Primary.'

'I can take her next week. I'll try and get Amber over for tea. How did it go at the school?'

'She was standing on her own again when I picked her up.'

'Any luck with the other nannies?'

'I'm trying. But they're dead cliquey.'

'What about the mums?'

'That lot wouldn't be seen dead talking to the help.'

'God, that place is snotty. Bloody four-by-fours and skiing in Val d'Isère.'

'Tom's right about the security. They stopped me again as I was going in. You'd think they'd know my face by now.'

'That's what we're paying for, I s'pose. Thank goodness she's meeting some nice normal kids at dance.'

'Tea?'

'If you're making some.'

On her way to the kitchen Gracie gives in to one of the unspoken pleasures of Falcon Square and trails her hand over the rubbed wooden sweep of the bannister, picturing the generations of women who have lived in this house, gentle ghosts who would never be more to her than names on a set of deeds, calling up the stairs to their children, throwing back the shutters to let in the light, planting the saplings that have grown into the tall lime trees at the bottom of the garden, their footsteps loosening the toffee-brown boards that creak beneath her feet.

She pulls her notebook from her bag. 'Let's invite her whole class to her party. That should get them on side. We can combine it with a housewarming – kids and families in the afternoon, adults in the evening. Could you have a look at entertainment options – maybe a circus workshop or one of those conjurors who does illusions?'

She hears Tom's key in the door. Her eyes pull towards him as he walks into the kitchen, tall, handsome, masculine, capable, tugging at the tie beneath his unbuttoned collar. He's the kind of man women notice. The kind who, like his twice-divorced father, will improve with age. Is she crazy to fill the house with other women? She snaps off that thought at the root. 'Forget the tea, let's have a drink.'

He glances at the notebook.

'What are you hatching now?'

She finds a smile. 'Elsie's party. We're going to have a barbeque.'

He pulls a bottle from the rack and reaches for the opener. 'When were you thinking?'

'Her birthday's on a Sunday so what about the Saturday before? That'll give us four weeks to get organised.'

'I'll give Stella and Todd a call. They'll want to know what to give her.'

'How about a new bicycle?'

'Isn't that what we're giving her?'

Gracie etches a doodle in the corner of the page. 'I was thinking we might buy her a puppy.'

Tom turns slowly to look at her. 'You're kidding.'

'She's always wanted one.'

'And you've always been dead set against it.'

'It'll help her make friends. Kids love going to houses with pets.'

'Yeah, but a puppy's a full-on commitment. Let's get her a rescue dog.'

Gracie stares at him appalled. 'Haven't you heard those horror stories about cuddly rescue dogs suddenly turning on the children?'

'Don't be ridiculous. They do tests to make sure they're safe around kids.'

'There'll always be unknowns, some trigger that sends them crazy.'

Tom rolls his eyes. 'So who's going to house-train this puppy?'

Heather butts in excitedly. 'Elsie and I can do it. Shall I have a look at some breeders' websites?'

'It's OK,' Tom says, his eyes still on Gracie. 'I'll do it.'

Gracie feels the linger of his gaze as she scores through another item on her list. 'Thanks, love, that'd be great.'

The Lynda Burton School of Dance is housed in a set of knocked-through rooms above a carpet shop, its windows decorated with a crudely painted top hat and a pair of disembodied ballet shoes teetering across the glass. Elsie runs up the narrow wooden steps, squeezing her bag past the line of parents coming down the other way. Some of them stare openly at Gracie, some look away and a balding man in paint-spattered overalls makes the kind of face that usually precedes a shout of 'Hey, aren't you thingy off the telly!' Gracie cuts him short with a quick smile and follows Elsie down a narrow corridor lined with chipped, wood-effect panelling hung with yellowing certificates and faded blow-ups of past productions – grinning rouge-cheeked kids in garish costumes, arms flung wide for the camera. She lowers herself onto one of the wooden benches in the small, dimly lit changing area and sits forward holding her breath. The sour smell of sweaty feet, floor polish and cheap body spray is almost un-breathable. She uses a finger to shoehorn Elsie's feet into her ballet slippers, tightens the ribbons at the end of her plaits and guides her towards the stream of children tripping into the studio, where music blares from the speakers, the rattling overhead fan pushes the sweaty air around and sinewy, leather-skinned Lynda Burton runs around in a red leotard like a manic chorizo whipping up enthusiasm. 'Come on, everybody, big breaths. Let's shake out those joints.'

Gracie leans against the doorjamb studying the dancers. One boy, razored hair tilting into a quiff, stands watching Gracie watching him in the wall of mirrors. With a grin he backflips across the room to a chorus of *oohs* from the admiring girls and a stern warning from Lynda about the need for a proper warm-up as she shoos him off to the advanced class. Gracie's eyes dart over to Elsie standing on her own chewing the end of her plait. Gracie searches the room for other girls her age. She feels a prick of disappointment. Maybe this isn't going work out. Give it a few weeks, she thinks. There's sure to be plenty of regulars who miss the odd session. Lynda Burton smirks a little when she sees her and hurries over. 'Nice to see you. If you want to stay there's coffee and a kettle in the kitchen.'

Gracie steps away and wanders over to the kitchen where two women are leaning against the stained countertop sipping from chipped china mugs.

'Hello.'

The women exchange glances and shuffle down the counter to let her get to the kettle. The thinner one gives her a nod. The plump one folds her fleshy arms and takes Gracie in, not unfriendly, just curious. 'You're slumming it, aren't you?'

'*Dawn!*' Her friend looks apologetically at Gracie who is opening cupboard doors, looking for a mug.

'This place is just like the dance school I went to as a kid, even the cupboards smell the same,' Gracie says.

'Your kid coming here's been the talk of Dunsmore. Even the teachers have been going on about it.' Dawn jerks her head at her friend and laughs. 'I said to Leslie, I bet that's Lynda spreading rumours to drum up business.'

'I hope not. I asked her to keep it quiet,' Gracie says.

Dawn's chin lifts, a touch of aggression. 'What school's she go to then?'

'St Mathilda's.'

Dawn gives Leslie a knowing look. 'There you go. This lot's either at Dunsmore or The Falcon Academy.'

'Blame my husband. I really liked the look of Dunsmore.'

Gracie passes its gates every day, even stops sometimes to watch the children in the playground forming and dissolving their little knots of allegiance, and still wonders if she should have fought harder to overcome Tom's worries about security. She flips on the kettle and sniffs the open milk carton.

'I wouldn't risk it,' Leslie says.

'It's all right,' Dawn grins. 'She'll turn it into cream cheese.'

Gracie laughs. 'I was thinking sour milk muffins.'

'I did your garden pie the other night, used up all the crap at the bottom of the fridge. My kids actually asked for seconds.'

'That's why I do the leftovers slot. It really pisses me off how much food gets wasted. You look in the bins behind any supermarket and there'll be enough food in there to feed an army.'

She's cracked the ice, got them on side, sworn a little but not too much, gauged it right. Footsteps sound on the stairs and thud across the changing area. The door of the studio bangs open, lets out a blast of 'Saturday Night Fever' and swings shut behind a latecomer.

14

Juliet sees her through the half-open door. She pushes between the lines of coat pegs, taking in Gracie Dwyer's shiny hair, the cared-for complexion, the casually expensive jeans, the manicured fingers cradled around the white china mug and those moonfaced women circling closer, like eels moving in on a juicy lump of meat.

Would Gracie turn? Would she look? Would she recognize her? Juliet backs away and slips downstairs. She leans against the window of the carpet shop sucking on a cigarette. She drops the half-smoked butt in a pool of melted ice cream, hears it fizzle and die and walks back up the stairs, breathing hard as she nears the kitchen. She pushes the door wider. How small Gracie is. *Petite*, the papers call her. Juliet edges forward, close enough to see the little mole, perfect as a dot of ink, just above her top lip. Close enough to breathe the smell of her, like rain on parched turf; tiny molecules of thrilling, addictive freshness kicking the air as she moves.

Gracie looks up. The flinch is almost imperceptible. *Careful.* Juliet pulls away, offering Gracie the chance to clap her hand to her chest and light up with recognition or at least to rumple that smooth brow and shake that shiny hair to show that somewhere inside her a memory has stirred.

'Hi,' Gracie says.

It's the coy smile that seals it, the implication that of course Juliet knows who she is, whereas Juliet is just another nameless nobody eager to pep up her dreary day with a little of the Gracie Dwyer charm. Juliet smiles back, adding the expected widening of the eyes at finding a famous face in Lynda Burton's shitty kitchen. 'We don't get many celebrities in here.'

Gracie ticks her head towards the music. 'My daughter's just started.'

Oh, yes. Let's not forget Elsie. The perfect cherry on your perfect cake.

That lumpy cow Dawn is staring at her, all folded arms and sagging belly. 'What are you doing back?'

Good to see you too. Juliet pushes past her to the kettle. 'I couldn't keep Freya away.' She moves swiftly, reaching for a mug, blocking Dawn out, her eyes fixed on Gracie. 'I didn't know you lived round here.' The lie comes easily.

'Just moved in.'

'Where were you before?'

'Greenwich.'

In your house of glass with its alarms and cameras and big high walls.

'Why the move?'

'We wanted to be close to the new bakery.'

'So whereabouts are you?'

Juliet sees the uneasiness, the pulling back. *What's the matter? Scared to tell a stranger where you live? I wouldn't worry. Everybody knows you've moved to Falcon Square. Nice. If you can afford it.* Juliet's hand flies to the buzzing

72

phone in her pocket. She glances at the screen. *Damn!* It's work, or at least a chance of it.

'Sorry. Got to take this.' She hurries into the changing area, pressing the phone to her ear.

'Aren't you the lucky one?' Dawn mutters.

Gracie looks up from her mug. 'Sorry?'

'Miss High and Mighty. Never gives the rest of us the time of day.'

'Oh.' Gracie's eyes stray to where Juliet is stabbing the air as she talks into her phone. There's a weariness about her – her roots need retouching, the orange varnish on her toenails is chipped and her skin has the coarsened pallor of a heavy smoker, saved by the kind of tip-tilt nose, flat stomach, high rounded breasts and long skinny legs that Gracie has always envied. She turns back to Dawn. 'So, what about this show? Will it be any good?'

'Not if my two are in it.'

Gracie laughs. You wouldn't catch a St Mathilda's mum knocking her offspring's talents.

'Hey, Gracie, fancy a go at this?' Leslie taps a card pinned to the corkboard advertising Lynda's 'pole dance your way to fitness' classes.

Gracie laughs. 'I'll stick to Pilates.' Though it's her self-defence that she practises every day. *Flick, kick, twist. Turn your weakness into power. Stay alert.*

The dancers thump their way through a selection of numbers from *Grease* before a round of self-applause signals the end of the session. Gracie reaches the studio doors just as they fly open. Elsie charges out through the crush.

'Amber's asking her mummy if she can come to tea. You said she could!'

'Of course.' Gracie looks round and smiles at the

exquisite-looking black woman being propelled towards her by a tall skinny girl in pink Lycra.

'That's so kind of you. Amber would love to come.' The woman's accent is American, caramel smooth, somewhere from the South.

'How about Thursday?'

'Great. Then Elsie must come to us, though my cooking won't be a patch on what she's used to.'

'Don't worry, I have my disasters.' Gracie blushes. 'That sounded awful. What I meant was, I'm sure your cooking is fabulous.'

The woman's laugh is rich and relaxed. 'I'm Laura by the way.'

Juliet pushes past. 'See you next week,' she says over her shoulder. The little girl she's dragging by the hand is bony and pale. Her dark hair could do with a wash, her black nylon leotard sags around her thin buttocks and a greying plaster flaps from her scuffed knee.

'Bye,' Gracie murmurs and smiles happily at Laura, elated that her hopes for the dance class seem to be working out. Still smiling she takes out her phone and punches in Laura's number.

Pauline Bryce Diary
Jan 15th

*I've got my plan all worked out, so first step I bunk
off college and go to the library. When I tell the
librarian what I'm after she gives me this understanding
little smile and scrabbles off into the basement. After
a while she's back with* Family Secrets: a Study of
Repressed Memories. *It's an interesting read. All about
how your mind blocks out bad things that happen to
you when you're a kid. Then I spend a couple of hours
brushing up on the law. It's very educational, the
library. Better than the useless crap they teach you at
school. There's plans to close this one down. I think
that would be a shame. So on the way out I sign the
petition.*

15

Juliet is drumming her fingers on the wheel, impatient for the lights to change when a sleek blue Audi draws up beside her. She catches the glare of the woman at the wheel. OK, so she's finishing a fag with her kid in the car. Big deal. She pings the cigarette through the open window. It hits the Audi's bonnet and spins away in a shower of sparks.

'Here you are, love.' She passes a box drink over her shoulder.

In the rear-view mirror she watches Freya pierce the seal on the box, a rush of heat beneath her skin as she asks, 'What's the new girl like?'

Freya puts the straw to her lips and sucks happily, rocking her head in time to some inner song.

'The new girl. *Elsie.*' Juliet raises her voice over the rattle of the engine. 'Dark plaits, pink leotard. Is she nice?'

Freya stops sucking and wiggles her front tooth with her thumb.

'Would you like to be her friend?'

'Liane's my friend.'

'Elsie could be your friend too.'

'Liane says I can be her friend forever. Even if I stop ballet again.'

'You're not going to stop ballet again.'

'If you don't have money, I don't mind.'

'I told you. It's fine. I've got a big new project lined up.'

'What's for tea?'

Juliet's thoughts flick to the dwindling contents of the freezer. 'Spaghetti meatballs. And if you're a good girl you can have some ice cream.' She makes a sucking sound and waggles her shoulders – a feeble pretence that another ready meal and the scrapings of a budget tub of vanilla are some kind of treat.

The woman in the Audi draws level again, shaking her head and tutting. The porridge-faced kids she's got in the back are probably going home to steamed salmon and organic broccoli, paid for by some sodding banker. But it's not just the money. Juliet has never been much of a cook and she's been so busy chasing work she hasn't had time to get to the supermarket. Maybe tomorrow she'll make Freya her favourite cauliflower cheese and pick up a bag of apples or tangerines. Something healthy. The thought jolts her back to Gracie Dwyer.

When she's home again, slamming the door on the microwave, sweeping plates into the sink, pushing work files to the edge of the table, her phone beeps. A brush-off from Ryder's. *Fuck! Fuck! Fuck!* She wrenches the plastic tray out of the microwave and stares down at the sloppy mess of meat and sauce, biting on her lip as the burn of disappointment gives way to a sharpening sense of purpose. She tips the meatballs onto a plate and carries it over to Freya, who's on the sofa glued to *Hollyoaks*.

'Elsie's mummy seems nice.'

Freya's eyes swivel glassily from the television to her plate. *Enough for today*, Juliet thinks. *Small steps.* She retreats to her bedroom with her laptop, kicking the chair round so it faces the little desk she uses when she needs privacy, aware now of just how wound-up she feels. She rifles through her cuttings drawer, snatching up a photo of Gracie hosting a charity auction, microphone in hand, looking for all the world like a fifties pinup with her taffeta swing-skirt, crimson lips and Betty Page hair-do.

She slams the drawer shut. A Google search throws up some shots of Gracie with that mouthy journalist friend of hers at some glitzy restaurant launch, the trailer for her latest TV series and her top tips for making a perfect bloody pavlova. After that it's mainly stuff Juliet has picked over a hundred times: fawning interviews about her charity work and pieces about the sale of the Wharf House. She gazes at a carefully staged press shot of Gracie and Tom, arm in arm on the steps, before stabbing the photo off the screen. Breathing fast she spools down to the coverage of the stalking campaign – the little maggot gnawing at the core of Gracie's glossy world: the leaked messages, the apology from the police, a psychiatrist's comments on the mind-set of the stalker and acres of tabloid prurience dressed as sympathy – the kind of exposure that money can't buy. The kind that works wonders for TV ratings and book sales. Her fingers tighten on the mouse. Gracie's just been appointed patron of the Stay Safe support group for victims of stalking. Juliet can guess who put her forward for that and even she has to admit it's a genius move. But Gracie Dwyer hardly needs a PR machine to power her success. It's as if she's golden, blessed, untouchable.

Sticky clots of resentment stay with her all evening, thickening her misery as she puts off the moment when she'll have to tell Freya Ian's news.

'Daddy's back from Sydney,' she says in a strained upbeat voice as she tucks her into bed.

Freya stops bouncing her hippo on the pillow and looks up with a sleepy smile. 'Can he come and see my dance show?'

'You can ask him when you see him. He's going to take you out this weekend.'

'Can you come too?'

'No, love. I've got too much work on.' *If only.* Juliet hitches her legs onto the bed and wriggles down so they lie face to face. Freya gazes at her with steady brown eyes, blinking as Juliet reaches over to brush back a strand of hair that has fallen across her cheek.

'He told me something really exciting.' For a moment the words sit on her tongue, too painful, too powerful to speak. 'He and Merion are going to have a baby. It'll be your little brother or sister.'

Freya pushes her nose into the hippo's fur and turns away to the wall. Juliet pulls her close, feeling the warm press of her back. 'It doesn't mean he'll love you any less. And if my new project works out we'll have all the money we need to do lots of fun things together. You and me. We might even be able to buy a flat of our own, maybe with a little garden.'

She lies in the half light, feeling the stillness of Freya's held breath and the flutter of her ribs when she finally speaks. 'Is my daddy going to marry Merion?'

Juliet's voice rises high. 'I don't know.'

Kids are strange. Instead of worrying about sharing her daddy, she's tuned straight in to Juliet's fears about Ian wanting a divorce, as if somehow she senses her mother's dread of a judge getting involved in the decision about custody.

Restless now, she kisses the top of Freya's head and slips away to the sitting room where she lights a cigarette and logs onto Merion's Facebook page. She clicks through the posts. No mention of wedding plans or even of the pregnancy and she is calm, calm, calm until she sees a post from last week and has to get up and there's no room to walk off the panic so she's beating at the wall with the side of her fist. Ian and Merion are buying a house in Sydney – a five-bedroom executive home. Juliet doesn't give a damn about the price tag or the size of the pool. It's the developer's blurb that is tearing her up, the chatty *The perfect home for a growing family, designed to accommodate the needs of children from tots to teens*, that drags a silent yell from her throat.

16

Gracie had hoped that the Introduction to Adoption talk would be held somewhere large and impersonal. Instead it's a cosy round-table gathering in one of the council meeting rooms, a high-ceilinged chamber filled with early evening sunlight. Just fifteen potential adopters; mainly women on their own sipping water from plastic cups, and a few fidgety couples whispering together as they study the handouts. A little of the tension breaks when a red-faced man bursts in demanding to know if this is the stand-up comedy workshop. A ripple of giggles and shaking heads sends him back down the corridor.

Tom doesn't even smile. Gracie feels his nervousness and tries to distract him. 'I'm popping down to the events site tomorrow to see how they're getting on with clearing it. We should take Elsie down there one weekend. It's such a beautiful spot—'

He shushes her as a large black woman enters the room. She has crisp greying hair braided tight to her scalp, and a mouth that seems to smile even in repose. She introduces herself as Thelma Johnson. Her assistant Carol, a smaller, neater, younger woman, gives off a palpable air of calm. These are good people, Gracie thinks. The ones who care.

Thelma welcomes everyone and talks of the adoption process as a journey that only the robust, committed and able will complete. 'This is no time for self-delusion,' she says, her dark-circled eyes taking in each face in turn. 'It's our job as social workers to get a sense of you, to make sure that you are the person you say you are and, just as crucially, to find out if you are the person you *think* you are.

'What is your understanding of parenting? Do you have the emotional resilience to deal with stress, conflict and rejection? Do you have in mind a fantasy child that no reality can ever meet? Are you truly capable of love?' The eyes of her audience flit away to settle on walls and thumbs. 'If you see adoption as a way to get over the loss of a child, a parent, a job or a relationship, think again. This is not about what you want. It's about what the child needs.'

Tom's chair creaks as he leans back. He catches Gracie's eye, seeking reassurance, which she cannot give. She turns her attention back to Thelma who is talking about babies given up voluntarily, describing them as 'relinquished', a word that whispers softly in Gracie's ears, hinting at snapped threads and an endless ache of loss.

'Even voluntarily relinquished newborns nearly always go into foster care to give the birth mother the opportunity to reclaim her baby,' Thelma is saying. 'So it's very unlikely that you will be offered a child under two. But whatever the age of the child, where possible we encourage a meeting with the birth mother, and feel it's important for that child to maintain contact with its birth siblings. Could you cope with that?'

Gracie twists at her rings.

'Ask yourselves. Are you truly willing to devote yourself

to the needs of a child who comes with a genetic endowment and a history separate from your own?'

Gracie and Tom walk out of the meeting with their fists full of forms and their heads full of words that have grown heavy with new meaning.

17

Juliet delivers Freya to the dance studio and heads to the kitchen. She stands by the window watching the reflection of the door in the grimy glass, swinging round with a ready smile when it opens.

It's Dawn, tatty hair, Chinese tattoo stretched across her blotchy arm, dumping her bag onto one of the plastic chairs. She grunts at Juliet, 'Not like you to be early.'

Juliet shrugs, rips open a strip of nicotine gum and folds it into her mouth. *Stay calm.* If it's anything like last week Elsie will turn up with that snotty nanny who buggers off straightaway. She looks around her at the smeared sink, the dusty strip light, the desiccated mop sloped against the wall. She's stupid to think that Gracie Dwyer would come back. Her nails press into her palms. Stupid to stand here waiting.

Juliet moves to the door. A flick of dark glossy hair, and there she is, pulling Elsie onto a bench, helping her into her ballet shoes. Juliet steps back, taking a moment to compose herself before she flips on the kettle. The music starts up, thumping out the passing minutes. Dawn settles down with a biro and a word search magazine and Leslie turns up complaining about the traffic. Juliet takes out her phone, pretends to dial a number and wanders out into the changing area. It's empty. Gracie must have popped out to the shops.

She hurries down to the street. She'll wait by the door, catch her as she comes back and they'll hurry upstairs together, chatting and laughing the way the other mothers do.

Juliet smokes and paces as she scans the pavement. Gracie doesn't come. Ten minutes before the lesson is due to finish Juliet climbs back up the stairs. At the top she hears Gracie's laugh – the careless confident laugh of success. And then she sees her, in the kitchen, chatting to that moron Leslie. *Damn!* She hadn't left at all. She must have been in the loo. Juliet squeezes past her. The women barely acknowledge her arrival although Gracie mutters 'Help yourself' and gestures at a Tupperware box that's empty except for a couple of broken brownies.

There's a tremor in Juliet's hand as she takes one and bites through the dusting of sugar into nuts and chocolate. *OK, here's my chance.* She lowers her eyelids and makes a warm throaty sound as if swept away by ecstasy. 'You going to be selling these at the new bakery?'

Gracie glances up. 'Of course. They're one of our best-sellers.'

'Don't know why you're bothering with that dump.' Dawn takes the last brownie, scooping up the crumbs in the box with a licked finger.

Gracie smiles. 'It was all my husband's idea. He's an architect. It's the kind of project he loves.'

'When's the work starting?' Juliet says.

Gracie sighs. 'As soon as we get planning permission. It was all going through fine but suddenly there's been a whole load of objections.'

Juliet inspects the tooth marks in her brownie. 'Let me know if you need any help with that. It's what I do. PR.'

The music snaps off, replaced by the usual whoops and applause. Gracie disappears into the changing area, Leslie and Dawn behind her. Juliet stays back, squeezing what's left of her brownie into a pulp. She timed it wrong. Messed up.

The studio doors swing open. Elsie scampers out arm in arm with that kid Amber. Freya is behind her, talking to her friend Liane. Gracie approaches Amber's mum, all smiles. Juliet cranes up a little and sees her reach into her bag. She's pulling out a batch of brightly coloured envelopes, pressing one into Laura's hand, trying to make herself heard over Elsie's showy squeals of excitement.

Juliet pushes out into the changing area, moving against the jostling tide of children until she's near enough to hear Gracie saying '. . . your husband too, if he can face it. There'll be plenty to keep the kids entertained—' she laughs her high fluttery laugh, 'hopefully the food will be all right too.'

Juliet slides her eyes to where Leslie and Dawn slouch against the wall, watching the same scene. Gracie glances up and sees them too. But she's not looking away. She's walking over to them, flicking through the envelopes. She picks out two. One purple, one orange. A flash of glittery ink as she hands them over.

Leslie and Dawn exchange looks of triumph as they rip them open. 'Nice one,' Leslie says. 'Hey, Liam,' she waves the invitation and shouts across the room, 'come and see this.'

Shit! If Juliet hadn't had to take that call last time Gracie was here she'd have been in the kitchen with her, getting friendly, and this week there'd have been an invitation for her and Freya in that overpriced designer bag. 'Quick, Freya, find your shoes!'

Gracie is close. Juliet edges closer, letting her bag slip

from her shoulder. As she bends to retrieve it there's Liam barging between them. In one swift movement she lurches forward, knocking him off balance. He stumbles into Gracie, sending her invitations flying.

'Liam!' Leslie shrieks.

'Not my fault!' He shoots a venomous look at Juliet. 'It was her. Stupid cow.'

Juliet, red and flustered, calls out to Leslie, 'Sorry. It's such a scrum in here.'

Gracie is on her knees, picking up invitations. Juliet shoves Freya forward. 'Can you help, darling. Look, there's a couple right under there.'

Freya scrabbles beneath the bench and shuffles back, grasping two gaudy, dust-smeared envelopes. Juliet points at Gracie, 'Give them to the lady.'

Freya holds out the invitations.

'Come on, love, time to go.' Juliet lays her hand on Freya's head as if to guide her away, exerting just enough pressure to keep her face to face with Gracie.

Gracie sits back on her heels, flushing a little as she takes the envelopes from Freya's hand. 'Thank you.' With an embarrassed smile she says, 'Look. . . um . . . my daughter's having a party. Would you like to come?'

Freya glances up at her mother.

'You'd love to, wouldn't you, darling?' Juliet says – a passable imitation of the breathy mum-speak she hears so often and hates.

Freya nods. 'Yes.'

'*Please*,' Juliet adds, as if manners are her top priority.

'Great.' Gracie shuffles a blank invitation to the top of the pile and takes a gold glitter pen from her bag. Her fingers hover. She looks up at Juliet.

'Freya,' Juliet says quickly.

Gracie writes *Freya* in big letters at the top of the

invitation, slips it into a sugar-pink envelope and writes it again. She smiles at Juliet, a distracted book-signing smile. 'Do come too. There'll be plenty of adults there.'

'Thanks,' Juliet says, meeting her gaze then looking away with a chirpy, 'It's a while since I've been to a party.'

On the way home Juliet takes a detour through Falcon Square. The Whittakers' tall, double-fronted house looks beautiful in the evening light. Mellow brickwork, arrowhead railings, lead window boxes overflowing with heavy white blooms and trailing ivy, a climber rose twisting over the fanlight. A world away from Tom's prize-winning house of glass in Greenwich.

18

Gracie always longed for a proper garden. Not a paved courtyard like the one they'd had in Greenwich or the cluttered roof terrace of the flat she'd lived in before she married Tom. What she yearned for was a wide lawn, leafy borders, mature trees and a place to grow her own herbs and vegetables. At Falcon Square she has all those things, plus a mossy cherub spouting water into a shell-shaped trough, a summerhouse and a gardener employed to keep the whole thing looking fashionably unkempt.

A horde of athletic young men in day-glo shirts, baggy trousers, shades and trilbies have spent the morning erecting a striped gazebo next to the summerhouse, laying the dance floor, trailing bunting and fairy lights through the trees and blowing up huge bunches of pink and gold balloons that quiver in the breeze like globs of dividing cells. By two o'clock the band is tuning up and the first wave of guests is pouring through the French windows, gasping at the delights on offer.

'Have you seen Daphne's new bloke?' Tom catches Gracie's arm as she sweeps past him with a bowl of marinated ribs. She pivots round. This one must be at least ten years Daphne's junior, surfer blond, tanned biceps straining the rolled-up sleeves of his faded denim shirt. Daphne sees them looking and drags him over, unable to hide a smug smile. 'Tom, Gracie, this is Dieter.'

'Great to meet you,' Dieter says.

'You too.'

'He's over from Munich for a conservation conference,' Daphne says.

Gracie's brows lift, signalling – *Sexy* and *green. Where do you find them?*

Daphne grins and whisks Dieter away to dance.

On her way back to the kitchen Gracie bumps into Tom's friend Geoff from ACP. It's the first time she's seen him since the business with Alicia.

'Hi, Gracie, you're looking great.'

She searches his face for hints of pity or embarrassment and blinks nervously, unsure of what she sees. 'Thanks, Geoff.'

She's moving quickly through the crowd when Kelvin, her producer, wobbles past on a unicycle. Gracie jumps back laughing, almost treading on the fingers of a woman sitting in the grass.

'Oops, sorry.'

It's Juliet from the dance class. She's made an effort and she's looking pretty good – her hair is up, the red linen dress shows off her figure and the toenails peeking through the front of her strappy high heels are freshly varnished. Her daughter sits beside her, gazing entranced at a fairy princess juggling glitter balls.

'Hey, you haven't got a drink!' Gracie says.

Juliet looks up. 'It's OK. I'll grab one in a minute.'

'I'll get it, what do you want – wine, beer, Pimm's or punch?'

'Pimm's please.'

Gracie smiles at Juliet's daughter. 'What would you like . . .' a pause for a fraction of a second then a quick relieved smile as she says her name, '*Freya* – do you want to come and choose an ice cream soda?'

Freya looks warily at Gracie's outstretched hand, only taking it when Juliet gives her a little push. 'Go on, sweetheart, don't be shy.'

Gracie shoulders her way to the bar, helps Freya to choose a raspberry chocolate float and chats to Heather's boyfriend Lyall, who is manning the soda fountain, while she collects a couple of glasses of Pimm's. On the way back to Juliet she makes a detour to deliver Freya to the face-painters under the gazebo.

'Thanks, she loves having her face painted,' Juliet says, taking the glass Gracie hands her. 'We haven't seen you at ballet for a while.'

'Work's been crazy.' Her eyes flit across the nearby faces. 'Hey, Kelvin, come and work your charm! Juliet, this is Kelvin the creative genius from Mange Tout TV who produces all my shows. He's also the one to blame for the band.' She pushes the second glass of Pimm's into his hand and dashes away to greet Laura and a tall older man in a neatly pressed check shirt who must be Amber's dad.

19

Faces whirl past as Kelvin twirls Juliet around the dance floor: famous names waving across the crowd, dressed-down media types murmuring into their phones, celebrity mums cooing over that ludicrously over-the-top cake – a prancing, rainbow-maned unicorn with a golden crown spiked with six candles on its head – and Elsie in gleaming white dungarees and sequined high top trainers queening it over swarms of pushy children clustered around the entertainers. This isn't a magazine spread. This is Gracie's life. And here she is, Juliet Beecham, finally on the inside, seeing it for real.

A craggy-faced blond man in faded denim flicks her a glance, tips a bottle of beer to his mouth and disappears into the crowd and there's Gracie – greeting, laughing, hugging – mistress of it all. While Kelvin is flirting over her shoulder with a waiter half his age, Juliet slips from his grasp, takes another glass from a passing waitress and makes her way towards two stocky men – white shirts, cropped hair, a little too muscly. Juliet knows security when she sees it and she'd noticed them by the door discreetly checking out the guests when she handed in her invitation.

The men separate, nodding and smiling, never quite

mingling. She ducks past Dawn and Leslie, knocking back punch in their sweaty, over-made-up best, and approaches the older of the men. He wears an earpiece, holds a can of Coke in thick fingers and doesn't take long to meet her gaze.

'Hi.'

'Hi.'

'Parent? Friend? Celebrity?'

He grins white teeth. 'Staff.'

'Caterer or clown?'

His smile widens. 'Definitely not a caterer.'

With a tilt of her head she says, 'So let's see your act.'

'You don't get to see me perform unless something goes very badly wrong.'

She moistens her lips with a gulp of wine, wishing her tongue didn't feel so rubbery. 'You any good?'

'The best.'

'Cop?'

'Used to be.'

'Are you here because of the stalker?'

'Better safe than sorry.'

She sips her drink and gazes across the crowd. 'How would you know who it was?'

'We wouldn't. Not unless he tried something. But if he did, we're here. Fucking weirdo. Going after a lovely woman like that.' He's watching Gracie running barefoot across the grass, a flutter of billowing skirts as she reaches out to hug a tall, ruddy-faced man who's got Ian's colouring, build, and similar dark unruly hair. Juliet throws a mental switch. She's not here to think about Ian.

'Who's that she's talking to?'

'Hugh Dugdale. The MP.'

'I knew I recognised him. I've seen him on the news.'

'The bloke with them is the comedian, Rory Devine. He's always at Gracie's parties.'

93

'Do you work for her a lot, then?'

'On and off.'

Juliet scans the crowd. 'How many security people has she got here?'

He sips his can of Coke. 'What's it to you?'

'Oh you know, too many long lonely evenings with nothing to do except watch cop shows.'

'That kind of thing can make you very edgy, damage your health.' His eyes linger on hers as he hands her a card. 'You ever need my services, you give me a call.'

She looks down at the name before she drops the card into her bag. 'Thanks, *Chris*.'

'And you are?'

'Juliet.'

He strolls away, one hand in the pocket of his jeans.

A woman stumbles past, screeching with laughter. She pounces when she sees Juliet lighting a cigarette. Juliet offers her the pack and the lighter. With a shiver she realises that this is Daphne Dawes. Gracie's best friend, darling of the TV chat show circuit, guaranteed to come out with an outrageous opinion on anything from Islamic State to vaginal orgasms. 'Thanks.' Daphne takes a long drag and blows out the smoke from the side of her mouth, her gaze cool and appraising. 'You with Mange Tout TV?'

'No. My daughter's a friend of Elsie's. That's her over there with the princess juggler.' Juliet sees the blond man in the denim shirt elbowing his way towards them. Daphne glances round. Ramming her arm through his, she drags him away.

The band takes a break. The dancers ebb from the dance floor, little cliques forming and breaking up as they gather around the barbeque. Through it all one fair head dips and rises, pumping hands, kissing cheeks, slowing now and then to share a joke but never quite stopping in his ceaseless quest to establish new contacts, consolidate old ones and hoover up the latest gossip. Jeremy Daley. CEO of Daley Associates PR. Anxious to avoid him Juliet dodges away. Elsie staggers towards her on mini stilts, her face a mask of tiger stripes.

'Hey, you look great,' Juliet says.

Elsie wobbles past her. 'Granny, look at me!'

The word swings Juliet around. Elsie is tottering towards a handsome, well-preserved couple laughing together on the fringes of the plate-spinning class. The man is clumsy, jerking his stick around, dropping his plate. The woman, silver blonde, straight-backed, fine-boned, keeps hers aloft without effort.

Juliet wanders towards her. 'You're a natural.'

The woman laughs. 'It's all that deportment they made us do at school.'

She has a faint accent – American? Canadian? 'So you're Elsie's grandmother?'

'That's right.' The woman smiles down at Elsie, full of possessive pride. 'I'm Stella. This is my husband, Todd.'

Juliet sways a little, her spiky heels sinking into the lawn. She's steadied by Stella's firm grip on her arm. 'Whoops. Are you all right?'

'Yes, yes, I'm fine. Are you visiting or do you live over here?'

'We moved to London when Todd retired.' She ruffles Elsie's hair. 'Mainly so we could spend more time with this one.'

Juliet takes a gulp from her glass. These aren't Gracie's parents, she's sure of that. Maybe Tom was adopted? Yes. She could just imagine these two proving to the world how liberal they were by picking out a cute little mixed race baby and sending him to an English public school. 'You're . . . Tom's mum and dad, right?'

The woman's eyes seek her husband's. He says softly, 'Actually, we're Louise's parents.'

'Louise?'

Stella says quietly, 'Tom's first wife.'

Juliet knows he'd had one, with all the press making

Gracie out to be some kind of saint for taking on a widower and his 'poor motherless baby'; how could she not? It makes her puke. Grabbing herself a good-looking architect and getting a ready-made family and his undying devotion all thrown in isn't exactly an act of martyrdom, especially if you can afford a full-time nanny. 'Oh. I . . . didn't realise.'

Todd forces a smile, anxious to keep things jolly. 'Can I get anyone another drink?'

Stella hands him her empty glass. Juliet flattens her hand over hers and shakes her head. 'I'm fine.' When he's gone she says, 'Great party.'

Stella's smile is gracious. 'Grace is an excellent hostess.'

Grace? Noting the missing syllable Juliet fishes a little. 'And this house. What a find. Living nearer to the studios must make things so much easier for her.'

'It's listed, I believe.'

Juliet follows Stella's gaze to where a giggling Gracie is spinning across the dance floor in the arms of Rory Devine.

'Did you ever see the Wharf House?' Stella is saying.

Juliet plumps for part of the truth. 'My daughter only just met Elsie at dance class but I saw the photos in the paper when they put it up for sale. Amazing.'

'I'll never forget the day Louise found that plot. She called me the minute she got back, so excited, so full of ideas for the dream home she wanted to build.'

Thrown a little, Juliet says, 'Was she an architect too?'

'A photographer. Louise Harper?' Stella searches for recognition in Juliet's face. Seeing none, she goes on undeterred, 'I'm sure you'd recognise her work if you saw it. She was so gifted. But as Todd always says, she would have excelled in any field she'd chosen.'

Aware of the fragility of the moment Juliet murmurs, 'I'm so sorry. You must miss her.'

'It's a terrible thing to lose a child. Unnatural. There's a wound inside you that stays raw even though you know the world must go on.'

'Do you have other children?'

She shakes her head. 'We never felt the need. Even as a baby Louise was quite extraordinary.'

'Having Elsie must be such a comfort.'

'Yes.' Stella smiles brightly.

'So sad for you. And for Tom. It must be terrible to lose a wife so young.'

Stella nods. 'He's a wonderful father. We offered to take Elsie to live with us for a while to give him time to grieve, but he couldn't bear to be parted from her.'

'What a blessing Gracie's so good with her. She obviously adores her.'

Stella is stepping away. 'Would you excuse me? I think Todd wants to introduce me to someone.'

Juliet watches her go. Christ. Stella is one bit of Gracie's life she definitely doesn't envy. She sees Amber's mother Laura, stunning in bright orange, and behind her that MP Hugh Dugdale fooling around on a unicycle. He wobbles towards the barbeque, swerves and falls off. And there's Gracie laughing as she rushes from the dance floor to drag him to his feet. Daley's weaselling in there too, gripping Dugdale's arm, clapping him on the back, sharing in the joke like they're old friends.

She catches sight of Tom and weaves through the crowd, strangers pressing in on her, as she veers across his path. His arm brushes hers. He's taller than she imagined, and his face is gentler; warm and well shaped.

'Great party,' she says.

'All down to Gracie.' He's directing his gaze over her shoulder. 'She's brilliant at this kind of thing.'

She can't stop herself staring at him, edging a little closer, inhaling the smell of his cologne.

'So how are you finding it living up here?' She's tottering on her heels. 'A bit different from Greenwich.'

'We're settling in.'

'I just met Stella and Todd. It's lovely that you keep in touch.' She's annoyed at the floppiness of her tongue, the way it's slurring her words. 'My ex's parents would have a heart attack if I invited them to a party.'

'Stella and Todd are good people.'

The band bursts into an enthusiastic rendering of 'Take a Chance on Me'. She laughs, suddenly bold. 'Want to dance?'

He steps away as if he hasn't heard her. 'The barman's calling me. Help yourself to food.'

She watches him go. Food. Maybe that's what she needs. She hasn't eaten since breakfast.

Daphne tugs at Gracie's arm. 'For Christ's sake do something about your friend.'

Gracie spins round. Juliet is hanging onto Dieter, lipstick smeared, eyes glazed, hardly able to stand up.

'Oh my God.'

'She was pissed when I talked to her an hour ago,' Tom groans. 'Now look at her. I'll call her a taxi.'

'No, leave it,' Gracie says. 'She can't take her kid home in that state. We'll have to let her sleep it off. Daph, tell Dieter to take her inside. I'll get Heather to put her to bed.'

Dieter pulls Juliet's arm across his shoulder and heaves her towards the French windows. She's lost one shoe and broken the heel of the other. To Gracie there's something far more humiliating about her trailing, mud-stained sole than her slack mouth and slurred muttering.

'Who is she anyway?' Daphne snaps.

'One of the dance mums. Her daughter's that funny little thing, over there.' Sensing their stares, Freya looks round, sees her mother being helped away by Dieter and starts to run after her.

'Oh Lord.' Gracie cuts her off. 'Freya, it's OK. Your mummy's not feeling very well. She's just going to lie down for a bit then she'll be fine.'

'You wish,' murmurs Daphne striding up the steps after Dieter.

Gracie takes Freya's hand and hurries her away to join the juggling class.

As dusk falls the trees blossom with fairy lights, small children are whisked away and a new wave of adults drifts in.

'That drunk's still totally out of it,' Heather says as she hands Gracie a bowl of plum sauce for the kebabs.

'I suppose we'll have to leave her to sleep it off.'

'What about her kid?'

'She'll be in the den with the others.'

'No. I just checked. I can't see her anywhere.'

'Oh, no.' Gracie drops the bowl on the counter and rushes away to scour the garden. Heather joins her, searching behind bushes and under tables until they find Freya in the summerhouse, curled up frail and miserable on the floor, her eyelids swollen with crying.

'Poor wee mite.' Heather scoops her up, rubbing her back as she carries her back to the house. Gracie follows her into the den where Elsie, Amber and a couple of girls from Elsie's old school lie stretched out on blow-up mattresses in front of a DVD.

'Hey, guess what?' Gracie says. 'Freya's going to stay over because her mummy's not feeling very well.' She glares at Elsie, daring her to complain.

Heather deposits Freya on a pile of cushions and brushes the hair from her face. 'You stay there, sweetheart. I'll fetch you some pyjamas.'

Pauline Bryce Diary
22nd Jan

The knock comes at ten past six. I can see them through the living room window – three policemen and a policewoman and I get scared something might go wrong so I slip into the hallway behind Mum. They ask her if Ronald Bryce lives here. She says yes, what's this about and they tell her they've had a tip-off about Ron purchasing illegal porn and they've got a warrant to search the house. Mum goes berserk, screaming that they've got no right to go round accusing innocent people. Ron pats her shoulder and tells her to keep calm – it's all some stupid mistake – but the policemen snap on surgical gloves and start tearing the place apart while the policewoman takes the three of us into the kitchen, and all the time she's giving Ron these funny sideways looks. We're stuck in there for ages and I'm looking out at the garden, getting a bit worried and then finally two of them come barging in and go down to the shed. Ten minutes later they're back with the photos in a plastic bag. Ron goes this really funny colour and he looks at Mum with this pathetic begging face and tells her it's bollocks, which is weird because I've never heard him swear before. He's in such a state it's not until they're putting him in the car – and not being too nice about it – that he shouts out to Mum, telling her to phone his cousin Malcolm who's a solicitor. It's nearly midnight when they get back from the station and I'm starting to get worried again. But it's OK. Good old Malc told the police anyone could have walked through our back gate and planted that stuff in our shed and they didn't have a case because there wasn't any forensic evidence to link it to Ron.

Course there wasn't. My plan's not going to work if he actually goes to jail. Mum and Ron never drink except at Christmas but they get through half a bottle of sherry sitting at the kitchen table trying to work out what sort of sicko would plant filth like that in Ron's shed then tip off the police.

20

At nine the next morning Gracie tiptoes upstairs and cracks open the door of the spare room, wrinkling her nose at the sour smell of vomit and the dishevelled bump on the bed. The rough scrape of Juliet's breath tells her that she's still out cold.

Gracie pads down to the kitchen. Tom looks up from his toast. 'She awake?'

'No.'

'Shall I tell the breeder we'll be late?'

'Why should we let her mess up Elsie's birthday surprise? If she's not up by ten we'll leave her a note and take Freya with us.'

'I'm not leaving that woman on her own in our house.'

'It's all right. Lyall stayed over with Heather.' Gracie heads off down the hall, calling over her shoulder, 'I'll tell them to keep an eye on her.'

Gracie busies herself with the toppling pile of presents in the hall, thinking over the events of the party as she divides the housewarming bottles of single malt and elegantly packaged candles from Elsie's birthday gifts. At least a few of the girls from her class turned up. As for Gracie's long-term plans, it will take weeks, maybe months to see how they play out. She lifts a long box wrapped in pink Disney paper. She freezes, all her senses alive. A pair of hollow eyes is staring up at her through the parcels. Eyes she recognises. Eyes that belong to the crude little figurine Louise brought back from Borneo. Her heart beating fast she pulls it free and unhooks a metallic gift tag from its outstretched fingers. The message, in small cramped writing, is unsigned.

Great to see your new house. Enjoy!

Tom clanks down the hall lugging a crate of bottles. 'What's that doing there?'

'I . . . don't know.'

'Well I'm glad it's turned up. I thought it had got lost in the move,' he says, opening the front door.

She gives a little shake of her head. How can she tell him that she hid the loathsome thing in one of the giant planters they left for the new owners? The wretched removal men must have fished it out and put it in the garden somewhere. Yes, she tells herself, that'll be it. And the tag from another gift will have got snagged in its fingers when some joker from last night brought the statue inside. So why is her heart still hammering so hard that it hurts?

Tom calls up the stairs, 'Elsie, Freya, shoes on! Time to go!'

By the time they've got everyone into the car, Gracie is calm again, annoyed with herself for imagining a threat that isn't there. She glances at Tom as she buckles her seat belt. He's watching the girls in the mirror, enjoying the symmetry. Two children in the back, two adults in the front. She turns to look at them too, glad that they've started the adoption process. Sure now that the time is right to move things on.

* * *

The breeder is out in Kent, a small cottage with a dresser stacked with mismatched crockery and a squirming mass of fur in a basket beside the Aga. Elsie and Freya drop to their knees squealing with delight. Tom takes control, chatting to the breeder while he picks up the fat-bellied spaniel puppies one by one in his big strong hands. A rheumy-eyed mother dog with trailing teats pads across the flagstones to sniff the strangers. Gracie puts out a nervous hand, pulling it away as the dog emits a wheezy rumble that might have been a growl.

Finally Tom and Elsie agree on a plucky little female who has burrowed her way through her siblings to nibble at Elsie's fingertips with sharp tiny teeth. Tom grins as he puts away his chequebook. 'Come on then, let's get her home.'

Freya is hugging a wriggling male, refusing to let it go.

'Put him back now,' Gracie says gently. She helps Freya to lift the little dog into the basket, rubbing her back as she stands up bereft.

On the journey home Elsie responds to Tom's reminders about sharing by letting Freya take the puppy onto her lap a couple of times then wrenching it away almost immediately.

'What are you going to call her?' Gracie asks.

'Tallulah,' Elsie announces.

Tom groans in mock horror.

Laughing, Gracie glances from her husband to the children. They're laughing too, and for the first time in months she's swept up in a surge of joy. She closes her eyes, daring to believe that the contentment she thought she'd lost for ever is back within reach. A sudden punch of panic snatches it all away and leaves her gasping at the memory of coming eye to eye with Louise's mocking figurine.

21

Juliet opens heavy lids. A shifting blur of French grey wood-work and sunlight through tall windows edges into focus; white blinds, stripped boards, an antique mirror over a marble fireplace. Simple. Expensive. Magazine chic. She turns slowly, dreading what she's going to find. The other side of the bed is empty. She's passed out on plenty of strange beds over the years, but rarely woken up in one fully dressed and alone. She pushes back the covers. A wave of nausea batters her body and slowly recedes, leaving a backwash of fury and self-loathing as she remembers the party and realises where she is and what she's done. She sways to the window. The garden is deserted, the dance floor gone, the chairs and tables stacked up by the side gate, awaiting collection. A second wave of sickness rolls and rises bringing a scatter of memories: talking, dancing, eating, laughing with some foreign guy – German? Dutch? – then suddenly feeling like shit. Oh God. So much for pacing herself. A slow burn of embarrassment creeps through her limbs as more of last night comes back: waking in the dark, throwing up in a plastic bowl left thoughtfully beside the bed. She turns and checks the floor. The dirty bowl has been replaced by a clean one that now sits reproachfully on a folded towel. What a screw up. How much did she drink? She remembers a couple of glasses of Pimm's before she hit the wine but she can usually hold her drink. Maybe it was the food. She almost laughs. The tabloids would have a field day with that – *Gracie Dwyer Poisons Kids' Party Guests*.

Oh God. Freya! She lurches onto the landing calling her name. The house stays wrapped in silence, the kind that tells you nobody's home. No mass food poisoning then. Shame. She's not worried, though. Perfect hostess Gracie Dwyer will be looking after Freya, just like she looked after Juliet.

She drags herself down the landing in search of a bathroom, stumbling into an airing cupboard and what must be the nanny's room – rumpled bed, snaps of doughy redheads of various ages and sizes Blu-Tacked to the wall and a neatly folded note wedged beneath the door. She picks it up and smooths it out.

Back around 1.00 pm. Juliet still asleep. Please keep an eye on her till we get home. G.

She glances at the alarm clock: 11.30. Plenty of time to take a little look around Gracie's home. She refolds the note and wedges it back where she found it. Maybe getting pissed wasn't such a screw up after all.

She finds a bathroom, splashes her face with water and peers into the mirror, hating the drawn grey creature that stares back. Idiot! She rips off her soiled dress, pulls on the cotton bathrobe hanging on the back of the door and hurries downstairs. The sunlit kitchen is pristine, all the party leftovers cleared away. Every scrap of them. Except her. Her handbag sits on the granite countertop holding down another note, this one addressed to her.

Juliet
  Taken Freya with us to pick up Elsie's present.
Give Heather a shout if you need anything.
Gracie

Trouble is, Gracie, Heather's not here.

She takes out her phone. Damn. The battery is almost dead. She makes for the pinboard: notes from the school, contact details for plumbers, cleaners and babysitters, a calendar covered in more of Gracie's neat, controlling italics and what must be Heather's scrappier handwriting. Dentist's appointments, term dates, school trips, Gracie and Tom's schedules, Heather's days off. A carefully managed system of adult lives orbiting around that little brat Elsie.

Working swiftly she photographs each item, lifting the pages of the calendar to cover the next two months. She checks the time again, cursing as her battery dies. Her body is screaming at her to go back to bed. She ignores it. She wasted last night. Phone or no phone, she's not going to waste what's on offer today.

She stuffs her dress into a bin liner, flicks Gracie's note to the floor and with a quick glance at the front door drags herself upstairs. If anyone catches her she'll say she didn't see the note and she's searching the house for Freya.

The master bedroom is disappointing: oak boards, walk-in closet, enormous French bed, books and magazines stacked on the floor – a room still waiting to belong. The ensuite is more interesting. Damp towels on the rack, Tom's shirt and jeans crumpled on the floor. She feels an almost erotic thrill as she slides her hand into the back pocket, brings out a handful of change and lets the coins trickle back inside. She lifts his razor, taps the blade with a fingernail and sets it down beside the can of shaving foam. Rubbing a dollop of Gracie's moisturiser into her face she opens the mirrored cabinet above the sink. No contraceptive pills, no condoms, no cap. She tears off a piece of tissue and wipes away the finger marks she's left on the glass. The room starts to spin. She grips the edge of the roll-top bath until it stops.

Gracie's closet is a mix of designer labels, high street basics and colourful vintage pieces, no doubt picked out by some overpaid stylist employed to maintain the casual quirkiness of Gracie's look. She slips her toes into a silvery green stiletto. It's far too small. She kicks it back onto the rack and moves on to the drawers. Silky bras and knickers in oyster and black that catch on the roughened skin of her fingers. Her mouth floods with saliva. She runs back to the bathroom and vomits yellow bile into Gracie Dwyer's white porcelain toilet.

Elsie's room is a little girl's dream: star-spangled gauze draped above a double bed, stuffed animals crowded against the footboard, a worn brown bear on the pillow, glitter-dusted wings hanging from the wall. Juliet inspects the photos on the mantelpiece – Elsie, Gracie and Tom screaming in the gondola of a fairground ride and behind it, almost hidden from view, a black and white studio shot of a woman with sharp cheekbones, shoulder-length fair hair and a quizzical smile. Louise. The resemblance to Stella is inescapable.

She opens a door across the landing, thrilling to the realisation that this is Gracie's study – a wall of half-filled bookshelves, a big vintage desk and a cream chaise longue scattered with bright cushions, resting on a faded Persian carpet. On the desk a wedding photo, bride and groom on the steps of Chelsea registry office – Gracie radiant in calf-length ivory lace, Tom, happy and handsome at her side, and Elsie on her hip in a blush-pink dress and a little crown of rosebuds, reaching pudgy starfish hands to catch the confetti thrown by the smiling guests. Juliet's eyes focus in on a couple in the crowd. It's Stella and Todd, leaning against each other as if, without support, they might fall. Bloody hell. That must have put a damper on the day.

A couple of pens and a handful of coins rattle against a pack of ink cartridges as she opens the top drawer of the desk. She fingers the roll of fifty-pound notes thrown in beside a tatty antique cookbook – Mrs Mary Henderson's *Practical Cooking and Dinner Giving*. The handwritten note on the flyleaf: *A little something to say thank you for last night. H xx*, fires a slew of images – an exclusive supper, trusted friends sharing secrets around Gracie's kitchen table, safe in their impenetrable bubble of power and privilege. She drops it back and slams the drawer. The lower drawer resists her sharp tugs on the handle. She puts her finger to the tiny brass-rimmed keyhole then runs it across to the shiny new lock shaft protruding from the top right-hand corner. Her irritation fades a little as she kneels to inspect the underside of the desk and sees a slip of paper taped to the wood. She picks it off with her nail. Pencilled on the back there's a seemingly random series of numbers and letters. The kind of password IT professionals recommend. The kind they advise their clients not to tape beneath the desk their computer sits on. She scribbles it down on a Post-it note, drops it into her bin liner and sticks the password back where she found it.

Tucked beneath a pile of fan mail she finds the business plan for the new bakery. It doesn't take long to loosen the binder and run the pages through the photocopier. It's a risk, but one worth taking. While it's printing she stands by the window, checking for movement in the square as she sifts through the bills, letters and circulars in Gracie's in-tray.

She puts the plan back where she found it and drops the

roll of copies into her bin liner. Clasping it tightly she hurries up the narrow stairs that lead to the attic. Exposed rafters, sunlight muted by the half-drawn blinds, a dormer window looking out across London and a wall of poster-sized photographs. Male and sparse and still. This room is obviously Tom's.

She inspects the bronze trophy on the desk, reluctantly ignores the slim silver laptop and moves on to the plan chest, delighting in the oiled glide of the runners as the drawers give up their contents: photographic prints, layered between sheets of dark pulpy paper – unsmiling portraits, faces etched with misery, parched landscapes. Each one numbered and signed by Louise Harper, her firm slanting signature dominated by the down strokes of the *L* and the *H*. And there are sketches of the Wharf House, or rather the essence of it; an idea of shape and light and river, drawn in soft lead on thick, ragged-edged paper, initialled with the same strong sloping *LH*. Beneath that she finds blueprints for the building, Louise's sketchy idea transformed into an architectural drawing. She closes the drawers and kneels to inspect the framed prints stacked against the wall. Stella was right. Louise had been good at what she did. Exceptional in fact, as well as looking like a supermodel. *How does that feel, Gracie?*

Juliet scurries downstairs, pushing open a door in the little passageway by the kitchen. It swings back onto a flight of stone steps. She feels along the brickwork for the light switch. The flagstones below are littered with packing cases, some sealed with bands of shiny brown packing tape, some left tantalisingly open, some emptied, flattened and stacked in piles.

Outside a car door slams. Dizzied by a swoop of nausea she closes the cellar door and hurries into the kitchen.

* * *

Elsie marches down the hall with a small black and white puppy in her arms, cradling it with all the pride and trepidation of a new mother bringing home her firstborn, Tom to one side of her, Freya in borrowed shorts and T-shirt dancing attendance on the other, and Gracie bringing up the rear. Juliet half stands up as Tom comes in. 'Thanks so much for looking after Freya. I'm so mortified about this. I don't know what to say.'

'Look, Mummy.' Freya runs to her, bright-eyed, smiling a joyous, gappy smile. 'Elsie got a puppy. It's called Tallulah.'

'Lucky Elsie.'

Gracie shifts Freya gently aside, her eyes on Juliet's bathrobe. Juliet plucks at the fabric. 'I hope you don't mind . . . my dress was a mess. Disgusting actually.' She lifts the knotted bin liner and pulls a remorseful face. 'I . . . I don't know what happened. I hardly drank anything. Did anyone else get sick?'

Gracie's eyes widen at the implication. 'Not that I know of.'

'Sorry, I didn't mean . . .'

Tom is jumpy, looking around the kitchen. 'Where's Heather?'

Juliet gives him a vaguely bewildered smile. 'I don't think she's here. I haven't seen anyone.'

He glowers at Gracie who frowns confusion. He turns away, pulling out his phone and strides into the garden.

'Look,' Juliet says. 'I hate to ask but could I take a shower and borrow something to go home in?'

'Oh.' Clearly exasperated, Gracie tears her eyes from Tom. 'All right. I . . . I'll find you something.'

Gracie hurries her up to her own bathroom, turns on the shower and pushes a towel into Juliet's hands. Juliet leans against the tiled wall, watching as Gracie throws open

111

the door of her closet and tosses a black wrap skirt and a white top onto the bed.

'You broke your sandals.'

Juliet flinches, imagining herself tripping up and going sprawling in front of Gracie's smart friends. 'Oh Lord.'

'What size are you?'

'Seven.'

Gracie tosses down a pair of espadrilles. 'I'm a five but these should get you home.'

'Thanks,' Juliet says. 'God, I feel so embarrassed.'

Gracie puts up her hands palm outwards, a gesture of *don't worry about it* but there's a rigidity in her splayed fingers as if she's warding Juliet off. 'We've all been there,' she says.

Juliet doubts that very much. She showers slowly, relishing the pressure of the water, the sharp piney soap washing away the staleness and soothing her pounding head. Naked, she walks into the bedroom and stands in front of the full-length mirror, pulling on the top and wrapping the skirt around her waist, smoothing it over her hips, looking at herself this way and that. It seems natural to pull open a drawer and help herself to a pair of knickers. She shoves her feet into the espadrilles, treads down the backs and there she is. In Gracie Dwyer's bedroom, wearing Gracie Dwyer's clothes. She still feels like shit but if she goes on playing the penitent, she's sure she can turn this around.

Hugging the knotted bin bag close she comes downstairs. Through the open French windows she sees Tom, Gracie, Elsie and Freya eating lunch on the lawn under a wide white umbrella. She hovers in the doorway shielding her eyes from the sun.

'I've heated you up some soup,' Gracie calls. 'It's in the saucepan on the stove.'

Juliet is about to refuse but the soup smells good and

112

suddenly she feels hungry. She pours the thin broth into the bowl Gracie has left out on a tray beside a spoon and a plate of salted crackers, squeezes the bin bag under her arm and carries the food outside. The sun is too bright for her and there are no spare chairs at the table so she takes the tray over to the lounger under the trees. She tastes a spoonful of the soup. It slips down, soothing her raw, empty stomach. Gracie looks up.

Juliet waves the spoon and says weakly, 'Thanks for this. It's just what I needed.'

Gracie doesn't seem to hear her. Elsie leans down, tempting the puppy with a piece of chicken, 'Talloooolah!'

Tom pounces, quick and firm. 'No, Elsie. You mustn't feed her from the table.'

Elsie sticks out her lip, screws up her eyes and folds her arms.

Juliet finishes the soup, sets the tray on the grass and lies back listening to the sounds of the garden: Elsie and Freya discussing whether to have chocolate or vanilla ice cream with their strawberries, the dog yapping, distant traffic, the buzz of a bee in the lilac. Watching the clouds makes her feel drowsy, drifting, detached.

'Gosh, look at you!' Gracie's voice cuts the quiet, springing Juliet from sleep. Freya is whizzing down the path on Elsie's bike, upright and steady.

'Who taught you to ride like that?' Gracie is saying.

Freya throws back her head. 'My daddy. He got me a bike for Christmas.'

Juliet looks away. It's not Ian who spends endless Sunday afternoons in the park watching the rest of the world play happy families so that Freya can practise.

Elsie drags at Gracie's arm. 'It's not fair. It's *my* bike!'

'You have to let Freya have a turn.'

Freya coasts around the corner with a wave in Tom's

direction. He looks up from his newspaper. 'Hey, Freya, that's fantastic.'

Elsie lets out a wail of frustration.

'OK, honey. Your turn now,' Gracie says. She's helping Freya off the bike but she's looking over at Juliet, her mouth firm and red.

Juliet swings her legs off the lounger and stands up. A rush of nausea brings the grass towards her. Her whole body is shaking. Gracie runs over to catch her. 'Are you all right?'

'No.' She falls back onto the lounger waiting for Gracie to tell her to go upstairs and lie down.

'I'll give you a lift home,' Gracie says, brusquely.

Juliet clutches her stomach and calls half-heartedly, 'Freya. We'd better be getting back.'

'But, Mummy, I have to say goodbye to Talloooolah.' The way she's aping that monster Elsie makes Juliet feel even sicker.

'Hurry up then.'

Gracie calls after her. 'Your balloons and party bag are in the den, and can you bring your mummy's handbag?'

Juliet hauls herself towards the house, still holding the bin bag to her chest like a badge of shame, afraid that Gracie might offer to carry it and discover the souvenirs she's taking home. But Gracie strides ahead, stopping to whisper in Elsie's ear as they get inside. Juliet follows slowly and finds Freya kneeling on the kitchen floor nuzzling Tallulah's neck.

'Come on,' she says. Freya clings to the puppy, pushing her face into its fur.

'Hey, Freya,' Elsie says. 'You can come and see Tallulah any time you want. You can be her . . . godmother.' She glances up at Gracie, clearly delivering the line she's just been fed to get rid of her mother's unwelcome guests.

114

Gracie cups Elsie's cheek. 'That's so sweet of you, darling.'

Once in the car Juliet points the way with grunts and waves of a shaky finger, grateful, despite herself, for Gracie's firm capable hands helping her up the steps at the other end.

22

Gracie unhooks Juliet's handbag from Freya's shoulder and pulls out a pair of keys on a blue glass fob. Freya shakes her head. 'Not those.'

Gracie scrabbles among the jumble of tissues, cigarette packs and loose coins till she finds another set and opens the front door of the building.

Freya scurries inside and waits as Gracie slips her arm around Juliet's waist and pulls her into the shared entrance. Dizzied by the movement, Juliet reaches for the wall and vomits a brown splash of liquid. Gracie twitches with disgust as she steps across the mess to unlock Juliet's door. She follows Freya into a narrow hallway – woodchip paper half stripped from one wall, scuffed skirting, bare floorboards ridged with black varnish, framed posters knocked and left askew.

Juliet staggers into a bedroom that smells of cigarettes, sleep and damp towels, collapses onto the unmade bed without kicking off her borrowed espadrilles and curls forward gripping her stomach. Gracie picks up the corner of the trailing duvet and drops it across her legs.

'I'll make you some tea,' she says.

Freya leads her into the gloom of a small sitting-room-cum-kitchen furnished with flea market tat abandoned at various stages of renovation. Faded velvet curtains block the sunlight while a saucer of cigarette stubs and an open bottle of wine sour the stuffy warmth. Gracie inspects the greasy plates and cheap mugs ringed with brown stacked in and around the sink. No pots, pans or signs of preparation. She wipes the vomit from her toe with a piece of kitchen paper and drops it into a pedal bin crammed with pizza boxes and empty bottles of cheap white wine. Looking about her she realises how hard Juliet is struggling to cope, how close she is to the edge. She fills the kettle, assailed by thoughts of the little flat she'd shared with Harry Flynn and how, when he walked out on her, she'd been plunged into a deep depression and let things get on top of her. But she'd got lucky. Her first book deal had funded the deposit on her flat in Holloway and the commissioning of *Cooking with Gracie* had set her on the path to a brand new life.

She takes Juliet a cup of tea, finds her sleeping and leaves it by the bed. When she comes back Freya raises her mournful little face and asks, 'Is my mummy sick?'

Gracie looks down at her and feels an overwhelming urge to scoop her up and carry her away from this mess. Instead she strokes her hair. 'She's got a tummy ache but she'll be fine.' She bends closer. 'I've had an idea. Why don't we make it nice for when she gets up?'

Freya brightens. 'OK.'

Gracie looks down at the spatters of Juliet's vomit on Freya's T-shirt. 'Shall we find you some clean clothes first?'

Freya leads her to a box room barely big enough for the narrow bed and ugly brown chest of drawers. Gracie feels a throb of sadness as she looks at the hippo sitting on the pillow, the tangle of naked plastic dolls bruised with felt pen and the washed-out ponies on the rumpled duvet. Freya lifts her arms and allows Gracie to pull the dirty T-shirt over her head and help her out of her shorts. Skinny and pale in her knickers, she pulls an unironed dress from a drawer. While she puts it on Gracie folds her pyjamas, smooths the sheet, pushes the stained pillow back into the pillow case and refastens the poppers of the duvet before shaking it onto the bed.

'OK? Ready?'

'Yes!'

They march back to the main room, arms swinging, soldiers on a mission.

Gracie drags back the curtains and opens the doors to the balcony. The low, unceasing rumble of traffic. A grind and squeal of brakes. A woman's high-pitched laughter. An angry shout that gets no answer. She looks across the roof-tops to the spire of St Stephen's on Falcon Square, picturing Tom and Elsie playing with Tallulah in the leafy garden of number 17.

She turns back inside, coming close to tears when she sees Freya pushing a chair towards the sink. 'It's OK, sweetheart, I'll wash up. You collect the dirty cups and plates.'

They work together. For Gracie, with her twice weekly cleaner and Heather to keep things orderly in between, there's intense satisfaction in working through the layers of grime and shaping order out of the chaos. She puts away crockery, empties ashtrays, wipes shelves and tidies tins and jars. She rearranges cushions to hide the rips in the sagging sofa, picks up the desk diary from the floor and gathers up the post – mostly final demands – scattered around the laptop. There's an assortment of thrillers and self-help manuals on the bookshelf, the only recipe book a copy of *Cooking with Gracie* with 'Property of Tower Hamlets Libraries' stamped on the flyleaf.

The bathroom is grim – white tiles capillaried with cracks,

thin towels and a smeared fan-shaped mirror, hanging from a knot of string above the sink. She throws away old toothpaste tubes, picks up scattered tampons and snaps the lid back onto a tub of anti-depressants. She wipes, tidies and straightens, collects up the slithers of water-softened soap then sweeps the sitting room while Freya catches the rubble of crumbs in a dustpan.

Gracie smacks the dust from her hands. 'There, what do you think?'

'It's nice,' Freya says. 'Look, Mummy.' She runs towards her mother who is clutching the doorjamb, leaning her head against her knuckles.

Juliet groans and looks away. 'I can't believe you've done this.'

'Are you feeling better?' Gracie asks.

'A bit. God knows what's wrong with me. I thought I was OK then, wham, it hit me again. I hope I'm all right by tomorrow. I've got a website to finish.'

'I'd better get home. I've left your keys on the counter.' Gracie picks up the bulging rubbish bag. 'I'll dump this in the dustbin.' She looks back at Freya and waves as she opens the front door. 'Be a good girl for your mum. She's still not feeling very well.'

In the car Gracie checks her phone, closes her eyes and sits for a minute before she starts the engine and heads back to Falcon Square.

23

Four bloody quid for one gerbera! Juliet buys eight fat pink heads, paying extra to have them wrapped in cellophane with a fraying length of straw. Holding the bouquet high she mounts the steps of number 17, aware as she lifts the brass knocker of a tightness in her chest. It's the nanny who comes to the door. *Damn!* Gracie's wall calendar said she'd be working at home this morning and Juliet had hoped to find her alone.

'Hi. I'm Juliet, I just—'

'I know who you are.'

Juliet winces at the sudden burst of memories: this girl's capable hands wielding a cool flannel, her clipped Scottish voice telling her to get some water down her, that pink freckled face glowering into hers.

'I came to apologise for what happened.' The girl continues to stand sentry. Juliet cranes past her, raising her voice above the roar of roadworks in the square. 'Is Gracie—?'

The girl turns and calls, 'Gracie!' in a voice that signals, 'There's a problem here.' Gracie appears in the hallway behind her, striped apron over jeans, floury hands, hair pinned up, tiny gold earrings, leaf shapes, glittering in the sunlight. Juliet says quickly, 'Hi, I just wanted to apologise and to thank you for everything you did, especially looking after Freya.'

'It was no problem, she's a lovely girl. We were happy to have her.'

Juliet knows the code. This is what you say when some feckless pain in the neck dumps you with their kid, but at least the snippy nanny is backing off and disappearing upstairs. She thrusts out the flowers. 'I brought you these.'

Gracie wipes her hands down her apron and takes them. 'You didn't need to do that.'

Somewhere behind her a timer shrieks. She glances over her shoulder, distracted. In that moment Juliet steps onto the mat, opening her bag. 'I've brought your clothes back too.'

'Sorry, that's the oven,' Gracie says, drawing back.

Juliet rummages in the bag. 'And something for Elsie, well Tallulah really. Freya chose it.'

Impatience creases Gracie's brow. She turns down the hall, giving off a heady rush of that fragrant Gracie smell. 'You'd better come in.'

Trembling with the effort of staying calm Juliet shuts the door, and follows Gracie's neat little frame into the kitchen. In her hurry to get to the oven Gracie has dropped the flowers in the sink, careless of the blooms that have taken such a bite out of Juliet's housekeeping. She's pulling on oven gloves and bending into the oven. As she lifts out the cake tin Juliet sits down at the table, rooting herself firmly among the mixing bowls, egg boxes, digital scales and open notebooks, before she takes out the bag containing Gracie's freshly laundered skirt and top (she's keeping the knickers, what the hell) and the pink rhinestone-studded dog collar she's just picked up from Bargain Pets. She pushes the collar towards Gracie. 'Sorry about this. When Freya shops it has to be shiny.'

Gracie, busy prodding the springy dome of sponge, barely glances up. 'Elsie loves shiny,' she murmurs.

121

Juliet nods towards the flowers. 'Shall I put them in water?'

'Oh. OK.' *She's forgotten them already.* 'Use that blue jug. Do you . . . want a cup of tea?'

The pause is perfect. Long enough to sound hospitable. Short enough to imply that she really doesn't have time.

'I'll do it.' Juliet gets up. For a second they are so close she is tempted to take the soft flesh of Gracie's underarm between her fingers and pinch it hard. She reaches the counter and – unable to resist – looks back. Gracie, who is watching her, gives a quick embarrassed smile. 'Red teapot. Tea's in the jar.'

The rising whoosh of boiling water filling the pot and the clink and scrape of metal on china as she stirs bring back memories of her mother's kitchen, which is probably why she always makes tea with a silent tea bag swirled in a mug. Keeping to small mechanical movements, she opens the double-doored fridge stacked tidily with tubs, cartons, cheeses in little straw boxes and mysterious packages wrapped in waxed paper. Wine bottles rattle enticingly as she reaches for the milk. Organic. From a West Country farm. The kind they don't stock in the garage shop.

'Sugar?' she says, as if for one moment, this is her home and Gracie the outsider.

'No thanks.'

She sets down Gracie's mug and sits with her own, running her finger around the rim. 'I still can't work out what happened on Saturday. I can usually hold my drink.'

Gracie doesn't meet her eyes. 'Please, don't worry about it. In fact I forbid you to mention it again.'

'Well, thanks for being so understanding.'

The puppy skitters over to sniff Juliet's foot. She shakes off her sandal, rubs the pink bulbous belly with her toe and makes a decent stab at looking enchanted, an indulgent

122

smile still fixed on her lips as she asks, 'How's Tallulah settling in?' *Tallulah*. For Christ's sake.

'Apart from peeing everywhere and chewing up my Ferragamo sandals she's doing fine.'

Juliet laughs lightly, as if she too has Ferragamo sandals scattered about her 'lovely' home. 'So how are you enjoying your new house?'

'Loving it. Give me old over new any time, but don't tell my husband.'

Juliet strokes her fingers along the worn grain of the wooden table that could easily seat twenty. 'Did you bring all this furniture from Greenwich?'

'God, no. Pretty much everything we had at the Wharf House was custom made to Tom's design. The buyers made us a ridiculous offer for it so we said yes. Selling "fully loaded" the agent called it.'

'How did Tom feel about that?'

'Sad in some ways, but flattered that the new owners wanted to buy in to his whole vision for the place and anyway he knew it wouldn't look right in a period house. Luckily the people we bought this place from were dealers so they were happy to sell us some of their pieces, like the amazing French beds and that table. Gorgeous isn't it?'

It all just falls into place for you, doesn't it, Gracie? Juliet gazes around her at the clever layout of the L-shaped island, the huge double oven, the hanging racks of pans and the wall of glass-fronted compartments filled with every imaginable ingredient. 'Was this kitchen here already?'

'God, no.' Gracie laughs. 'It's the one thing I insisted on having done before we moved in.'

The nanny pokes her head round the door. 'I'll drop Tom's suit off at the cleaners before I get Elsie. Do you need me to babysit tonight?'

'No thanks, Heather,' Gracie says. 'Tom's in Dublin so

it's rubbish telly, a bottle of wine and an early night for me. Bliss.'

Juliet watches Heather go, rankled by the casual offer of babysitting and the idea that telly, a bottle of wine and a night in on your own could constitute some kind of treat. But how would Gracie Dwyer know how it feels to be trapped indoors night after night because you can't afford a babysitter, sitting there watching your life tick away, so lonely you want to bang on the door of the next door flat, just to have someone to talk to, and you'd do it too if your neighbour wasn't a tight-lipped old bitch who disapproves of the way you look, dress, drive and bring up your kid.

Juliet takes a drink of tea. 'Single mum's dream.'

'Sorry?' Gracie is cracking eggs, letting the whites slither into a copper bowl.

'Babysitter on tap.' Juliet sips again, gratified when Gracie finally nibbles the bait.

'It must be tough bringing up a kid on your own.'

'Some people manage fine,' Juliet says, carefully. 'For me, it's a struggle.'

'No family to help out?'

Juliet leaves a pause. Just a tiny beat and fills it with a faint sad smile. 'No. It's just me and Freya.'

'What about her dad?'

'Ian? He spends half his time in Australia. Got a business and a girlfriend over there. She's pregnant.' *Where did that come from? Calm down.*

'I'm sorry,' Gracie says.

She's whisking now, holding the bowl in the crook of her arm, springy wire scritch, scritch, scritching against the sides. *Why doesn't she use the bloody great mixer she's got sitting on the counter?*

'Don't be. Leaving him was the best thing I ever did.'

'Still, it's difficult splitting up with someone you've loved.'

124

Juliet can't make out if it's a knack Gracie's picked up from interviewing guests on her show or whether she means it, but her sympathy seems genuine. Maybe it's the novelty of it, like watching a documentary about desperate lives to make you feel better about your own.

'Not when he's a control freak.'

Gracie adjusts the bowl. 'Was he violent?'

'He's cleverer than that. Prefers the kind of abuse that doesn't leave a mark. Though when you meet him he comes across as a real charmer. It took me five years to realise the truth.'

'That long?'

'You know how it is. You're besotted with someone, the relationship starts going wrong so you start making allowances and changing the way you are, hoping you can turn things around.'

'But you never can.'

'No. I hoped having Freya would make it better but he got worse after she was born. He thought that with a baby and no job I'd never get it together to leave him.' A flash of pain she hadn't planned for cuts her breath.

'But you did,' Gracie says.

'Yeah.' Juliet looks out at the garden. She breathes in and exhales slowly to steady her voice. 'God knows how. Though it helped when he started going back and forth to Sydney. Gave me the space to try and get my career back on track. I'm in marketing and PR.' She looks up into Gracie's face, curious to see if this triggers a response.

Scritch, scritch, scritch. 'Oh right. Who for?'

'Gibson Rourke before I married. I'm freelance now.'

'Must be tough in this climate.'

'Yep. Specially when you've been out of the loop for a while. So I do a bit of telemarketing and web design and spend the rest of the time trying to get PR jobs.' She pulls

125

a rueful face. 'Not exactly the glittering career I had planned. But if you're self-employed you've got to be out there, networking. That's not easy when you've got a kid. Still, we get by.' She stares into her mug. This little heart to heart is going so smoothly it's almost beginning to feel real. 'Though poor Freya was devastated when she had to give up ballet for a while. But she's a good kid. Never moaned once.'

Gracie sprinkles sugar into the egg whites. Juliet readies herself, taking another long breath to stem the adrenaline. 'No reason why you should remember . . . but we've met before.'

Gracie flushes and looks sheepish. 'Sorry, I've got a terrible memory for faces. Where was it?'

'The North London Business Hub. I'd put a few feelers out, trying to get my career back on track so I could leave Ian, and they asked me to run a seminar. Ironic really – Best Practices in Self-Promotion.'

'The Hub.' Gracie prods the air with the whisk. 'Gosh, that would have been what, five years ago?'

'Six. We got chatting.' Juliet gives a little laugh. 'In the loos, I think.' She remembers every detail, the mirror, the tiles, the smiles, the promises. 'I was trying to get enough of a client base together to convince the bank to give me a mortgage and you were developing ideas for a TV show, about to publish your first cookbook and trying to raise money to get your bakery off the ground. Kind of a turning point for both of us.' Gracie looks flustered. *Gently. Small steps.* 'You were looking for someone to handle your marketing and PR. We talked through a few ideas, swapped cards.'

Gracie's eyes slide curiously over Juliet's face. 'Your hair was different. And—'

Juliet cuts her off, not wanting to hear how badly she's ageing. 'I sent you a few thoughts I pulled together' – *a comprehensive brand strategy I dropped everything to work on.*

She takes another slow sip of tea. 'Called too. Left a couple of messages.' Gracie's eyes dart away as if to escape what she knows is coming. 'I didn't hear anything, then a couple of weeks later your assistant emailed me to say no thanks.'

'Oh God. How awful. I had no idea. All I can say in my defence is that things got a bit crazy around then. I . . . I was recovering from a bad break-up, sorting out last-minute hiccups with the book and trying to fulfil a whole load of new catering contracts so I got someone in for a couple of weeks to help out.'

Juliet watches her carefully, searching for a sign that she is lying but her upset seems genuine. 'Who did you get to do your PR in the end?' she says.

'Someone my editor recommended. Jeremy Daley?' Gracie says it with a questioning upswing, as if Juliet might not have heard of him.

Juliet manages a nod. She's monitored every project Daley has ever done for Gracie, watched him use that success to build his one-man operation into exactly the kind of boutique PR company she's always dreamed of running. 'I've come across him a couple of times. He's done all right for himself,' she says brightly. 'And things certainly worked out for you.'

Gracie blushes. 'I've been very lucky.'

Yes, Gracie, you certainly have.

Juliet's smile is generous. 'Look, I'm taking Freya to the new Disney film on Friday. She'd love it if Elsie could come too. She could come for tea after school, see the movie and maybe stay the night.'

She studies Gracie's expression, barely able to resist the urge to laugh. The thought of entrusting her precious child to a woman like Juliet, letting her sleep in that grotty flat and eat cheap, packaged food is bringing panic to Gracie's eyes and a fluttery rush to her voice. 'Oh . . . that would have been lovely . . . but I've already booked tickets to see it on Saturday.' A flush slinks up her cheeks.

Juliet keeps her eyes fixed on Gracie's face, making sure she knows that she's seen right through the smile to the lie. 'What a shame. Freya will be so disappointed.' She scoops the puppy onto her lap. 'Is it all right if I take a photo of Tallulah in her new collar to cheer her up?' She fiddles with the stiff buckle, flipping the squirming animal onto its back as she fastens the collar around its neck. Surprised by the sharpness of its teeth she plonks the puppy back on the floor and fires off a series of shots. Willing herself to speak coolly she says, 'How's the planning application going?'

Gracie rolls her eyes, clearly relieved at the change of topic. 'Nightmare. Someone's dragged up some old statute forbidding "the manufacture, distribution or sale of alcohol" on the premises. But if we're going to offer a bistro menu in the evenings we have to be able to serve booze.'

Juliet keeps her voice as level as she can. 'If you need someone to help push it through just let me know. I've done a lot of lobbying for local developers and I've got some great contacts at the council.' No response. She checks the time. 'I'd better go. I've got to pick Freya up and break the news to her about the cinema. I'll tell her we'll try to organise something with Elsie for another time.' Rising from her chair she makes for the door, swiping through the photos of Tallulah as she goes. 'Aw. She's going to love these. Honestly, Tallulah and Elsie, that's all she ever talks about.'

Gracie drops the whisk. 'Look, that film. We could . . . go together.'

Juliet turns in the doorway and looks up from her phone. 'Are you sure?'

'I'll get a couple more tickets for Saturday and if we come back here for tea Freya can see Tallulah. It'll be fun.' She's making an effort to sound enthusiastic, not doing too badly. 'Shall we meet you at the cinema at two?'

'Freya will be thrilled.' Juliet throws her a pathetically grateful smile, no hint of triumph at all, and reaches in her bag for her purse. 'Here, let me . . .'

'It's fine.' Gracie waves an impatient hand. 'We can sort that out later.'

'Okay. Don't worry. I'll let myself out.'

Gracie tugs the pillow up behind her head and holds her book against her knees. Tom watches her as he crosses the room and slides into bed. 'What's up?'

'Juliet. She came round today.'

'What did she want?' He reaches for his magazine.

'To apologise. She brought flowers and a collar for Tallulah.'

'Why's that upset you?'

'Her life's such a mess. It can't be good for Freya living in that chaotic flat. Dirty sheets, cheap takeaways, chaos everywhere. Imagine if it was Elsie.'

'It's not your problem.'

'She was so broke Freya had to stop ballet for a while.' She lowers her head, her fingers restless on the duvet. 'It's tough being a single mum. Even tougher if you're broke, lonely and struggling to get work. It makes me wonder how well I'd have managed it.'

It's so rare for her to talk about the miscarriage she'd had before she met him that he drops the magazine and runs his hand down her arm. 'You'd have been brilliant. You were always going to make a success of your life.'

'I've been lucky. Right place. Right time. But you know what really gets to me? It turns out we'd met before.'

'When?'

'Ages ago, at some conference. I was trying to raise backing to expand the stall into a bakery and looking for someone to handle my PR and she was trying to restart her career after having Freya. The awful thing is she looks so terrible I didn't even recognise her. But back then she came over as really smart and together, just the kind of person I wanted to be working with.'

'She must have changed.'

'Don't be mean. She's had a hard time. It's no wonder she drinks. That's the thing. I was going to call her. But I didn't.'

'Why not?'

'I left the conference early and I saw her in the car park with a man. He was obviously her husband and they were having this huge fight.'

'What about?'

'I don't know. He was shouting at her then he pulled her into the car and they sat there yelling at each other. There was something, I don't know, really vicious about him. Then they drove off. After that I thought . . . I thought if she was involved with someone like that I couldn't trust her judgement.'

'Looks like you made the right decision.'

'How can you say that? She was trapped in an abusive marriage with a small baby, desperate to get her career back on track so she could leave him.' She looks up at him. 'I could have helped her, Tom. If I hadn't been so snotty and judgemental things might be very different for her now. But I got lucky and she's barely holding it together.'

'That's not your fault. However bad things were, you'd never have got so pissed you passed out at a party and forgot your own kid. No wonder she can't get work.'

'I want to help her.'

He rolls his eyes.

'She's depressed, Tom. It could happen to anyone. You love someone. You trust them enough to build a life with them then it all comes crashing down and you hit rock bottom. If no one gives you a break maybe . . . maybe you never come up again.' Pent anger splinters her voice. He reaches for her hand.

She frowns and looks away, 'I'm sorry. It wasn't a dig, it's just—'

He doesn't let her finish. 'I screwed up, our life took a knock and now we're making things stronger than they were before. I promise you, nothing's going to come crashing down.' Her head stays bent as she feels the rub of his thumb across her knuckles. The pressure increases. 'The adoption people called. They want to book a date for our first assessment.'

She slides her hand away.

'You haven't changed your mind have you?'

'Of course not. I want this as much as you do. But what if something goes wrong?'

His eyes travel down to the book in her lap, open at a chapter headed, 'Bonding with Your Adopted Child'.

'Is that what you're worried about?'

'Aren't you? This kid will be upset, maybe bereaved, struggling to adjust to a new life. It won't be easy.'

'I know.'

'Do you really think you can learn to love a stranger's child as much as you love Elsie?'

'I'm going to do my best,' he says with certainty – impatience almost. He finds her hand again. 'And you of all people know that you're more than capable of loving another woman's child.'

Gracie gazes over his shoulder at their reflection in the pitted mirror above the chest of drawers, his head close to hers, his bronze flesh and dark hair sharp against the white of the linen.

Pauline Bryce Diary
January 23rd

*Mum stomps in around 8.30 telling me I'm going to
be late for college. I do a bit of sobbing into the pillow
and she just stands there – no sympathy – and says
what's the matter with you? I tell her I'm stressed out
because I've been having these bad dreams – really
horrible ones where I'm trapped in a room and it's
cold and there's a big shadow between me and the
door, and it feels like I'm in Ron's shed. And now I'm
thinking maybe . . . maybe it's not a dream, maybe
I'm remembering something that happened in there
when I was a kid. She goes crazy, eyes popping out of
her head, yelling about everything Ron's done for me,
how he's always treated me like his own daughter. So
I get dressed and go downstairs and grab some cereal
and I'm reading the book on repressed memories while
I eat it, then I lay the book cover-up on the table and
get some juice from the fridge. Mum's watching me
with this odd look on her face and she picks up the
book and I'm expecting her to go crazy again but
instead she goes very quiet. And I say I've been getting
flashbacks about Ron for a while and maybe it's time
I talked to child services or a counsellor or something
because the book says it's bad for your mental health
to bottle it up. And then she gives me this sour little
smile, murmurs something about me turning out just
like my dad and walks out. I make a cup of tea and
try out the slow breathing I read about in this article
'Serenity – the Key to Lasting Joy'. Half an hour later
she walks in, throws a fat envelope at me and tells me
to get out and to take my evil lies with me. There's
nine hundred pounds in that envelope – a bit more*

than I'd expected, not as much as I'd hoped. I take a look around that cramped little kitchen and I think, remember this moment, Pauline. You've taken your first steps and you've reached your first target. Then I go upstairs to pack.

24

For once Juliet is enjoying her evening. The sitting room, still reasonably tidy after Gracie's clean-up, is bathed in light, she's treated herself to a decent bottle of wine and the sounds of the other lives being lived in the flats around her feel comforting rather than excluding. She is on the sofa, laptop on her knees, glancing from Gracie Dwyer's business plan to the planning pages of the council website. Tom Whittaker's design for the chapel is clever and bold and the projected figures for the business stack up well. Of course they do. But now that Juliet is working on a little project of her own, the thought of Gracie Dwyer notching up another triumph is almost bearable.

The details need a bit of fine-tuning but she's mapped out the basics: get close enough to Gracie to scrape up some dirt on her – *come on*, no one achieves that kind of success without having *something* to hide: sexual, social, fiscal, professional, Juliet's not fussed. And she's not asking for a whole skeleton, just a few stray splinters of bone tucked away at the back of those carefully ordered, hand-painted cupboards. Some dark little secret she can work up into something juicy before she leaks it to the press from a Daley

Associates' email account. And then, as Gracie's life hurtles into a shit swamp – taking Jeremy Daley's reputation with it – who better than Juliet, loyal friend and trusted PR, to drag her, bruised and busted, back out? And you know what? In the end, letting the world see that Gracie's human might even do her good. Juliet can't be the only one gagging to take a hammer to that weapons-grade sugar coating. So right now it's all about digging into the soft underbelly of Gracie's life, chipping away at the stresses and heartaches, checking out her friends and her finances, finding out the real secrets behind her success.

Since her chat with Gracie it's been easier to think about the night of the party and the image that keeps breaking through the flashes of dancing, laughing, flirting and vomiting is the look on Stella Harper's discreetly made-up face when she talked about her dead daughter. Juliet sets down her glass and Googles Louise. Her fingers brush the photo that appears on the screen; communion with this woman she never met, this chip of grit embedded deep in the clay of Gracie's existence.

Curious to know how Louise died, she spools down, imagining a car crash in a foreign capital, a stray bullet or a light aircraft downed in a desert, shocked to discover that it was none of these things. Among the obituaries and alarmist tabloid headlines she finds the coroner's report:

Internationally renowned photographer Louise Stella Harper, aged 37, died in the main bedroom of apartment 8, The Dye Works, N5 on 4/8/2011 between the hours of 11pm and 5am, of asphyxiation due to an inflammation of the throat caused by a wasp sting. At the time of death Ms Harper was sleeping under the influence of Zopiclone. The drug was given to her on prescription by her GP following a period of insomnia two years before

135

her death. The wasp is likely to have entered through the open window. She had a known allergy to insect venom described by her doctor as moderate in nature, resulting in swelling of the localised area. The police were alerted to the tragedy at 8.00am the following morning when a neighbour heard the cries of her 10 month old daughter Elsie. The deceased's husband Thomas Whittaker was away on business at the time.

'Jesus.' Juliet gazes into the eyes of this strong-jawed, clear-eyed woman, strangely moved by the tragic absurdity of her death.

For once Juliet drops Freya at school on time. She queues in the garage shop cradling milk, fish fingers and frozen chips, impatient to get back to her laptop. The place is packed. Why don't they open another bloody till? When she finally gets to the counter the cashier checks the food through, flicks her greasy fringe and mutters, 'Pump?'

'Five.'

'Forty-eight seventy-three.'

Juliet slides a credit card into the reader and keys in her pin. The cashier pushes a wad of gum through her teeth and sucks it back. 'Declined.'

Juliet whips out the card, wipes it down her jeans and slots it back. 'Try again.'

The cashier glances at the screen, inspects a bitten finger-nail and shakes her head.

'Shit.'

'You got cash?' she says wearily. 'Another card?'

'Not with me.' Juliet's phone buzzes in her pocket.

The cashier, suddenly animated, is on the intercom calling, 'Mr Malhotra, lady can't pay.' A big-bellied man stomps through a door at the back, angry, loose-lipped and sweaty.

'Why did you fill up if you don't have money? It's a

criminal offence.' He jabs a thumb at the sign behind the cashier: *We always prosecute.*

'It's OK. I'll call my bank.'

She turns her back to him and leans away while a voice in a faraway call centre insists she reported the card missing two days ago.

'No, I didn't. Reactivate it right now!'

'I'm sorry, madam, I'm afraid I can't do that. A replacement card will be sent to you within five working days.'

'It's the bank's mistake. Why should I have to wait?'

'I'm sorry, madam. Is there anything else I can help you with today?'

She cuts the call. It's Ian. Has to be. Doing this to piss her off. She turns back to the manager. His eyes glide down her body. She glowers at him, letting her thoughts spin away to a place where she's punching his sagging face until the blood spurts.

'It's a mistake,' she says. 'They think I reported it stolen.'

'You pay the money or I call the police.'

'I'll go home and get cash.'

He twists his flabby lips. 'You think I'm stupid? You think I'm going to let you drive off and not come back?'

'I'll leave the car here then.'

'It's blocking the pump.'

'Here.' She thrusts the keys into his plump hairy hand. 'Move it yourself.'

The people in the queue edge sideways to let her pass, enjoying the guilty thrill of her humiliation. Her phone buzzes again. She checks it as she crosses the forecourt. Three alerts. All from 'Spark'. She's never heard of it.

Welcome to your new account. It's time to ignite!
Add more photos to your profile.
Ned says hi.

Who the hell is Ned?

For once there's a bit of cash in the flat, forty quid for sorting out the virus in her landlord's computer – how many times has she warned him about downloading cheap porn? She empties Freya's piggy bank to make up the rest and swaps her sandals for trainers. It still takes time she can't spare to jog back to the garage.

The manager hovers beside her as she pays and shakes her keys in her face. 'Next time, lady, you bring your money.'

Fuming, she tugs the keys from his fingers and gives his bloodied mental image another kick in the throat. With a yank of the wheel she's swinging out of the exit when she thumps her hand against the dashboard. She's forgot to get cigarettes. Her phone beeps. 'Spark' again. She screams at a man who steps off the pavement, and hits the horn. He raises a finger and swears back.

As soon as she gets home she checks out 'Spark'. It's a dating site for 'adults who like to share'. An account in her name logs in automatically, the photo, one she doesn't recognise, looks like it was snatched on the street. Has Ian been following her? Paid someone else to? *Hello Juliet! See who's been checking you out.* She spools down, shuddering at the sexual preferences listed as her 'likes'. She clicks through the garbled filth to the profiles of men who have viewed her page and finds 'Ned' – thick-necked, bovine, 'into horny older babes'. She jabs the keys and deletes the account, her heart a hot knot of fury. Ian is crap at IT, too arrogant to learn, which means he's paid someone else to hack her computer. The thought stays with her, a low hum of disquiet as she scours her hard drive, scanning it for the breach in security that allowed the hacker in. She finds nothing. She lights a cigarette, turning the lighter in her fingers. Ian doesn't splash money around for no reason and there are far cheaper ways than this to piss her off. An image worms its way through her confusion – his lawyer citing this filth in a custody hearing. Hard evidence that she's an unfit mother. *Fuck you, Ian. Fuck you.*

25

The Saturday paper is wedged in the letterbox. Gracie works it free, cursing the endless supplements she never gets time to read. A postcard falls from the folds. No stamp. Hand delivered. Addressed to Mrs Tom Whittaker. The words 'Wishing you every happiness in your new home!' written in tight tiny script above an illegible squiggle of a signature. She turns it over and flinches at the grainy reproduction of Louise's best-known photograph – the dead tree root sprouting one indomitable sprig of green. She flips the card back again, a terrible caving-in of her lungs as she reads the slogan printed in the corner – 'The past is always with us for it feeds the present' – and a logo for Wise Words Cards. Drained of breath, Gracie is turning away, faltering towards the kitchen when Tom comes up behind her. He pulls the newspaper from under her arm and tugs the card from her fingers. 'Who's this from?'

'I can't make out the name. It was hand delivered.'

'Probably one of the neighbours. Nice that this picture's still so popular, though I don't remember getting any royalty cheques from Wise Words Cards.' The half smile dies when he sees her expression. 'What's up?'

She can't tell him she's afraid. That being sent Louise's best-known photograph as a housewarming card or finding Louise's favourite figurine in her new home fills her with the same sickly dread as opening one of the stalker's packages. 'It just creeps me out when I can't work out who things are from.'

He kisses her forehead. 'You mustn't let yourself get paranoid.'

'I know.' She forces a smile. 'Are you still all right to take Elsie swimming?'

'Course. What are you doing today?'

'Finishing off that progress report on the chapel for the backers, then this afternoon I'm taking Elsie to the cinema with Juliet and Freya.'

'What?' He pulls a face, somewhere between amused and irritated.

'She asked us. I felt bad about saying no.'

When he's gone she takes down the postcard, gazes at the photo and studies the cramped handwriting that looks so worryingly similar to the writing on the gift tag she'd found attached to Louise's figurine. Is this part of a new, more subtle phase of the stalker's campaign, designed to stir up her insecurities about the past and tarnish her hopes for the future? Was he at the party? In her home? Eating her food, drinking her drink, dancing on her lawn? Was he here just now, pushing this postcard through her door?

You're being ridiculous!

Her hands move swiftly, ripping the card into tiny pieces. She drops them into the bin, stiffening herself against a wave of new fears: fear that she can no longer trust her own judgement, fear that she really is getting paranoid. *Stop this! You can't afford to confuse the real and the imagined. Not now. Not when there's so much resting on every decision you make.*

*   *   *

Elsie kicks the steps of the cinema. 'I want Amber to come. Freya's a baby.'

'She's actually a couple of months older than you.'

'She cries all the time.'

'Shush. They'll be here in a minute.' Gracie glances hurriedly up and down the street. 'She was only crying because she was upset about her mummy being ill.'

'Her mummy was *drunk*.'

'Elsie!' Gracie leans down, shocked. 'Who on earth told you that?'

'Amber's daddy told Amber's mummy. And Amber's mummy said—'

'I don't want to hear it. It's naughty to listen to grown-ups' conversations. I want you to be nice to Freya *and* her mummy and to promise that you will never, *ever* repeat what Amber said.'

'Why?'

Gracie softens her tone, 'Because Freya's mummy gets a bit sad sometimes and it will make her even sadder if she thinks people are talking about her. OK?'

Elsie pouts and looks away.

'There they are.' Gracie waves as Juliet comes running across the road, pulling Freya by the hand.

'Sorry,' Juliet pants. 'Parking was a nightmare.' She's done something with her hair. It suits her.

'No rush. I've got the tickets.'

Juliet reaches for her purse. Gracie lays a hand on her wrist. 'Honestly, don't worry about it.' She looks from Elsie to Freya. 'Who wants popcorn?'

'Me!' Elsie cries.

'I'll get these,' Juliet says quickly. 'Sweet or salted, Elsie?'

'Sweet. And I want a Fanta.'

Gracie pulls her close and whispers, horrified, 'You know

you're not allowed those kind of drinks. You can have juice. And what's happened to the magic word?'

Elsie wraps her arms around her chest, stamps her sequined trainer and glares at Freya, who is staring at her, wide-eyed and admiring. Gracie looks apologetically at Juliet, who smiles indulgently and heads towards the counter. As they squeeze into their seats Gracie stems the ripple of nudges with a little good-natured eye-rolling at the difficulty of juggling drinks, bags and buckets of popcorn. The lights in the auditorium dim to black and the screen explodes with a riot of advertisements for overpriced plastic toys and creepily wrinkled dolls that look like newborns. Gracie glances at Elsie and Freya who sit enthralled, and catches Juliet staring at her through the darkness. They both blink, embarrassed, and look away.

After tea – tagliatelle with broccoli, kale and toasted pine nuts, which Freya gobbles down without a murmur, followed by homemade raspberry ice cream – the girls tumble out into the garden. Gracie lets out a sigh. 'It's so good for Elsie to have a lovely little girl like Freya to play with. To be honest she's not really making friends at her new school. I wish Tom had let me send her to Dunsmore. Everyone says it's great.'

'I've heard St Mathilda's is pretty stuck up.'

'Do you know people with kids there?'

'I did a website for a builder whose son's just started. His wife took a job as their catering manager so they'd get a chunk off the fees and the other kids were teasing him about his mum being a dinner lady.'

'God, how awful. But I'm not surprised. Trouble is, Tom insisted on sending her somewhere with brilliant security and he's got a point. We can't afford to take chances.' She catches herself straying into places she doesn't want to go and says hurriedly, 'I've been thinking about what you said

143

about Freya having to give up ballet for a while. Doesn't your ex pay you maintenance?'

'When it suits him. He prefers spending his money on flashy presents.'

'Aren't the child support people pretty tough on that kind of thing?'

Gracie watches Juliet and senses that something isn't right. It's there in the tightening of her lips, the flustered way she's picking at the skin around her thumbnail.

'I've never got the authorities involved.'

'But—'

'We're not actually divorced. Not yet. Anyway on paper his business runs at a loss.'

'So why not go for a divorce and get a proper settlement? It's a crime to hide your assets from the court.'

'I'd rather stand on my own two feet.'

'But you're entitled.'

'It's complicated.'

'What do you mean?'

'Ian would do anything to stop me getting half of what he has.' A deep breath, a grinding of her jaw. 'Even sue for custody of Freya.'

'He wouldn't win.'

Juliet looks away. 'Not a risk I'm willing to take.'

'You've done a great job bringing her up, anyone can see that.'

'Look, I didn't cope very well after she was born, post-natal depression I suppose. The doctor gave me anti-depressants and I got a bit . . . dependent. It was bad. I . . . spent a couple of weeks in hospital and when I left him Ian threatened to use it against me to get Freya back.' Unable to meet Gracie's enquiring eyes she flicks back her hair. 'But let's not talk about him. How's it going with the new café?'

144

'Not great. There's been a whole load of new objections.'

'To what?'

'You name it. The extension at the back, worries about increased traffic, noise from the air conditioning in the bake house. There's talk of a petition.'

'Petitions only go so far – it's letters from individuals that count.'

'Really?'

'Yes. Is it just a couple of busybodies putting up multiple objections?'

'I think they're all from different people.'

'That's a bit more problematic, but, like I said, I've done quite a bit of work for local developers. If you want I could pull together some strategies you could use to help get it through.' With a stiff little shrug she adds, 'On spec. No pressure.' But she's taken a breath and she's holding it with quiet desperation.

Juliet really wants this, Gracie thinks. Needs it too, but she can't let it look like charity. She stands to clear the table, her attention caught by a shriek of laughter from the girls in the garden. She watches them for a moment – Elsie in the stripy playsuit Stella brought her back from Rome and Freya in her washed-out shorts and cheap chain-store sandals – and then gives Juliet a casual nod. 'Sure. Why not?'

26

That Sunday Gracie packs up a picnic and drives Tom and Elsie out to the Cotswolds, spreads a chequered rug on a velvet meadow that slopes down to the river, hands him a tiny tartlet laden with bacon, leeks and splinters of roasted garlic and tells him her news.

'The Americans have bought the show. We start shooting *Cooking with Gracie USA* in the spring.'

He wipes the crumbs from his lips, pulls her towards him and kisses her hard on the mouth. 'Amazing! I thought it was dead in the water.'

'Me too.'

'Go on. How much?'

Her voice is steady. Her heart is not. 'A lot more than we thought. With syndication it could be serious money.'

His grip slackens as she names a figure. He swallows hard. 'Why now, after all this time?'

'Who knows? Maybe someone re-crunched the numbers or an exec got replaced.'

He sits up, squinting into the sunlight. 'If we'd known we could have hung on to the Wharf House, rented it out.'

She lays her hand on his chest. 'Tom. I'm so sorry.'

'Come on, Daddy!' Elsie is tearing across the grass, raising her voice over Tallulah's yaps.

Gracie calls out, 'Don't go too close to the water!' She catches Tom's hand. 'As soon as I heard I tried to buy the Wharf House back. I told them to name their price. They wouldn't budge.'

Tom's hand slips from hers. He watches his daughter with an odd fixity, as if she is the only thing he can bear to look at.

'But there's this.'

Tom, getting up, murmurs dully, 'There's what?'

She flings out her arm. 'The woodland, the stretch of river down to the bend and planning permission to convert the cowshed into a house.' She'd planned to take it slowly when she told him, build up to it, but it's all coming out in a pleading, breathless rush. 'It belongs to one of my backers. I told you – he wanted the company to lease it for a couple of years to try out our wedding and events idea.'

He's staring past her, blank and tight-lipped.

'Don't you remember me telling you?' Her voice cracks. 'A semi-permanent marquee?'

He shrugs.

'But when I realised I couldn't buy the Wharf House back I asked if you and I could buy him out. Keep the site for ourselves.' She looks up at him, almost pleading. 'He said yes.'

He gazes around him at the dancing sunlight filtering through the willows, the long tussocky grass sprigged with buttercups circling the ruined cowshed and the perfect view of the glittering water.

'Let's do it, Tom.' She rushes on. 'Let's build a new house on the river. Get a boat and make new memories for . . . the four of us.'

For a moment he says nothing then he lifts her hand and kisses her palm.

'Daddy! Come on!'

They leave Tallulah tethered to a tree, dreaming twitchy dreams in the shade, and run to the river pulling off their clothes. The water is cool and green. Elsie bobs between them in her float suit, scrambling onto their backs when she gets tired. They climb onto the opposite bank and gaze across to the sloping meadow, imagining their new house framed by the blue sky and the trailing willows. As the sun drops they swim lazily back and clamber up the bank. Gracie wraps a towel around Elsie's shoulders and sits on the jetty to comb out her plaits. She closes her eyes as she bends to kiss the little hollow at the nape of her neck, overcome by the memory of the first time she held Elsie in her arms. The need to love and protect that frail bundle had been sudden and shocking, filling the emptiness inside her like a torrent of water bursting into a dried-up river bed, bringing back colour and purpose and life.

Tom stands above her, silhouetted against the sinking sun, towelling his hair. 'Shall we take a look round the village before we go?'

'Elsie's tired. We should get back. I've brought her a snack for the car.'

'Come on. I'm starving. Let's find a pub. She can sleep on the way home.'

Gracie gives in and they drive into the village, past rows of honey-stone houses and a post office with a white picket fence and geranium-filled window boxes. Tom slows in front of the Swan, a glossy gastro pub with a garden to one side. Gracie leans across him to get a better look. Waiters in black aprons weave between crowded tables, balancing trays on upraised palms.

'Fancy it?' Tom says.

Gracie glances at Elsie, drowsy eyed in the back seat,

and feels a little lurch of love. 'I think there are two pubs – let's see if the other one's any quieter.'

Tom drives on, pulling out to avoid a flurry of cyclists with blistered flame-red shoulders.

'Down there.' Gracie runs a wrist across her forehead and points to a turning.

'You OK?'

She nods and rummages for her sunglasses. 'Too much sun, I think.'

The Caxton Arms is much smaller and scruffier than the Swan. No waiters in aprons here, just basic bar food and a florid, fair-haired landlord who needs a shave to take their order. They choose from the minimal menu and take their drinks into an overgrown garden hazy with honeysuckle. In the far corner a rubber tyre dangles from the branches of a bent oak, beside it a well-worn climbing frame and slide. Three couples, who all seem to know each other, chat across bench tables while a horde of children run riot, stuffing themselves with crisps as they chase an old brown Labrador.

Tom chooses a table with a view of the river and sits with Tallulah on his lap, watching the swans glide past while Elsie sucks her thumb and stares round-eyed at the other children. Gracie watches them too, imagining long summers and endless weekends in their new house, these kids knocking at their door and Elsie and her new sibling running out to play in dusty flip-flops with Tallulah at their heels. She looks at Tom, gripped by sudden doubts. Is this the right time to be buying in Caxton? Is it too soon, or too much, to be embarking on this new venture as well as everything else she's taking on?

Their food arrives. Chicken pies – homemade but nothing special – a basket of potato wedges and a bowl of over-cooked broccoli and carrots. The woman who brings them is mid-fifties, cheesecloth shirt over ripped jeans, blonde-grey hair tumbling from a scrappy knot, silver earrings swinging.

'Down for the day?' she says absently.

Tom picks up his glass. 'Well, yes and no. We're going to buy the land up the road and build a house.'

Gracie beams at him. The landlady's eyes find focus on his face. 'The Gibson plot?'

'That's right,' Gracie says.

She seems surprised. 'I heard that had sold a while back.'

'It did but the buyer's agreed to sell it to us.' Gracie spoons coins of carrot onto Elsie's plate.

'Oh, right. Weekenders?'

'Afraid so. We both work in London.'

'Don't apologise.' The landlady sticks out a freckled hand heavy with silver rings. 'Jess Villiers. That was my husband Matt who took your order.'

Tom shakes her hand, grinning broadly. 'I'm Tom. This is my wife Gracie and our daughter, Elsie.'

The woman pauses, screwing up her eyes at Gracie. 'I thought I recognised you. You're Gracie Dwyer.'

Gracie laughs and pushes her sunglasses onto her head. 'That's me.'

'Welcome to Caxton. I hope you'll be very happy here.'

Gracie grasps Jess's fingers and feels a ridiculous urge to cry. 'Thank you, Jess.' Smiling, she looks across the trampled grass. 'Now, what Elsie and I are dying to know is, *who are all these children?*'

Jess presses a hand into the bow of her back and scans the garden. 'I don't know all of them but the two redheads and the blonde girl belong to the Durrants over there. Those older boys are with Phil and Julia Morris at the table by the fence – and the boy on the slide and the dog are mine.'

Gracie looks across at the boy. He is about ten, sturdy and tall with dark eyes and thick brown hair falling from a middle parting. Jess laughs, 'I know what you're thinking but he's mine all right – a late lamb, bit of a miracle really.'

'What's his name?' Gracie asks.

'Jamie.'

'He's gorgeous,' Gracie says. Not because it's expected. Because it's true. She tries to imagine what it would be like to have a son – they seem so different from girls, alien almost.

'He's a handful, I can tell you that.' Jess laughs. 'Next time you're down, Elsie must come over to play.'

'You'd love that, wouldn't you, Elsie?'

Elsie jumps down from the table. 'What's your dog called?'

'Rosie. Do you want to say hello?' Jess leads Elsie to where Rosie lies panting in the shade. Jamie wanders over to join them. Gracie watches them crouch down to stroke the Labrador's fur; the little girl she loves, and this sturdy sun-kissed boy. She looks up. Tom is watching them too. A slow smile as he chinks his glass against hers and she tells herself that building a house on the Gibson plot is exactly the right thing to be doing.

On the way home Tom is like a man reborn, talking excitedly about the new house. She detects something more though, in the small smiles and glances he throws at her as he drives. When they hit the motorway he runs his hand down the curve of her thigh and whispers, 'You know, for a while after . . . I messed up, I thought I was going to lose you.'

Gracie glances at Elsie, asleep in the back with Brown Bear grasped to her chest, and lays her hand over his. 'My biggest fear was that *I* was going to lose *you*.'

* * *

151

Pauline Bryce Diary
January 24th

I'm off the train, lugging my backpack through pouring rain, and I'm straight into the nearest recruitment agency. I hang around for ages waiting to be seen and when I get to the counter this girl with squinty eyes and too much makeup flicks her hair extensions, gives me this sneery up and down look and says she might be able to get me a few shifts cleaning offices. Bitch. It's the same in the next three places I try. Then I fork out twenty quid for a bed in a scuzzy hostel and I sit up all night going through job ads in the papers and trying to make sure no one nicks my stuff.

27

'Juliet?'

'Hi, Gracie.' Juliet switches her phone to her other ear and reaches for her cigarettes.

'Sorry I didn't get back to you sooner. I've just had a look at this proposal you sent me. I didn't realise how much lobbying work you'd done.'

'Right.'

'Do you fancy coming over to the bakery for lunch?'

'No problem. When?' Juliet bites her lip.

'Any chance you could do today?'

Jesus. Juliet stands up to see in the mirror. She looks dishevelled, puffy. If her plans work out the first thing she's going to do is treat herself to a little tuck around the eyes. 'I'm just finishing something. Would one thirty be all right?'

'Great. Do you know the café? It's near Camden tube.'

Yes, Gracie. I know the café. 'See you in a bit.'

She grabs a narrow black skirt from her cupboard and kicks through the clothes on the floor searching for her cream top, fuming at the grease spot. *Shit!* It'll have to do.

* * *

The café is crowded, Tom's hand visible in the stripped-back décor. A chalkboard offers freshly pressed pomegranate juice. Rustic loaves and pyramids of overpriced cakes float on glass shelves above hordes of punters dithering between pulled duck in a sodding muffin and something dark and gritty that looks suspiciously like black pudding on lumps of toast. She calls to the woman at the till. 'I'm Juliet Beecham. Here for lunch with Gracie.'

The woman's eyes take her in then dart to the stairs. 'Top floor.'

A quiver of excitement as Juliet passes the sign that says 'Private' and keeps on going, up another floor. The first door off the landing opens onto a pretty little shower room, the second leads to a small white-tiled kitchen area, clean as a laboratory with charts on the wall and something simmering in a pot on the stove. She taps on the third door.

'Come in.'

Gracie, at her desk and on the phone, wrinkles her nose in apology and points to a worn leather chair. Juliet looks around. It's a good room, bright, busy, and of course, organised. A row of glossy red filing cabinets, books in neat piles, a scrubbed wooden table for meetings, giant stills from the series propped against the wall; sexy, curvy, sweet-faced Gracie blown up to monstrous proportions, and a simpering photo of Elsie on the desk.

'Great. Call me tomorrow to confirm dates.' Gracie puts down the phone.

'Thanks so much for coming in.'

'No problem.'

Gracie leans into the intercom. 'Sal, could you send us up some lunch?'

The phone rings again. A grimace. 'Sorry.'

Juliet wanders to the window and looks down into the yard. Sunlight strikes the roofs of the liveried vans lined up outside the kitchens. Gracie's Volvo, parked further along, has its own space in the shade, marked by a plaque on the wall.

A girl arrives with a tray, striding over to the table to set out ragged strips of cured meat and crumbly wedges of cheese piled on a board, a basket of bread and a dish of some kind of salad. She sees Juliet eyeing the bowl and says eagerly, 'Split wheat and beetroot.'

Juliet adjusts her ponytail and looks away. Is this how it is when Daphne drops in for lunch? Or do the favoured get to choose their food? Still, at least she's been spared the black pudding.

Gracie jumps up from her desk. 'Sorry, today's turning into a bit of a nightmare but, now you're here, I want you to try something for me.' She disappears across the landing and returns with two earthenware bowls.

'Porcini,' she says as she ushers Juliet over to the table and sets a bowl of muddy-looking soup in front of her. She takes her own and sits across the table, her cheeks flushed, her fingers fidgety. Juliet unfolds her napkin, presses her lips together and waits.

'I'll get straight to the point,' Gracie says. 'I'd like to take you up on your offer of help to get this thing through.'

Juliet gazes at the oily globules floating in her soup. 'What about Daley Associates? I wouldn't want to tread on any toes.'

There's an impatience in the way Gracie tosses her head. 'This is a one-off job that needs local knowledge and good contacts at the council. Jeremy will understand.'

'If you're sure.'

'Well, maybe keep it under your hat till it's done, just in case he gets prickly.'

'No problem.' *We can't go upsetting Jeremy. Not yet, anyway.*

155

'Basically I want you to go ahead with all these proposals – starting with the personalised response to each objector. But I need this to happen fast. When can you start?'

Juliet moistens her dry lips. 'Now. If you want.'

'Fantastic.' Gracie smiles that heart-stopping smile. 'I'll take you through the plans.'

Juliet takes the sheets she passes her, her spoon hovering over her bowl as she turns the familiar pages. 'Can I take a copy of this?'

'That one's for you.'

Juliet gazes into Gracie's face as she talks. There's a change in her, an animation she hasn't seen before. *Is this what you're always like in the office? How will you be when your image gets trashed, your fans turn against you, and you have to fire Daley for screwing you over? Will you crumble and fold or will you turn feisty and fight back? Either way you're going to need a bloody good PR to steer you through the storm.*

'OK,' Juliet says. 'I'll work on it over the weekend.'

'What about Freya?'

'She's seeing Ian.'

'All weekend?'

'He's taking her to *The Lion King* which means he'll keep her out till God knows what time on Saturday and send her back exhausted on Sunday. Why the hell he didn't get matinee tickets I just don't know.'

'Things no better on that front?'

'Worse, if anything. Still—' her smile, despite her determination to stay cool is broad and unstoppable, 'the better my work's going, the less hold he has over me.' She swallows a spoonful of soup. It's smoky and a bit too peppery but actually not bad. Not bad at all.

28

'For heaven's sake. Leave the cushions alone.' Tom is even more nervous than Gracie, bobbing up to look through the window every time he hears a car in the square.

Gracie tugs at the hem of her dress – a high-waisted vintage shift she's teamed with a little red cardigan. It's the third outfit she's had on in the last hour and she's still not sure if it's right. She jumps at the sound of the doorbell. 'Oh God.'

'I'll go.'

Gracie is on her feet again when Tom ushers in a tall fair-haired woman in her mid fifties. Her leopard print blouse, big black-framed glasses and skinny black trousers aren't quite what Gracie was expecting, though exactly what that was she's not sure.

'Gracie, this is Mrs Mills.'

'Please. Call me Beverley.' She takes Gracie's hand in firm fingers. Gracie panics that the squeeze she gives back is too tight, too sticky or too quick. Beverley Mills glances at the balanced perfection of the sofas, the precision arrangement of books on the shelves. 'It's not usually like this,' Tom says hurriedly, 'Gracie got a bit carried away with the tidying up.'

Though it's how we like it, Gracie thinks. All our mess out of sight.

'Shall we go into the kitchen?' Beverley says. 'It's always nicer to chat over a cup of tea.'

She follows Gracie down the hall, taking out her pad while Tom fills the teapot and puts out a plate of Gracie's ginger and walnut biscuits.

'You may find some of my questions intrusive,' she says crisply. 'And rightly so. We're placing a child for life.'

'Of course.' Tom hands her a mug and sits down beside Gracie, cupping his hand a little awkwardly over her clasped fingers.

'Let's start with you, Tom.' Beverley taps her notes. 'You already have a daughter by your first wife.'

'Elsie. She's just turned six.'

'Her mother died when she was how old?'

'Ten months.'

'Would you mind telling me how it happened?'

And there she is, Gracie thinks. The ghost of Louise summoned to the table by a stranger.

Tom's Adam's apple dips and rises as he unpacks the story in small, speak-able chunks. 'A wasp stung her in the mouth while she was asleep. She was allergic. Her throat swelled up and she suffocated.'

It must take a lot to unsettle someone whose job it is to pry but Beverley Mills seems moved as well as startled. 'I see,' she murmurs. 'I'm so sorry.'

'It was tough.' Tom smiles bravely and tightens his grip on Gracie's hands. 'I don't know what I'd have done without Gracie. She's been a brilliant mother to Elsie.'

Beverley waves the pen. 'So when did you two—?'

As if to spare the spectre of Louise, he lowers his voice. 'We got married when Elsie was two and a half.'

Beverley glances at her notes. 'Gracie, you have no

biological children.' It's a statement not a question, demanding no more from Gracie than a wide-eyed look of engagement, which is all she can manage.

'Have you ever been pregnant?'

'I had an ectopic pregnancy in my twenties.'

'Is there any reason why you can't have another child?' Beverley continues crisply, oblivious to the weight of Gracie's grief, the quiet pain she carries within her. But how could a baby that-never-was compete with the manifest tragedy of a dead wife?

'I've been told there's no possibility.'

'I see.' A beat. 'How would you describe your relationship with Elsie?'

Gracie draws back a little. 'She's my daughter,' she says simply. 'I love her.'

'Honestly, you should see them together,' Tom says, throwing Gracie a smile.

Beverley makes a note. 'Do you have a preference as to the sex of your new child?'

Gracie looks up at Tom. 'I think my husband would rather like a boy to balance the sexes in the household.'

'Yeah, even the bloody dog's a girl.' Tom looks panicked that he's sworn until Beverley laughs. 'But honestly,' he says hurriedly. 'We don't mind.'

'What kind of support networks do you have – friends, siblings, parents?'

'Unfortunately my mother died a couple of years ago,' Tom says, 'and my father splits his time between London and St Lucia, but he's a retired paediatrician, brilliant with kids and he loves being a grandparent, doesn't he, Gracie?'

She nods. Fond as she is of Tom's father, she's not sure a second grandchild will ever compete with the attractions of his fishing boat and third, much younger wife.

'Gracie, what about you?'

'Bit short on family. I'm afraid. Both my parents died some time ago.'

'No siblings?'

She shakes her head.

'I've got a sister in Bristol. She's got three kids,' Tom says.

'So no close family nearby?'

Tom says eagerly, 'My first wife's parents are still very much part of our lives. They think it would be wonderful for Elsie to have a sibling.' Gracie looks up, surprised and hurt that Tom has discussed their plans with Stella and Todd. She thought they'd be telling them together, as a team. He carries on, oblivious. 'Especially her father. He was adopted himself, so he's totally on board.'

This too is news to Gracie, who takes a moment to digest the idea of burly patrician Todd as a helpless orphan.

Beverley makes another note. 'The important thing is to make sure that everyone in your lives is sensitive to the needs of the adoptive child. You can help by involving them early on, so that by the time the child arrives they are completely at home with the idea.' She sits back. 'If you pass the assessment you would obviously be in a strong position to help a child of mixed heritage to maintain a sense of identity and belonging.'

'Will it help our application?' Tom says.

'We have a lot of children from black or ethnic minority backgrounds in need of placements, so all other things being equal I'd say, yes.'

'What we would offer any child is love and security,' Gracie says. 'Isn't that what matters?'

'Of course. But we're legally required to give full consideration to the child's ethnicity when deciding on a match.'

Tom pushes the biscuits towards her. 'If we pass the assessment, how long before we're offered a child?'

'Anything from six months to a couple of years.'

'That's crazy.'

'You may want to consider a concurrent application to be fast-tracked as foster parents.'

'How would that help?'

'The child could be placed in your care while you wait for the adoption process to be finalised.'

Tom is nodding at Gracie, excited now.

'The drawback is that the birth mother could claim the child back at any time. It's something for you to think about. Now,' she folds her hands together on the table. 'There is the question of your public profile, Gracie.'

Tom jumps in. 'We do everything we can to protect our private lives. We never allow the papers to print pictures of Elsie and the school we've chosen is used to dealing with children whose parents are far better known than Gracie.'

Beverley draws a breath. 'What about this problem you've had with a stalker?'

After a cautious pause Tom comes out with the line they've prepared together. 'Everyone in the public eye gets unwanted attention now and then. We were just unlucky that the press latched onto the idiot who picked on Gracie. Anyway, it's over now.'

'Did the police find the culprit?'

'No. But there's been nothing for months.'

'That's right,' Gracie says and in that moment she almost believes it to be true.

'We will be asking the police for an assessment of the threat.'

'Of course,' Gracie says, refusing to meet Tom's frown.

'And we'll be interviewing your nanny,' she glances at her notes – 'Heather Patterson.'

'No problem,' Tom says. 'She loves the idea of Elsie getting a sibling.'

Beverley declines his offer of more tea and asks to see the room they're planning to give to their new child. Gracie leads the way, but Tom quickly edges her aside, showing Beverley the choice of spare rooms and taking her on a tour of the rest of the house.

As the inspection ends Beverley focuses in on Gracie. 'I get the feeling Tom is the driving force behind this application and that you feel more . . . reticent about it.'

Gracie flushes. 'Absolutely not. It's just . . . such a huge step. For us and the child. I . . . I want to get it right.' Her eyes well with tears. 'Having lost a baby of my own I'm nervous about getting too excited in case . . . it doesn't happen.'

Beverley pushes her glasses up her nose. 'I think that's to your credit. We see far too many people who want to rush into adoption without taking on board what a fraught and difficult process it can be.'

Tom beams at Gracie. 'If you need proof that she's got the love and commitment to take on another woman's kid, just look at the way she is with Elsie.'

Beverley nods. 'I'm going to leave you with some forms and an information pack. I want you to read it very carefully and then let me know if you are interested in the fast-track fostering option. It's very early days and there are no guarantees but at this stage I see no reason why we can't begin the vetting process and put you down for our Adoption Preparation training course.'

29

Freya spots him straight away. He's lounging on a bench, burly, handsome, sunburned, chatting to an elderly couple who are watching a group of boys kick a football around. She runs towards him. 'Daddy!'

'Hey, Princess.' Ian leaps up and swings her round. The elderly couple look on approvingly, totally taken in by his adoring father act. He scowls at Juliet. 'You're late.'

Juliet has done her best, brushed her hair and put on makeup, but he's still looking at her as if she's dirt, and so are the couple on the bench. What's that bastard been saying about her?

He pinches Freya's cheek. 'Looking forward to *The Lion King*?'

Freya looks down and kicks the grass with her toe.

'Don't you want to go?'

'Can I have new trainers instead, Daddy? Ones with . . . with *sinquins*.'

He frowns, trying to work out what she means then laughs, a manly indulgent laugh, and glances at the old couple. 'Tell you what, why don't I take you to *The Lion King and* buy you the sparkliest trainers we can find?'

Freya's look of joy cuts Juliet far deeper than Ian's smirk of triumph.

'Hungry?' he says. 'I thought we'd get something before we head into town.' He is all smiles. 'Why don't you come too, Juliet?'

Juliet glares at him. Holding her gaze he puts his mouth to Freya's ear and says in a stagey whisper, 'Maybe not. Mummy looks tired. Best if she gets some rest.'

Tired. It's Ian's favourite starter word, one that if they were alone, would lead on to *irritable, drunk, crazy.* A word that triggers the familiar constriction in Juliet's chest, as if he has reached inside her and turned a screw.

Hot and angry she stands on the path and watches the man who tried to destroy her walk away with her child. She turns and runs back to her car and drives for a long time, heading nowhere. It's nearly six when she finds herself in an all too familiar street. She pulls up at the kerb. Her eyes travel up the concrete façade of Ian's apartment block and settle on the windows of the flat she left on a cold wet day with Freya in a sling and her suitcase balanced on the buggy. Her hand slides into her bag. Her fingers find the blue glass fob attached to her keys to Ian's flat. She squints a little, unsure if the movement she sees in his window is a reflected glimmer of evening sunlight piercing the gathering clouds or the flick of a blonde head moving back from the glass. Is he cheating on Merion? She watches and waits. The clouds close over, the flicker stops.

Apart from the couple in the penthouse, the block houses a mainly transient community of business people on short-term leases; new faces in the hallway, new names on the mail boxes. There's no one to recognise her as she approaches the entrance, any more than she recognises the man pushing through the swing doors, or the woman throwing a headscarf over her thick fair hair, pulling up her collar and unfurling her umbrella as she steps out, head down, into the gust of summer rain. Juliet watches her go. Is she Ian's new bit on the side? Unlikely – he likes his women tall.

30

'Did the new menus come?' Gracie throws off her jacket and takes the coffee Sally hands her.

'Not yet. I was about to call the printers.'

Gracie registers Sally's simmering excitement, the self-conscious pursing of her lips. 'Oh my God!' She puts down the coffee cup and grabs Sally's hand, holding it up so the tiny, square cut diamond catches the light. 'When did this happen?'

'Last night.'

Gracie pulls her into a hug. 'When's the big day?'

'Not for ages. We'll have to save up.'

Gracie starts in on her post, tearing the Sellotape from a neatly wrapped package. 'Don't worry about the catering. My present.'

Sally's look of delight gives way to welling tears. Gracie pulls out a well-thumbed cook's journal and glances at the note:

Dear Gracie, One for your collection. It belonged to my aunt who was famous for her parkin . . .

She puts the book to one side and tosses the packaging into the bin. 'If it's ready you can have the reception in the chapel.'

'Oh, Gracie. I . . . I don't know what to say.'

'Hey, come on. After everything you've done for me it's the least I can do.' A vision of that elegant white space garlanded with flowers melts into memories of her own wedding reception – the joy, the clinking glasses, the absolute confidence that her trust in Tom would last forever. With a swift jerk she slits open a plain buff envelope and feels inside it for a note. There's nothing. She tips it up. Something bounces onto her desk, a bead, with a rounded stalk like a tiny mushroom.

Sally leans closer. 'What on earth . . .?'

Gracie turns it over with the blade of the letter opener. Half a minute of silence and then a low moan escapes her lips as her finger darts forward to press a key on her desk phone. As the number rings she uses the letter opener to flip the envelope and re-reads her name, handwritten in square, impersonal capitals.

'Hi,' Heather's voice crackles through the speaker.

'Can you go up to Elsie's bedroom?'

'I was on my way out.'

'Please. It's important.' She looks up at Sally as she speaks. 'Can you see if Brown Bear's missing an eye?'

'What?'

'Someone's just sent me a boot button.' She listens to the thud of Heather's feet on the stairs, the creak of Elsie's door, the rustle of fabric.

'Heather?'

A choked, barely audible sound.

Gracie holds her breath.

'It's gone. And the fur's ripped as if it's been torn out in a hurry.'

167

Sally puts one hand to her mouth, the other on Gracie's arm.

Gracie's voice is pained, unnatural. 'Can you remember when you last saw him with two eyes?'

'I . . . her birthday. . . after the party.'

'You're certain?'

'I retied the bow round his neck. After that I . . . I'm not sure. The fur's so thick you really have to look to see it's missing.'

'Can you remember where she's taken him since then? Swimming, the park, someone's house?'

'I don't know. She's getting self-conscious about carrying him around . . . he'd have been in her backpack . . . oh God.'

'What?'

'Last week I found him stuffed at the bottom of her school bag.'

'When?'

'Um . . . Tuesday.'

'I'll call you back.' Gracie dials Jamieson's mobile, sharing panicked glances with Sally as she waits.

He doesn't pick up. She leaves a message asking him to call her urgently.

Gracie stands a little apart from the other parents, nannies and au pairs waiting at the steps of St Mathilda's. Usually she makes a determined effort to connect. Today she's too tense to negotiate her way through their tight little power groups. Standing on tiptoe she waves eagerly as Elsie comes skipping down the steps.

'Hello, darling. Have you had a lovely day?'

'I've got to draw six metal things for homework and write down what they're used for.'

'Why don't you start in the kitchen? Plenty of metal things in there.'

In the car Elsie chatters about the story she's writing, the girl who was sick all over her desk and the boy who got sent to the headmistress for dropping his biscuit in the fish tank. Gracie can't bear to pollute this outpouring of innocence with questions about Brown Bear.

With a heaviness inside she follows slowly behind as Elsie drops her bag and scoops Tallulah from her basket. Heather is being determinedly upbeat, murmuring to Gracie, 'At least our mass party invite's paying off.' She's waggling a bright pink envelope addressed to Elsie in childish purple felt pen. 'Hey, Elsie, guess what—'

With a sudden lunge Gracie darts in front of her, blocking Elsie's view. 'I . . . I'm going to do my special tacos for tea.'

She pivots round, eyes locking on Heather's as she plucks the envelope from her fingers, carrying it by the corner like something contaminated and drops it onto the counter. Holding it down with a tea towel she slits it open with a knife from the rack and eases out a square of white card. A large yellow emoticon grins up at her; one eye a staring circle of black, the other a winking slit.

She flips it over. No message.

She's aware of Heather's wordless horror as she takes a Ziploc bag from the drawer and slides the card and the envelope inside it.

'How did you know?' Heather whispers.

'The writing.' She presses a finger to the plastic, tracing the wobbly lines of the *E* and the trailing tail of the *S*. 'It's like someone *pretending* to write like a kid.'

She turns back to Elsie. 'Now, what about this homework?' Grabbing a pair of metal tongs she sweeps in on her, snapping them like jaws. 'How about these?'

Leaving Elsie and Heather to trawl for cookie cutters, spoons and sieves, Gracie runs up to her study, leaves another message on Jamieson's mobile and calls Tom, who says he'll

169

come home as soon as he can. She holds a bright, steady smile firmly in place as she goes downstairs to cook the promised tacos, turning continuously from the stove to admire Elsie's drawings and glance nervously at the kitchen clock. *Where are you, Tom? I need you.*

Elsie is in the bath when Gracie hears the front door slam and the sound of his footsteps on the stairs. She looks up, her smile faltering as he appears in the doorway. 'Oh, Tom—'

His fingers find her shoulder, the pressure of them firm and reassuring. Slowly she takes a breath and, leaning down to Elsie, she says very gently, 'Poor old Brown Bear's been in the wars. He's lost an eye. When did that happen?'

Elsie moulds the bath bubbles into a teetering dome and shrugs.

'Can you try to remember, darling?'

'Did you take him with you when you went swimming with Heather?' Tom says. 'Or when you went to the park?'

Elsie pushes out her lower lip. 'Can't remember.'

Gracie closes her fingers around the soap and feels the softened edges slip against her palm. 'Heather says you've been taking him to school.'

Elsie looks up, frowning. 'I'm not a baby.'

'It wouldn't be babyish to pop something into your bag to give you a bit of courage when you've just started a new school.'

Elsie scrunches up her face. 'I *didn't* bring him. He just came.'

'Can you remember which days he came to school?'

Elsie shakes her head.

'Did anything special happen while he was there? Something extra nice for lunch or a lesson you particularly liked?'

Elsie shrugs again. Her eyes brim with tears.

'Don't cry, darling. Nobody's cross with you. We just want to find out when his eye went missing. Did you show him to anyone?'

'No.'

'Where do you leave your bag when you're at school?'

'On my peg.'

'Where's your peg?'

'In the cloakroom.'

'OK.' Tom lowers himself onto the edge of the bath and trails his hand in the water. 'Do you remember when we talked about strangers?' Elsie nods solemnly. 'So what do you do if a stranger tries to talk to you?'

'Yell and run.'

'Clever girl.'

'But what's even more important than that?'

'Never wander off on my own.'

'That's it,' Gracie says. 'And never get into a car or go anywhere with anybody unless Daddy or Heather or I have said you can.'

'I know that.'

'Yes, but it's easy to forget. Even if it's someone you know, remember, just say no and run back into school.'

Gracie wipes away a tear with the back of a soapy hand and pulls a towel from the rail, furious that she has to put Elsie through this. Tom lifts his daughter out of the water onto Gracie's lap. She wraps her in the towel and rocks her close, the way she did when she was tiny. Elsie wriggles. 'Not so tight, Mummy.'

Tom kisses the top of Elsie's head and pulls open the door. 'I'll give Jamieson another try.'

Gracie closes her eyes, experiencing a floaty, untethered feeling. She hurries Elsie into bed and curls up beside her on the unicorn duvet to read her a story. After less than a chapter Elsie falls asleep, Brown Bear flopped over the crook of her arm, his single eye staring up at the stars on the ceiling.

Tom is jittery, pacing the kitchen with his phone to his ear. He glances up as Gracie comes in. 'Jamieson wants to meet us at the school first thing but I'm supposed to be flying to Dublin. I'm trying to see if Geoff can go for me but he's not picking up.'

'Don't worry. I'll go on my own,' Gracie says.

'Are you sure?'

'No point letting this creep mess up both our days.'

'How on earth did he get into St Mathilda's?' Heather says. 'That place is like Fort Knox.'

Tom drops his phone on the counter. 'We don't know for sure that it happened at school but if it did, he could easily have paid a caretaker or a cleaner to search her bag for something to vandalise.'

'Do you think Jamieson will tell the adoption people?' Heather says.

Tom makes an exasperated noise. 'Course he bloody will.'

Pauline Bryce Diary
February 25th

So I spend another day trudging round flats, getting nowhere and I'm down to the last place on my list. It's in an old warehouse miles from the tube and right next to a ratty kebab shop. But I'm not put off by the stink of fat or the drunks bedding down by the ATM because at least there isn't a queue a mile long waiting to view it. As they buzz me in this Disney princess with hair to die for comes running out like she can't get out of there quick enough, shouting 'Dunno, I'll let you know', and I'm thinking maybe I'm in with a chance. Then I go upstairs and I see these two girls in the doorway – one of them's all vintage curls, fake pearls and a flowery frock that sets off her big tits and tiny waist and the other one's some kind of pixie/ emo hybrid with a perfect skinny body, thigh-length boots and a shaggy black fringe hanging over one eye. They don't say a word, just watch me coming. I feel nervy and when I say I'm Pauline Bryce, Vintage gives Emo a look – like me and my name are some kind of joke – and tells me to come in. So I do and the place is unbelievable. Dark red walls, cushions on the floors, low lighting, drapey curtains and this junky old furniture they've painted gold, like it's a club. This fit bloke with long curly hair looks up from the camera he's fiddling with and gives me a smile as I go past and I'm thinking this is what I want. What I came to London for. This world. These people. So I ask a few questions and it turns out they're art students and they make a bit extra renting the flat out for shoots and parties. Then they take me into the kitchen and Emo opens a door and says this is it, like she's doing me a

173

big favour. I'm gobsmacked. It's tiny, barely big enough for the single mattress laid out on the bare boards. There's a six-inch square window and a couple of hooks on the door and that's it. But I don't care. I want to be part of this. Then she starts asking me questions – what I do, where I'm from – but I've hardly got a word out when Vintage looks at her watch and says they'll get back to me. It's a brush-off. I want to lean over and twist those fake pearls round her throat till she chokes.

31

'You stupid, stupid bitch!' Ian's fury jolts through Juliet's body, violent, electric.

She holds the phone away from her ear. 'Ian—'

'As long as you're hurting me you don't give a shit what happens to Freya.'

'What the hell has got into you?'

'I knew you were a spiteful cow but I never thought you'd go this far.'

She puts her head down and walks faster. 'What are you talking about?'

'They've taken the lot. Computers, accounts, files.'

'Who?'

'The fraud squad.'

'What's that got to do with me?'

His voice is suddenly weary. 'Who else would want to fuck me over?'

'You've got plenty of enemies. That's what happens if you treat people like dirt.'

'Well, just remember. If I go down, you and Freya will suffer just as much as Merion and the baby.' He cuts the call, leaving a hollow whirr on the line.

She walks into a Starbucks and orders a double-shot espresso, her hand shaking as she takes the cup out to one of the pavement tables. She lights a cigarette and takes a deep drag. He's right about the money. Times would get bloody tough for her and Freya if he went to prison. But she's sure it won't come to that. She knows how he works, how careful he is about leaving any kind of trail. She takes the smoke deep into her lungs and for one delicious moment imagines how good it would feel to be free of him.

32

A sweep of wood panelling gleaming in the slant of light from the tall windows, silver trophies displayed in under-lit glass cases, tall lilies arranged just so in a slender vase. The room is far larger and tidier than the headmistress's office at Gracie's old school but it has the exact same intimidating feel, made even more alarming by the sight of Jamieson setting down his cup and standing up to greet her.

Mrs Ogilvy – immaculate grey chignon, pearl-studded ears – waves a hand towards the other chair. 'Do come in, Mrs Whittaker.' Her expression is business-like and her eyes behind her glasses steady and unblinking, as if she and Jamieson have been discussing Gracie's misdemeanours and are yet to decide how best to deal with her. Gracie crosses the carpet and lowers herself into the chair.

'Can I get you something? Tea? Coffee? Water?'

'No, thank you.'

'Inspector Jamieson tells me you've received some disturbing packages relating to Elsie. Do you have the items with you?'

Gracie takes out the plastic bag containing the boot button and its envelope. She places it on the desk. 'It arrived at my office yesterday morning.' She pulls Brown Bear from her bag and lays him beside the button. 'It's the eye from this toy, Elsie's favourite.' The words are coming out in strained staccato breaths. 'And this was sent to the house.' She holds up the second plastic bag to show the winking emoticon, flipping it over so they can see the envelope. She looks from Jamieson to Mrs Ogilvy. 'This is the first time that any of this has involved Elsie so you can imagine how frantic we are.'

Mrs Ogilvy studies the items on her desk. 'When did the bear's eye go missing?'

'Our nanny says it was there on the fifteenth. After that we're not sure.' Gracie pushes her finger into the folds of fur around the bear's empty eye socket. 'Unless you're actually looking it's hard to see it's gone.'

'I understand how distressing this must be,' Mrs Ogilvy says, 'but I can assure you that once inside these gates Elsie is absolutely safe. Our security is second to none.'

Gracie smiles diplomatically. 'Yes, I know. It's one of the reasons we chose St Mathilda's school and, of course, we're trying to get her to remember all the other places she might have taken the bear. But so far, all we know for sure is that she's been bringing him into school. Definitely last Tuesday and possibly on other days too. So we can't ignore the possibility that somebody here could have been involved.'

Mrs Ogilvy's lips tighten over slightly protruding teeth. 'I would be very surprised if that were the case. Every one of our employees has been thoroughly vetted.'

'She says she left him in her bag in the cloakroom.'

'Are the cloakrooms locked, Mrs Ogilvy?' Jamieson asks.

'No. No. They're not,' Mrs Ogilvy says, a little flustered now. 'There's never been a need.' About to go on, she seems to reconsider and turns abruptly to her keyboard. 'Elsie may have taken her bag on an excursion – yes.' Visibly relieved she taps the screen. 'Last Tuesday her class attended a poetry workshop at the Barbican. And the Friday before that they visited the British Library. But if her possessions were tampered with at either of those locations it is still extremely worrying.'

'I'd like to speak to all the teachers who accompanied the children on those trips,' Jamieson says. 'And to anyone else who has had access to Elsie's bag over the last two weeks.'

'Of course. Would you be able to come back later this afternoon – say three thirty?'

'Fine.'

Mrs Ogilvy takes off her glasses and lays them on the table, giving herself time to shape her words. 'There is one thing that concerns me.'

Gracie tips forward, searching the headmistress's face.

'Did Elsie tell you that I had to have a little talk with her last week?'

'No.'

'She got very upset when she didn't earn a smiley face sticker for good behaviour and she took one from another child. Her form teacher was concerned enough to bring the incident to my attention. Of course, it may be a coincidence but—'

'No.' Gracie draws a shaky thumb across the plastic bag, her mouth quivering as she looks up at Jamieson. 'These things I get sent, it's always something to prove how much this person knows about my life, how close they can get to me.'

Mrs Ogilvy says hurriedly, 'It still doesn't mean that someone at St Mathilda's is responsible. Classroom gossip can spread beyond the school gates very quickly, particularly when a child with a well-known parent is involved. But rest assured that we will be stepping up our security and making sure that the children's belongings are supervised at all times.'

Gracie closes her eyes and says croakily, 'I just want Elsie to be safe.'

Standing up, Jamieson slips the plastic bags into his briefcase and extends his hand to the headmistress. 'Thank you, Mrs Ogilvy, you've been very helpful.' His pale eyes shift to Gracie. 'I'll be in touch, Ms Dwyer. Call me if there are any developments.'

Gracie nods him a goodbye and stays in her seat, looking straight at Mrs Ogilvy. 'I don't understand why you didn't tell us that Elsie was getting into trouble. I know she's been having problems settling in but she's not usually naughty.'

Mrs Ogilvy's expression remains bland.

'I was going to wait another week or so to see if things settled down. But if you and your husband would like to come in and have a chat with me and her form teacher we would be happy to see you at any time. Why don't you stop by my secretary's office on your way out to make an appointment?'

Gracie leaves the car, slips on her dark glasses and sets off down Upper Street, badly in need of strong coffee and a few minutes to herself. It's still early, the sunshine holds only a promise of heat and yet she is sweating, still keyed up, her brain over-revving as she replays the meeting in her head. Shutters rattle and rise as she hurries on past restaurants, kitschy little gift shops and estate agents. A dog trots out of an alleyway and sniffs along the kerb and far above her, in the pale haze of the sky, a helicopter whirs and glitters. For a moment she gives herself up to the bustle of the streets, the brief luxury of being part of something that makes no demands on her. The dog barks loudly. Gracie sees it skitter towards a cluster of pigeons pecking at a flattened burger. They rise in a fluttering swirl and swoop towards her, a musty whir of beaks and feathers, flapping wind in her face. Gracie flings up her arm and dodges away in disgust, a horrified shiver running through her limbs as she shoves open the door of the nearest coffee shop and rams it shut behind her. She stands for a moment with her back to the glass, waiting for the panic to recede, her breathing still juddery as she joins the queue at the counter.

She's paying for her coffee, almost back in control, when she feels her phone vibrate. It's Daphne. She hesitates, sees the repeated missed calls and, with a tiny sigh, picks up. 'Hey.'

'Didn't you get my text?'

Gracie squeezes her phone under her chin and keys her pin into the reader. 'Sorry. Phone was on silent. It's been a bit hectic. What's up?' Gracie nods a thank you to the barista and takes her coffee to an empty table.

'Burridge.'

'What's he done now?'

'His wife suspects.'

'Suspects he's cheating on her or suspects he's cheating on her with *you*?'

'She doesn't know it's me, thank God. But she went through his credit card bills and so he's cancelled Barcelona. Fucking wimp. I needed that weekend.'

'What happened to Dieter?'

'*Dieter?* He's in Munich.'

'Go and see him instead.'

'This isn't about sex! Sherys is leaving and Rachel Byrne's going for her job. If she gets it I'll have to leave.'

'Don't be so dramatic.'

'You know I can't work for her. She'll make my life hell. I need time alone with Burridge to convince him to give me the editor's job. What does that dowdy cow know about lifestyle?'

'Is it up to him?'

'Pretty much.'

'You did a brilliant job covering Sherys's maternity leave.'

'Yes, but Rachel's got half the top brass rooting for her. Hang on.' Gracie hears the slam of a taxi door, the tapping of heels up stone steps. 'Can't talk about it now,' Daphne hisses. '*Please* don't say anything. Not even to Tom.' Her voice reverts abruptly to its normal strident pitch. 'I meant to tell you, I saw that woman who got pissed at your party—'

'Juliet?'

'Yeah. She was hanging round the lifts by my office. The minute she saw me she scuttled off down the stairs.'

'When?'

'Yesterday.'

'You sure it was her?'

'Hundred per cent. I would have gone after her but I had a meeting.'

'She was probably too embarrassed to say hello.'

'I don't care about that. What the hell was she doing here?'

'I don't know.'

'How much do you know about her?'

'I told you, Elsie and her daughter go to the same dance class.'

'Yeah, but when did her kid *join* this dance class?'

'For heaven's sake. It was ages before Elsie. She's been going for a couple of years.'

Daphne grunts. 'What else do you know about *Juliet*?'

'Single, separated, does PR. She's helping with the planning application for the chapel.'

'Are you crazy?'

'She's having a tough time. She needed the work.'

'So?'

182

'I had to get *someone* to deal with the objections.'

'Why not Daley?'

'His people are crap at small stuff and, anyway, Juliet's got great local connections *and* she's done this kind of thing before.'

'You need to be more careful. You should have seen the way she was looking at you at your party. Trust me. She's not stable.'

Gracie laughs. 'You just don't like her because she was all over Dieter.'

'No! There's something . . . *creepy* about her.'

'Oh, come on, Daph. Have a heart. She's broke and she's lonely.'

'Got to go. See you later.'

Gracie sips her coffee and stares out at the thickening traffic. It *was* a bit odd Juliet turning up at Daphne's workplace, unsettling enough to vie with her concerns about Elsie throwing tantrums at school.

The disquiet goes on bubbling in her mind as she drives to the studios and it's still there as she makes her final check of the ingredients laid out on set.

Come on, Gracie. Focus. She scoops a heap of flour into the scales. As the floor manager counts her down she turns to camera and snaps on a smile.

'There's no mystique about making perfect pies, pastries, cakes and meringues and no reason why a novice can't produce great results. That's because baking is a science, and like any science, accuracy is everything. If the recipe calls for cold butter or room temperature eggs there'll be a good reason for that. If it tells you to cook in a low oven for an hour don't turn up the heat and do it for forty minutes and expect good results. So remember, to guarantee success don't ever cut corners. And above all get your timings spot on.'

33

Juliet has been toying with the idea of spinning this out, pretending she's using her skill and contacts to deal with the planning objections. But the thought of sitting at Gracie's kitchen table, close enough to see every twitch and hesitation on her face when she tells her the truth about the objectors, is far too appealing. Anyway, whichever way she plays this, Gracie's going to realise how wrong she was to pass her over for that self-serving dick Jeremy Daley.

She's offered to make tea. While the kettle boils she checks her phone and sends off a couple of emails, shifting around a little, so she can see Gracie reading the report she's just handed her.

'So are you saying these people don't exist?' Gracie says.

'They exist all right. They're all property owners and all on the electoral register.' Juliet carries the teapot over to the table. 'It's the email addresses that are fake. That woman who emailed four times . . . Irene Franklin, she's in a dementia ward. According to her daughter she's never used a computer in her life. As for the letter writers, most of them work abroad and the only one who lives locally didn't have a clue what I was talking about.'

Gracie grows very still. Juliet steadies the lid of the teapot with a finger as she pours. 'It looks to me as if this whole thing's being orchestrated by someone who's out to make your life as difficult as possible.' She watches and waits. The tightening around Gracie's jaw is almost imperceptible but there's a new, strained quality to her voice when she asks, 'Any way of finding out who it is?'

'The council chucked the envelopes so we've no way of knowing where the letters were posted, and I . . . took the liberty of . . . getting a friend to trace the IP addresses on the emails. It looks like they were all sent from internet cafés.'

'So what do we do?'

'I've sent everyone on the list a form to sign confirming that they've got no objections to the change of usage or the planned conversion. Apart from that my advice would be to keep quiet about it.'

Gracie looks curiously at her.

'Honestly, things like this leave a nasty taste and we don't want *any* negativity associated with this project. Not at this stage.'

'There's a new detective running the case. He's promised to keep everything confidential.'

Juliet blinks a couple of times, as if unsure what Gracie means, before summoning her most startled expression. 'You think it's your *stalker* who did this?'

That word finally on her lips. Powerful. Exciting.

Gracie looks down at her hands.

Juliet says carefully, 'Is that still going on?'

Gracie doesn't answer immediately. When she does her voice is very quiet. 'The case is still . . . open.'

'Oh, right.' Juliet waits for her to say more, to tell her how it feels to look at every passing stranger and wonder, 'Is it you? Are you the one who thinks I deserve to die?'

Gracie says nothing, just runs her hand across her face.

185

Juliet tips her head to one side as if in sympathy, tempted to let her stew. She quashes that idea. What she needs right now is Gracie's gratitude. With a bemused shake of her head she says, 'I just assumed it was a developer making trouble, hoping to get his hands on the site.'

Gracie lifts her head, eyes wide and hopeful. 'You think?'

'They play dirty all the time.'

'That would make so much more sense.' Gracie's face relaxes, there's even a glimmer of a smile. 'Tom's right. I *am* getting paranoid.'

'Well,' Juliet says firmly. 'The important thing is, I've stopped the damage' (just the right amount of emphasis on the *I*) 'and I think you should leave it at that. When there's no way of proving anything getting the police involved is only going to stir up the kind of attention you don't need.'

Gracie nods thoughtfully and shifts back in her seat. 'What about the alcohol ban?'

'I've been on to the trustees and explained why a licence is vital to the business. They've suggested you go along to put your case in person. But from what they're saying I think it's just a formality. I've listed all the points I think you should make at the back of the report. Once you've had a look I'll tidy them into a document you can distribute at the meeting.'

Grace fingers the papers. 'You're doing a great job on this. If you can get your invoice to me by Friday I'll make sure it's paid by the end of the month.'

This is so far from the outpouring of hand-grasping, eye-rolling gratitude Juliet is expecting that for a moment she can scarcely take it in. All that work and not even a thank you? Ablaze with anger, she stares fixedly into the garden where a man in overalls is weeding the borders. Another dispensable nobody, clearing away the dross from Gracie's life. She glances at Gracie's wall calendar and the list of names and contacts pinned to the corkboard beside it: the hand-picked

186

team of minions standing by to keep the Gracie Dwyer show on the road. She checks the time. *Shit!* Why doesn't that phone ring? She has to leave soon to pick Freya up.

'Do you remember my friend Daphne?' Gracie is saying. 'You met her at the party.'

Juliet turns back slowly. 'Yes. I recognised her from the TV.'

'She saw you the other day.'

Juliet grows uncomfortable. 'Oh, yes?' *What is this?*

'At the paper.'

So that's why Gracie's holding back. Daphne's been warning her off. 'She should have said hello.'

'She tried to. She said you rushed away.'

'I didn't see her.'

'How . . . how come you were there?'

'Their advertising people were doing a presentation. You wouldn't believe the money they throw at these things – lunch, freebies.'

Gracie's hands move oddly. 'You were in editorial. By Daphne's office.'

What if I was? I couldn't miss a chance to see where your best friend worked – who knows what little insights I might have picked up? 'They gave us a tour. I nipped off to the loo and got lost.' With a questioning smile she says, 'Did Daphne think I was . . .' she hesitates before opting for a mildly amused, 'up to no good?'

Gracie blushes. 'She was just . . . surprised to see you.'

'I've probably still got the invitation.' Juliet flicks through the emails on her phone. 'Here you go.'

Gracie grows redder and shies away as Juliet thrusts the handset towards her. 'Honestly. Don't worry. It's fine . . . it's just Daphne . . . being Daphne.'

Juliet imagines the eager intimacy, the sly digs at Juliet as Daphne shared her little revelation. Something needs to be done about that woman. Juliet can't have her getting in the way when she rides in to rescue Gracie's reputation.

Embarrassed, Gracie has taken refuge in Juliet's report. 'Maybe we should put the points about the apprenticeships and the link-up with the local sixth form college nearer the top.'

'OK.' Juliet eyes the kitchen clock. 'I'll get Freya and pop back.'

'Don't worry. I'll email you the changes.'

Damn! Juliet takes her time gathering up her things, dropping her pen and looking around for her notebook. Heather appears in the doorway, a stolid unsmiling presence. A couple of times as she stomps from the fridge to the counter Juliet catches her looking at her. She makes sure she's the first to look away.

The house phone rings. Finally! Juliet bites her lip. Heather picks up. Her replies are curt, she sounds annoyed.

Gracie looks up. 'Everything all right?'

'That was Magda. She can't do Tuesday.'

'Why not?'

'Job interview.'

'Couldn't she have given us a bit more warning?'

'She's only just found out. Don't worry. I'll ring round.'

'Problem?' Juliet says, without a blink.

'Heather has college on Tuesday afternoons so her friend Magda comes over to let Tallulah out then she picks Elsie up from school and gives her her tea.'

'Can't Tom do it?' She's putting her laptop into her bag, zipping it up.

'He's away all week and I'm filming on Tuesday.'

'There must be plenty of people round here who'd love a few hours' work.'

'It has to be someone we know and trust.'

Heather clanks and clatters. 'Worst comes to the worst, I'll cut college.'

'Don't be silly, haven't you got an exam?' Gracie says.

Juliet slips the strap of her bag onto her shoulder. 'What time does Elsie get out of school?'

'Not till four thirty, it's tennis club, but I won't get back till at least six.'

'I could do it,' Juliet says.

'You?' Heather says, addressing Juliet for the first time since she came in.

'Freya gets out at three fifteen.' *No tennis clubs at Dunsmore*. 'So I'd have no problem getting to St Mathilda's by four thirty.'

Juliet's gaze travels from Heather, who has the look of a starving dog sniffing at a lump of poisoned meat, to Gracie who seems equally torn.

'Honestly,' Juliet says as if she's shrugging off their concerns about imposing on her. 'I can work just as well here as at home and Freya would love to see Elsie and Tallulah.' She fastens a smile on the puppy, counts the seconds of silence and gets to five. *Thanks Daphne, this is all your doing*. 'Well, the offer's there,' she says, injecting just enough hurt into her voice to show that Gracie's reticence hasn't gone unnoticed. 'Just let me know.'

Heather stalks out with the phone clamped to her ear. Gracie sees the look on Juliet's face and says in a fluster, 'No, look, it would be great if you could do it. I'll dig you out a spare key and show you how to work the alarm.'

Juliet follows her down the hall.

'If you're here on your own you can set it to go off if anyone tries the doors or windows.'

'Great.' Juliet smiles her most forgiving smile and commits the code Gracie gives her to memory. A bit more gratitude would have been nice but all in all her plan is back on track. Let's just hope Magda doesn't get too excited about her job interview.

34

Once Freya is in bed Juliet logs on to Daphne Dawes' Facebook page. It's exactly what she expected: parties, restaurants, fashion shoots, ski trips. Eight hundred and twenty friends. Two hundred likes when the sneery bitch posts a shot of her new haircut. She takes a long sip of wine and goes back to researching Louise Harper, skimming through a story she tells one interviewer about getting bitten by an insect on a shoot in Malawi and her hand blowing up like an inflated rubber glove. Stuck in the middle of nowhere she pays a young street vendor to operate the camera but he insists on framing the shots his way before grudgingly agreeing to take a few the way she wants. Two months later it's one of his pictures that wins an award.

Juliet is studying the shot of Louise standing in a dust-blown market presenting the grinning boy with his prize money when the doorbell drags her from her laptop. She steps onto the balcony and leans out to see the chequered blue and yellow of a police car parked below. She breathes in, holding the air in her lungs for a count of five, before going back inside. She smooths her hair, removes the ashtray and wine glass from the table and presses the button on the entry phone. 'Hello?'

'Mrs Murray?' The tone is crisp, professional.

'Who is this?'

'Police. Can we come in?'

Juliet presses the buzzer and hears footsteps in the shared hallway as she opens her front door. A short, sharp-faced woman in a grey suit holds up her ID.

'DS Flanagan,' she bats a hand towards the young male officer hovering beside her, 'and PC Dowd.'

'If it's about the break-in at number 40, I'm afraid I didn't see or hear anything.'

'It's about your husband.'

'Ian?' Juliet's voice catches. 'What's happened?'

They step inside. Flanagan closes the door behind her before she says,

'He's been arrested.'

'Oh.'

'May we come inside, Mrs Murray?'

'I use Beecham now,' Juliet says, quickly. 'Ian and I are separated. Have been for over five years.'

Flanagan follows her into the sitting room and glances around, nodding when Juliet motions her to the sofa.

'Sorry about the mess,' Juliet says. 'I've been working. I haven't had a minute to tidy up.'

The two women sit facing each other while the young policeman perches on one of the wobbly dining chairs.

Juliet looks blandly from one to the other. 'I'm not involved in Ian's business. Not any more. Even when we were together I was a director in name only.'

'So you know we've been looking into his affairs?'

'He called me after you confiscated his computer . . . he was angry. He thought it was me who'd tipped you off.'

Flanagan's eyes behind her stumpy lashes are grey and

steely. 'If it *was* you, Ms Beecham, we'd be very interested to know whether—'

'It wasn't. I told you. I'm completely out of the loop as far as his business affairs are concerned.' Juliet gets up and goes over to the kitchen area. 'Tea?'

'If you're making some.' There's a pulse of silence. 'Maybe it wasn't his business affairs you were worried about.'

Juliet switches on the kettle. 'I don't understand.'

'Maybe you . . . wanted to give us a reason to search his computer.'

Juliet takes down three mugs. 'No. Sorry.' She longs for a cigarette but she's wary of seeming nervous. 'He's based in Australia now. Before last week I hadn't seen him for months.'

'The thing is,' Flanagan says, 'we found some photographs on his hard drive.'

Juliet feels a charge in the air, smells it almost, like the crackle of electricity before a storm. 'Photographs?'

'Indecent images. Of children.' Juliet drops her head in a stunned kind of way, her mouth a frozen circle. 'Not a huge amount, but we rate this material on a spectrum of one to five. Some of the photographs we found were a three.'

'Oh my God.' Juliet grabs at the counter for support.

'Did you ever have any suspicions that your husband might have had an unhealthy interest in children?'

Juliet flounders for a moment, wondering how to play this. 'He's a controlling man, Sergeant, I . . . I wasn't always happy about the direction he wanted to take our sex life,' she glances at the young policeman who reddens, 'but I never thought for one minute . . .'

'Our concern is for your daughter.'

'Oh, God.' Juliet's hand flies to her mouth. 'She stayed over at his flat last weekend.'

'How was she when she got back?'

Juliet gazes away, puckering her face. 'She seemed fine. But she's naturally so quiet it's difficult to tell when she's upset.' She turns back to Flanagan. 'Where is he now?'

'At the station. But he'll be out on bail until the case comes to court.'

'I don't want him seeing her!'

'That will be up to the judge. Your husband's got a very smart lawyer who will probably press for visitation rights. The court may rule that he can see Freya under supervision.'

'Why would they do that?'

'He's denying everything. He claims that someone has hacked his computer and done this to discredit him.'

'So he won't . . . go to prison?'

'We're gathering evidence. Payment for some of the material has been traced to a credit card in his name which he says he never ordered but it's linked to his British bank account, and we're getting our colleagues in Sydney to search his computer over there. But even if he's convicted it's a first offence, the number of photographs is small and the period of activity limited so he may get a suspended sentence.'

'You mean he'll get off scot-free?'

'He'll go on the sex offenders' register.'

'What will that mean for him seeing Freya? And me? For Christ's sake, he's got a vicious temper. If he thinks I'm the one who tipped you off—'

'Here, let me.' The young policeman eases the box of tea bags out of Juliet's twitching hands.

'If he turns up, call us.' Flanagan hands her a card. 'And let your daughter's school know that he is no longer authorised to pick her up.'

'If he's touched her I'll kill him.'

'It doesn't always follow, Ms Beecham. She *will* need to

193

be questioned, however. Standard practice in cases like this. Social services will be in touch in the morning.'

Juliet takes the mug of tea the young constable hands her. The sweetness of it makes her shudder but rallies her thoughts. 'Merion,' she gasps. 'His girlfriend in Sydney – she's pregnant.'

'Does she have other children?'

'No. She's not much more than a kid herself.'

Flanagan glances at Dowd then away. 'Well, thank you for your help, Ms Beecham.' She moves to the door, leaving her tea untouched. 'If there's any news we'll let you know.'

Juliet gazes up at her. 'Will it be in the papers?'

'Probably. Cases like this always attract attention.'

After they've gone Juliet sits shivering on the sofa with her mug of tea. As the warmth of it begins to steady her she does her breathing exercises and allows herself to imagine Ian shouting and raging in the interview room, protesting his innocence. She wants to feel elated, free, triumphant. Only she doesn't. She feels hollow and alone. She tiptoes into Freya's room. In the dim orange glow from the street lamp she watches her daughter sleep. The sight of that grave little face so innocent and vulnerable tightens the pressure around her heart.

Pauline Bryce Diary
March 6th

*Rain again. Funny, I thought once I got down South
the sun would shine. But I've been wrong about a lot
of things. The only coat I've got is the parka and I'm
not turning up for a posh interview with the fur
smelling like wet dog so I leave it in the hostel and
by the time I get to Soho I'm soaked and my hair's
like rats' tails smeared flat on my head with my ears
sticking out like handles on a jug. The size zero cow
in the leather mini at reception leaves me to sit and
steam in the lobby for an hour. Then this really, really
beautiful woman comes out – she's about thirty, dressed
like something out of a magazine and she actually
smiles and shakes my hand – like she's a normal person
and I'm another normal person. And she takes me into
her office and asks me if I want a cup of tea or maybe
coffee. And I know I'm looking at her like I'm an
idiot and I'm saying yes, no, either, I don't mind, but
the words aren't coming out right because in the whole
time I've been here she's the first person who's not
looking at me like I'm something stuck on the bottom
of their shoe. And I'm starting to think that maybe
she'll give me a chance and in ten years' time I'll be
the one with the white swivel chair and the big glass
office. Then the phone rings and she says yes, yes, yes
into the receiver and gets up and says God she's sorry
but something's come up and can I come back later,
about four. So I go outside and traipse around Soho
for five hours and then go up again and I'm soaked
and so cold I can't feel my feet but I'm still warm
inside with this dream of how she'll save my life. I
tell Size Zero I'm back to see Ms Beautiful and she*

gives a sniff and says Ms Beautiful's been called away to New York. Crisis cover for some executive who's been injured in a car crash. She'll be gone for months.

I'm back out on the street and it's raining worse than ever and I go into a pub on Tottenham Court Road and ask for a Bacardi Breezer and then another one. I sit in the corner as the place fills up and I'm talking to this secretary and her friend, telling them how crap everything is and I buy us all drinks and I talk some more and little by little they shift away and one of them whispers something in the other's ear and they say they have to meet some people in Victoria. Then these two boys come over – suits, nice shoes – and they buy me drinks and ask my name and they start moving closer, one either side of me, and one of them says I have lovely hair and I think that's nice though I know it's just mousy brown and scraggy. Then the other one – quick with no warning – puts his hand up my top and I shove him away and say what the fuck and he says don't flatter yourself, darling, there's nothing there. Then they both laugh and the other one pats my other tit and says bloody hell you're right and they laugh again and get up and go. I sit there and want to cry but don't. And when I get up I feel sick and I go outside and throw up on the pavement. Then I get the tube back to the hostel.

35

'Who the hell does that woman think she is?' Gracie wrenches at the strap of her seat belt and snaps the buckle into place. 'Elsie's no more spoilt than any of the other kids in that place.'

'You have to admit, she does have a problem sharing.' Tom pulls out of the school car park, raising his hand to the security guard.

'She's an only child, of course it's difficult to share if you don't have to do it every day.'

'Which is why we have to tell her about the adoption. She needs to get used to the idea that there's going to be another kid around permanently.'

'It could be months before we even hear if we've been accepted.'

'The sooner we start involving her the easier she'll find it to adjust.'

'What if it all falls through?'

'Maybe a bit of disappointment is what she needs.'

'She's six years old, Tom. If those stuck-up kids at her school don't like her we've just got to make sure she sees more of her out-of-school friends.'

They bicker gently as he drives. Outside the sky is darkening. By the time he pulls onto the forecourt of the chapel rain is falling in thick heavy drops. No longer in the mood for their planned discussion about floor plans and flow patterns, Gracie hitches her jacket over her head and runs across the tarmac, squeezing herself beneath the shelter of the narrow porch, urging Tom to hurry as he fumbles with the keys and pulls open the door.

It's his body that reacts. A folding in as if he's been punched. Gracie's eyes follow his to the back wall. The message is daubed in dripping red capitals, a crude imitation of blood. It takes her a second to make sense of it – the elegance of the words in such jarring contrast to the clumsy lettering.

I am closer than breathing, nearer than hands or feet.

'What the—' He crosses the room and dabs the paint with his fingers. 'It's still wet. How the hell did they get in?'

Gracie's eyes dart to the splintered shutter hanging open on the far side, the jut of broken lead and the scatter of shattered glass, wet from where last night's storm has driven rain across the floor. 'It's him.'

Tom turns on her, surprised. 'Don't be silly. It's some religious nut who doesn't want us turning this place into a café.'

'How do you make that out?'

'It's a mis-quote. From a poem about God. "Closer is *he* than breathing, nearer than hands or feet."' He keys the words into his tablet and hands it to her. 'See. It's Tennyson. I keep telling you, you can't let yourself get paranoid.'

She stares at the screen then at him, her thoughts gluey, slow to seep to the surface. 'Since when have you been an expert on Tennyson?'

He drags a worn-down broom from the piles of junk and sets about sweeping up the glass. 'I must have told you this story,' he says, amusement pulling at his mouth.

'What . . . story?' She tries her very hardest to smile.

'When we were at university this tutor of Louise's wrote a book about retracing Tennyson's travels in the Pyrenees and asked her to do the photos. So I went along for the ride thinking it would be a laugh.' He's shaking his head. 'It was a nightmare. The old buffer had a clapped-out Morris Minor that he refused to drive above forty and all the way there he insisted on playing this one tape over and over of some actor reciting Tennyson to "get us all in the mood".' He throws down the broom. 'By the time we got there he'd converted Louise but I was ready to kill him.' His laughter – deep and easy – bounces off the walls.

Even as Gracie closes her eyes and tells herself that no one else could know this, that the link to Louise is too tenuous to have any relevance, her thoughts scurry from the arrival of that postcard with the photo of Louise's dead tree root on the front and that creepy motto about the past feeding the present on the back, to the sudden appearance of Louise's gurning figurine in the hall, and she battles the rising dread of a threat that she can't define or confront or ever dream of voicing to Tom.

She opens her eyes. Tom is watching her. And now he's coming over, catching her in his arms. She leans into his chest, hoping that the frenzied rattle of raindrops on the roof will mask the rapid drumming of her heart.

36

Juliet savours the sound of the dropping tumblers as she turns Gracie's keys in the locks of Gracie's home. She gives the shiny black door a sharp push. There's a pause before the alarm goes off. Like a toddler filling its lungs before it screams. She taps in the code and resets the alarm. This time she's come prepared – her phone fully charged and her handbag packed with all sorts of useful tools. She starts in the sitting room, determined to dig beneath the effortless order of it all – even the glossy hardbacks on the dark-painted shelves are arranged to please. Her eyes dart along the spines and snag on a familiar name: Hugh Dugdale, the posh blustery MP who was at Elsie's barbeque. He's written a book on the Iraq war. She takes a shot of the matey dedication to Tom and Gracie on the flyleaf. He comes across as Mr Clean on the news but with politicians there's always a chance of something shady going on.

She makes her way to the kitchen where the puppy is yelping and pawing the mesh of her cage.

'Forget it, Tallulah. You're in for the duration.'

There's one of Gracie's notes on the table: *I've made popcorn chicken as a special treat for the girls and lasagne for you. Help yourself to anything else you want. So grateful, Gracie xx*

Two kisses. Penitence for her misgivings.

P.S Watch your stuff – Tallulah is still destroying everything she can get her teeth into!

Juliet opens the fridge and lifts out an orange Le Creuset dish, just right for one, swathed in cling film, labelled 'Juliet'. For a second she imagines warming it up then and there and eating it under the trees with a glass of that Sancerre she can see in the fridge door. She shoves it back. No time for lunch.

On her way up to Gracie's study she glances over the bannister. Reassured by the glowing dot of green on the alarm she settles herself at Gracie's desk, takes out the bag of old keys she's brought with her and spends a few minutes trying them in the locks of the drawers. A couple of them send her heart thudding as they slide into one of the barrels. But they all refuse to turn.

She boots up Gracie's computer and taps in the password she's learned by heart. Scowling at the cutesy screensaver of Elsie and Gracie sharing a dripping ice cream, she tries the document folders. They're password protected. Damn. She clicks on the email icon. A second disappointment. Gracie has changed her account. The oldest message only dates back four months. She combs methodically through the messages, struck at every turn by how little of herself Gracie gives away.

She checks her browsing history: St Mathilda's parent portal, daily searches of Gracie's own name and bouts of obsessive Googling of someone called Ryland Stott, who turns out to be a copper-skinned, New-York-based TV executive. She hunts him down in Gracie's inbox, hoping for a hint of flirtation, but his communications are so terse they're almost meaningless. She follows one thread of forwarded memos and messages back to last year. Surprised that Gracie doesn't seem to use an agent to thrash out her deals, she skims through a gushing focus group report citing off-the-scale ratings for Gracie's 'likeability' and a bit of to-ing and fro-ing about embargoing the announcement but two things are clear. One, Gracie is a steely negotiator, and two, she's sold *Cooking with Gracie* to the US for a staggering amount of money.

She checks the clock. Oh God! It's time to pick up the girls and she hasn't even started on the boxes in the cellar.

Freya peers up at the golden pineapples topping the gateposts of St Mathilda's while the man on security inspects Juliet's letter of authorisation with the surly concentration of a Soviet border guard. Juliet parks badly and hurries Freya past the gleaming new science block to the main entrance, where she and her letter are subjected to a second inspection before Elsie is finally handed into her care.

'Come on then, let's get you home,' she says, aware as they cross the car park of how battered her old Micra looks beside the gleaming line-up of Audis and BMWs.

'Hop in, Elsie.'

'I'm thirsty.'

'You can have a drink as soon as we get home. Put your seat belt on.'

'I want one now.'

'Let's get home quickly then.'

Freya watches and listens, round-eyed with fascination. Juliet feels the thump of Elsie's feet against her back.

'Please don't kick my seat, Elsie.'

The pressure increases. 'Elsie, I've asked you nicely. Please don't kick my seat.'

The kicking stops but the sour little face Juliet catches in the rear-view mirror stays sucked into a pout.

As soon as they get back Elsie drops her racquet and school bag in the hall and runs to the kitchen, ignoring Juliet's call of 'Elsie! Pick up your things.'

Juliet picks them up herself, setting them down on the kitchen table as Elsie drags Tallulah out of the puppy cage and Freya looks on. Juliet pours tumblers of juice – raw, cold pressed apple, cucumber and chard. *For fuck's sake.*

'Here, Elsie, if you're thirsty have a drink.'

Elsie snatches the pink tumbler, leaving the blue one for Freya, and struts into the garden. Freya runs in her wake. It breaks Juliet's heart to see her daughter hovering longingly every time Tallulah is snatched from her arms and being forced to surrender every toy she touches. She intervenes only once when a push sends Freya toppling to the ground, although, as she runs to help Freya up, a glare at Elsie and 'Gently now. Play nicely' is all the reprimand she allows herself. She rubs Freya's knees and plants a kiss on her grazed elbow. *I'm sorry, my darling. I promise this is all going to be worth it in the end.*

She's serving up the popcorn chicken when Gracie calls, flustered and apologetic.

'There's been a glitch in the recording, we need to reshoot two items and Heather won't be home until late. Is there *any* chance you could stay on till one of us gets back?' Juliet can sense her wincing. 'If it's a problem I can reschedule for tomorrow but I'd have to pull out of this lunch I'm hosting and it's a big fundraising thing for Stay Safe.'

The thought of Gracie letting down one of her precious charities and pissing off all those celebrities is tempting, but can't compete with the appeal of the unexplored packing cases in the cellar. 'Oh . . . I . . . of course . . . it's fine,' Juliet hits a perfect note of good-natured martyrdom. 'Freya can sleep on the sofa until you get back.'

A hesitation. 'Why don't you put her to bed with Elsie

and both stay over? That way she can sleep, you can relax and I won't have to worry about getting back. There's a nice bottle of Sancerre in the fridge and some new tooth-brushes in the cupboard in my bathroom.'

'If you're sure,' Juliet says, adding – for her own sake – 'I'll put Elsie on so you can tell her what's happening.'

She waits while Elsie sulks and whinges to her mother, then hurries both girls through their tea and a shared bath and leaves them whispering and giggling beneath Elsie's designer duvet.

There's a coolness about the cellar. Juliet pauses on the wooden stairs to take a photograph of the layout of the packing cases, a flash of brilliance in the half light, before she makes for the ones marked *Gracie*. Setting down her wine glass she takes a packet of razor blades from her bag and slides one out. Deftly she slices the seals on the nearest case, folds back the cardboard flaps and lifts out a set of iron saucepans and a brass tea urn encased in bubble wrap. She packs them back, takes out the roll of tape she's brought along and reseals the flaps. She moves on, gratified to find that the next case holds box files: a row of shiny jewel colours packed spine upwards, coded alphabetically in Gracie's neat black lettering. They're full of folders stuffed with cuttings and research notes, labelled by theme, ingre-dient or utensil – *Paring knives*, *Parsley*, *Quince*, *Radicchio*, *Sumac*, *Tarragon*, *Umami* – with matching handwritten lists pasted inside each lid. The box files below them are plain mottled grey and labelled by date. She runs her eyes along them, eager to see what Gracie thought worthy of keeping from the year they first met; the year Gracie got her big break. The year Juliet's life imploded. There are two. She hooks her finger through the metal eyelet and lifts one out. The folders inside chart the birth of Gracie's first cookbook and her dreams of opening a café. Juliet stops to sip her wine and turns to the second box file, flicking through a thick wedge of complaints about Gracie's recipe for chocolate torte published in the *Evening Standard*. She lingers over the three-page outpouring of vitriol from Elizabeth Pitt (Mrs) who made 'your inedible dessert', served it to her husband's boss and claims it ruined his chances of promotion. *Oh, dear.* She runs a professional eye down the template letter of apology clipped to the complaints, which lays all the blame for the mistakes (too many eggs, not enough butter) firmly at the door of the printers. Her amusement sours when she sees the handwritten note at the bottom: *Hope this helps, Jeremy x*

Jeremy fucking Daley.

The letter is competent enough – but there's nothing of Gracie's trademark warmth about it. Juliet would have added a lot more contrition to get the complainants on side and arranged for Gracie to write a follow-up piece on famous culinary disasters. *What the hell did you do to keep her business, Daley?* All the old anger rises like scum as she yanks open more folders looking for his pitch. She's tossing aside an old pub menu when a glimpse of orange on glossy black snatches her breath. It's the programme for the conference where she and Gracie first met. Dazed by the hiss of blood in her head she reads through the list of talks and seminars, peering closely to find 'Juliet Beecham' among the contributing speakers. A few millimetres of type that summon all the fear and excitement of ditching her married name; the first tentative step in her bid to put the dark months of depression behind her and escape her toxic marriage. There's a business card tucked between the pages. She flips it over.

It's hers: *Juliet Beecham, PR and Marketing Solutions.*

The shock of it, of finding it here in Gracie's home after

all this time, almost overpowers her. She turns the folder over, curious to see how her own dreams had been filed. There's a single letter on the label, a neatly inked 'R', repeated on the list inside the lid of the box file. 'R' for what? 'Rejects'?

Unable to smile at her own bitter joke she sits back on her heels, certain that if she stops thinking about it the real answer will snap into place. She tips up the folder, shaking out a couple of invitations – a glimpse of the glamorous life Gracie was living while Juliet dragged a colicky baby between short-term lets, writing pitches through the night because she couldn't afford childcare, too frightened to ask Ian for money in case he took Freya away. The events are an unlikely combi-nation – a private view of 'Images of Old Age', by some octogenarian called Olga Maswell at the Forward Gallery, and the launch party for *This Is Me,* the autobiography of that trashy TV presenter Lana Laughton. She fingers her business card, gratified that Gracie kept it, and at the same time annoyed that she buried it amongst this load of junk. 'R' – what the hell does that stand for? Bloody infuriating that it's the only file Gracie didn't bother labelling properly.

She empties the second box file for 2010, fuming at the estate agent's bumf for a 'delightfully compact one-bedroom flat in a spectacular industrial conversion in Holloway'. The difference a place like that would have made to her grim first years with Freya. The difference a nice flat – or maybe a little house with a garden – would make to her and Freya now.

She checks her watch and moves quickly on to a packing case marked *TOM – Fragile This Way Up.* There's a pleasing snap as the tip of the razor pierces the tape. She sets aside a small architectural model encased in Perspex and takes out a battered camera box. Excited by the name on the label, she flicks up the latch and lifts out the camera, im-agining Louise Harper's expert fingers choosing a lens, fixing it on and lifting it to her eye to capture a haunting frame of displacement, hunger, desolation. She picks at the foam in the lid. It's stuck fast, though the block at the bottom lifts away easily, revealing documents and a velvet drawstring bag. She shakes two matching gold wedding bands into her palm (Gracie and Tom's are platinum) and tries on the smaller one, turning her splayed fingers from side to side, giggling nervously when it jams beneath her knuckle and has to be licked and gripped before she can wiggle it free. And there's a shopping list, pencilled in a hurry – honey, Persil, bananas, milk. *Does Gracie know you kept them, Tom? These little things that mean so much?*

She's flicking through an envelope of what she reckons must be pre-Elsie shots of a young-looking Tom and Louise on a rocky beach, somewhere in the Mediterranean – a crop of blue-shuttered, whitewashed cottages on the hillside above – when a whispering freezes her fingers. She turns in panic. Two dwarfed misshapen figures stand at the top of the cellar steps shrouded in drapery.

'I'm telling my mummy.' Elsie's voice, shrill with accusation.

Juliet says evenly, 'I was looking for a mop and I saw a mouse scuttle into this box.' The girls yelp and step back.

She runs up the steps. They've daubed their faces with blusher, lipstick and eye shadow and wrapped themselves in an assortment of Gracie's evening wear – Elsie in a long blonde wig, Freya in a green velvet hat, both askew.

'What on earth is going on? You're supposed to be asleep.'

Freya cowers. Elsie stays defiant. 'Playing dress-up. My mummy lets me.'

'Not at this time of night, she doesn't.'

'You didn't read us a story. I can't get to sleep without a story.'

Juliet claps her hands together. 'Out! Both of you. Now!' Pulling the cellar door shut behind her she shoos them upstairs, pushing up behind Elsie and snatching off the wig, which hangs soft and heavy in her hands, real hair by the feel of it, expensive. 'Where did you get this?'

'It's my mummy's.'

'Did she say you could play with it?'

Elsie lifts her shoulders, an exaggerated shrug. 'She won't mind. She's got lots.' She holds Juliet's stare.

Juliet shoos them into the bathroom. 'In there and take those clothes off. Now!'

Freya, close to tears, steps out of the black-beaded shift she's wearing while Elsie stands and pouts. Resisting the urge to slap her, Juliet holds her wriggling body firm with one hand, using the other to strip her of the green silk cocktail dress and Vivienne Westwood jacket. She soaps a flannel, ignoring Elsie's yelps as she scrubs her face. She's just as brutal with Freya, refusing to be pacified by her sobs of 'Sorry, Mummy' as she marches them back to bed.

Juliet stands at the bedroom door. 'If either of you set one foot out of this room there's going to be trouble.' She snaps off the light and goes to close the door. Something stops it, one of Elsie's sequined trainers. She kicks it out of the way.

Furious at the precious minutes slipping away, she turns down the landing to Gracie's room gathering up clothes as she goes. God, what a mess. Closet door hanging open, skirts, tops, jackets and shoes slung across the bed, floor littered with spilled eye shadows and lidless lipsticks.

She moves quickly, replacing lids, shaking out clothes, combing her fingers through the ruffled wig. Looking round for its box, she catches herself in the mirror. She can't resist. Twirling her ponytail into a knot she pulls on the wig, adjusting the crown with the flats of her hands. The transformation is startling, the face beneath the feathery fringe almost that of a stranger. Juliet stares at her reflection and giggles out loud, imagining the things she could do, the places she could go, the people she could spy on, or occasionally even become, if she bought herself a wig like this.

'Take that off!'

She spins round, slapping her hand to her chest. Heather stands in the doorway. 'Oh, you gave me a shock!' Burning with embarrassment she pulls off the wig and shakes out her ponytail. 'Elsie and Freya were in here playing dressing-up. I was trying to clear up the mess.'

Heather moves forward, curiously light on her feet for someone so thickset. She plucks the wig from her hand. 'I suppose you never thought to come up and check on them?'

Juliet bridles. 'I thought they were asleep. Freya never gets up once I've put her to bed, and anyway she wouldn't dream of touching my things.'

Heather's face darkens at the implied criticism of Elsie. 'Go home. I'll sort this out.'

Juliet lifts her jaw. 'Actually, we're staying the night.' She stalks out, pauses on the landing and looks back. Heather is stroking a brush through the wig, each flyaway hair gleaming like spun sugar in the lamplight.

Still smarting, Juliet carries on down the landing and stands with her hand on the knob of Elsie's door. She turns it silently, and goes in. The girls are sleeping, the only sounds the purr of their breath and the swivel-eyed tick of the ladybird clock on the wall. Juliet gazes down at them, Freya curled on the edge of the mattress and Elsie, selfish little bitch, sprawled on her back, fists flung wide, hogging the rest of it. If Juliet hadn't been so busy picking up after her she'd have remembered to reset the alarm.

She gropes in the gloom for the sequined trainer and hurries downstairs. She stops outside the kitchen, electrified by the sliver of light beneath the cellar door. She listens hard. Senses sharpened, she makes out the faintest creak of the ceiling and the slam of a drawer. Willing Heather to take her time she creeps down the steps. Her handbag, wine glass and phone sit beside an open packing case, obvious and incriminating. Clumsy with panic she rams everything back, rucking the tape as she reseals the flaps. No time to fix it. She grabs the glass, throws the razor blade and tape back into her bag and pockets the phone. With a hurried backward glance she switches off the light and slips into the kitchen. Stopping briefly to tuck Elsie's trainer beneath the tartan blanket in Tallulah's cage, she pours herself a large glass of Sancerre and puts the lasagne in the oven. While she waits for it to warm up she looks up the Forward Gallery and Lana Laughton on her phone. The gallery is a grotty little place in the East End run by some kind of charity, and it turns out that Lana Laughton doesn't just present those raunchy reality shows, she owns the company that makes them – Wink Productions. She must be raking it in.

As she's stacking her plate in the dishwasher a key turns in the front door. Gracie's voice, husky with tiredness, calls, 'Hi, Juliet. You are a total lifesaver.'

Juliet calls back, 'Tea? Coffee? Wine?'

'Tea would be wonderful.' Gracie flops into one of the kitchen chairs and kicks off her shoes.

'There's some lasagne left. Do you want it?'

Gracie pulls a face. 'No thanks, I've been picking all day. Did the girls go down all right?'

Juliet smiles awkwardly and turns away to put on the kettle. 'Actually they got a bit overexcited. I thought they were asleep but they were playing dressing-up and made a hell of a mess in your room. Heather's up there now and she's not best pleased with me.'

Gracie laughs, rubbing her hand down her foot. 'Oh, don't mind Heather. Elsie's obsessed with dressing-up at the moment, it's driving us all nuts.'

Juliet spoons tea into the pot, a casual look up as she says, half laughing, half apologetic. 'She was wearing a wig. It looked expensive. I hope she hasn't damaged it.'

She's aware of Gracie's hand growing still; a paralysis that creeps along her arm and tenses her whole body.

'If I had gorgeous hair like yours I wouldn't bother with a wig.'

'I don't,' Gracie says, after a silence. 'At least, not any more.' Her hand regains movement. 'For a while I got a bit paranoid about being recognised when I went out on my own. The wigs . . . got me through a tough patch.'

'Oh, God. I'm so sorry,' Juliet murmurs. 'I should have thought. I can't imagine how you coped with all that. It must have been awful.'

Gracie sits staring at nothing. Juliet watches her, ready to catch the gush of pain. *How did it feel, Gracie? Come on, you can tell me.*

'So how have things been with you?' Gracie says. The moment is gone, replaced by one that Juliet has been dreading.

'Actually, not so good.' She keeps moving, dipping down to get the milk, rinsing a spoon. 'There's something I need to tell you, before you see it in the papers. I told you, didn't I, that the fraud squad was investigating Ian's business?'

'Did they find something?' Juliet can tell that Gracie's mind is elsewhere.

'Yes. But not fraud.'

'What then?'

Juliet rubs her dampening hands down her jeans and forces out the words. 'Child pornography.'

'What?' Gracie's voice is sharp with shock. Juliet has all her attention now.

'Of course, he says he's innocent but they traced the transactions to one of his credit cards.'

211

'My God, did you ever suspect?'

'Never. And now, just thinking about being with him makes me feel sick.'

'Where is he now?'

'Out on bail.'

'What about Freya?'

'It's OK. Social services sent someone to talk to her. They're as certain as they can be that he never touched her.' She presses her fingers to her skull to ease the growing tightness.

'Thank God for that.'

'But he's insisting on seeing her.'

'Surely they won't let him.'

'As long as the visits are supervised the court says he can.'

'Oh, Juliet. If there's anything I can do, anything at all, just ask.'

Juliet nods, tearful. 'I was worried that once you knew, you might not want anything to do with us.'

'Don't be ridiculous. It's not your fault.' Juliet feels the weight of Gracie's fingers on her arm, consoling and supportive. She looks up. Heather is standing in the doorway holding her phone.

'Magda just called me.'

'Did she get the job?' Gracie says.

'It was a mix-up.' Heather's eyes find Juliet's. 'The company had never heard of her. They weren't even hiring.'

'How odd.'

Juliet rubs her temples. 'I think I might go up to bed.'

'Are you all right?' Gracie murmurs.

'Just a bit . . . achy.'

She moves unsteadily towards the door. From the stairs she looks down into the kitchen and sees Gracie lift the wine bottle to the light, checking the level.

Pauline Bryce Diary
March 11th

I get a call this morning. Some posh girl being dead friendly saying it's Imogen and she's sorry it's taken her so long to get back to me. I haven't got a clue who she is till she starts on about a flat share in Mile End. Then it clicks. She says I'd been top of their list till her sister decided to move in but now her sister's dropped out, so long story short the room's mine. I can't believe it. I pack up my stuff and after I finish my bar shift I check out of the hostel and go down there. As soon as I walk in Imogen (Vintage) and Suzy (who's dropped the emo/pixie look and gone full on dream-girl hippy) are offering me wine and while they're showing me the rotas for hoovering and washing up and giving me a key the place is filling with people who look like models. I look around and suddenly it feels like Lancaster is a million miles away and I'm finally going to get a taste of the life I want.

37

Tom and Gracie sit on the sofa in the den, balancing plates of seared scallops on their knees while they catch up on the latest Nordic thriller. Except for the muted dialogue and Tallulah snuffling on the rug, the house is quiet.

'Hang on,' Gracie reaches for the remote, 'why isn't he telling the police what he saw in the garage?'

'Don't know. Pause it a sec while I get us a refill.'

He brings the bottle from the kitchen and tops up their glasses. She holds the programme on pause, loath to spoil the moment, but she has to tell him. 'While you were away Juliet told me something terrible.'

'Let me guess. She got pissed at another party.'

'Tom!'

'Done for drunk driving?'

'Stop it. Her ex was arrested.'

'Oh,' he says, not much interested. 'You said he was violent.'

'It's not that.' She turns the remote in her hands. 'The police were investigating him for fraud and they found. . .' she swallows hard, then she says it, 'child pornography on his hard drive.'

She can see his smile withering, feel his body filling with protective outrage. 'Has he been anywhere near Elsie?'

'No. Never. But he's insisting on seeing Freya.'

'The courts can't let that happen.'

'Well they are and there's nothing Juliet can do about it, though the visits have to be supervised.'

'But if he's touched Freya—'

'There's no evidence that he has. He's pleading not guilty. He says he's been set up.'

'That poor kid. Imagine growing up knowing your dad's a paedophile.'

'I don't even want to think about it. She's such a sweet little thing.'

'Shame about her mother.'

She turns her face to his. 'I know Juliet's not your favourite person but she did do a brilliant job on the planning objections and right now she needs all the support she can get. I don't think she's got much in the way of friends or family.'

'You do what you like, but I'm not having Elsie going anywhere near her flat. Not ever. Christ, what if he turned up?'

'I know. I'll make sure they always come here.' Gracie presses play. On the screen a well-dressed middle-aged couple sit stiffly in matching armchairs staring straight ahead. 'What's the matter with them?'

Tom takes a swig from his glass. 'It's Danish. They're probably dead.'

Gracie mouths *Sorry* across the packed church hall and shakes her head at the elderly man who is pointing at the chair she's saved for Juliet. She waves at Amber's parents and peers through the crowd. Dawn is in the front row, chatting to an older version of herself who grips her bulging handbag as if preparing to make a dash for the door. 'Can you see Juliet anywhere? I can't save this seat much longer.'

Tom doesn't bother to look up from his phone. 'Why couldn't she just turn up on time?'

'That's not fair. She had a late meeting. That's why Freya came with us.'

Gracie twists right round to look at the crush by the entrance. It's standing room only now. She turns back, surprised to see Daphne half way along the row, thrusting her handbag into people's faces in her hurry to get to the empty seat.

'Daph! What are you doing here?'

'Elsie told me I had to come.'

'She didn't think you'd actually turn up.' She lowers her voice. 'You're going to be bored stiff.'

'A promise is a promise. Anyway, I wouldn't miss this for the world.' She gazes archly at a pair of gum-chewing young mothers, bare midriffs, slashed skinny jeans, tossing their hair back as they poke their mobiles. Their partners sit hunched at the end of the row, hands hanging between splayed legs, heads tipped back. 'God, who are these people?'

'Oh, shut up. I want Elsie to grow up in the real world.'

Daphne's eyes widen in mock horror as Lynda Burton appears on stage, in a red satin sheath.

'What the hell is she wearing?'

'Daphne, I'm warning you.'

Lynda taps the microphone, wincing at the screech of feedback. Gracie drops her voice. 'Any news on the job?'

'The interviews are next week.'

'Have you talked to Burridge?'

'Can't. He won't let me near.'

'So you've just got to wow them at the interview. You can do it, Daph. You're brilliant at what you do.'

Daphne shrugs and sighs as the curtains stutter open and three strobe-lit boys jerk across the stage in perfect staccato unison. Their routine, led by Leslie's son Liam, is surprisingly witty and slick.

Daphne raises an eyebrow and joins in the burst of applause. Gracie twists around again looking for latecomers as a troupe of teenage girls in wispy tulle teeter onto the stage. With sinewy concentration they switch from sweeping pirouettes to bursts of robotic aggression, and take a bow to rapturous whoops and whistles as a woodland backdrop is cranked into place. Elsie and Freya appear among a wobbly row of little girls, cardboard mushroom hats tied tightly beneath their chins. Shiny with makeup they shuffle into position, lips pouted, heads tilted, stiff fingers jammed coyly into red-dotted cheeks. Gawky and determined they thump and totter through their routine, Elsie constantly pushing forward to eye the others, still unsure of the steps. Gracie bites her lip, willing her to catch up.

'Christ, imagine what the lovely Louise would have made of this,' Daphne whispers. Gracie nudges her hard, though the same thought has occurred to her.

The music tinkles to a stop. The mushrooms drop into awkward little curtsies to take their applause and Elsie, peering into the audience, sees Gracie and waves. Tom cheers loudly and they both wave back. Freya's eyes dart wildly along the rows looking for Juliet. Gracie rises up in her seat so that Freya can see a friendly face.

'Wave at Freya,' she whispers. Tom waves and widens the zoom on his camera to include her in shot. Freya breaks into a sudden smile and waves hard, not at them but at a figure standing at the back, clapping his hands above his head. Gracie squints into the darkness. 'Oh, God.'

Tom whispers, 'What's wrong?'

'I think that's Freya's dad. What's he doing here?'

Daphne swings round to get a better look. 'The paedophile? God, it just gets better and better.'

The mushrooms skip off into the wings. The hall vibrates to a blast of 'Saturday Night Fever' and a slowly descending mirror ball scatters shafts of light across the dark. Tom, grim-mouthed, is on his feet pushing along the row and striding up the aisle towards the doors where Juliet is squaring up to Ian, spitting fury.

'Wait here,' Gracie says, but Daphne comes too, treading on toes, mumbling apologies. Juliet's voice rises above the applause, a raw guttural cry. 'Get out! Get out!'

Ian's face is placatory, bewildered. 'I just wanted to see her dance.'

'You can't be here!'

'I promised Freya . . . then I got the email . . . and I thought if I stood at the back—'

'Wait till the police hear about this.'

There is a sudden tightening of his jowls, a naked fury, as if something has been ripped away. 'You bitch. It was you! *Don't miss out. Come and see your child perform!*' Flecks of spittle fly from his fleshy lips. 'You sent it so you could call the cops on me.'

'What the hell are you talking about? I don't want you coming anywhere near Freya.'

He lurches forward as if to strike her. Tom steps between them, one palm raised high like a traffic cop, the other flung protectively in front of Juliet.

'Time to go.' His voice pulses with anger.

Ian glares at him. 'Who the fuck are you?'

Tom drops his hand onto Ian's shoulder. 'I said, it's time to go.'

Ian smacks the hand away, his face contorted with pure animal fury. Tom stares him out, his eyes never moving. 'Gracie, call the police.'

She fumbles for her phone. Suddenly Ian is wilting, as if the air has been punched out of him. 'I swear to God I

218

never knew that filth was on my computer. Somebody set me up.' His eyes are lifting, his words stuttering to a stop as if to allow a slowly forming thought to take shape. 'It's her.' He glares at Juliet, his finger trembling as he jabs it at her face. 'She planted that muck!'

'You sick bastard!' Juliet flies at him. Gracie pulls her back.

His eyes move pleadingly to Tom. 'She's good at that stuff, hacking computers, faking emails.' He pushes his face close to Juliet's, jowls wobbling. 'Do what you want. Call the cops, plant your filth, peddle your lies. You're never going to stop me seeing Freya. I love her. She's mine. She's my kid.' His voice breaks as he turns and walks away, letting the outer doors bang shut behind him.

The whoops in the hall grow deafening as a boy in a white waistcoat and flares punches the air. Gracie slips her arm around Juliet's shoulders and looks up at Daphne. 'Can you and Tom fetch the girls? I'll go back with Juliet.'

Daphne compresses her lips. 'Back where?'

'Falcon Square. I promised them we'd have pizza.'

Daphne looks at Tom in exasperation. Gracie glares at them both and tightens her grip on Juliet's arm. 'Shall I drive?'

'I'll be fine,' Juliet says.

'Come on. What we need is a drink.'

Back at the house Juliet hurries into the garden to call the police. Tom sends the girls to the den and Gracie stands by the doorway watching the wandering dot of Juliet's cigarette glow in the gloom. Tom comes up behind her opening a bottle. 'Do you think it *was* her who emailed him about the show?'

Daphne dumps her bag down. 'I wouldn't put it past her.'

'Why on earth would she do that?' Gracie says.

'How about to trick him into breaking his bail conditions and losing it in front of witnesses?' Daphne says.

Tom reaches for the glasses. 'Daph has got a point.'

Gracie looks out at Juliet. There's something utterly forlorn about the way she's leaning against the summerhouse finishing her cigarette. 'Could you honestly blame her if she did? If I were her I'd do anything to protect my kid.'

'It's weird,' Tom says. 'When I saw him watching those little girls, grinning all over his face, I wanted to kill him. But when I got close and he looked at me, I could see he wasn't just angry, he was really upset. And I thought, Christ, supposing that stuff really *had* been planted on him. Can you imagine not being allowed to see your own kid because of something you didn't do?'

Gracie watches the wine swirl into the glass in his hand. 'Paedophiles are good at pretending. That's why so many of them get away with it. It was his credit card don't forget, *and* his laptop and anyway he *can* see Freya, just under supervision.'

She moves off to answer the doorbell. The house fills with the smell of warm pizza as she rips the lids off the boxes and hooks down the cutter but her efforts to keep the conversation going fall flat. Juliet sits hunched at the table barely touching a thing. Daphne stays huffy and tight-lipped. Freya, sensing tension, picks at the congealing strips of cheese and Elsie scuffs her feet against Gracie's chair and whines about the hardness of the crust.

'Go on, you two,' Tom says, handing them spoons and tubs of ice cream, 'go and finish your DVD.'

Juliet reaches for the wine.

'You should go easy on the alcohol, Juliet,' Daphne snaps. 'We wouldn't want a repeat of what happened at Elsie's party.'

Juliet keeps her eyes on the bottle and refills her glass.

'I need something to calm me down. God, I didn't even get to see Freya dance.' She looks at Gracie with pleading desperation. 'Don't tell her I was late, will you? I promised I'd take photos.'

'Don't worry. We took loads.'

Juliet presses her napkin to her eyes. 'This thing with Ian is a nightmare. They should never have given him bail, you saw what he's like.'

'You've told the police,' Gracie says. 'Now you've just got to put it out of your mind.' She gathers up the plates. 'Try and do something nice with Freya at the weekend.'

'Oh, God. Monday's an inset day. Three days rattling around the flat, waiting for him to turn up.'

Daphne's voice is dismissive. 'Take Freya away then.'

Juliet shakes her head. 'Where would I go?'

'You must have family.'

'God no.'

'Friends then.'

"Most of them took Ian's side after the split.'

Daphne lifts a *Well there's a surprise* eyebrow at Tom.

Gracie shoots her a warning glare, irritation with Daphne adding heat to the surge of emotions pressing in on her. With a defiant jerk of her head she turns to Juliet and says in a voice too loud and too upbeat, 'Why don't you come down to Caxton? Elsie's broken up already so I was planning on staying till Monday anyway. She'd love to have Freya to play with.'

Daphne's mouth drops open and clamps shut.

Juliet's eyes slide towards Tom who's looking horrified. 'I . . . I wouldn't want to impose.'

'You won't be,' Gracie insists, pushing the enthusiasm. 'Tom's coming down on Sunday but he can't stay. So I'd love a bit of adult company. There's this gorgeous little pub we can go to for lunch – my treat.'

221

'You know what?' Juliet says, with a wan grateful smile. 'That would be a lifesaver.'

Gracie carries the plates over to the dishwasher, refusing to look at Tom or Daphne on the way. 'Brilliant. I'll pick you up around nine on Saturday. Bring your swimming stuff and plenty of sunscreen, the forecast's looking good.'

Smiling up at Tom, Juliet says, 'Thanks so much for what you did tonight. I don't know what I'd have done without you.'

'No problem,' he says, but Gracie catches the look he exchanges with Daphne, who is shaking her head and getting up to leave.

38

Juliet sits back in the quiet comfort of the passenger seat, watching Gracie's profile as she swings the Volvo effortlessly into the fast lane, wind rushing through the window, fluttering that cascade of hair and flushing those dimpled cheeks. This is how Juliet's life would have been if Gracie had returned her calls, how it will be if her plan works out; the two of them heading off with their kids for weekends in the country – straw hats, laughter, sun cream. Juliet glances round at Freya, whose eyes flit from Elsie's pink heart-shaped sunglasses, to the iPad in her hands and the puppy curled in her lap. There's no envy in her expression, just adoration.

Turning back she catches a sunny flash of yellow from the banana keyring dangling from the ignition. So many keys in that bunch. Picturing the locks they open she looks away. 'I hope Tom isn't too pissed off.'

'What about?'

'You inviting us to Caxton.'

'We had a chat after you left. He's mainly worried about Ian.'

'Aren't we all?'

Gracie drops her voice. 'Maybe you need some counselling to get through this.'

Juliet doesn't want counselling. She wants a life. This life.

Gracie's phone buzzes.

'Shall I answer it?' Juliet says, reaching down a little too quickly for Gracie's bag.

'Don't worry. It's probably the café.'

Juliet lets the bag drop. 'Don't you use the hands-free?'

'Not if I can help it. Being in the car is just about the only time I ever get to myself.'

Juliet gazes out of the half-lowered window at the fields of yellow rape. 'It's ages since I've been to the countryside.'

'Did you go as a kid?'

Juliet shrugs. 'Not really.'

'Are your parents still alive?'

'My mum is.' She squints into the strobing trees. 'We don't get on. Never have. What about yours?'

'Both my parents died years ago. I miss them a lot.'

'Shame they didn't live to see your success.'

'Mum wouldn't have been impressed. She wanted me to be a teacher – as if! I'd have hated it.'

'Was it her who taught you to cook?'

Gracie laughs. 'You're joking. With her it was all grey meat, limp lettuce and vegetables boiled to mush.'

'So how come—?'

'I used to bake with my dad's mum. Granny Grace. Though she always said I shouldn't waste my time cooking, I should go on the stage. Honestly, can you imagine! Anyway,' a sudden eagerness in her face, 'I did a couple of cookery courses in my twenties, then I started experimenting on my own and things finally took off when I got my market stall.'

'I'm a disaster in the kitchen. Specially baking.'

Gracie smiles into the distance. 'You've just got to stick to the recipe and get your timing right.'

She turns off the road. They bump down a narrow track overhung with branches and burst out of the dappled gloom into a lush green meadow fringed with woodland that slopes down to the river. Gracie turns past the shell of a dilapidated stone barn circled by a mesh of stakes and tapes and pulls up beside a long, gleaming white caravan. Elsie tumbles out of the car, tugging Tallulah on the lead. Freya skips along behind. 'Don't go near the river,' Gracie calls. 'As far as that fallen tree and no further.'

Juliet follows her into the caravan; two neat double bedrooms, a cleverly arranged area for sitting and eating, a shower room and a kitchen far better equipped than the one in her flat. 'Wow,' she says. What else *is* there to say?

'We hired it, just for the duration of the build.' Gracie throws her keys into her bag and sets it down on the table. 'I promised Elsie she could share with Freya, so no arguments, you've got the second bedroom and I'm having the sofa bed.'

Juliet barely has time to mouth a half-hearted protest before Gracie is off again, eager to show her around the site. She puts up a pretty good show of enthusiasm, oohing and cooing as Gracie points out imagined sitting rooms, terraces, bathrooms and stairs and asks what she thinks about a door here or an extra window there. 'And come and see this.' She leads her through the trees to a newly paved area, canopied by a pergola, with a long wooden table and benches down the middle. At the far end there's a large 'igloo' of creamy concrete standing on a base of weathered stone. This is weird even for Gracie.

'You built a giant pizza oven before you made a start on the house?' Juliet says.

Gracie laughs her flutey laugh. 'I had that put in when we were planning on using this site for events. But it won't go to waste. I've been using it for breads, barbeques, roasts, even cakes. It's what my next book's about – wood-fired cookery from all around the world.' She's gazing at the oven, with an odd sort of brightness in her eyes. *You're not putting this on*, Juliet thinks. *You actually get a kick out of this stuff.*

'I had it hand-built by these two amazing old guys from Sicily.' Gracie strokes her hand down the base of the oven as if expecting the rough grey stones to arch and purr. 'They charged a fortune. But they are the best.'

Of course they are. Juliet smiles and nods. *Perfection in all things for Gracie Dwyer.*

Juliet looks on as she packs the oven with kindling and wood from the log pile, fires it up with a shot of flame from a gas gun and pokes the blaze with a stick.

Gracie rubs the dirt from her palms. 'Why don't we have a swim and cool down a bit before lunch?'

Freya hasn't swum for a while. When she squeezes into her costume it cuts into her shoulders and pulls between her legs. 'Don't fuss,' Juliet whispers. 'Swim in your knickers.'

Freya is close to tears, ashamed and embarrassed, when from nowhere Gracie leans in with a pair of nail scissors, snips the straps free and ties them into a halter at the back of her neck. Problem solved. Freya smiles up at Gracie and scampers away. Juliet feels suddenly bereft. As if she's been robbed of something she didn't know she'd had.

'They grow so fast, it's crazy,' Gracie is saying as she runs after the children, whisking a bottle of sunscreen from her hand-woven basket of smug-mum holiday essentials. Tanned and healthy as a peach in her black plunge-neck one-piece, she sprays both girls and massages the cream into their skin, her hands moving in brisk circles as if she's oiling chickens.

Juliet follows, still in her jeans and vest top, and sits on the bank blowing up Freya's armbands. Elsie, who's wearing a brand new, top-of-the-range float suit, calls out in a cross little lisp, 'Mummy, someone's tied their boat to our jetty.'

She's just like her mother, convinced that the good things in life are hers by right and everybody else can go to hell.

Gracie looks up and laughs. 'I think that boat's ours, love! Daddy said he'd got you a surprise.' She points to the *Elsie* painted in curly letters on the bow. Right on cue the girls erupt in a chorus of delight. Juliet avoids joining in by tugging an armband onto Freya's arm and latching her lips to the valve.

'If you're good he'll take us out in it tomorrow,' Gracie says. 'How's your rowing, Juliet?'

'Non-existent.' She manages a smile.

'Aren't you coming in?' Gracie drops her basket on the grass and clambers down the bank to the muddy little curve of beach. 'The water's lovely.'

'Can't swim . . . got a bit of a . . . phobia.' She twitches and looks away, ambushed by a childhood memory of those bitches at the pool, their laughter echoey and remote as they push her beneath the water and hold her down.

Totally oblivious to the shittiness of the world outside her gilded cocoon, Gracie takes Elsie and Freya by the hand and leads them into the river. For an hour the three of them splash and swim and giggle together in sprays of water sliced by sunlight while Juliet sits and watches, a cigarette in her fingers, her chin pressed to her knees, skin-pricklingly aware of the corner of Gracie's handbag peeking through the fun floral beach towels in the basket that sits just a hand's breadth away.

At lunchtime Gracie gathers them all around the big wooden table, whips balls of dough from a plastic cooler and gets them pulling and patting and stuffing them with lumps of mozzarella and dollops of sauce and folding them into calzones which she bakes in that bloody great oven. Freya watches in awe as Gracie tips hers, crusty and golden, from the paddle onto her plate. 'Look, Mummy, look what I made!'

When they have eaten Gracie sets out deckchairs on the jetty. 'Careful, kids, it's pretty deep down this end,' she warns. The girls lie on their bellies for a few minutes kicking their legs and peering over the edge into the water, then run back to the grass to practise cartwheels.

Juliet settles back with a cigarette, aware that Gracie is throwing her sideways glances, unable to relax. She turns to look at her. 'All right. Out with it.'

'Is it that obvious?' Gracie pulls her sunglasses down from the top of her head. 'Tom always says I'd make a rubbish poker player.'

'Go on. Tell me.'

'Look,' Gracie says, her smile cautious. 'I want to give you this.' She pulls a little black pouch from her basket, hesitating before she drops it into Juliet's lap. 'I don't need it any more.'

Imagining some kind of beauty product, Juliet unzips it, bemused to find a vaporiser complete with a charger and three bottles of e-liquid. She frowns. 'I never had you down as a smoker.'

'It used to be the odd one at parties but then I started wanting more so I bought that and weaned myself off.'

Juliet unscrews one of the bottles and sniffs the liquid.

'I tried pretty much all the flavours,' Gracie says, 'I found the menthol the least disgusting.'

Juliet unfolds the instruction leaflet and murmurs, 'Thanks.'

'If you can't give up altogether at least it should help you to cut down.' A pained half smile. 'You need to look after yourself, you know. Especially after what's happened with Ian. Whatever would Freya do without you?'

Gracie shows her how to screw the tubes together and pump the little reservoir with liquid. 'Go on, give it a try.'

Juliet switches it on and draws the vapour deep into her

lungs. As the nicotine hits she looks into Gracie's earnest, encouraging eyes and for a moment the sense of drowning in a hostile darkness recedes. She feels grateful, elated even. Then the old resentments rush in, sharpened by this fresh glimpse of the way things could have been. This reminder of everything she's been denied.

At bedtime, while Juliet hovers uncertainly by the bedroom door, Gracie climbs between Elsie and Freya, clutching a book. 'Who wants a story?'

Freya holds back, shy at first until Gracie throws out an arm and pulls her in. Juliet watches as Freya snuggles closer, her eyes fixed hungrily on the book, her mouth slackening as Gracie turns the pages with as much wonder as a kid.

Later the two women eat lamb tagine on the jetty: candle-light, couscous and bottles of wine; red for Gracie, white for Juliet – she remembered! For a while, after they have eaten, they listen to the soft knock of the boat against the wooden struts, the ceaseless sounds of water, insects and the faraway weir. Juliet bears it for a while until, emboldened by alcohol, she asks her about the stalker. Just comes right out with it.

Gracie is silent at first, staring at the shred of moon rippling on the blackened wrinkles of the river. Then out it pours, how hard it's been, how much the experience has changed her, how the feeling of invasion has taken something from her that she will never get back. Juliet doesn't point out how much she has left.

'But it's stopped now?'

For a fraction of a second Gracie looks utterly vulnerable. A little twitch of her head and then she's back in control. 'Yes.' She nods sharply, as if reassuring herself. 'There's been nothing for months.'

Pauline Bryce Diary
March 15th

I call Mum today. Just for a chat. She says Ron's angina's flared up so he's taking early retirement. She blames me, says it's the stress of what happened with the police and now they're having to sell up and move to Cornwall because everyone in Lancaster has stopped talking to them. She's so bitter, so busy thinking about her own small-town problems, she never even asks me how I am or what I'm doing.

39

Tom arrives next morning with hugs and kisses for Gracie and Elsie. Freya watches him, wide-eyed and hungry. Tom, to give him credit, picks her up and swings her around. She beams with happiness. He greets Juliet with a wave of his hand. She turns away, worried that she too might appear wide-eyed and hungry.

'Who wants a ride in the boat?' he calls, unlocking the new wooden shed and reaching for the oars.

Under cover of Elsie and Freya's screams of excitement, Juliet backs off, making excuses – she's not feeling that great, she's got work to catch up on, she'd upset the balance in the boat.

There's a scrambling down to the jetty, a fastening on of life jackets. Juliet stands on the bank as Tom, murmuring 'Whoa there' and 'Steady', hands first Gracie then the children into the boat. She watches the 'Elsie' rock and settle as he takes the oars. There are no last-minute entreaties for her to join the party, though there would have been room, just about, for her to perch in the bow.

She walks back to the caravan. Like she said, she has work to do and she wasn't lying about feeling unwell.

There's a heaviness in her limbs, a throbbing in her head. Too much sun. She'll have to be careful.

She locks the door behind her and closes the slatted blinds. Her eyes scan the room for Gracie's bag. She unlatches the cupboards and overhead lockers, stuffing back the cascade of blankets, pillows and towels. She tries to think logically, her eyes flitting, searching, finally settling. She pulls up the edge of the bench. And there it is, nestling in the furrows of a folded duvet. *Whatever happened to trust?* She tips out pens, notebooks, mints, hairbrush, lipstick, a worn Mulberry wallet packed with the plastic of privilege and finally Gracie's keys. She parts the slats of the blind and peers across the meadow to the river. All clear. She unclips the keys from the banana keyring, lays them out on the white laminate table and carefully photographs each one. With a sense of being one step nearer to where she wants to be she selects 'International express delivery' on the app on her phone and uploads the photos. *Ping. Ping. Ping.* Now all she has to do is wait.

Jiggling the keys in her hand, she checks through the slats of the blind – still no sign of the boating party. Her fingertip catches an indentation at the top of the banana. She probes it with her nail, twists the little black stalk and pulls out a thumb drive. In seconds she's slotting it into her laptop, running the cursor down folders of video, photo and audio files. She clicks open the photo file. It's full of shots of Elsie – knowing smiles, pert poses, endless different outfits. Juliet skims through at least fifty of them before she finds a few blurry snaps of a man and a boy messing around in the snow, then it's back to bloody Elsie, with Stella and Todd this time, unwrapping oversized Christmas presents, simpering in a party frock, perching on Todd's knee.

Shrieks of laughter burst across the water. *Damn!* She should have downloaded a copy when she had the chance.

As it is there's barely time to eject the drive, throw everything back into place and unlock the door before Tom, Gracie, Elsie and Freya come running up the field yelling that it's time for lunch.

The pub they go to is homely and rundown. Juliet feels a flutter of what feels like recognition as they pull up in the car park, memories of happier times perhaps, when she and Ian used to drive out to country pubs for lunch in whichever leased convertible he happened to be driving that month.

Tom and Gracie are on first-name terms with most of the couples in the beer garden – Roger and Jenny, Bill and Annie, Adam and Jody, a sea of baggy khaki shorts and shiny suntanned faces. While Tom heads inside to order drinks Elsie and Freya scramble onto a tyre dangling from a tree and cling on nervously while it swings. A boy runs towards them. Juliet stands up ready to intervene but the boy, when he turns, is laughing. She stands transfixed. He has dark hair, straight brows and wide-set, long-lashed eyes like Freya's, but he's dimpled, tanned and athletic, the kind of boy Ian always dreamed of having. Would things have been different if they'd had a son like this? She squirms away from thoughts of Ian and locks her gaze onto hand-some wholesome Tom who is making for the wicket gate in the hedge carrying an armful of bats, balls and stumps.

'Where's he off to?' she asks.

'Rounders,' Gracie says, rolling her eyes. The children run over to help him and the men at the other tables nod and raise their thumbs as they down their beer.

A woman arrives with their drinks. Hippy type, too much silver jewellery, a frizz of blonde hair, grey at the roots. She and Gracie kiss like old friends. 'Jess,' Gracie says, 'this is Juliet.' Jess's gaze lingers longer than her smile, as if she's been told about Juliet and warned that she has problems.

'Great to meet you,' she says. As they turn to watch the children Gracie's hand comes to rest on Jess's arm, affectionate, companionable. Juliet sucks on her vaporiser and sips her lager. Gracie calls to Elsie and Freya to come and get their drinks. The boy comes too. Gracie ruffles his hair. Jess calls him Jamie. He calls her Mum. Juliet is surprised. Jess looks too old to have a kid that young. In the scrabble for bags of crisps and glasses of lemonade Juliet's lager gets slopped down her clean white top. She dabs it with a napkin. The stain is embarrassing and in this heat she'll stink like a brewery. And now everybody is carrying their drinks out to the field and picking teams for the rounders. She sweats as if she's back at school. The loner who never gets chosen. Instinctively she backs away.

'Hey, come on, Juliet.' It's Roger or Bill or Adam beckoning her over, telling her she's next in to bat. She stands in line behind a small boy who whacks the ball almost to the river and runs and runs, skinny legs pounding. She claps with the others and tries to cheer. The sound sticks in her throat. She's picking up the bat. Her head swims, the handle slips but she manages to graze the ball. Her legs pump. For a second she's running, her team is cheering. She trips. Her knee gives under her. A thwack of ball against base. A triumphant yell of 'Out!'

Her face burns as Jenny or Annie or Jody come to help her up. She holds up her hand, warding them off, and limps back to the edge of the field to sit out the rest of the game.

She sucks her vaporiser and watches Gracie and Tom. He touches her often – a casual arm around her shoulder when they're lining up to bat, a hug of triumph when she scores a rounder. He doesn't seem to notice that she rarely touches him. Gracie glances round, catches Juliet's eye and waves. Juliet waves back.

* * *

Lunch is a raucous affair, rickety wooden tables pulled together, enormous burgers and piles of chips, kids running and screaming, Tallulah yapping at a tired old Labrador who waddles away, sick of the noise and pestering.

It's nearly five o'clock when they say their goodbyes. As they cut across the fields Juliet manoeuvres herself next to Tom, enthusing about the layout of the new house. 'I never saw the Wharf House' (squinting over the wall from the towpath or being shunted around with a crowd of ten on the estate agent's open day hardly count) 'but the photos were stunning. It must have been tough giving it up.'

She's touched a raw place. She can tell.

'Yeah . . . it was.'

'Couldn't you have hung on to it?'

'Couldn't afford to.'

'But Gracie's US deal—'

Gracie has caught up with them. Juliet stops, afraid she's said too much. It's OK. The US show's been announced in the press. She didn't need to read Gracie's emails to guess that the money would be substantial.

'We didn't realise it was going ahead.' Tom's voice is flat.

With a quick darting movement Gracie lays her hand on his sleeve. A gesture of condolence. Juliet keeps walking. Far away, drifting on the breeze she hears the wail of a fretful child and the *pock pock* of a tennis ball. There's a throaty cry when it hits the net. Something inside her shifts. A ratchet trying to engage with a slowly turning cog.

Juliet can't wait for the evening; just the two of them again, Gracie opening up over a bottle of wine. Isn't that what women friends do? Share their secrets? Bare their souls?

But it's Juliet who drinks too much and gets angry and upset about Ian, the controlling behaviour, the lies and manipulation.

'You have to move on,' Gracie says gently. 'Has there been anyone since?'

'No one serious.' Juliet pictures the teacher at Freya's school, thinning hair, an earring, a tang to his breath that made her cringe and the string of brash divorcees and lonely widowers who had offered themselves on 'executive' dating sites.

'There will be,' Gracie says. 'Someone who'll treat you the way you deserve.'

'We're not all as lucky as you.'

'Tom wouldn't have looked at me twice if he hadn't been a widower.'

Taken aback by her honesty Juliet murmurs, 'How did you meet him?'

'We were neighbours.'

Juliet laughs. 'Well I definitely won't be running off with any of the miserable sods down my street.'

'I never thought for one minute we'd end up together. I'd practically starved myself to scrape up the deposit on this tiny attic flat in Holloway and Tom and Louise were the glamorous professional couple in the huge apartment downstairs. I used to see them having a drink on their terrace in the evenings, Louise looking fresh and elegant even after a day at home with the baby.' She falters, a rueful smile. 'They used to call me "the girl upstairs".'

Juliet turns to look at her. 'Did he tell you that?'

'Course not. But one night I heard Louise offering him one of the little Gruyère and pumpkin gougères I'd taken down for her to try. When he asked where she'd got them from she said, "The girl upstairs." Honestly, if a man like Tom hadn't been tied to his flat, struggling to bring up a baby on his own, I'd never have stood a chance.'

Juliet looks into her glass. 'What was she like?'

'Louise?' Gracie shrugs. 'Oh, you know, beautiful, clever, talented, tall. She was nice too, knew a lot about food.

She's about the only person I've ever met who was totally truthful about the things I asked her to taste. I'd sit there while she took a bite, then she'd give it to me straight.'

'It must have been awful finding her.' Juliet's grip tightens on her wine glass. Has she given herself away? All those hours she's spent poring over the press reports of Louise's death – the upstairs neighbour who alerted the police. Who else could it be? Gracie, lost in her own thoughts, says only, 'You have no idea.'

'So what happened?' Juliet whispers.

Gracie unstoppers the wine bottles and tops up their glasses. She hasn't described the events of that terrible day since the inquest. Five years on she's amazed how precisely the words re-form on her lips, how right it feels to sit here in the moonlight and share her story with Juliet.

'Tom was away that night. I'd seen him leave the day before, swinging his overnight bag and looking up to wave at Louise and Elsie as he jumped into the taxi. Next morning I woke up just before seven and heard the baby crying. Nothing unusual about that, I often used to hear her having a bit of a grizzle first thing. It was a beautiful summer morning, I'll always remember that. I scrambled out onto the strip of walled roof outside my kitchen window to water my herbs and then I sat up there with a mug of tea, making plans for the day. I must have been there about twenty minutes when I realised the crying wasn't trailing off like it usually did. If anything it was getting louder. The building was L-shaped and from where I was sitting I had a pretty good view of the Whittakers' terrace. The windows were open and I couldn't see or hear anyone moving around, and there were none of the usual smells of coffee and toast drifting up from their kitchen. I opened my notebook and began one of my *to do* lists but the baby's howls were so worrying I couldn't concentrate. By ten past eight I was getting really concerned so I ran downstairs and pressed their doorbell. The sound was almost drowned out by the baby's yells but I still wasn't sure whether to call the police or to wait. What if Louise was in the shower, or trying out some trendy new *leave your baby to scream* regime? I rang the bell again, gave it another five minutes then dialled 999. When I told the operator there was a baby screeching itself sick in what seemed to be an empty flat she said they'd send somebody round straight away. I think that's when I started to panic. I was still in the T-shirt I'd worn to bed and I remember thinking I should go back to my flat and pull on some clothes before the police arrived but Elsie's cries were so desperate I just sat on the Whittakers' doorstep, unable to move.'

She glances up. Juliet is gazing at her, attentive and unblinking.

'Ten minutes later a young constable came pounding up the stairs in his shirtsleeves. PC Harris, his name was. He tried the bell, then he thumped on the door and shouted "Police! Open up!" and he kept on thumping while he asked me about the family.

'I told him Tom was away and Louise wasn't the sort of woman who would ever leave her baby on its own. He wanted to know if there was a way into their flat over the balconies so I took him up to my kitchen to take a look. He was so big he could hardly get through the window but he managed it somehow and he clambered along the parapet to test an old drainpipe that ran down past the Whittakers' terrace. He gave it a shake, took one look at the wobbling bolts and decided it would never take his weight. It's funny. Even in a crisis it's the little things that stick in your mind. I can still see the dark triangle of sweat on the back of his shirt as he leaned out to grab that pipe.' She takes a sip of

238

wine, remembering how she'd reached out to steady him, glanced down and seen Louise's toppled figurine, staring up at her from the decking below.

'We ran down to their front door and he smashed his truncheon into the glass door panel, thrust his hand through the hole and unlocked the latch. By now Elsie was totally hysterical. He told me to stay back. But I couldn't bear it. I went in after him and I was there, right beside him when he found Louise collapsed on the floor. It was horrible.' Gracie's fingers fly to her cheeks. 'Her face was bright red and all swollen up and Elsie was squirming and screaming in the cot by the bed. For a moment it felt unreal, as if I'd stumbled onto a film set. I doubled over trying not to be sick and he was radioing for an ambulance and gesturing at the cot yelling, "Take the kid! Get it out of here!"

'Back then I knew nothing about babies, but I scooped up this screeching, wriggling bundle of fury and darted around the flat grabbing nappies and a bottle from the fridge. I was in such a state, when he asked me where Tom worked my mind went totally blank and it took a minute before I could remember the name of the practice.

'By the time I got Elsie up to my flat the poor little thing was starving and her nappy was this big sodden lump, but somehow I managed to change her and warm up the milk. I can't tell you the relief when she clamped her lips round that bottle and finally stopped screaming.

'I was sitting on my living room floor, jiggling her in my arms, still struggling to cope with the horror of seeing Louise's dead body, when PC Harris came in holding out his phone. It was Tom on the line, begging me to stay with Elsie till he got back. I said of course I would and when the woman from child services turned up I told her I was a friend of the family, which wasn't strictly true. I'd hardly ever spoken to Tom and I'd only got to know Louise because

239

I'd asked her to hang on to a set of keys so she could let a plumber in.' Gracie goes quiet, her head moving slowly from side to side. 'She'd offered me coffee and asked me to hold Elsie while she went off to make it. I remember struggling to balance her on my hip as I walked round the room looking at her amazing photos. When Louise came back with the coffees I joked about getting her to take the pictures for my next cookbook and she laughed and said *Any time* because she loved food and was always up for a challenge.

'So after that I used to pop down now and then to ask her to test out my experiments. Just the night before she died she'd tried out my new take on samosas.'

'Poor Tom,' Juliet murmurs. 'He must have been in a terrible state when he got back.'

'Awful. I've never seen anyone look as sunken and grey as he did when he walked into my flat that afternoon. He didn't say a word, just took Elsie out of my arms and left. But over the next few days I tried to do what I could, running down with bowls of soup and hunks of pie and helping him to deal with Louise's parents who were literally out of their minds with grief. I used to take Elsie for long walks across London just to give him space to do some grieving of his own. And when he did start to talk he just wanted to pick over what had happened – what if Louise hadn't slept with the window open? What if she hadn't taken the sleeping tablets? What if she'd managed to shove something down her throat to keep the airway open till she found her anti-histamines? All I could do was listen. Then gradually he started fretting about the Wharf House. He wanted to finish it as a memorial to her and live there with Elsie but the construction costs were spiralling out of control and he was worried he'd have to sell it on half built.'

'So when did you two . . . get together?'

Gracie shrugs and smiles. 'To be honest it was so gradual I couldn't really tell you. I mean, yes, we'd been spending a lot of time together, getting closer, but I couldn't believe it when he asked me to marry him. I told him to see how he felt in a year or two. But he said he didn't want to.'

'So there's hope for me yet,' Juliet says. 'I've just got to keep my eye out for a hunky widower.'

'Well, it can bring its own problems.'

Juliet leans in a little. 'What do you mean?'

'They come with baggage – not Elsie, God, no, I didn't mean her.'

'Stella and Todd?'

Gracie looks up.

'I met them at Elsie's party.' Juliet smiles. 'Before I passed out. We had quite a chat.'

'They've been lovely to me. I know how hard it must have been for them seeing me step into Louise's shoes.'

'Stella said they offered to have Elsie live with them.'

'They were healthy and well off with time on their hands. You can see why they thought it would be the perfect solution. But of course Tom wouldn't have it.'

'I couldn't stick having them watching over my shoulder all the time.'

Gracie laughs. 'It's not like that. They've been a fantastic help. It was Stella who found Heather for us when our old nanny left. We've even been on holiday together.'

'Christ. Rather you than me.'

The sun is setting. Juliet squints into the fan of brilliant orange fading to pink beyond the far bank of the river. 'What I don't get is why anyone with a ten month old would need to take sleeping tablets. When Freya was that age I used to drop off the minute my head hit the pillow.'

'She'd been prescribed them before she got pregnant. Tom says he remembers seeing them shoved at the back of the bathroom cabinet. But Elsie had just started sleeping through and he thinks Louise must have dosed herself up and gone to bed early to try and catch up on all the broken nights.' Gracie watches a bat swoop across the water in the half light. 'When something like that happens it makes you realise how fragile our hold on life is. Even when we're young and healthy. Some freak accident or a sudden illness and bam!' She snaps her fingers. 'We're gone. Just like that.'

40

Juliet swings herself onto Gracie's sleek silver mountain bike and follows the children across the car park of the Caxton Arms. Like everything else in Gracie's life this bike ride has been organised down to the last detail. Jamie Villiers has been cajoled into coming too. Freya's on his old bike, Elsie's showing off on her shiny pink one, Gracie is riding Jess's rattly old bone-shaker and somehow Matt Villiers has found them all helmets. Juliet's head throbs – too much wine and her shoulders smart where the straps of Gracie's spare backpack grind against her sunburned flesh. Thoughts jolt around her head as she bumps along the track: the disgusting way the Whittakers spoil Elsie, Gracie's massive US deal, the cost of their palatial weekend getaway, the look on Tom's face when he talked about the Wharf House, Gracie's quiet unburdening about Louise's death.

They enter the shade of the woods and stop for juice and biscuits. Juliet skids to a stop, giving the noisy back wheel an exploratory kick as she takes a deep slug from her water bottle and pulls out her vaporiser.

Gracie turns, straddling her bike, and smiles approval. 'Well done. What were you on, fifteen? Twenty a day?'

Juliet manages a shrug that might have passed for agreement and takes another suck. Gracie pulls the lid off a Tupperware and offers Juliet a biscuit. 'Almond and quinoa. Lots of protein.'

'I'll pass, thanks.'

'All right, kids?' Gracie calls.

The children flop and sigh and munch their protein bars, hot, red-cheeked and happy.

They're off again, playing I Spy – shouting Ss and *skies* and Ts and *trees* over their shoulders. Juliet adds 'idyllic' and 'a day to remember' to the phrases she's got lined up like words on a Scrabble rack waiting for the most gainful moment to be played. When they stop by a bend in the river for lunch Gracie spreads a tartan rug under the trees and Juliet swings the pack from her shoulders. As she unloads the picnic she feels Freya's eyes on her, and senses the game she's playing, pretending that she too has a mother who gets up early to stuff home-baked flatbreads with sautéed courgettes and snap protein bars into Tupperwares – Juliet the earth mother. For one unruly minute she plays along and tries on Gracie's skin, smoothing the picnic rug, fussing with napkins, and shaping mini frittatas and curly slices of pepper into grinning faces on biodegradable, button-spot plates.

Then of course there's more ruddy swimming. Gracie in a red swimsuit this time, fifties-cut with a white frill across the bust. Juliet fixes her grin in place and waves from the bank while Gracie plunges into the water with the children, sleek as a seal with her pups. When the children climb out Gracie strikes off downstream, strong arms whirling through the water. After a while she flips onto her back and lets the current carry her around the curve of the bend. Juliet feels her absence, even before her manicured toes have drifted out of sight. Heaviness pulls beneath the lingering throb of her headache. Today is their last day in Caxton. Tomorrow she will wake up back in her own crappy life. She looks away to where Freya and Elsie are on their knees inspecting something in the grass that Jamie is poking with a stick. 'Stay out of the water, kids.'

She wheels her bike over to a patch of shade and lights up a real cigarette while she squats down to take a look at the back wheel. There's a satisfying logic to the intermeshing parts, achingly familiar from kneeling over her grandad's toolbox as a tiny child, handing him pliers and wrenches while he screwed and tightened and rubbed oil from his fingers with a frayed rag; a good memory, buried deep beneath the bad.

'What's up?'

She drops her cigarette in the dirt, smashing it out with a guilty swivel of her trainer. Gracie is coming across the grass, a towel over her shoulder.

Juliet spins the wheel. 'It was making a funny noise. I thought there might be something trapped in the spokes.'

Gracie throws her head forward and rubs her hair hard with the towel. 'I'll get Matt to have a look at it when we get back. Fancy a cup of tea? I brought a Thermos.'

Of course you did. The children come running over, burbling about building a den under the trees.

'OK,' Juliet says.

Gracie, of course, says the right thing, the motherly thing. 'Put your shoes on and don't go where we can't see you.' She spreads the towel, pulls a shirt on over her swimsuit and sits down, still damp and breathless, to rummage in the backpacks for cups. 'It's doing Elsie so much good, being with other kids. I worry that we spoil her, especially Tom.'

Juliet stretches out beside her. 'All the more reason to have one of your own.'

Gracie is quiet for so long that Juliet rolls onto one elbow to look at her.

'I can't.' Gracie slits her eyes to the sun. There is a moment while she watches the clouds and Juliet nibbles quietly on a stem of grass. 'My problem. Not Tom's.'

A prickle of heat runs down the inside of Juliet's arms. 'I'm sorry,' she says.

'Don't be.' Gracie unscrews the Thermos; quick efficient twists of her hand. 'I did get pregnant once. By an actor called Harry Flynn.'

'What happened?'

'He was heading for Hollywood and a baby didn't figure in his career plans. So he wrote me a cheque, told me to get an abortion and walked out the door.'

'Did you?'

'What?'

'Get an abortion.'

'God no.' Wisps of steam rise from the tea she's pouring. 'I went to John Lewis and spent the lot on a cot, a buggy and a changing table.' She passes Juliet the plastic cup. 'I had no idea how I was going to bring up a baby on what I earned from a handful of catering jobs and a cake stall in Broadway Market but I was too blissed out to care. It's funny. Until I got pregnant I didn't think I had an ounce of maternal instinct in me and then it just . . . took over.' Gracie catches Juliet's stare and answers the question that hovers unspoken in the air. 'The pregnancy was ectopic.'

'Oh . . . oh, how awful.' Juliet lays a hand on Gracie's arm and experiences, for a moment, the power of her pain.

'I . . . I don't talk about it very often.'

Juliet looks into Gracie's eyes. Beneath the distress she sees something she can't quite pin down. Gratitude? For listening? For being here?

'So, did Hollywood happen for Harry?' she says with a

disparaging *whoever heard of Harry Flynn* inflection. She gets it right, even elicits a smile – the sympathetic friend who understands Gracie's anguish yet refuses to let her wallow.

'The last I saw of him he was the harassed single dad in a washing powder ad – the one where he forgets to wash the kid's football kit until an hour before the match.'

Juliet's heart goes out to Harry. She knows that ad. She knows that actor, washed up and not yet forty, probably watching Gracie's success from some dingy rented flat, kicking himself for what might have been. She shapes her mouth and brows into a look of concern. 'You shouldn't give up, you know – it's amazing what they can do these days.'

Gracie shakes her head. 'Not for me.'

'How can you be so sure?'

'The ectopic pregnancy ruptured the tube. I had no idea there was anything wrong until I collapsed in the street and a passing stranger called an ambulance.'

'But if you've conceived once—'

The quiver of pain again, like a breath of wind on water. 'When they opened me up they discovered it was a miracle I'd ever got pregnant at all. The surgeon told me my chances of ever producing another viable egg were zero. Those were his actual words.' She mimics a gruff impersonal voice. 'Zero, Miss Dwyer.'

'Oh, Gracie.'

'I went to pieces but I'm not sure he even noticed. He was too busy checking his watch.' She drops back into gruffness. 'Your biological clock hasn't just stopped ticking, Miss Dwyer, it's been trampled in the dirt and crushed to powder.'

Despite the mimicry and the dry little joke her fragility bleeds through. She looks down into her tea and says softly,

'I was very low for a while. But when my book contract came through I picked myself up, gave the cot, buggy and changing table to Oxfam and threw myself into my work.'

Juliet swallows the temptation to share the story of her own rocky road to motherhood and says only, 'That was years ago. They come up with new treatments all the time.'

'Every specialist I've seen says the same.' She waves a dismissive hand. 'It's my womb as well, apparently. Some condition I can't even pronounce.'

So there are some things even you can't buy, Gracie Dwyer. Ah well, chin up.

Juliet waits for tears, misery, rawness but Gracie drains the last of her tea and says, 'It's not the end of the world. I've been lucky. I've got Elsie.'

How about a hint of bitterness, Gracie? All those times you saw other women with the one thing you wanted and couldn't have? Don't tell me that didn't piss you off.

Gracie trashes that thought as smartly as if Juliet had said it aloud. 'I never needed the whole pregnancy and birth bit to think of her as mine.' Her voice slows and dips almost to a whisper. 'Louise didn't believe in christening babies – she thought you should, you know, be christened when you were old enough to decide for yourself but at our wedding reception we had a little naming ceremony for Elsie – got Daphne and Tom's sister who were our witnesses to be her godparents, just to make sure she didn't feel left out. And as I held that gorgeous little girl in my arms and Tom raised a toast to her health and happiness I remember being overwhelmed by the almost frightening sensation that I had everything I could ever want.'

Juliet's body grows rigid with a yearning more powerful than envy. She jerks herself upright. 'How does he feel about having more kids?'

'He'd love another one,' Gracie says into the quiet.

248

So it's not all roses at Falcon Square. A little nod of sympathy as she probes deeper. 'Have you talked about adoption?'

'We're being assessed. But it's a long slow process with no guarantee of success.'

'I thought they were crying out for adopters.'

'They're very strict about giving the birth mother every chance to change her mind, specially with newborns.'

Gracie's gaze returns to the sky. Is she fantasising about how pregnancy would have been for her, cossetted and pampered by Tom, discussing the ups and downs of it all on daytime TV, putting her feet up to draft that bestseller about eating for two? Or is she too smugly content to dream of how things might have been?

'You've never thought about surrogacy?'

'We looked into it. I can see it might work if the surrogate was your sister or a close friend, someone you could totally trust, but if you're dealing with strangers the whole thing's so fraught and unregulated. Did you know that the surrogate and her husband are the baby's legal parents? If they refused to hand it over there'd be absolutely nothing you could do.' She shudders a little. 'I couldn't bear it.'

'Haven't you got a sister?'

'No, and I don't think Daphne's going to be offering me the loan of her womb any time soon. Not if it means giving up booze and sex for nine months.' She's smiling at the thought, unaware that her shirt has slipped open and the fleshy curve of her upper breast is turning crimson in the sun. It's going to be agony in the morning. 'Did you have an easy pregnancy?' Gracie asks suddenly.

It's as if she's torturing herself, Juliet thinks. 'A bit of morning sickness. Other than that no problems at all.'

'Lucky you.'

'It didn't stop Ian insisting I stop work.'

249

'Why?'

'At first I thought it was because he cared. I should have realised it was just another way of tightening his hold over me.' Her breathing quickens. 'He was obviously screwing around but when I challenged him about the texts and the restaurant receipts he'd tell me I was a fantasist, that I'd lost my grip on reality.' *Hey, calm down.* She blinks a few times and swallows. 'By the time Freya was born it was as if I wasn't me any more.'

'How was the birth?'

'A doddle, thank God. A three-hour labour and she just popped out.'

'Freya looks like him,' Gracie says from nowhere.

'That's what he wanted. Another little Ian. Like an idiot I thought giving him one would make things right.' She wrenches up a handful of grass. 'Looking back I can't help wondering if he had some other sick reason for wanting a kid. Fucking pervert. Thank God I left him when I did.'

'How was he after Freya was born?'

'Furious she wasn't a boy. That's when he started telling people I was drinking too much and hooked on anti-depressants.' She lights a real cigarette, sees Gracie frown and stubs it out on a stone. 'For Christ's sake, what did he expect? Freya wouldn't stop crying and he was never there. No wonder I got depressed. Then there was a problem with his business and he got totally irrational about the cost of . . .' she pulls back '. . . of the baby. That's when I knew I had to leave.'

Gracie is watching a cloud that looks like a slowly unfurling flag. 'It must have been a nightmare.'

'That's when I met you.' *The golden girl on her way up who could have taken me with her.*

Gracie turns to her – big apologetic eyes – about to speak. Juliet cuts her off. She doesn't want to hear it. 'Yeah. It was tough.' Juliet looks across to where Freya is cartwheeling across the bleached grass, her thin legs stiff as rusty scissors, and it feels almost as if she's seeing her daughter for the first time. She smiles an unguarded smile. 'Worth it, though.'

'You've never wanted more kids?'

Juliet's laugh is harsh. 'I love her to bits but you've probably noticed I'm not exactly supermum.'

She feels the touch of Gracie's fingers, so light it's almost a caress. 'You've done a great job with Freya. She's lovely.' Gracie jumps up. 'Come on, let's take a look at this den.'

Juliet rolls onto her knees and falls back. As she struggles to catch up, Gracie pulls ahead, dark hair tossing about her shoulders. Suddenly it's a race. Gracie wins with ease, crawling into the wobbly wigwam of branches while Elsie dances up and down hollering, 'My mummy won!'

Juliet barely registers the taunt. She crouches in the prickly gloom testing the weight and the shape of Gracie's unlooked-for revelation about her infertility, turning it over and over like a pebble in her pocket. She needs more. More of this. More time to prise open the cracks beneath Gracie's perfect exterior.

Pauline Bryce Diary
March 29th

I'm skint so I ask Suzy to lend me something to wear to her party. She's not happy about it but she gives me this green dress. It's too short and a bit tight but I haven't got anything else, so I wear it. I've got myself a drink and I'm talking to a bloke called Jacob who's getting pretty friendly, when I see Imogen collecting money for a booze run so I go off to the bathroom. While I'm in there I hear voices outside. One of them's Suzy's and she's moaning about 'The Maggot' who's embarrassing her by getting pissed and trying to chat people up. I get a nasty prickle up my arms. Then this other girl says 'What the fuck's she doing here anyway?' and Suzy laughs and says who else was going to cough up fifty quid a week to sleep in a cupboard? And in anycase they've got her doing most of the cleaning and it's not for long because Imogen's boyfriend's moving back in and he'll need the room to store his film gear. So I wait till they've gone then I creep out of there, shove all my stuff in my backpack and dump it by the front door. Then I go into Suzy's room and step over a bloke and two girls sharing a spliff. They're so stoned they don't even notice when I throw open Suzy's huge fucking wardrobe and take the scissors to everything in it. Then I put my coat on and tell Imogen that I don't mind doing the booze run for her and not to worry, I'll carry it all back in my backpack. She smirks at her mate, holds out the wad of notes she's collected and tells me to get plenty of vodka. I take the money, pick up my backpack and leave them to it.

41

Gracie folds the map back into her pocket and pushes off down the track, pleased and more than a little surprised at how well this weekend is turning out. She doesn't regret opening up to Juliet. She hadn't planned to do it but it had felt right somehow; a rare moment of release and she could see that Juliet had been happy to listen, that Gracie's honesty had meant something to her. She can hear the children behind her panting and giggling. Apart from a couple of minor tantrums Elsie has been sharing well, especially when Freya has shown a spark of feistiness, and of course, having Jamie around to add a bit of big brother calm to the mix has helped no end.

The short cut down to the pub is slightly steeper than she'd imagined and the ground is rutted and dry, pegged with scrubby trees on either side. Every now and then Gracie calls over her shoulder, warning everyone to take it slowly and follow exactly where she goes. She's concentrating hard and it's a while before she looks back to see that Juliet has fallen behind. She slams on her brakes. 'Hang on, let's wait for Freya's mum.'

Tired now, the children skitter to a stop, straddling their bikes and looking back as they suck the last dregs from their water bottles. Juliet is a dark flash speeding through the trees. She swerves out of sight. A silence as they wait for her to reappear, then a yell and a muffled thud.

'Mummy!' Freya screams.

Gracie is turning her bike around. 'Stay there!' she shouts, her voice sharp and frightened. 'Stay there all of you.' She's pedalling fast up the slope, rounding the curve.

Juliet is on the ground, lying oddly, one arm flung above her head. Gracie throws down her bike, unhitching her backpack as she kneels beside her. Juliet's eyes flutter open. She groans and turns her head.

'Don't move. Where does it hurt?'

'Everywhere.' Juliet reaches up a wobbly hand to unbuckle her helmet.

'Keep it on till we get you to A and E.'

Freya, who has broken free from the others, comes running towards them. Gracie holds her back. 'Gently, love. Don't pull Mummy about.' To Elsie and Jamie who come pedalling over the ridge she calls, 'It's all right! I'll get Matt to fetch us in the Land Rover.'

She settles the picnic rug around Juliet's shoulders before moving away to get a phone signal.

Freya drops her head into Juliet's lap and begins to sob. Wincing a little, Juliet rubs her back. 'Don't cry, you big silly, I'm all right.'

'He's on his way.' Gracie slithers sideways down the sandy scoop of the bank, rights the fallen bike and spins the back wheel with her foot. 'What on earth happened?'

'The brakes failed.'

'Oh, my God.' Gracie tries to push the bike forwards. The front wheel jams, too bent to turn.

Their arrival in A and E causes a flurry of excitement. When they call Juliet's name, she dumps her foul-tasting beaker of machine coffee and hobbles off, leaving Gracie signing autographs and flashing that famous Gracie smile.

As she emerges from the treatment room with bandages on her wrist and ankle and a bottle of painkillers in her hand, a woman on crutches backs into the toilet down the corridor. Speeding up, Juliet follows her inside. Both cubicles are engaged. The crutches stand propped against the sink. It's the action of a moment to take one and slip back to the corridor. She shoves her good hand through the grey plastic cuff, getting up a loping rhythm as she enters the waiting area. She looks across the rows of plastic chairs. For a few furious seconds she thinks Gracie has gone, then she spots her behind the reception desk, holding a pink china cup, full no doubt of fresh coffee, brewed specially for her by one of the hovering staff.

Gracie looks up, a pout of sympathy. 'What did they say?'

'My rib.'

'Broken?'

Bruised actually, but Juliet's not going to split hairs. It still hurts like hell. She nods. 'And a buggered wrist and ankle' (suitably vague – those cuts are pretty deep) 'and sprains in places I won't even mention.'

Juliet looks around, aware of the watching eyes of the receptionists.

'How long before the rib mends?' Gracie says, coming round to her side of the counter.

'Six weeks.' Juliet sighs and looks away.

'What about the ankle?'

'I can't drive or put any strain on it.'

'Poor you. Is it agony?'

'I'll manage. Freya will have to help me. She's a big girl now.' A pained intake of breath. 'I'll ring round and see if there's anyone in her class she can walk to school with.'

Gracie makes a sympathetic tutting noise.

'It's not being able to drive that's the problem. Do you think Heather would mind picking her up from school on Thursday and taking her to dance class?'

'Of course. If there's anything else we can do just ask.'

The eyes of the staff stray back to their screens but their energy remains fully focused on Gracie.

Come on, Gracie. Juliet pushes her fingers to her forehead. 'They've given me a leaflet about symptoms of delayed concussion. I . . . I just hope Ian doesn't turn up making trouble.'

Gracie is flustered, taking just a little too long to find her keys in that big squishy bag of hers. It takes Juliet sucking her breath and looking at the dosage on the painkillers to finally push her into a response.

'Look, why don't you stay with us for a few days? This is all my fault anyway. I feel terrible. My bike's worked brilliantly up till now.'

Juliet has never been the object of so much open-mouthed envy. For a minute she wonders if Gracie is merely playing to the crowd and as soon as they're outside 'a few days' will shrink to 'one night only'. But all the way back to the pub she's making plans, going on about sleeping arrangements, fitting the Dunsmore school run into Elsie's hectic holiday schedule and deciding what they'll need to pick up from Juliet's flat on the way back.

'How's Heather going to feel about having me under her feet all day?' Juliet asks.

'She'll be fine,' Gracie says, adding quickly, 'though probably best if you work in my study.'

'What about Tom? Won't he mind?'

'He'll understand. Anyway he's back and forth to Dublin at the moment.'

Shame. Still, his absence will give Juliet more time alone with Gracie. More time alone in Gracie's house. More opportunities to move her project on to phase two. As the painkillers kick in she settles back in the padded seat, floating woozily on a warm wash of satisfaction, doors opening in her head to bright visions of the future.

The minute they turn into the Caxton Arms car park Matt comes hurrying out. He leans in through the driver's window, sweaty and agitated.

'I just took a look at your bike. I'd say it's been tampered with.'

'*What?*' Gracie turns off the engine. 'How?'

'The wheel and cable look like they were deliberately loosened so they'd let go once your speed picked up.'

'That's horrible. Who would do that?'

Juliet picks at her bandage and shakes her head. 'I knew there was something wrong with that wheel.'

'Could have been kids messing around,' Matt says. 'Or it could have been someone who wanted you to come a cropper. If you'd been on the road, you could have been killed.'

You, Juliet thinks. *Not me.* He couldn't care less about me.

'You need to be careful, Gracie. Next time, check your bike before you take it out. Or drop it in here and I'll do it for you.' He swings round as Freya and Elsie come running across the tarmac. For a moment Gracie sits with her hands on the wheel, her mouth set in a grim line, then she snaps on her 'Brave Gracie' smile and opens the car door.

42

Once back at Falcon Square Gracie goes into overdrive, chivvying the girls into bed, bringing Juliet tea, taking her bags to her room, even offering to help her up the stairs, though Juliet refuses, insisting she needs to get the hang of doing it on her own. She's half way up, balancing herself between the crutch and the bannister, when Gracie's mobile rings – four shrill bursts of two bleeps and a pause. It stops. Juliet looks back. Gracie is sitting lost in thought, her mobile in her hand, lit by the pool of light from the arc lamp which hangs above her. As Juliet passes from the staircase to the landing the phone rings again. Into silence. Seconds later the landline starts up. Finally Gracie picks up. Curious to know who she's avoiding, Juliet slips into Gracie's and presses the speaker. It's Tom:

'You have *got* to be kidding me.'

'What else could I do?' Gracie's voice is weary. 'It was my bike, my fault it happened. She didn't even want to go cycling.'

'I suppose she was pissed.'

'Of course she wasn't.'

'How long's she going to be there?'

'A few days, a week. You'll be away for most of it and it'll be great for Elsie having Freya around.'

'What if the husband turns up?'

'He doesn't even know she's here.'

'I don't like it, Gracie. The woman's a walking bloody disaster.'

'She could have broken her neck.'

'I'm more worried that it could have been you.'

'If she goes back to her flat who's going to look after Freya?'

'I've got no problem with the kid. It's the mother who's a flake.'

Juliet waits for Gracie to fly to her defence, to snap back that she's a friend, an ally, a confidant.

'She's on her own, Tom. She's got no one.'

'God, you and your bloody waifs and strays.'

He hangs up. Juliet flicks off the speaker, all the satisfaction she'd felt in the car cooling and curdling inside her. She hobbles into the spare room and stares at her reflection in the gilded mirror above the chest. *A flake. A walking disaster. One of Gracie's waifs and strays. 'R' for 'Reject'.*

The square below is quiet but sounds drift in from the main road: passing lorries, rowdy pub goers, drunken shouts, distant laughter. She strips off her clothes thinking sour thoughts about the women Gracie really does count as friends, the ones Tom greets with kisses. She can see that Daphne Dawes has her uses but what's so bloody special about that raddled old hippy Jess Villiers?

Gracie has unpacked Juliet's things, put her medication on the bedside table and ranged the little phials of e-liquid along the top of the chest of drawers, a hint no doubt that she doesn't want Juliet smoking in her precious house. Juliet washes down her painkillers with a slug from the bottle of Evian she finds beside the bed and checks Jess out on

Facebook. She's got two pages, one personal – rarely updated – and one for the pub. Interestingly, she's the licensee, not Matt – does that blunt manner and grizzled exterior conceal an iffy past? Her photos are mainly of birthdays and Christmases – Matt and Jamie showing off the reindeer motifs on their dorky matching sweaters, Jess bearing the turkey to the table with a set of light-up antlers clamped to her head. Silly cow. She must be fifty-five if she's a day. God, how Juliet loathes Christmas. All that fuss and fakery. Smiling through the loneliness, getting through the day. If it wasn't for Freya she'd spend it in bed. Exhausted, she logs off and eases herself back onto the pillows. The pills dull the pain in her rib but they can't erase the aftertaste of Tom's exasperation or the repetitive echo of Gracie's voice breaking through her dreams. *She's on her own, Tom. She's got no one.*

43

Juliet opens her eyes and lies for a moment, gazing up at the fluted cornice, excitement kicking in as she maps out how she's going to use her first day at Falcon Square. She reaches for her phone, shocked to see it's nearly half past eight. Freya's going to be late. She wriggles into a pair of jeans and limps downstairs, oddly perturbed to find her daughter washed and dressed – uniform newly pressed, hair in ribboned pigtails – spiralling honey onto a bowl of porridge.

'Are you better now, Mummy?'

'Not yet, sweetheart.' She bends painfully to kiss her daughter's freshly scrubbed cheek. 'But I will be soon.' Her eyes sweep the kitchen as she holds Freya close. *If I get this right,* everything *will be better soon.*

'Help yourself to coffee, toast, yoghurt, whatever you want,' Gracie says. 'How did you sleep?'

'The bed was brilliant, but I had no idea a . . . broken rib could hurt so much.' She winces and touches her fingers to her chest. 'I had to prop myself up all night just to be able to breathe.'

'Best take it easy today then.'

261

'I can't. I've got a website to finish.' Juliet smiles pointedly at Heather. 'Don't worry. I won't get in your way. I'm going to be working in Gracie's study.'

Heather turns away. Gracie doesn't notice her surliness, she's too busy dotting the girls' porridge with blueberries.

Juliet glances at the calendar: all those informative little squares brimming with holiday drama workshops, art classes and tennis lessons. *What a busy little bee Elsie is.* 'So what exciting things are you and Heather up to today, Elsie?'

Elsie lifts her shoulders in that irritating shrug.

'They're going over to Wimbledon this morning,' Gracie says, brightly.

'Her granny's booked her in for a riding lesson.'

Elsie turns to Freya with a boastful little shimmy of her head. 'My other mummy had a horse of her *own* when she was little. Its name was Muffin.'

Juliet shoots Gracie a glance. There's not a tic or a twitch, just a bland, 'That's right, darling', before she drops her hands onto Freya's shoulders and smiles at Juliet. 'Don't worry, they'll be back in plenty of time to pick this one up from school.'

Juliet, who could have done with a few more specifics about the timings of the riding lesson and the details of their lunch plans, sees Heather watching her, piggy-eyed with distrust, and merely returns Gracie's smile. 'I'm so grateful to be here, I just don't know how we'd have managed on our own.'

'Honestly, it's the least I can do. I've left you some soup in the fridge. Make sure you eat it. You need to keep your strength up.' Gracie kisses Elsie, dabs a knuckle to Freya's cheek and sweeps her keys into her bag. 'Bye, girls. Be good.'

Juliet pours herself a coffee. She sips it quickly, one eye on the clock, her stomach seizing with impatience as she hobbles down the hall to kiss her daughter goodbye and watch her scamper down the steps after Heather. At least that dumpy cow's being kind to Freya, probably pities her for having such a crap mother.

She shuts the door, sets the alarm and hurries upstairs, eager to use the precious minutes of Gracie's phone-free commute to check her emails. It's predictable stuff: requests for interviews, a note from her publisher, a revised shooting schedule, the minutes of the Stay Safe AGM. Juliet is dying to click the speech bubble icon and read Gracie's latest texts. She daren't, though. Gracie will be arriving at the bakery at any moment.

She logs off and tries the handle of Gracie's bottom drawer. It's still locked. She swings round in the swivel chair, ready to make a start on Gracie's files. Reckoning she's got a good three hours, she runs her eyes across the coloured box files ranged along the bottom of the bookshelves. None of the old grey ones are there. Has Gracie chucked them out?

Sucking on her vaporiser she heads down to the cellar, relieved to see two open packing cases marked 'Gracie' pushed into a recess. The battered grey box files are still there, dating back a promising thirteen years. She settles down with her back to the wall and starts with the earliest, hoping for a youthful indiscretion, a druggy boyfriend or a slip-up in accounting that might give her something to work with. She wades on through cookery school certificates, rental agreements, photos of Gracie on her market stall looking painfully young, a copy of the article by Daphne bloody Dawes that launched Gracie's career, a couple of shots of her all loved up with that drippy actor Harry Flynn, press mentions of her daytime cookery slot and hundreds of clippings about cafés and artisan bakeries. Why hang on to all this crap? Juliet moves on through the years. There's still nothing. Not a smudge or a smear to sully Gracie's gloss.

She reaches the files for Gracie's year of triumph. Six

years on it still turns Juliet's stomach to look at that neatly inked date, but she can't stop herself burrowing down to the folder containing her own business card, a point of pride to find something, anything, that might elevate the meaning of its label to more than 'R' for 'Rejects'. It's not looking hopeful. Apart from the dreary exhibition at the Forward Gallery and Lana Laughton's garish book launch invitation, the offering of the bar menu is pretty uninspiring: sandwiches, jacket potatoes, pies. Juliet turns it over, part of her brain dismissive of the sepia picture of a country pub even as the other half is registering the name on the sign: the Caxton Arms. A fly buzzes at the bare bulb hanging above her head. She watches it zig-zag closer to the light as she runs her fingertip around the edge of the card. Did Gracie think about teaming up with the Villiers to revamp the restaurant at the Caxton Arms? Or investing in Laughton's Wink Productions? Is that what she was doing with all these businesses – bearing them in mind for some future project?

Certain that the answer needs only the tiniest nudge to bring it bobbing within reach, she takes a photo of each item in the file, making sure to capture every inch of text. She's returning the folder to the packing case when a new thought strikes her. Is this about PR? She searches the Daley Associates client lists – past and present. She should have known. None of these outfits has ever been cool enough for Jeremy Daley. She swipes his smug, Botoxed face off the screen. His smile stays with her – the self-satisfied smirk of the man who took everything that should have been hers and turned her life to shit. She digs out the apology he wrote for the chocolate torte disaster, fretting over the arrogant scribble at the bottom: *Hope this helps, Jeremy x.* Her eyes lock on the date. June. Gracie can't have been that impressed with him if she was approaching Juliet at the Hub two months later. *What swung it for you, Jeremy? Why did Gracie reach out to me then suddenly pull back?*

She snatches up the 'R' file again then tosses it aside and leans back, closing her eyes. Is she crossing into crazy? She's found her business card stashed in the files of a woman who throws nothing away. So what? This need for it to mean something is starting to eat into her, take over, get in the way. She can't let that happen. Not this time. *Focus on the plan, Juliet. Just focus on the plan.* She does the breathing, forcing air in through her nose and out through her mouth, visualising Jeremy Daley's horror when he opens the papers to find that a leak from his company has shafted Gracie, lost him his flagship client and destroyed his reputation. It'll take more than a half-baked letter of apology for him to 'disappear those negatives'. Calmer now, she stands up and dusts down her jeans. Time to get out of here. Heather and Elsie could be back at any moment.

She warms up the soup she finds in a jug labelled *Juliet*. It's spicy tomato – a bit too spicy for Juliet, but she eats it anyway. On her way upstairs she takes an apple from the fruit bowl and nibbles it as she wanders over to the book-shelves in Gracie's study. She's not obsessed, this is research, she tells herself as she bumps her finger along the spines of book after sodding book about food; its production, history and preparation, stopping with a satisfied grunt when she finds what she's looking for – a well-thumbed copy of Laughton's *This Is Me* – a luscious-lipped pout-and-cleavage combo on the embossed jacket.

To Gracie, Best wishes from a domestic disaster! Lana xx.

She turns it in her hands. Did Gracie drop Lana, like she dropped Juliet? Or are they still friends, extravagant kisses at parties, nodes on an exclusive network of influential women in the media?

She carries the book to the chaise longue, lifts her bandaged foot gingerly onto the cushions and skims the pages, searching for references to Gracie. Soon though she finds herself settling back onto the cushions, sucked in by the juicy revelations – every toe-curling intimacy of Laughton's body, mind and marriages offered up for public inspection. Juliet doesn't know who she pities more, her long-suffering husbands or her poor kids. The older two – twin girls – must have been taunted mercilessly about their mother's affairs, abortions and experiments with drugs. The younger one, a boy, has all that to come.

Half an hour of reading tells Juliet more about Laughton than being in this house is telling her about Gracie. She gazes around her at the ordered busyness of Gracie's study, the pinboard bristling with invitations, the smiling photos. *Where's the real you, Gracie? The doubt? The dirt? The pain and disappointment? There must be more to your past than the startling little snippet you let slip at the weekend.*

Gracie stands on the John Lewis escalator looking down at the shoppers below. She should be down in the basement buying a new juicer and here she is, getting off at the third floor to wander the children's section. She drifts past racks of clothes for newborns, tiny Baby-gros, cute little dresses, lacy shawls, bootees, and hats no bigger than her own cupped hand. Things she has never needed to buy. Things she never *will* need to buy. She shakes that thought away. She's not here to mourn the past. She's here to prepare for the future and now, for the very first time, she's allowing herself to think about furnishing a room for a second child.

Her head fills with blinds, duvet covers, rugs and friezes. She walks the aisles and looks and touches, holding up

T-shirts, testing the softness of vests, examining toys. She doesn't buy, though. Not yet. That would tempt fate, risk heartache. She's made a pact with herself not to purchase anything for this new child. Not so much as a toothbrush until it's legally and permanently hers.

44

'Mummy, I got a gold star for reading!'

Juliet jolts awake, the copy of *This Is Me* sliding to the floor as Freya rushes in to share her news.

'Wow, darling.' Juliet reaches out and gives her a bleary kiss. Freya skips to the door, summoned by Heather calling her down for tea.

God, Juliet feels shitty. Angry too, that she's wasted her afternoon. She'll have to make up for it tonight. And this time she'll hold off on the drink and let Gracie do the talking.

By the time she's roused herself enough to rinse the furriness out of her mouth, brush her hair and go downstairs, Gracie is home and Elsie and Freya are sitting side by side at that huge kitchen table, drawing with fierce concentration, looking up only to rattle their fingers in the box of crayons.

'Sorry. I put my feet up for twenty minutes. Next thing I know I've been asleep for a couple of hours.'

'Don't apologise.' Gracie glances up from the sink where she's shucking peas for some fussy rice thing she's got steaming in a pan. 'Your body's still in shock. You need to rest.'

Juliet props the crutch against the wall and sags into a chair, bracing herself for the inevitable explosion when Elsie and Freya's fingers collide on the same crayon or the felt tip Freya's using sparks a sudden craving in Elsie.

Gracie tips a handful of raw peas into her mouth, frowning as she crunches them down. 'Are you feeling all right?'

'I think it's these tablets, making me feel a bit weird.'

'Get your GP to change the prescription. There's a cab number on the notice board. Put it on my account.'

Juliet glances over at the board, taking in Gracie's keys lying on the counter, itching to get another look at that thumb drive. 'Thanks. I think I will.'

'Let's see these drawings, then,' Gracie says.

Elsie holds up her picture, simpering and pointing. 'That's me, that's you and Daddy, that's Granny and Grandpa and that's Heather, Daphne and Tallulah.'

'Lovely, darling. What about yours, Freya?'

Juliet smiles encouragement as Freya shyly lifts her paper, jerking back sharply when she sees what her daughter has drawn.

Elsie casts a critical eye over the picture. 'Who's that?'

'That's me and my mummy and that's my daddy and Merion and my baby sister.'

Elsie purses up her mouth and snaps, 'You haven't got a baby sister.'

'I do, don't I, Mummy?'

'Well, not quite yet.' Juliet turns her frozen smile on Elsie, quietly wishing she could throttle her. 'But it's true that Freya's daddy and his girlfriend are having a baby who will be Freya's new sister or brother.'

Elsie screws up her eyes, envious for a moment. Then she lashes out. 'I don't want my daddy to have a girlfriend.'

There is a second of brittle silence before Gracie claps

her hands together. 'All right, everybody! Tidy-up time!' She turns smartly back to the pea pods but not before Juliet has seen the quiver of her jaw.

All this shucking and husking and blanching and dicing. *What is it you're avoiding, Gracie? Fear of your stalker? Or is it worry about your handsome husband? All those nights he spends away? What he's doing? Who he's with?*

'I'm out tonight,' Gracie says as she shakes the colander of peas under the tap. 'Will you be all right?'

Juliet looks down, ramming lids onto felt pens, her mouth clamped shut against the choke of disappointment. 'Sure.'

Gracie is looking at her from across the room. 'I took some beef in red wine out of the freezer for you, lots of iron, and there's plenty of veg and some of that Sancerre in the fridge. Help yourself to anything else you want.' She glugs oil into a pan. 'I'm determined to feed you up, you know. You really don't look well at all.'

'I'm fine,' Juliet says. 'I've got that website to finish. Is it OK if I use your study again?'

'Of course.'

'It's such a great place to work. So organised. I keep meaning to sort out my filing system but I never get round to it.'

'It's worth doing. It saves so much time in the long run.'

Juliet's eyes dip away to the garden. 'So what's your system?'

Gracie laughs. 'It's probably best described as intuitive.'

Intuitive. Juliet laughs too, a light throwaway chuckle. 'How does that work?'

'Not sure, but I can always find what I'm looking for.'

'Really?'

'Tom doesn't get it, he teases me for being a hoarder, but when I'm working on a project I can't order my thoughts unless I've got bits of paper to shuffle around.'

'You mean for your books?'

'Yes, and articles, recipes, business pitches. It's the way I process things.'

'I must try it.' Juliet flashes Gracie her girliest smile. 'Off somewhere glamorous tonight?'

'God no. Supper and a film with Daphne. I'll put the girls to bed before I go. Don't worry about checking on them. Heather's here.'

Is that a dig about what happened last time?

It doesn't take Juliet long to draw Gracie out, establish the film and the venue and work out when it will be safe to look at her emails.

It's only later, after Gracie has gone, that she notices Freya's drawing stuck on the fridge. Somehow Gracie has managed to hide the images of Ian, Merion and their baby beneath an overlap of novelty magnets, photos and postcards. How tactful. But next to Elsie's crowded portrait, she and Freya look pathetically lonely. *She's on her own, Tom. She's got no one.*

A murmur of canned laughter filters from the television in Heather's room as Juliet shuts herself in Gracie's study and jams a magazine under the door. It won't stop Heather from barging in but it might slow her down. She tips out the pen jar on the desk; there's always a chance that Gracie has backed up her banana keyring files onto another thumb drive. If she has, she isn't keeping it here. At precisely 8.45, when the movie Gracie's seeing is scheduled to start, she clicks open Gracie's latest texts: a jokey note from Kelvin and an outpouring of angst from Daphne Dawes.

PLEASE say you're free tonight. Need to vent.
Fucking Burridge gone cold on promotion. Says it'll look suspicious!!!

271

She lingers over that one. Snide, judgemental Daphne. Elsie's godmother, Gracie's closest friend, Tom's eye-rolling ally. *You should go easy on the alcohol, Juliet. We wouldn't want a repeat of what happened at Elsie's party.*

She spools through Daphne's messages – needy outpourings, bitchy comments, witty one-liners and huffy put-downs, a snapshot of the kind of friendship Juliet has never had. She moves on to Gracie's emails, checking through her pithy correspondence with senior studio executive Ryland Stott and working back through a message thread that began months ago with an internal memo about the contractual details of the off-network reruns. She's combing through the details, astounded by the eye-watering fees Gracie stands to earn if the US version of her show sells in even a quarter of the target territories, when her phone alarm shrieks a warning. Quickly she logs off. The movie credits will be rolling, the audience shuffling into the aisles, dipping into bags and pockets, turning on their phones. She switches swiftly to her own laptop and pulls up the staff list for Daphne's paper. Tony Burridge – designer glasses, grey suit, flabby jowls – is the editor of the magazine.

She is still up when Gracie gets back. They drink a glass of wine together, Juliet finishing off the bottle of white, Gracie fetching red for herself. Juliet listens to her account of the film, laughing in all the right places though her head is still full of Gracie's US deal. All that money. No wonder the studio were hammering out the syndication deal before they even told Gracie they were buying the show.

'Juliet?'

Gracie is waggling the bottle, offering her more wine.

'Oh sorry,' Juliet smiles and holds out her glass.

Pauline Bryce Diary
May 3rd

I really get my hopes up for this one, even shell out on a haircut and new shoes and I walk in there and the minute I open my mouth it's obvious I'm ten times smarter than any of the airhead bimbos sitting around in that waiting room. I give all the right answers, ask all the right questions and tell them about the business and computing classes I'm starving myself to pay for and I still don't get the fucking job. And now that slimeball Ricky is telling me he's cutting down my shifts at the bar because I'm not 'friendly' enough to the customers and we all know what that fucking means. How am I supposed to 'turn the things I hate about my life into the tools to change it' when the whole thing is shit?

45

On Wednesday morning Elsie has a forty-five-minute tennis lesson scheduled for ten o'clock. Juliet adds twenty more for travel and ten to buy the whiny brat an ice cream, giving her a safe window of an hour to explore Tom's study. But the afternoon is going to be a total write-off. Somehow – God knows how – Heather has managed to cajole a couple of nannies from St Mathilda's into bringing their kids round. She's done it on purpose, Juliet's sure of that. Still, she might as well use the time to get the doctor to change the prescription for her painkillers.

She uses the phone in the kitchen, making sure Heather can hear her asking about cancellations for the afternoon surgery – *see, Heather, I really am injured*. As she gives the receptionist her details she fiddles with the stack of scrap paper the children were using for drawing. You've got to laugh. Gracie Dwyer – two homes, three cars – thinks she can save the world by recycling a few old meeting agendas. She glances round to see Heather filling Elsie's pink plastic water bottle. With a casual sweep of her bandaged hand she spreads the pages, examining Gracie's spiky little doodles in the margins and looking for Daley's name in the lists of

274

attendees. Her eyes flit past a letterhead – broken black letters on a disc of red – then slide back to settle on the words. *The Forward Gallery.* It's a note from the trustees thanking Mr and Mrs Tom Whittaker for their generous support. She reads it again. If Gracie is one of their sponsors, active in keeping this place afloat, what's the 'intuitive' reasoning behind filing one of their invitations with Juliet's business card and an old pub menu? As Heather goes to the door to tell Elsie to bring down her tennis racquet Juliet quickly folds the paper and slips it into her pocket. Perhaps it isn't 'R' for 'Rejects' after all.

Aware of Heather's eyes on her back, Juliet calls the cab number on the noticeboard. It feels good giving 17 Falcon Square as the pick-up address, even better saying *Yes* when the controller asks if it's on account. He calls her Ms Dwyer. Why bother to correct him?

Wincing at the slam of the front door, she hangs up. With the departure of Heather and Elsie a deep, inviting calm descends on the house. Morning sunlight warms the wooden stairs as she carries her coffee up to Tom's attic. She goes over to his desk, examining the pin-sharp pencils, opening the potato print Father's Day card – *to my luvly daddy* – trying to get a sense of the man in Gracie's life. She gazes at the picture above his desk. It's a framed copy of *The Sunday Times* feature on his prize-winning Wharf House. They've reprinted one of Louise's shots of the construction site beside a photo of the finished building at dusk with the setting sun hanging in the darkened expanse of glass. It looks stunning, though she's not sure she could have stuck living on that gloomy stretch of river in a dead woman's house, however cutting-edge the design.

She wanders to the window and stares down at the rusty reds and mottled browns of the slanting rooftops below, each one touched by the summer heat, each one housing secrets, hopes and surrendered dreams. Her eyes return to the photo of the Wharf House. Shame the US studio didn't confirm Gracie's contract before they sold it. Poor Tom.

Of course, the delay panned out just fine for Gracie. She'd ended up with an eye-watering US deal *and* the chance to get shot of her husband's dead wife's house. Deep down what woman wouldn't be pleased about that, especially if the dead wife had been as talented and attractive as Louise?

'Change of plan,' Juliet says as soon as the cab driver pulls away from the kerb. 'Can you take me to E1 instead?' She'll tell Gracie she had to pick something up for work, offer to reimburse the fare and play grateful when she tells her not to be silly.

'Whereabouts?'

'Shadwell station.'

She doesn't want her true destination showing up on Gracie's account.

Juliet gets out at the station and follows the line of overhead railtracks through a tight cluster of fifties council blocks, tiny shops spilling fruit, plastic buckets and phone accessories onto the pavement, madrasas housed in decaying Georgian mansions and a sprinkling of pop-up cafés.

The Forward Gallery, housed in a railway arch between a dodgy-looking meat warehouse and a wine bar specialising in biodynamic wines, is showing paintings by a Palestinian artist – Ensaf Hadawi. A photo of her hangs by the door, a bird-like woman gazing down at the ruins of a bombed-out village, eyes slit against blinding sunlight. Juliet limps forward on her crutch to inspect the canvases – bright sunbursts of colour, each with a central core of black, brown and red like a crust of old blood.

'Wonderful aren't they?' An eager woman – ruby-red lips, platinum hair – is offering her a catalogue.

Juliet takes it. 'I didn't realise the trust supported foreign artists.'

'When we can.'

'That's brilliant.' Juliet is floundering, suddenly unsure of why she's even here. 'And you're totally dependent on donations?'

'We take a small commission from the work we sell but it's our sponsors who keep us going.'

'Friends of mine . . . Tom and Gracie Whittaker?' she makes it a question. 'I think they sponsor you.'

There it is. That sickening simper that appears whenever she mentions her connection to Gracie.

'Very much so,' the assistant says. 'They're big supporters of what we do.'

'Actually I was wondering about an artist you exhibited years ago – Olga Maswell? "Images of Old Age"?'

'Before my time but the name rings a bell.'

'Do you still have any of her work?'

'I can have a look.'

Juliet follows her through an archway into a dingy, cave-like space taken up with cupboards, plan chests and storage stands. The assistant points to a rack of prints on the wall. 'Her sketches should be in there and any tapestries will be in one of these drawers.' While she's craning and crouching to check the labels, Juliet flips through the rack, slowing down to look at a series of poster-sized photographs of a wild rocky shoreline, stopping completely on a sharply shadowed cliff slanting down to the sea.

'Who did these?' she says over her shoulder.

The assistant glances up. 'Louise Harper. We held a retrospective of her work to mark the fifth anniversary of her death. Tom and Gracie sponsored the whole thing.'

How very noble of you, Gracie.

'Such a terrible waste of talent,' the assistant bobs down to try a lower drawer. 'Her photos still sell really well.'

Juliet goes on turning through the pictures in the rack, shaken by the rumble of a train passing overhead. The sound fades to unsettling stillness as she studies Olga Maswell's dismal little sketch of gnarled hands gripping the stem of a death's head cane.

'Ah, here's the tapestry.' The assistant lays a package reverently on the trestle table and loosens the tissue. Juliet gazes down at a coarse web of brown string, interwoven with ripped-up prescriptions, photos, get well cards, pill packets, saggy lengths of Germolene-pink knicker elastic and strips torn from rubbery support stockings. *OK, Olga! We get it. Old age stinks.*

'It's so haunting,' the assistant says.

Stumped for words Juliet murmurs, 'It certainly . . . makes a statement. How much is it?'

The assistant dips back into the drawer and pulls out a wad of stapled sheets, chewing her lip as she flips through them. 'OK, so there were three small tapestries. *Remnant* and *Unseen* were sold . . . so this one must be *Frailty*, which is . . .' She looks up with an eager *Ooh, what a bargain* smile on her face '. . . three hundred pounds.' The door of the gallery clangs open. 'Back in a mo.'

Juliet is turning through the lists of pieces, purchasers and prices when her eye catches on a familiar name. Hugh Dugdale, Gracie's MP friend. He paid £200 for an Olga Maswell sketch called *All That Is Left*. *I bet that one cheers up a room.*

The assistant is back, frowning slightly when she sees what Juliet is holding.

'Oh sorry,' Juliet says. 'I . . . I noticed Hugh Dugdale bought one of Maswell's pieces. I met him the other day, at a party at Gracie and Tom's.'

The assistant smiles, placated by the magic words. 'He buys something from every exhibition. It gives young artists such a boost to see that first little red dot appear at their opening.'

'Does he go to *every* opening?'

'Tries to. He's chair of our trustees.'

'Oh. Oh, I see. So it was probably him who got Gracie and Tom involved.'

'I wouldn't know.'

'Well, thanks so much. I'll have a think about the tapestry.'

'Of course.'

The assistant hands her a flimsy pamphlet. 'Do take one of the Maswell catalogues. We've got so many, they're only cluttering up the storeroom.'

'Oh, great.' Juliet smiles wanly and hobbles to the door.

That night, over bowls of slow-cooked squid with fennel, Gracie asks almost shyly if Juliet would try out some new ideas she's experimenting with.

'Why not?' Juliet says, flattered but not sure how she's going to bluff her way through this one.

For the next couple of hours Gracie chops, stirs, sautés, spritzes with lime, sprinkles with parsley and spoons aromatic little morsels onto dishes as Juliet forks up tiny mouthfuls, nodding thoughtfully and gazing off into the distance as she chews. What the hell is she supposed to say? Especially with Gracie sitting there, sipping wine and leaning close. 'Too salty? Try it with a bit more of the sauce. Does it need more basil?' A couple of times Gracie apologises for pressing her. 'Sorry, but it's so helpful having a live-in guinea pig.' It doesn't seem to occur to her that these subtleties of texture and flavour might be lost on Juliet's smoke-scorched taste buds.

She bites into a squishy nugget of sweetbreads spiked

with tarragon, a contemplative, mmm sound vibrating in her throat as her stomach quivers in revolt. 'Doesn't Tom try things out for you?'

Gracie laughs. 'He loves his food but he's never been one for analysing what he eats. Daphne's pretty good, but she's so busy these days I don't like to ask.'

Daphne. Always bloody Daphne.

Before she goes to sleep Juliet spends a couple of hours gathering words from foodie websites – sharp, clean, crunchy, gelatinous, silky – a ready vocabulary for use next time she's asked to pronounce on Gracie's experiments. Now and then as she reads, her attention catches on the letter *R*, her brain refusing to halt its frantic sift and search for the meaning of the label on that file.

46

Gracie throws back her head and pulls long steady strokes of her brush through her settling cloud of hair, taming it into a single glossy hank before coiling it expertly onto the top of her head and reaching for the pins. She's doing it without thinking, her mind on the book in her lap, sent to her by one of the psychologists involved with Stay Safe. It's the paragraph about stalkers who prefer to inflict mental rather than physical harm that holds her, twisted minds who subject their targets to prolonged psychological torture, changing tactics, feeding their victims' paranoia, in the knowledge that by remaining invisible they take on the power of their victim's darkest dreams. She snaps the book shut and she's dragging her thoughts away, trying to lose herself in Tom's plans for the chapel, the long refectory tables, the use of mirrors, whether she should go for black or white marble for the countertops, when her phone rings.

'Daph. A bit early in the morning for you, isn't it?'

'Burridge's wife knows it's me.'

'How?'

'A snidey dig on some gossip site and now the whole thing's snowballing.'

'Can't you deny it?'

'Too late. It's totally blown my chances of getting Sherys's job.'

'Who tipped them off?'

'He says he's been super careful. I know I have.' There's a pause. 'The only person I told was you.'

Gracie drops her hairbrush, shocked by the ice in Daphne's voice. 'I haven't mentioned a word to anyone. I wouldn't. You know I wouldn't.'

'Not even Tom?'

'I swear.'

'There's stuff on Twitter about him cancelling our trip to Barcelona. You're the only person who even knew we were going.'

'Then it *must* be Burridge.'

Daphne's voice rises, sharp with anger. 'He had too much to lose. We both did.'

'Daph. Please, I would never—'

The line goes dead.

Gracie drops onto the edge of the bed, still holding her phone. A floorboard flexes on the landing. She lifts her head. 'Heather?'

'Sorry. Only me.' Juliet pokes her head around the door. 'I was after something to settle my tummy before I head off to Freya's end of term assembly, but I didn't want to interrupt.'

Gracie blinks, distracted. 'Oh . . . try the cupboard in the kitchen . . . the one next to the fridge.'

Juliet's head disappears. Gracie stares at the door for a minute then redials Daphne's number. She doesn't pick up. She tries again as soon as she gets to the Mange Tout offices and then again before the start of her meeting. Every time she calls it goes to voice mail.

*　　*　　*

282

Juliet gets a cab to Dunsmore school and limps into the hall. Secretly rather enjoying the looks of sympathy from the other parents, she makes her way to the front row and rests the crutch against her chair. As the headmistress welcomes everybody to the school and the first batch of award-winners shuffles towards the podium, Juliet's mind drifts away picturing more trips to Caxton over the coming weeks and for once the thought of the summer holidays doesn't fill her with dread. Her attention snaps back to the podium. Freya is stepping up to receive her red rosette for reading. She turns to throw Juliet a proud gappy smile. Juliet waves and claps. Her heart aching, she raises her phone to capture Freya's moment of triumph.

Freya moves back to join the rest of the award winners who stand thrilled and self-conscious at the side of the podium, thrusting out their chests as the Year Three teaching assistant sits down at the piano and begins to plonk out the intro to 'I Believe I Can Fly'. Juliet groans. Why do they always pick this mawkish crap? The children's voices rise high and hopeful over the screechy whistle of recorders and the random ding of fiercely gripped triangles. *Don't believe any of it!* Juliet wants to shout. *Life's a bitch and you've got to fight and claw and scratch and grab or it will screw you over!* The music swells through the hall. Juliet watches her daughter, her beautiful, innocent, sweet-natured daughter, throw back her head and sing out with all her might that if she just spreads her wings she can touch the sky. As if swept away by sudden grief Juliet feels her eyes smarting and like a bloody fool she starts to cry.

Damn! That girl Donna is back on the Mange Tout reception desk. Gracie can see her girding her fury, ready to spill the latest on her messy break-up. *Sorry, Donna, I can't face a tirade about the cattiness of your ex's new girlfriend or what his mum said about yours, not today.* Putting on a spurt Gracie calls, 'Must rush', and makes a dash for the exit. With a gasp of relief she bursts into the sunshine and clatters down the steps into the hot bright glare of the car park. She stops and squints into the sunlight, confused by the ruffled lump of grey marring the gleaming lines of her car bonnet. She moves closer. A spasm of revulsion constricts her gut. It's a pigeon. She doesn't need the flies circling its flesh to tell her that it's dead. She twists round, the panicky need to get rid of it tripping her feet as she lurches down to pick up a dented Coke can. Trying not to vomit she holds the can at arm's length and edges around the car to jab at the bird. For a moment it sticks stubbornly to the hot metal, one jagged wing stabbing the air each time Gracie jolts the putrid carcass, then it drops with a soft thud onto the tarmac. She hurls the can away and dashes back into the studios.

Ignoring Donna's excited demands to know what's wrong, she backs into the cloakroom. Arms held high she thumps the soap dispenser with her wrist, jerks open the hot tap, plunges her hands beneath the scalding water and scrubs and scrubs, imagining her stalker planning this, all part of his new subtle campaign to chip away at her sanity. She can see his hands opening a plastic bag and shaking that heap of maggoty flesh onto her car: the same hands that wrote that housewarming message on Louise's most famous photo, brought Louise's statue into number 17 and scrawled a creepy quote from one of Louise's favourite poets on the walls of the chapel. She leans forward and dry-retches into the sink.

She lifts her head and glares at herself in the mirror. 'Stop this!' she says aloud. 'A fox did it.'

Even as she's nodding at her reflection her mind is turning through Louise's life and work, rummaging for references to pigeons. Nothing comes to mind. *But there is a link to you, isn't there, Gracie? Can that really be a coincidence? Of course it isn't. He's playing with you. Can't you see? He wants you to dig deeper, to ask around and find some connection to Louise that everyone else will think is too tenuous to exist anywhere outside your own insecure imagination. And if you tell Tom how you feel, he'll think you're jealous, paranoid, unhinged.* The door swings open behind her. She flinches at the touch of Donna's hand.

'Was someone out there? Shall I call the police?'

'No, no it was nothing . . . a fox dragged a dead pigeon onto my car. It gave me the creeps, that's all.' She shudders. 'I've always had a thing about pigeons, ever since one got trapped in my room when I was a kid and this one . . . it was rotten . . . disgusting.'

Clearly disappointed that she isn't in for a tweet-worthy standoff with Gracie's stalker, Donna tilts her face to the mirror, twists her bottom lip to one side and runs an exploratory finger down her jaw. 'You shouldn't let pigeons worry you, aren't they like symbols of peace or something?'

Gracie slides her an uneasy look. 'I . . . I think that's doves.' She rinses her mouth, leaves Donna picking at a pimple and walks quickly to her car, her eyes searching left and right for a sinister figure skulking among the passing shoppers or a face watching her from the window of a parked car.

'Stop it! For God's sake, it was a fox!' She drives unsteadily to the nearest car wash and for a while she sits motionless, cocooned in the dimly lit tunnel of whirling brushes. But she can't shake off the doubt. Her heart grows jumpy in her chest as she pulls out her phone and keys in 'symbolic meaning of pigeons'. 'You're being an idiot,' she says to her reflection in the foam-spattered window. 'Look hard enough at this kind of stuff and you can find a link to anybody. But even your paranoid brain is going to be hard-pushed to link a bloody pigeon to you *and* Louise.' Her eyes work the page – anodyne stuff about home, hearth and family. 'See!' And then her gaze falls onto a line that douses her with dread.

In many cultures the pigeon is considered to be a spirit messenger that carries communications between the living and the dead.

She beats her hands against the wheel. 'No! No! No!'

That evening Juliet realises she's grown used to seeing Freya run in from the garden, wriggle into a chair and chomp down home-made ravioli stuffed with ricotta and mushrooms, butternut squash risotto or stir-fried tofu with noodles. All this good food and sunshine is turning Freya sleek before her eyes.

As for herself, her intake of real cigarettes has dropped to three a day (five at most) and she wears the vaporiser on a thong around her neck, sucking on it whenever she craves nicotine. She is probably still drinking too much, but it's good stuff – chilled, sipped and enjoyed, not the gut-rotting muck she's used to – so it surprises her how achy she still feels and how small her appetite has become. She'd laughed when the doctor in A and E said a fall could take it out of you. Looks like he was right. But she's not complaining. Given where the bike accident has got her she'd gladly have suffered worse.

Tom is on his way back from Dublin and earlier, when she offered to eat with the children and then make herself scarce, Gracie wouldn't hear of it, insisting that they all have supper together. Fine by me, Juliet thinks, savouring a little flicker of anticipation.

Once the children are in bed she takes time to tidy her hair and change her top, questions and possibilities circling her mind as she leans into the mirror to flick a dusting of blusher across her cheeks. On her way to the door she stops to check Daphne's Facebook page. No mention, of course, of her failed attempt to fuck her way to promotion or of her nasty little spat with best friend Gracie Dwyer. In fact, no new posts at all. Looks like Daphne Dawes is lying low. Juliet doesn't feel bad. Nobody died and she had to neutralise that sneery cow's influence on Gracie somehow. She logs off and limps downstairs leaning on her crutch.

Tom answers politely enough when Juliet speaks to him but for the most part he keeps his eyes on his plate of gingered pork, or on his wife who, to be honest, is looking a bit peaky and strained. He softens only once, glancing directly at Juliet when Gracie tells him how good it's been for Elsie having Freya around, how brilliantly she's been sharing. That's not quite how Juliet sees it but hey, if it keeps Tom happy. They discuss the progress of the chapel and it's not difficult for Juliet to nudge the conversation around to Caxton, what a wonderful weekend they'd had, what a shame about the accident, and it seems quite natural for her to say, 'It's such a gorgeous spot. Do you know that area well?'

Gracie puts some kind of flan on the table. 'No, not at all. I'd never been there till last spring when I went to see if the site would work as an events venue.' She slides a knife into the cherry-studded filling. 'Would you like some clafoutis?'

'Just a sliver,' Juliet says. 'So you didn't know Caxton before?'

'No. But from the minute I got out of the car and saw that beautiful stretch of river and the wood full of bluebells all bathed in sunshine I fell in love with it.' Her eyes find Tom's. 'But I never dreamed we'd ever be able to buy it and build a house.'

Juliet takes the bowl Gracie hands her. She spoons up a cherry and looks down at the red-veined socket in the batter. 'Maybe you dropped into the Caxton Arms years ago and forgot you'd ever been there.'

'I don't think so. Cream?' Gracie holds up a little white jug.

'No thanks.'

Tom pours a generous slug into his bowl and fixes Juliet with keen – but not overly sympathetic – interest. 'Any news on Ian?'

'The court is letting him see Freya,' Juliet keeps her voice resolutely matter of fact, despite the jolt at Ian's name. 'I wrote to the judge and told him it would only upset her but it didn't make any difference. So now I'm talking to social services about a venue and a chaperone that will be "acceptable to both parties".' She makes speech marks with her fingers. Looking up and seeing the uneasiness on Tom's face she says quickly, 'Oh, not here. God, no. I wouldn't dream of suggesting he came here.'

He seems placated, at least for now, but she doesn't want to push it. She leaves the rest of her clafoutis and refuses Gracie's offer of coffee, saying she's tired and might go up now. And it's true. She's exhausted. But thoughts of the Caxton Arms – the pub that Gracie forgot – have set the 'R' file cogs whirring into overdrive.

She lies alone in the lamplight, conscious of the comings and goings in the square – grunts of laughter, a clink of keys – straining to work out Gracie's 'intuitive' connection between her own, barely functioning 'Juliet Beecham PR and Marketing Solutions' and the other businesses in that file. *Come on, Gracie. What venture did you give up on that I can resurrect and run with if your rock-hard shield of smiley do-goodery proves too tough to crack?*

Juliet gives up, drops back against the headboard and

opens *This Is Me*. Is it too much to ask for Lana to stumble into Gracie Dwyer snorting coke at a drug-fuelled orgy? Laughton is just getting down to drunken sex in the back of a taxi with third husband-to-be Charlie when Juliet looks up, alert to the murmur of voices and the angry scrape of a chair. She swings her legs out of bed and pads to the door, turning the handle and slipping onto the landing. She stands peering down the darkened stairwell, unable to make out the words. It's all too muffled until the kitchen door flies open, throwing a slice of light into the gloom. Gracie's voice rings out: 'You're just incapable of seeing it from my point of view!'

Then there's movement. Juliet sees her in the hall. Tom is coming after her, reaching for her arm. 'We have to talk about this.'

'What's the point? We're never going to agree!'

'Just calm down, for God's sake.'

Juliet pulls away into the shadows and then they are gone, back into the kitchen, shutting the door.

First the argument with Daphne then a shouting match with Tom. All in all it hasn't been a great day for Gracie.

47

Juliet struggles from sleep, groggy and unrefreshed, reaching for a slippery thought – a face? a photo? – that slithers away as she opens her eyes. Somehow she has to get her hands on Gracie's thumb drive. There's a tension at the breakfast table; something strained and unresolved in Tom's offer to use his morning off to take the girls swimming and something hurt and unforgiving in the way Gracie keeps her eyes fixed on Elsie and Freya when she enthuses about the idea. In the tumble of excitement to borrow a costume and run out to the car, Freya forgets to say goodbye. Juliet calls her back for a kiss.

Gracie is working on scripts in her study so Juliet drops her laptop and phone into her shoulder bag and limps out to the summerhouse on her crutch, positioning the wicker sun lounger to give herself a perfect view of anyone coming into the garden. She likes it out here. She can relax and smoke a proper cigarette. More importantly, she can see without being seen and use her phone with no chance of being overheard. Once settled against the candy-striped cushions she calls the Caxton Arms. Gracie might not remember the pub but there's just a chance that Matt and Jess will remember Gracie.

'Hi, Matt. It's Juliet.' His silence really pisses her off. He knows damn well who she is. 'Juliet Beecham, Gracie's friend.'

'Oh. Right.'

'I'm just calling to thank you for last Monday. I don't know what we'd have done if you hadn't come to the rescue.'

'No problem.'

'Gracie's so lucky having friends like you and Jess in the village. Have you known her long?'

'Nope.'

'Really? I'd kind of imagined she'd been popping into your pub for years.'

'Never heard of her till she bought the Gibson place.'

'Gosh. You . . . seem so close.'

'Delivery's here. Got to go.' He hangs up.

Maybe that Caxton Arms bar menu was a recent one that got mis-filed in an old folder. But Gracie Dwyer doesn't make mistakes like that. And anyway the design is totally different from the menus the pub are using now.

The French doors swing open. Gracie appears on the terrace. She seems to hesitate for a minute before making her way across the lawn. By the time she reaches the summer-house Juliet is bashing out content for a local events website, starting up, surprised, when Gracie taps on the half-open door. 'Fancy some lunch? Tom's taking the girls to a café. I thought I'd make us an omelette.'

'Great.' Juliet reaches for the crutch.

Gracie leans back against the doorjamb, silent for a minute, then she says softly, 'I hope we didn't disturb you last night.'

'Don't worry.' Juliet lays a hand lightly on her rib. 'I'm not sleeping much these days.'

'So you did hear us.'

Juliet puts on her most stoical expression. 'Does Tom want us to leave?'

'It's not so much that . . . he, he's worried . . . about Ian turning up and causing trouble.'

'Ian doesn't know where I am.'

'I know. I explained that to him.'

Shit. This can't happen. Juliet swings her good leg off the lounger and rubs her bandaged foot. 'Look, Gracie. You've been fantastic, *really* fantastic to me and to Freya. My life – our lives – haven't been that great for the last few years but meeting up with you again has given me back a bit of hope, made me think that perhaps, with the help of good friends, I can turn things around.' She shoots out her hand, as if clutching at rescue. 'But the last thing I want is to make problems between you and Tom. If you want us to go, please, just say so.'

'You don't have to go. He knows you're only here for a few more days, until you're a bit more mobile.' Gracie looks up at the trees, her voice thickening. 'Honestly, you mustn't worry. It wasn't just about you. We were arguing over the adoption. All these decisions to make, forms to fill in.'

Juliet lets her heart settle then says softly, 'It must be very stressful.'

'They're right to be thorough but there's so much to think about.' Gracie pushes herself off the doorframe and turns back to the house, calling over her shoulder. 'Ready in ten minutes.'

Juliet waits five before she follows her into the kitchen. Gracie has set the table with chunks of olive bread and a salad – glossy green against the bright orange glaze of the bowl – and she's at the stove shaking a heavy black pan. 'Pancetta and spinach. Hope that's all right.'

'Great.' Juliet sits down, pulling back a little to let Gracie shake a folded froth of egg onto her plate, yielding to the silky touch of her hair, inhaling the freshness of her, catching the tension dragging at that wide sensuous mouth. 'You still seem upset. Would talking about it help?' Gracie's eyes shift from the pan to find Juliet's face. Juliet picks up her fork, worried she's gone too far. Crossed an invisible line. 'Sorry. It's none of my business.'

Gracie sighs. 'The adoption people say we have to appoint a guardian, someone who'll look after the child if anything happens to us. Tom can't see why I balk at the idea of asking Stella and Todd.'

Juliet doesn't have to feign surprise. 'Why on earth would you want *them*?'

'They're Elsie's guardians. If anything happened to us he thinks both children should stay together.'

'Would Stella and Todd be up for that?'

'Totally,' Gracie says, uncomfortably, 'they love kids.'

'Aren't they too old?'

'Stella's only sixty-four and they're both super fit – all those hours at the tennis club. But I'd rather ask Tom's sister. She's young and funny with a house full of kids and her husband's lovely.'

'Why not ask them to be Elsie's guardians too?'

'Oh God.' Gracie pushes at her hair, a flash of irritation. 'Stella and Todd would have a fit.'

'Really?'

'It was in Louise's will. With the kind of risks she took on location she'd thought a lot about this stuff and she left strict instructions that if she died and anything happened to Tom, Elsie would go to Stella and Todd.'

'Couldn't you talk to them about it?'

'It's a bit of a no-go area. After we got married Tom was pushing for me to adopt Elsie and they got really distressed about it. It didn't seem to matter that we'd never have stopped her being part of their lives.'

'Why don't you ignore what they want and do it anyway?'

'Tom would never do that. He doesn't want to upset them.'

293

'Doesn't that piss you off?'

'It's just the way it is. Day to day it makes no difference.'

'Not the same though.'

'No. No it's not.' Gracie closes her eyes and presses her lips together as if she's holding in some bottled-up thought that's bursting to get out. 'God, this is awful. I should be grateful they'll always be there for her, not bitching about it.' She looks up, slightly panicked. 'Promise me you won't say a word.'

'Of course.'

Juliet's gaze wanders to the crayon drawings on the fridge, hovering on the grinning stick figure of Elsie surrounded by her adoring family before coming to rest on the lonely little picture of herself and Freya. Gracie's waifs and strays. She is only half listening as Gracie complains about the tough time 'poor Elsie' had with the little horrors from St Mathilda's who came over to play.

'Kids can be so cruel,' is about all Juliet can trust herself to say. For a while they pick at their omelettes in silence, until she asks suddenly, 'Does appointing guardians take a lot of paperwork?'

Gracie blinks at her as if her mind's still stuck on Elsie. 'It's just a line in your will. It's finding the right people to do it that's the pain.' She looks sad somehow, lost, almost lonely. 'It has to be someone you trust one hundred per cent. Ideally, a relative or a friend who really cares about you and who'll do everything they can to bring up your child the way you want.' She stands abruptly, clattering the plates, taking them over to the dishwasher. 'One of my suppliers sent me some lovely pears from his orchard. Do you fancy one with some of that smoked Pecorino I bought at the farmers' market?'

Juliet doesn't want pears or bloody Pecorino. It was hard enough getting that omelette down. Is this how a stomach ulcer starts?

Pauline Bryce Diary
July 19th

So this morning I'm dragging myself back from a four-hour cleaning shift and I see a billboard with a perfect-looking woman in a white coat on it telling me that the way I've always wanted to look is closer than I think, so why not book in for a free consultation and hear how her team of skilled cosmetic surgeons can boost my confidence and transform my life? I stop right there in the street. This is why my plans have stalled. I've missed out a vital step.

48

On Saturday morning, as Juliet is getting dressed, she hears the murmur of voices in the hall. She tiptoes onto the landing. From her position behind the balustrade she can't see Gracie, but she can hear her. She's suggesting to Tom that they take Freya with them to lunch at Stella and Todd's. 'It'll be fun for Elsie.'

Tom's voice is low and resigned. 'All right, but no way are we taking her mother.'

'God, no.'

Juliet burns with humiliation, picturing the conspiratorial smiles as they break apart, hearing the lightness in Gracie's step as she runs to the den calling, 'Elsie, Freya, who wants to make a cake to take to Stella's?'

She waits for the squabbling in the kitchen to rise to a peak – Gracie insisting the girls take turns with the mixer, Elsie squawking that Stella is *her* grandma so she should go first – before she creeps downstairs. Gracie's bag hangs from the newel post. She hovers beside it, checking up and down for Heather or Tom, pulsing with nerves as she slides her fingers under the flap, roots around for the keyring and unclips the banana thumb drive. Eyes fixed on the half-open kitchen door, she pushes the drive deep into her pocket and makes her way back to her room. Downloading all those video files is going to take a while. She inserts the drive, slips the laptop into a drawer and covers it with a heap of knickers. Leaving it there to do its work, she heads down to the kitchen. Smiley Juliet, eager to join in the fun.

Juliet stands on the top step to wave them off. Freya looks up briefly, presses her face to the window then turns away – distracted by a game, a drink, a joke – before the car has reached the corner of the square.

Juliet slings her bag over her shoulder and makes for the kitchen, irritated to see Heather's lumpy boyfriend Lyall at the stove frying bacon like he owns the place and Heather laying the table on the terrace. They're both in tennis gear – not a good look for either of them – but it bodes well for their imminent departure.

She hobbles across the grass into the dusty quiet of the summerhouse. Keeping one eye on the terrace she swipes through the download of Gracie's photos. The file is so big she misses the shots she's looking for and has to start again, forcing her fingers to work slowly until she finds the images she glimpsed before. A man and a boy playing in a flurry of snow. She zooms in, cursing the weather, the distance of the figures from the camera and the terrible resolution. Her eyes lock on the grainy blur of red, beige and black as she tries to make out the hazy motifs on their sweaters. She didn't imagine it. They *could* be reindeer. The air in the summerhouse grows heavy, almost stifling. She drags hard on her vaporiser, almost sure that the motifs *are* reindeer. Chunky-knit reindeer sweaters. Just like the ones Matt and Jamie Villiers were wearing in Jess's Christmas photos.

Excitement fizzes in the pit of her stomach. Is this something? Or is she so desperate her mind's playing games?

She concentrates on the background. That definitely looks like tarmac beneath the sprinkling of snow so it could be the car park of the Caxton Arms. If it is then that dark patch on the right must be the gate to the beer garden.

The picture mists and swims. She screws up her eyes, suddenly unsure about the line of red on the left that looks like the side of a phone box. Was there one outside the pub? She can't remember and she's no longer entirely convinced about the heights of the man, or the boy. One seems too tall, the other too short. On the other hand they both look so bulky, wrapped up in those sweaters, scarves and hats, it's hard to tell. Her excitement slows but doesn't stall. Three things keep it ticking over – the Caxton Arms bar menu tucked away in a box file dated six years ago, Gracie's insistence that she first saw Caxton this spring, and Juliet's own hard wish to catch Gracie Dwyer out in a lie.

'What's up with this traffic?' Tom shunts the car forward and pokes his head out of the window.

Another night of bad dreams has left Gracie with a weariness and a sense of detachment, as if she is still trapped in the stifling dark while her life is unfolding elsewhere. Elsie is growing restless in the back, drumming her heels against the seat. With a huge effort of will Gracie turns around and says with a gaiety she doesn't feel, 'I went to the shops and I bought a . . . dragon!'

'My turn,' Elsie squeals. 'I went to the shops and I bought a dragon and a poo-ey potato!' She throws back her head and laughs.

'Yuck. Your turn, Freya.' Gracie glances back and sees Freya's look of panic. 'Just repeat the things we said and add something of your own. Anything you want.'

Freya scans the passing hoardings in search of inspiration. When she speaks it's with the breathy intensity of a witness swearing an oath. 'I went to the shops and I bought a purple dragon, a poo-ey potato and a . . . a green teapot.'

Tom grins and bellows, 'I went to the shop and I bought a purple dragon, a poo-ey potato, a green teapot and a *hungry lion*,' the sound ricochets around Gracie's skull as he rotates his head and lets out a roar. She opens her bag, looking for the headache medication she always carries. The blister pack is empty. Surely she had two left?

Tom turns between white painted gateposts onto the Harpers' wide gravel drive. Stella is coming out to greet them, immaculate in taupe cargo pants, a cream shirt and pearls.

'Darling, how are you?' She's striding towards Tom, narrow fingers coming to rest on his chest as she kisses his cheek, then she turns and throws her arms wide for Elsie, crouching low, supple as a thirty year old, to pull her grandchild close.

Todd is opening Gracie's door, helping her out, dipping down to look into the back seat. 'Who have we got here?'

'This is Elsie's friend Freya.' Gracie opens the back door. 'Hop out, love. Come and say hello to Elsie's grandpa.'

He takes Freya's hand between his, says gently, 'Hello, Freya, I'm Todd.' He whisks her around to the other side of the car. 'Freya, meet Stella, Elsie's granny.'

'Hello, Freya.' With one fluid movement Stella is standing up, shepherding both children towards the house, throwing a smile and a 'Hello, darling, you're looking lovely' over her shoulder to Gracie, who is bending into the boot of the car trying to calm Tallulah's yelping while she tries to open the jammed bolt of the dog cage. 'Tom, could you—?'

'Would you mind carving for me, Tom?' Stella calls. 'Todd's hopeless with lamb.'

And Tom is off, swept away by the remorseless current of Stella's wants and needs.

It's Todd who wrenches open the bolt and lifts out the squirming Tallulah in his big calloused hands. 'Any news on the adoption?'

'We're still being vetted.' She glances nervously at the house. 'But we haven't told Elsie yet so please don't say anything to her.'

'Aren't you supposed to be getting her used to the idea?'

'We will. As soon as we're sure it's going to happen.' She looks up at him, a little shyly. 'Tom told me that you were adopted. I . . . I didn't know.'

'It's not something I really think about.'

'Do you know anything about your birth mother?' she asks in a low voice.

'Only that she had three children and didn't want a fourth. My father was always a little coy about the details but I know that money changed hands. Fifty pounds, I believe. All arranged privately through the local GP.' Todd pushes open the front door and stands aside to let her in.

The house, a detached Arts and Crafts villa a short walk from Wimbledon Common, is cool and airy inside, nothing fussy or overwrought: delicate antique porcelain brought back from Todd's postings in the East, his collection of rare books – mostly poetry – housed in glass-fronted shelves, one or two interesting abstract paintings, and Louise's photographs displayed to catch every turn of Gracie's head.

'Did you ever try to trace her?' she asks.

He seems surprised. 'I had wonderful adoptive parents who loved me. Ties of blood to a woman who didn't give a damn always seemed like an irrelevance.'

Ties of blood, Gracie thinks. Her eyes drift to the kitchen. Through the open door she sees Elsie jostling Freya aside, eager to be first to be measured on Stella's Hogwarts height chart.

'Share nicely now, Elsie!' she calls.

'Tom was saying you won't be offered a new baby,' Todd says.

'No. The child we get will be anything from two upwards, maybe even school age.'

'Well, good for you, you're a wonderful mother. And Stella and I . . . we really want to be involved. What's the point in having a big house like this if we don't fill it with grandchildren?' His pale eyes grow distant, the tears, never far away, creep closer. He lifts Tallulah to his face, fusses her ears and says croakily, 'Probably best to keep this one in the garden.'

Gracie, who wouldn't mind letting Tallulah loose on Stella's Aubusson rugs, follows him into the Harpers' large sunny kitchen.

'You wouldn't have an aspirin, would you, Stella?' she asks. Within seconds a packet of Nurofen and a glass of water are being pressed into her hands. She swallows them quickly, though over-the-counter painkillers are almost useless when her head is like this.

Juliet repositions the laptop on her knees and stares at the screen. It's impossible to tell for certain if these figures in the snow are Matt and Jamie Villiers, but she's pretty damn sure they are. She's aware of the warmth of the summer-house, the trickle of sweat gathering between her breasts and the shape of possibilities shifting. *Why lie to Tom about first visiting Caxton this spring, Gracie? Why hang on to a bar menu from the Caxton Arms for six whole years then pretend you've never been there?*

Juliet closes her eyes and walks the village – rows of immaculate cottages and a few grander houses set back down sweeping drives. That posh gastro pub – the Swan, was it? The twee little shop selling everyday essentials like vacuum packs of organic salmon and fifty varieties of local honey. She enters the Caxton Arms – blackened beams; bottle-green Anaglypta; scorched bricks in the fireplace; bluff, beery Matt drying glasses behind the bar; the corridor leading out to the garden, the snug on one side and on the other . . . she struggles to remember . . . scuffed wooden stairs and a 'residents only' sign pointing up to the rooms they let out for bed and breakfast. The blurb on the pub's website promises *olde worlde* charm. The photos show faded flounces, tired décor and rickety four-poster beds, prompting hazy memories of a long ago one-night stand on a hotel four-poster with a hunky drummer called Jed, who'd had a wife and two kids somewhere in Wales. Disaster. He'd got carried away, swung Juliet sideways with her legs clamped around his waist and nearly knocked her out on one of the bedposts. Thank God she'd been too stoned to feel the pain. Her smile falters. It's months since she's had sex – the disastrous or any other kind. She refills her vaporiser, finishing one of the bottles of liquid Gracie gave her, takes a deep hit of nicotine and exhales. Sex – the cheating kind – that was what she and Ian had lied to each other about, probably what most couples lie to each other about. It's the logistics of it, the sneaky trips to seedy hotels and the shaky alibis, that catch people out. Her eyes dart back to the screen. A sudden image of Gracie Dwyer cheating on Tom on the saggy mattresses of the Caxton Arms brings a snort of laughter. She jerks upright in the lounger, falling back coughing as pain shoots across her rib. Oh God. But the image is delicious. Gracie, disguised in one of her wigs, nipping down a cold dusty corridor to a shared loo, keeping that old bar menu as a memento of their first night of passion. The laughter keeps coming, and yet as she gazes from the sunlight dancing through the overhanging trees to the fluttery distortions the leaves are throwing on the walls, the idea that Gracie might be having an affair keeps on rolling around in her head; a little nub of possibility gathering mass. The confused way she looks at Tom when she thinks no one is watching, her restless need for activity, all that time she spends alone while he's working away, and that night he called her mobile and she avoided picking up.

But why would she want Tom to build a house in the village where she's been meeting her secret lover? Juliet moves to the doorway and looks down at the path, jabbing the rubber tip of the crutch at the lines of moss veining the concrete. A thought slithers in on her. If Caxton's easy for this man to get to she could be building there to be near to him. Didn't she say she was hoping to spend most of her summers at the new house, with Tom visiting at weekends? Excitement flares then sputters out, doused by the memory of Matt's insistence that he and Jess had only known Gracie for a few weeks. Was he too insistent? Look how quickly he'd hung up when she'd tried to press him. Are the Villiers guarding Gracie's secret? Has she secured their loyalty by making them feel special? Gracie's good at that. Look how special she'd made Juliet feel when she reached out to her at the Hub. Promised her the earth then snatched it away.

Her phone beeps. A text from Ian.

Got court order to see Freya Tuesday. Don't piss me about.

Feeling as if she's been punched, she sinks back onto the lounger. What she needs is a lawyer. A good one. One that costs money. That's what everything comes down to in the end, she thinks bitterly. Money she hasn't got. At least, not yet.

49

Stella's lamb is perfectly seared on the outside, perfectly pink on the inside and perfectly carved by Tom. She's made rosemary potatoes, green beans and a *Tarte Tatin* to go with it, served on the terrace overlooking the garden into which Todd has poured his grief. Carefully tended banks of silver and green, pierced with peonies, stocks and clumps of gypsophila spilling over in a lacy foam of remembrance.

Stella keeps the conversation going with the deftness of a diplomat's wife, questioning them about the progress of the chapel and Tom's new project in Dublin. But all the while she's watching Elsie with a sort of glassy enchantment. Now and again she coaxes a smile out of silent, wide-eyed Freya and nods approvingly when Todd spoons the crunchiest potato onto Freya's plate.

After lunch they set off for the common – Tallulah straining at the leash, and the girls darting through the trees as they head for the pond. They throw bread for the ducks but it's the fish that come, dark shapes rising from the depths, Elsie and Freya squealing in disgust as pale gaping mouths break the surface of the water, snap shut around the softening crusts and flip back into the gloom.

Gracie hardly gets a chance to talk to Stella who is always up ahead, pointing out a flock of parakeets or calling to Tom to keep hold of Tallulah while she re-ties Elsie's trainers.

'Any more problems since . . . that business with the bear?' Todd says.

Gracie feels a fleeting pang of annoyance. Tom's been crazy with work since it happened so how does he find time to keep the Harpers updated? Chats in the car on his way to work? Todd at the breakfast table with his mobile on speaker while Stella throws in questions and fiddles with the coffee maker?

'It's worrying that it was something of Elsie's. But the security at the school is fantastic and there's a new detective on the case so we're in good hands.'

Todd reaches out a hand to help her up and over a muddy rut. 'We've always admired how well you cope with all that. Some people wouldn't, you know.'

He is so safe and so solid that she feels an almost unstoppable urge to hang on to his hairy, big-knuckled fingers and tell him about the things she's not coping with, all the little intrusions that feed her paranoia. To explain to him that it's not the obvious violations, the ones the world can see, that now fuel her nightmares. It's the subtle assaults, the hints and whispers that seem designed to mar her judgement and make her doubt her own sanity: the postcard with the illegible signature, the reappearance of Louise's gurning figurine, the graffiti daubed inside the chapel, the rotting pigeon left on her car, the constant sense of being watched and accused by someone whose malign intent is apparent only to her.

After tea and slices of the children's wonky lemon cake served in the garden, Gracie settles into a deckchair while Todd and Stella lug a rope-handled box onto the lawn and unpack hoops and croquet mallets. They applaud Tom's technique and take it in turns to show Elsie and Freya how to bend from the waist and put just the right amount of force behind their swing. Gracie closes her eyes, listening to the laughter and the gentle crack of wood on wood. I'm being ridiculous, she thinks. I have to stop imagining problems that aren't there. Everything is going to be all right.

Juliet dips her hand into the top drawer of Gracie's chest, lifting out the underwear, feeling the flimsy slide of the silk, imagining the barest touch of fingertips on the lace. Whose fingertips though? Gracie's husband's or her lover's?

From nowhere Ian's sneering face looms in her head, calling her crazy, telling her she's 'off on one' again. *Fuck you, Ian. I wasn't 'off on one' when I worked out you were screwing that bitch from De Loitte's.*

That's all she's doing now. Working things out. Asking questions. Testing a theory. Perfectly sane. Perfectly rational. Seeing the holes, like the problem with the dates. If the Caxton Arms bar menu in Gracie's files *is* a memento of time spent with her lover the affair must have started before Gracie met Tom. So why aren't she and this man together?

She runs the flat of her hand along the cool marble edge of the mantelpiece. Maybe he's married and he can't or he won't divorce his wife.

Someone famous then. Or at least in the public eye. That fits. She picks up the framed photo of Tom and Elsie, one finger tracing the line of his dark brows, the shadow beneath his cheekbones and the sculpted curve of his mouth. Any lover of Gracie's would have to have a hell of a lot of money or a hell of a lot of clout to compete with a man like Tom Whittaker.

She sits on the edge of Tom and Gracie's bed to go through the download from Gracie's thumb drive, clicking dismissively through rough cuts of inserts for *Cooking with*

Gracie and radio interviews about the work of Stay Safe, then she's back to the files of photos, spooling past the pictures of Matt and Jamie to shots of the gates of St Mathilda's and Dunsmore Primary, a couple of the chapel with a 'For Sale' sign nailed to its walls and one of a crowded high street taken from across the road on a zoomed lens pushed so far the pictures are almost a blur. She recognises the carpet shop beneath Lynda Burton's school of dance, the wink of fairy lights spelling out pre-Xmas offers on Axminster, a stream of parents heading to Lynda's door. There's Leslie and that nosy cow Dawn. She clicks to enlarge the picture, peering closer. Like the whisper of her own name heard beneath a clamour of shouts, she makes out what looks like the hideous brown coat she only puts on when it's really cold and the lovely pink scarf she lost on New Year's Eve. And then she's sure. There's her own face, dipped into the wind, almost hidden in the crowd, and Freya rushing along beside her carrying her ballet bag, late as usual. She spools on to some kind of event – a bar and a banner – Gracie's book launch. That's Tom's friend . . . what's he called? Geoff. He was at Elsie's barbeque with his kids. Then other faces she recognises from Elsie's party, a reporter from the news and the comedian Rory Devine. Juliet squints at the screen. That's Hugh Dugdale. She's sure Gracie danced with him a couple of times. She was definitely one of the people laughing with him, helping him up when he fell off his unicycle.

The thought goes all through her. Gracie Dwyer and a married MP? She closes her eyes imagining Hugh Dugdale's fleshy body swamping Gracie's toned little torso. If it's true it's perfect. But is it even possible?

Images of the barbeque flicker from light into darkness. For the hundredth time she curses herself for getting drunk, missing out, fucking up. She Googles Dugdale. He has a wife – groomed, hawk-faced Veronica. No sign of her at Gracie's party or in the shots of her book launch. According to the profiles of Dugdale, Veronica is wealthy, scarily well connected and the engine of her husband's ambition. She digs deeper. He's pretty cagey about his home life but finally she discovers three teenage children, one who's in and out of rehab, and another who is seriously disabled. The family home is a moated manor house in Suffolk that's been in Veronica's family for generations but his constituency is less than an hour from Caxton. He sits on the Children, Schools and Families Select Committee and he's tipped for a ministerial post in the next reshuffle. An affair would knock one hell of a dent in his glittering career. But a hunch is no good to Juliet. She needs to come up with hard evidence and her time in this house is running out. She flicks on through Gracie's photos, searching for more images of Dugdale, pausing briefly on a shot of Gracie leaning into the camera, her arms around Elsie, Freya and Jamie at the Caxton rounders match. It's a lovely picture, dappled sunlight, all four of them happy and laughing. Like something out of a bloody Boden catalogue. With one vicious jab Juliet closes the file, pierced by a shaft of envy at Gracie's ability to take pleasure in simple things, to enjoy time with her child instead of always searching for something more than the moment, something to hold back the emptiness.

Pauline Bryce Diary
September 18th

There's a new woman on my shift. We get talking, mostly about ways to make money and she tells me about these clinical trials that pay £2000 just to inject you with viruses and keep you wired up to monitors 24/7. She says she can't do it because she's over thirty and she gets asthma. And I'm thinking I'm young and I'm healthy and for £2000 I can cope with a bad dose of flu and a few days in bed. Use what you've got.

The scents of Tom and Gracie's bath oil, aftershave and perfume linger on the landing as Juliet stands at the arched window watching them leave to see Rory Devine live on stage, her hand pressed against the watery blue glass, Tom laughing as he opens the cab door, Gracie checking her phone as she trips along the pavement in ridiculous heels. The heady feeling of being part of their lives is already dying away, like pleasure in a fading dream. Stumbling down to the kitchen she hears Heather and Lyall laughing in the den, smells the fatty scent of their takeaway and imagines the life of this house going on without her, untouched by her absence.

She pours herself a glass of Tom's single malt and hurries up to Gracie's study, sipping the whisky as she pulls the battered old copy of Mrs Mary Henderson's *Practical Cooking and Dinner Giving* from the desk and rereads the note inside: *A little something to say thank you for last night. H xx*

Is that H for Hugh? Is 'last night' something more intimate than a kitchen supper with friends? A tryst at the Caxton Arms? But if it is, how the hell is she going to prove it? Her fingers close on the handle of the locked bottom drawer. Is this where she hides Dugdale's letters? Or where she keeps a throwaway phone with a single number in the contacts?

Tired and achy, she takes a fresh whisky to bed and tugs *This Is Me* from beneath her pillow. Six months on, Laughton has married Charlie. Desperate to prove her youth by having another baby, she embarks on fertility treatment, giving her readers a blow by blow account of the process that Juliet remembers so well – obsessing about timing, pinching up lumps of her belly for the subcutaneous injections, sinking that needle right in, dealing with the agony each time the bad news comes, capped for Laughton by the horror of hitting her forty-fourth birthday. The chapter about the holiday she takes to recover from the misery of it all comes as a welcome relief.

Juliet reads on, braced for more graphic details of Laughton's treatment – but no, she comes back from holiday and suddenly she's pregnant – Juliet skims over the high-tech, drug-infused birth, picking up the story with Laughton's return from hospital with baby Tybalt in a carrier. *Tybalt!* The poor little sod must be ten or eleven by now.

Juliet turns restlessly beneath the sheet, upset by the eruption of memories of her own years of IVF; the fear that she would never have a child of her own; the sense of dreams and expectations being dismantled, discarded, left to rot; and the sudden joyous reprieve when the pregnancy test finally came back positive.

Of course, the cost of the treatment was never a problem for Laughton, not like it was for Juliet and Ian, though he had been willing to borrow whatever it took to stop Juliet's failure becoming his. That's why he'd been so furious when Freya was born. As if Juliet had deliberately cheated him out of the son he'd bought and paid for. For those first overwhelming, sleep-deprived months the bastard had punished her by barely acknowledging the baby's existence. But later, when it suited him, he'd started acting like Freya was his property – his flesh, his blood, his possession. And now he's got this bloody court order to see her on Tuesday. *Why can't you just leave us alone!*

The front door slams. Tom and Gracie come stumbling and shushing up the stairs. She lies and listens in the heat, imagining the swish of clothing, cool linen, hot skin, pores opening, sweat mingling, strong brown limbs pressing on pale flesh, groans stifled because 'flaky' Juliet is sleeping alone along the landing, not to be disturbed.

50

Juliet's head is all over the place. As she steps out of the shower the tiles around her shiver and blur and she has to press her hand to the wall to steady herself. Oh God, what's the matter with her? She turns on the tap and scrubs cold water across her face. Her body feels a bit better, her mind's still not right. She stands at the window for a moment, listening to the Sunday clamour of the bells of St Stephen's and watching Tom playing rounders with the girls, before she pulls on her dressing gown and shuffles downstairs.

Gracie looks up from her notebook. 'Are you all right?'

'I felt a bit dizzy getting out of the shower.'

'I thought you got your GP to change your painkillers.'

'I'll . . . go back tomorrow.'

'Good. It's probably just the after-effects of the concussion but dizziness isn't something you can afford to ignore.'

Juliet starts away, disturbed to hear Gracie voicing her own unspoken fears: the steady grind of suspicion that this dry mouth and fractured vision might be due to something more than the painkillers – a virus? Something worse? She busies herself cutting bread she doesn't want to eat. 'I don't think the stress is helping. This thing with Ian. I didn't realise how much fallout there'd be.'

Gracie nods but doesn't answer. Too busy scribbling in her bloody notebook.

There's a clatter as Juliet drops the knife. 'Look, I know how much you've done for us already, but . . . well, you said if there was anything you could do to help with the Ian situation.' Gracie looks up again. 'He's getting his first access visit on Tuesday and I . . . I want to make it as normal as possible for Freya. Obviously it's a big ask and I know how busy you are but there's . . . no one else.'

Gracie puts down her pen. 'You've lost me. What is it you need?'

Juliet's jaw shifts. She hears her voice grow soft, almost pleading. 'Would you chaperone her?'

Gracie seems totally thrown, almost panicked.

'She knows you,' Juliet says before Gracie can speak. 'It would be so much less stressful for her if it's you rather than some stranger from social services. All you'd have to do is be there, just for an hour or two.' She waits, expectant. The pause grows uncomfortable.

'I'm . . . I'm sorry,' Gracie raises her hands, her fingers tightening into fists of embarrassment. 'With the adoption people scrutinising everything we do, Tom wants us to keep right off Ian's radar.'

Juliet jerks away, a burst of darkness fragmenting in her head as the anger that's always there flares up, a murky explosion of fury, frustration, exclusion, rejection. *You fucking owe me, Gracie Dwyer!*

Gracie's still going on '. . . is there really no one else?'

Breathe. Breathe. 'I shouldn't have asked.' Juliet moves towards the French windows, one step, then another, in search of air.

313

'Sit down, you look awful.' Gracie pulls her into a chair and squats beside her.

'Why don't you go back to bed and let me bring you up some tea. Don't worry about Freya, she'll be fine with us. We thought we'd go to the steam fair this afternoon.' She takes Juliet's hand and rubs it between her palms. 'I would have chaperoned her if I could. You know that. But I'm sure the person from social services will do her best to make things easy for her.' Mock scolding, she adds, 'And if you don't make that appointment to see the doctor first thing tomorrow, I will. Freya's got enough to deal with without her mummy getting sick.'

Juliet looks into the doe-like eyes of this woman who has everything that she doesn't – money, a husband, a lover, a life – and almost gags on the rush of resentment.

Juliet is dying to go back to bed but she can't afford to waste the time. As soon as Gracie, Tom and the girls leave for the steam fair, she's upstairs logging on to Gracie's computer. It's dangerous. Gracie could be checking her phone right this minute but she's probably too busy playing some chirpy car game with the children. She clicks the speech bubble and keys in *Hugh Dugdale*, an excited fist-clench when she gets a hit. Five messages from Dugdale in the last ten weeks. Only they're not quite the damning proof she's hoping for.

Lunch?

Call me.

Tomorrow any good?

Stefano's at 2?

And then, for a moment her brain stops completely.

Just talked to Daley. Call me.

She reads the line again, word by word, sensing urgency, conspiracy. Why didn't she see it before? Daley's been helping Gracie and Dugdale to cover up their affair, spinning away the rumours, keeping the press at bay. Pent breath hisses through her lips. That's how he managed to hang on to Gracie's business. Not blackmail exactly – Daley's far too smart for that – merely expectation on his part and a fearful gratitude on Gracie's.

Standing there, in that hot bright afternoon with the sounds of the London summer drifting in through the window, Juliet closes her eyes and for the first time in weeks, months, years, she feels close to Gracie. Close to her secrets. On the way back to where she should be.

Her eyes spring open. This still isn't proof. And she can't rely on that locked bottom drawer yielding what she needs. For all she knows it might just be jewellery in there, or the secret recipe for Gracie's bloody brownies. She goes over to stand at the window and gazes over the square. It's busy – a black-clad priest hurrying down the steps of St Stephen's, a deliveryman at the door of number 40, a woman leaving the flats opposite, a couple of boys on skateboards navigating the bumps in the road. It all looks so innocent. But what is she really witnessing? Is the priest everything he seems? Does that woman's husband know where she is? Are those boys going somewhere they shouldn't?

Who could tell her who Gracie sees and where Gracie goes? Who could supply a little substance to test out her theory about Dugdale? Feeling the quick exhilaration of an idea forming, she tips out the contents of her handbag, picking through the clutter until her fingers close around a crumpled business card. Bouncing impatiently on the balls of her feet, she dials the number.

'CGB Security.'

'Hey.' Juliet looks down at the card. 'Is that . . . Chris?'

'Who's asking?'

'Juliet Beecham. We met at Gracie Dwyer's barbeque.'

Gracie loves the soothing clatter of the Monday morning farmers' market, the thump of apples tumbling into a metal scale pan, the slam of a knife through a black-bellied papaya, the rustle and snap of paper bags being ripped from loops of string. She presses her thumbs to the centre of a melon, holding it up to sniff the honey ripeness. She'll make a cantaloupe and strawberry sorbet, a treat for Elsie and Freya. But even as she bites into the fat red strawberry the stallholder gives her to try and holds out her hand to take the paper punnet bloodied with berry juice, she's haunted by the thought of Freya stuck in some soulless room with her father and a cold-eyed stranger. Ian will get angry and Freya will be confused and upset. The courts must be mad to let him see her.

She walks on, viewing the stalls through her big square sunglasses. A couple of times, as she inspects an artichoke or picks through a box of leeks in search of the slenderest, she's tempted to call Juliet and tell her that she *will* chaperone Freya after all. She stops herself. Tom's right. She has to keep away from Ian Murray. Imagine the damage a vindictive man like that could do if he decided to turn his anger on her. She feels terrible, though. Poor Freya. None of this is fair on her.

51

On Tuesday morning, Gracie stays tactfully at the kitchen sink, leaving Juliet to open the door to Freya and the chaperone.

'It's not fair!' Freya yells, as she storms down the hall. 'Why can't I see my daddy on my own!' She crosses her arms and pushes her chin against her chest, the way Elsie does when she's upset, and rushes past Gracie into the garden.

The echo of Elsie in her movements, that stubborn little jerk of the head, shocks and touches Gracie. She plunges her hands into the water and pulls out the plug, reassuring herself of the rightness of her decision. It's hard though, so hard, not to get involved. 'Poor little thing,' she murmurs.

'This is nothing.' Juliet stands at the kitchen door gazing helplessly after Freya. 'Think what she'll have to deal with if he's convicted. People will make her life hell.' Tears slide down her cheeks.

Gracie reacts clumsily, knocking a cup onto the floor, almost crying herself as she bends to pick up the pieces. 'They might not make the connection.'

'Those gossipy cows at Dunsmore? Course they will.'

Gracie drops the broken shards in the bin and wipes her hands with a dishcloth. She has to say something, the right thing. Her mind races. 'She's lucky,' she says at last. 'She's got you. You're tough. You'll protect her.'

Juliet tears off a sheet of kitchen roll and blots her eyes. 'What if something happens to me?'

'Oh, come on. You can't think like that. What did the doctor say?'

'He's changed my prescription. If that doesn't work he'll get me back for some tests.' Juliet doesn't mention their discussion about her anti-depressants, the little boost she still needs to get through each day. 'But if this exhaustion and dizziness does turn out to be something . . . serious. Who's going to look after her then?'

Gracie folds and rehangs the dishcloth. 'There must be someone. An old friend, a relative?'

'It's easy for you, Elsie's got Stella and Todd and Tom's sister. I couldn't even find anyone to chaperone Freya.'

'I wanted to help. You know why I couldn't.' She means it, but her voice sounds false and thin.

'You could be her guardian.' Juliet flings this out like an accusation and stares at Gracie once she's said it.

Outside the clouds break and a slash of sunshine streams in through the French windows. Hot and tense Gracie looks away, unsure where to aim her gaze. '*Me?*'

'Yes.' Juliet comes towards her, visibly strengthened and straightened. 'For Freya's sake.'

'She's a lovely girl. I've grown really fond of her but—'

'It's just a formality. You said so yourself. A line on a piece of paper.'

Gracie steps back, her head shaking slowly. 'It's not just up to me. It would have to be Tom's decision too.'

'So talk to him.'

'There's no point.'

'Why not?'

'You know why not. If Ian decided to get nasty he could make things really difficult for us with social services. We could fail our vetting!'

'Ian wouldn't even have to know. It would be an agreement between you, me and Tom. The thought of Freya ending up in care . . .' she's shaking now, sobs of frustration. 'She needs to be with people she knows. People who understand.'

'Oh, Juliet. I wish I could help.'

'Let me talk to Tom.'

'No!' The movement of Gracie's hand is swift, catching Juliet's arm. 'Please. It's such a tense time for us, it will only make things worse.'

Freya's voice drifts in from the garden. They turn to see her chasing after Tallulah, pigtails flying, and suddenly Gracie's saying, 'Look, put my name down.'

It's as if the words have said themselves. She and Juliet stare at each other. Gracie's breath quickens. 'Just for now,' she adds hurriedly. 'That way you can stop worrying and it'll give me time to talk Tom round.'

'You're serious?' Juliet's voice is cautious.

'I couldn't bear the thought of Freya getting caught up in the care system, or worse still, Ian convincing the courts to give him custody.' She takes a deep shaky breath. 'You have to promise me not to say a word to Tom or anyone else until I've talked to him.'

'No, no of course not.' Juliet sinks into a chair. 'Oh, God. Just knowing that if . . .' She tips forward, screwing up her eyes as the tears come trickling down her cheeks.

'Hey, it's not going to happen. Now come on, you can't let Freya see you like this. Go upstairs and wash your face. I'll bring you a cup of tea.'

This place is worse than prison. The food's disgusting and I'm stuck here feeling like death, surrounded by deadbeats who'll do anything and I mean anything to get their hands on a bit of cash. One bloke, Serge, says he owes thirty grand to a poker syndicate. But he's not worried. He knows about these foreign clinics who pay big money for a kidney, a bit of your liver, things you can live without. I spent all last night thinking about it then this morning I ask him for the number. But now I've got it I'm not sure I'll ever get up the nerve to call.

'Can I come in?' Gracie calls.

Juliet turns from the window. 'Of course.'

Gracie has brought up two mugs. She hands one to Juliet.

'I don't know how to thank you.' Juliet sniffs and rubs her eyes. 'I'll get the paperwork done and drop you a copy.'

'Fine, but we're keeping quiet about it, remember?' Gracie sits on the edge of the bed and sips her tea. 'I've been thinking, next time Ian wants to see Freya, maybe you could pay Heather to chaperone her.'

'Do you think she would?'

'I don't know, but it's worth a try.'

'Sure,' Juliet says, not quite sure what she thinks about this idea.

Gracie crosses her legs and pulls at the hem of her skirt. 'You seem to be managing OK without the crutch now. Does that mean you can drive?'

'I . . . think so.'

'You must be dying to get back home.'

Juliet knows what's coming. She struggles to compose her face, finally managing a grateful smile as she turns back to Gracie. 'Staying here has been wonderful, especially for Freya. She's loved every minute.'

'Honestly, we were happy to help. But Tom is going to be home for the next few weeks and it might be easier to talk him round about the guardianship if . . . if we have the house to ourselves.'

So that's it. Job done. Juliet dismissed.

'There's no rush. He's not back until till Thursday night so if you stay until Thursday morning I can run you and your stuff back on my way to the café.' Gracie is striding to the door. 'If you want I can book Freya into Elsie's drama workshops for the next couple of weeks to give you a bit more time to rest.'

On her way to the bathroom Juliet stops at Elsie's

bedroom door, held by the movement of the ladybird clock; black swivel eyes, tick-tocking down the minutes to her departure from Falcon Square. Gracie agreeing to be Freya's guardian is something but it's not enough. Not enough to ease the pain of being ejected from this house, this life, this proximity. Not enough to secure Juliet a permanent stake in Gracie's world and a chance at a new life. She just has to hope that her night out with Chris will give her what she needs.

52

Eight minutes it takes for Gracie to drive Juliet home. Door to door. World to world. Life to life. And it's all such a rush. Even as she's dropping Juliet's bags in the hallway she's turning to leave.

'I . . . just don't know how to thank you,' Juliet says urgently, as if by speaking fast she can make her stay. 'You've been so . . . wonderful and this guardianship thing . . . it's like this huge weight has been lifted off my mind.' Her gratitude is heartfelt. She looks up, expecting to see compassion, friendship, understanding in Gracie's face. What she sees is pity. It's gone in an instant, replaced by a brisk smile but the memory throbs like a burn – Juliet, the flake. The lame duck. 'R' for 'Reject'.

'It was the least I could do,' Gracie says. 'Don't worry about picking Freya up from the workshop. Heather will drop her back.'

They kiss. Once on each cheek. There's no embrace, just the cool airy scent of Gracie drifting away as she opens the door. 'You look after yourself,' she says. And then she's gone.

Juliet stumbles into the living room. The darkness opens

up, the same gaping emptiness that engulfed her six years ago when it hit her, finally, that Gracie Dwyer was never going to return her calls. She throws open the doors to the balcony and stands looking out at the spire of St Stephen's. She can't do this. She can't let the old life suck her back. She breathes slowly. Telling herself it's going to be all right. If she sticks to her plan it won't be like before. Once she gets proof of Gracie's affair with Dugdale there'll be no problem leaking it to the press from a Daley Associates email. The challenge is going to be transforming herself from the charity case who provoked that sickening look of pity, into the indispensable friend and trusted PR Gracie turns to when her perfect life goes belly up.

Right now though, she's got an eleven o'clock appointment with her solicitor. By the time she leaves his office and walks out onto Upper Street she's feeling more upbeat, deciding to wait a day or two before she drops a copy of her amended will round to Gracie. For now it's enough to hold the documents in her hand, signed, witnessed and sealed.

The streets are full. She manoeuvres her way through the bustle, dodging a mobility scooter and leaping back as a bus scrapes the kerb. A taxi pulls up. An elegant older woman steps out in a tailored sky-blue dress. She casts her eyes up and down the street before turning into a café on the other side of the road. It takes Juliet a second to place her. It's Stella Harper.

Juliet cuts through the traffic and approaches the café door, snapping back when she sees who Stella is meeting. It's Heather. She leans in for another look. Heather's got the drinks in, ready and waiting, a latte in a tall glass beaker and tea in a little white pot. Juliet walks on, her fingers tightening around the envelope in her hand. They're friends. Stella and that snarky little bitch are friends. A coven of two.

* * *

324

Juliet sits up late, alone and awake in the green glow of the television, desperate to think up a way to recalibrate her relationship with Gracie. What she needs is a wrong she can right. Forget work, this has to be personal. She sips her wine, letting the little nuggets of negativity she's gleaned about Gracie's life click and tumble through her head. Next door there are voices, something drops and rolls, a baby whimpers.

Gracie is in denial about it but any fool can see that Stella Harper hates her guts. Gracie stepped into her dead daughter's shoes. Why wouldn't she hate her? And what's Heather's game? Is she Stella's eyes and ears, reporting back what goes on at number 17? Because that's what it looks like. Juliet tucks these little insights away. She can't use them. Not yet, anyway. Then there's Gracie's obsessive adoration of Elsie, as if she's blind to what a revolting little monster she is. It's Gracie's own fault for spoiling her. Overcompensating for the one big hole in her life.

Juliet thinks back to the sunlit intimacy of their conversation at Caxton: the sadness in Gracie's face when she'd talked about the baby she'd lost and her subsequent infertility, Tom's yearning for another child, all that probing about Juliet's own pregnancy and Gracie's tremulous admission that she doesn't talk about her miscarriage very often. But there she was, talking about it to Juliet.

Not to Daphne.

Or to Jess.

To Juliet.

It's almost dawn when the thought comes, slowly at first, an uneasy flicker that grows with the rattle of traffic, the first gleams of daylight and the sounds of the girl in the flat upstairs clacking her way back from another night out.

You're crazy. Ian's voice hisses in her head. The mocking smile, the finger circling his temple.

She gets up.

Makes a coffee.

Walks around.

The more she thinks about it the less ridiculous the idea seems. She checks her contacts, tries a number. It's no longer in use.

'Mummy.'

Freya stands at the door in her pyjamas. 'Is it time to get up?'

'Not yet, love. Go back to bed.'

'My bed's itchy. I want to go back to Elsie's.' Her lips wobble into a wail. 'I want Talloooolah!'

Juliet puts on her best Gracie voice, 'Why don't you cuddle down on the sofa and I'll make you a hot chocolate.'

Freya scrambles onto the cushions and sits pouting with her arms crossed tightly across her chest. Juliet opens the fridge. Her heart sinks. She forgot to buy milk.

53

Walking through Chelsea later that morning brings it all back, the adrenaline rushes of hope, the worry about money, the squeeze of her gut when she sees the lettering engraved on the glass door. A couple brush past her on the steps, tight smiles, clutching each other's hands. She follows them to the reception desk, overcome by the familiar smell of tension and hope. She doesn't recognise the blonde at reception. Why should she? It's seven years since her last appointment. The woman looks up, selecting from a ready store of smiles. The one she picks for Juliet is concerned.

'Are you all right?'

'Fine. I'm trying to get in touch with a nurse who used to work here . . . Dylan Holt?'

'Not since I've been here.'

A woman in scrubs pushes through the swing doors.

The receptionist beckons her over. 'Rhianne. Do you remember Dylan Holt?'

The woman looks Juliet squarely in the eye and shakes her head. 'Sorry.'

The receptionist calls into the back office. 'Eileen, someone here looking for Dylan Holt. Mean anything to you?'

A second woman comes out – older, brisker. 'May I ask why you want him?'

'I'm an old friend of the family. I heard his mother was unwell. I . . . I wanted to visit her.'

The woman shakes her head. 'He left almost five years ago.'

'Would your HR people have a forwarding address?'

'They don't give out personal information. The best they could do is pass on your number.'

Juliet writes *formerly Murray* beneath the *Beecham* on one of her cards and pushes it across the desk, though whether Dylan will remember her among so many she's not sure. 'Thing is, I'm not in England for very long so if you could ask around the other staff I'd be incredibly grateful.'

She stumbles out into an opulent world of stucco façades and neatly trimmed box trees, exhaustion rushing in to replace the excitement that has kept her going through the night. She's making her way back towards the King's Road, staring unseeingly into the window of a smart little boutique, when she becomes aware of a woman coming up behind her.

'You're looking for Dylan?'

Juliet turns. The woman is young, neat, business-like.

'Are you from the Selway?'

'I'm one of the lab technicians. Can I ask why you want him?'

'I . . . heard his mother wasn't well.'

The woman's eyes hold Juliet's. 'His mother died three years ago.'

'So you know him.'

The woman gives a non-committal shrug and glances back towards the clinic. 'I have to get back. What's this really about?'

'He helped me once and I . . . I want to know if he still has . . . contacts who could help me again.'

The woman eyes her steadily.

She's one of Dylan's scouts, Juliet thinks. She's worried I'm a cop. 'Look. You can check out my records. Ten years ago I registered at the Selway. I had three unsuccessful rounds of IVF and they put me on the waiting list for egg donation. But I didn't want to wait. I wanted to save my marriage, and my husband was willing to pay whatever it took to have a child.'

The woman says nothing.

Juliet leans in. 'Dylan offered to help us. He arranged everything.'

The woman looks over Juliet's shoulder. 'Did it work out?'

'The treatment – yes, I have a daughter. The marriage? No. We're separated.'

'So why do you want Dylan now?'

'I . . . I'm thinking about having another baby and I want Dylan to fix me up with the same donor but the number I've got for him doesn't work any more.'

'Give me your number. I can't promise anything but I'll see what I can do.'

Juliet hands her a card. 'Tell him I was Juliet Murray back then.' She watches the woman slip the card into her top pocket.

'Why did he leave the Selway? Did someone get suspicious?'

'I have to go.'

Juliet carries on walking east, into the glitzy heart of Chelsea, imagining the life that could be hers if she can just keep her nerve. She's stopping at a café scraping back the chair of a pavement table when her phone buzzes. 'Hello.'

'Mrs Murray. You were looking for me.'

'Dylan. Thanks for calling.'

'I hear you want the same service as before.'

'Yes. And the same donor.'

'Why don't we meet for a chat? I've got an hour or so at twelve.'

'Where?'

'How about Cleopatra's Needle?'

She cuts the call and lays her phone on the table, overcome by a giddying swell of certainty that this is what Gracie wants.

54

'We've got something very special to tell you.' Tom lifts Elsie onto his knee. Gracie edges close, laying her hand on that fragrant little head, feeling the firm bounce of her hair beneath her fingers.

Elsie sits up, arms folded, mouth pursed in expectation. In her world 'special' heralds something good. And so it should, Gracie thinks. She's devoted the last five years of her life to protecting this child, keeping the bad things at bay.

'Mummy and Daddy love you so much,' Tom is saying, 'that we want to give you a brother or sister.'

'A baby?' Elsie blinks at him. 'Is Mummy going to have a baby? Like Merion?'

'Merion?' Tom is bemused.

Scornful, Elsie folds her arms. 'Freya's daddy's girlfriend,' she says, as if he should know, as if this child of Merion's is something talked about all the time in this house. Maybe it has been, in those whispered conversations between Elsie and Freya, under the duvet, in the dark.

The mention of Ian is making Tom tense. Gracie steps in to steer the conversation back on course. She avoids his eyes and says uneasily, 'Not quite the same as Merion, Elsie. Your brother or sister isn't going to come out of my tummy.'

She glances up at Tom. His eyes implore her to go on. 'Our new child will be a little boy or a little girl who needs a new mummy and daddy.'

'Why?'

'Well, it might be because their mummy and daddy can't look after them properly or because their mummy and daddy have—' she pauses, softening her voice, 'because they've died.'

Elsie shoots Tom a knowing look. 'Like my other mummy.'

'Yes,' Tom nods, encouragingly. 'Just like that. And you and Mummy and I are going to love this new little boy or girl as much as we all love each other.'

Elsie blinks again, unconvinced. 'I want a baby. Freya's getting a baby.'

'We can't have a baby, love,' Tom says.

Elsie swivels round to look at Gracie. 'You got me when I was a baby.'

Tom's smile is tender. 'That's right but when the old mummy is still alive, the new mummy and daddy have to wait in case she gets well enough to have her baby back.'

She slides off his lap. 'Are we going to get it now? Can I choose?'

'No, love.'

Elsie pouts. 'Why not?'

'Because it's very special to be allowed to adopt a child and it takes a long time. But it means we can get ourselves ready. You can help Mummy choose things for their room and you can pick out some toys.'

'I want to pick his name.'

'This brother *or* sister will already have a name,' Gracie says gently. 'If we change it they might get all confused about who they are.'

332

'I want a boy.'

'You don't get to choose that either,' Tom says. 'Any more than you can when the baby comes out of its mummy's tummy.' He laughs. 'You get what you're given. And last time I got you.'

He scoops Elsie up and twirls her around, making growling noises into her neck. Elsie shrieks with delight and Gracie looks on, feeling as if her pounding heart will burst.

Juliet blinks into the sun as she weaves past slaloming roller skaters and tourists framing selfies against the backdrop of the Thames. For a few dazed moments she's gripped by the familiar feeling that the life of the city, with all its bustle and purpose, is rolling past her like the river, leaving her alone, untouched, unneeded. And then, through the crowd, she sees Dylan leaning against the base of Cleopatra's Needle, and her dejection dissolves. Everything is about to change. Afraid he won't recognise her, she's rising a little on her toes, holding up her hand. 'Dylan!'

He pushes towards her. 'Mrs Murray—'

'It's Beecham now.'

'So, how are you?'

'All right. And you?' Her eyes slide from his well-cut suit and buffed fingernails to the slim gold watch on his wrist. 'Things going well?'

'Not bad. I've branched out.'

Her brows lift.

'With all these new advances in transplant technology there's an awful lot of buyers out there needing help to find the right sellers.'

'Do you still offer donor and recipient anonymity?'

'Absolutely.'

'And no need for any kind of registration?'

He shakes his head.

She glances around and drops her voice. 'So if I wanted another baby, the father, the sperm donor, he wouldn't need to know it wasn't my egg?'

His eyes meet hers. 'If it's that important to you it would be safest to freeze his sperm so he's not at the clinic when the procedure takes place. You wouldn't want anyone letting anything slip.'

She watches a little boy trying to scramble onto the slippery flank of the statue of the Sphinx. 'And I can use the donor I had before?'

A pause. She looks up. He's running the back of his thumb across his forehead.

'Unfortunately that won't be possible.'

'Why not?'

'After we spoke I made some calls. She seems to have slipped off the radar.'

Juliet sways unsteadily. She blinks hard. 'What do you mean?'

'It looks like she used a false name.' A dismissive hand flick, as if to bat this elusive donor out of the equation. 'She'd be pushing it age-wise anyway. Far better to go with someone younger. I've got two students in mind for you. Smart, athletic, good-looking girls, your sort of height and colouring, both with at least one live birth behind them, ready to fly out to Greece whenever it suits you.'

'No!' her voice comes out choked. 'This baby has to be Freya's *real* sibling! It has to look like her. That's . . . important.' *Important that Gracie and Tom think that I'm the biological mother.* The thought of the unbreakable bond that she and Gracie will share brings back the dizzying conviction that this is what Gracie wants.

She feels Dylan's hand on her arm steering her towards an empty bench. 'I told you, the name and contact details

334

she gave me drew a complete blank. I'm sorry. I checked her ID at the time, I thought she was reliable. But don't worry. She couldn't fake her medical tests. She was in excellent health. So, would you like me to set you up with one of these other donors?'

A waterbus glides past. Possibilities slip away. She can't give up now. 'You said she was desperate for money. I remember. You said she'd do as many cycles as we needed.'

'She got greedy, kept upping her price, so I stopped working with her.'

Juliet flounders. 'But you think she went on donating?'

'Oh, yes. She was out to make as much money as she could in as short a time as possible.'

'Can you at least give me the name she gave you?'

A flash of expensively capped teeth. 'You know I can't do that.'

'Even if it was fake?'

The smile fades. 'Yes.'

'I don't remember you being so scrupulous back then.' She grips his sleeve. 'Pouncing on desperate couples. A whisper of hope and a flight to a discreet foreign clinic. No waiting list, no regulation. Is that why you left the Selway? Did they realise what you were up to?'

He leans into her and hisses softly, 'I just find suitable matches and point them in the right direction.'

'For a fee,' she snaps. 'Last time I looked that was still very much illegal.'

He gets to his feet, offended. Juliet blinks rapidly, regretting losing her temper. 'Sorry . . . look, I'm sorry. I can pay you. I haven't got the money right now but I . . . I can get it. I just need that name.'

'We're both wasting our time, Ms . . . Beecham.'

'Please.'

He shoves a card into her hand. 'Call me if you want to

go ahead with one of these other donors. Otherwise I can't help you.'

He's walking away, disappearing into the entrance to the tube. Juliet stands up. It's a blow to her plans but would it really matter if the donor were different this time? If Elsie is anything to go by, Tom's genes would be dominant. In fact Elsie doesn't look anything like Louise so there's no reason why this new child should look like its mother. The important thing is that Juliet would become an integral part of the Whittakers' lives, tied to them by a bond like no other. And if ever, *God forbid*, anything should happen to Gracie, she would be the one Tom would turn to. His friend and comforter. The second mother to his child. She calls Dylan, gets no reply and sends him a hurried text.

Sorry. Let's go ahead with one of your other donors.

55

Walking back from Camden Lock, Gracie is aware of how tired and stressed she feels. Juggling so many projects is taking its toll and her dreams are getting darker and coming almost every night. Even so there's a growing excitement at the thought of the coming year, when all the strands of her new life will come together. It's taken months of careful planning. The builders are making decent progress in Caxton, the chapel should be finished by early February and when she gets back from shooting *Cooking with Gracie USA* everything should be ready for the new addition to her family.

A figure appears in her peripheral vision. A vague impression of height, breadth, tattoos and piercings before a juddering thump of muscle spins her around. Her self-defence training kicks in. She reaches for her inner aggressor, ready to scream and claw and twist and jab, but the man is already a hundred yards down the street, shouting drunkenly into his phone. She pushes back the panic and makes for the safety of Gracie's Kitchen, forcing herself to take small measured steps. By the time she gets upstairs to her private shower room and splashes her face with water her breathing is almost steady and her heart is slowing down. She stares for a moment at her reflection then puts on some lipstick, tidies her hair and walks across the landing to her office to ring down for coffee.

'I'll bring it up,' Sally says. 'The builders called. There's a problem with the sewage at the chapel.'

Gracie groans. Tom should be dealing with this. She's got meetings to prepare for. She texts him quickly, and she's deep in a spreadsheet when the intercom buzzes.

'Gracie. Juliet Beecham's here to see you. She says it's important.'

Surprised and a little worried, Gracie flicks on the speaker. 'Send her up.'

She's watching the door, half standing up as Juliet comes flying in. 'Is it Freya? Has something happened with Ian?'

'No, everything's fine.' Juliet doesn't seem at all distressed, in fact there's an almost manic breeziness about her.

Gracie flops back into her chair. 'Thank goodness for that.'

'Have you got a minute?'

Gracie bounces her palms on the papers on her desk and smiles apologetically. 'Is it urgent? I've got a supplier coming in.'

'It won't take long.' Juliet thrusts out an envelope, as if it's something Gracie is expecting.

For a few embarrassing seconds she thinks Juliet is giving her money. 'What's this?'

'A copy of my amended will. I've had it stamped and notarised so it's all official.'

Gracie stares at the envelope, her mind for a moment numb. Then it snaps into gear. 'Oh . . . Oh. . . that was . . . quick.' Her fingers close around the envelope. She pulls out the document and there it is in black and white. She is now Freya's guardian. She looks up, horribly conscious of Juliet staring at her, that unnerving smile on her face. 'I . . . I

338

haven't mentioned it to Tom yet, so best keep this between us for a bit longer.'

'That's why I brought it here rather than the house.' Juliet's eyes still hold Gracie's as she moves to sit down. 'It's such a massive weight off my mind. I can't tell you how grateful I am.'

'Honestly. Don't worry about it.'

'I do, though. You and Tom have been so good to me. I don't know how I'd have got through the last few weeks without your help and I . . .' she's getting out her laptop '. . . I think I've found a way to repay you. Both of you.'

Gracie glances at the time and shifts uncomfortably, her gaze straying back to the spreadsheet. 'Really, there's no need.'

Juliet leans in close. Too close, her eyes wild and expectant. 'You know what you were saying about it being almost impossible to adopt a new baby . . .'

Gracie nods slowly, trying to fathom where this is going, even more bemused when Juliet opens her laptop like a salesman opening a case of samples and says, 'I might be able to help.'

'Do you know someone who wants a private adoption?'

'No. No. It's more . . . well,' her words come out in halting breaths, 'if you wanted to reconsider the surrogacy option . . .'

Gracie shudders a little. 'I told you,' she says firmly, 'I couldn't possibly pay a stranger to carry my baby.'

'Not a stranger. And there'd be no question of payment.' Juliet's head shakes exaggeratedly from side to side, her smile broadening. 'I like to think we've become friends, good friends and since you've offered to be Freya's guardian—'

Gracie's eyes find the envelope Juliet just thrust at her. Actually I didn't offer, she thinks, it was you who pushed for it.

339

'. . . and pregnancy was so easy for me, it would make perfect sense for me to be your surrogate.'

Gracie knows that she's gaping and recoiling but the voltage of shock is so high the words 'No! God, no' are out before she can stop them. Juliet is staring at her, hurt and bewildered. Gracie flushes, struggling to cover her horror. 'It's . . . it's an amazing offer, so kind, but I . . . I couldn't possibly accept.'

Juliet pulls an impatient face. 'I wouldn't smoke or drink if that's what you're worried about.'

'It's not that—'

'I know this fantastic clinic in Greece, totally discreet. No one would ever need to know except us.' She's turning the laptop around, showing her the clinic's website and speaking fast as if all it needs for Gracie to see sense is a little more explanation.

Gracie stares at the picture on the screen, groping for a way to make this stop.

'This way the baby would be Tom's biological child, just like Elsie, only it would also be yours from birth. Isn't that what you wanted? Someone you could trust to hand it over as soon—'

Sally's voice cuts in through the intercom. 'Mr Donahue's here. Shall I send him up?'

Gracie hits the speaker switch. 'Yes!' Never has she been so pleased to see a supplier. Standing up quickly, she steps back as if to put more distance between herself and Juliet. 'I've got a meeting . . . I can't talk about this now . . . I'm sorry. I. . . I'll call you.'

The silence that follows is excruciating. She's conscious of Juliet getting up, walking towards the door. She can't look at her. She struggles to murmur goodbye and can't get her breath until the footsteps on the stairs have died away.

Pauline Bryce Diary
August 22nd

*I wake up feeling even shittier than usual. The Six-Point
Guide tells you to deal with the bad days by going
through your diary and reminding yourself how far
you've come. But it's making me feel worse. In a year
and a half I've only hit one target – getting to London
– and now I'm here I can't move on because I don't
look the way I need to look and I haven't got the
money to change that so I'm stuck. And now I'm
looking at that number Serge gave me. So I make the
call. Just to see what they say. The woman I talk to
is a bit cagey but she books me in for some tests. She
says if I pass the medical they'll fly me abroad and
pay me ten grand – five now, five when it's over. If it
all works out I can do it again in a couple of months.
Half of me's thinking, where's the catch? The other
half's thinking, Do it. How else are you going to get
your hands on that kind of money?*

56

Juliet blunders into the road, shaking her head to dislodge the sound of Ian's laughter echoing through the sleep-deprived depths of her brain. She almost walks in front of a van. She reels back, nearly slips, barely able to focus on where she is. Then she's racing down the pavement, barging into a bar, the skin of her cheeks red and hot as if she's been slapped.

She orders a beer and sits alone in the gloom, ugly flashes of embarrassment breaking through the anger as she relives the disdain on Gracie's face. No point kidding herself, that's what it was – complete and utter disdain.

So why all the wide-eyed misery about her fertility? Why go on and on about Juliet's pregnancy if she hadn't been angling for her help? Gracie had practically spelled it out . . . 'a sister or a close friend', someone she could totally trust. *But that's what you do, isn't it, Gracie? You test people out to see if you can use them then you drop them and file them away under 'R' for 'Reject'.*

Who the hell does Gracie Dwyer think she is? Sneaking around with her lies and her lover, picking people over, discarding them like bits of rotten fruit. It's a game with

342

her, just like before, singling Juliet out, stringing her a line about working together, promising to keep in touch when all the while she was signed up with Jeremy fucking Daley. Tom needs to know that his angel wife is a liar and a cheat who messes with people's minds and fucks up their lives. But he won't believe 'flaky' Juliet, not without proof. He'd accuse her of being vindictive and jealous. She's aware of her lips and fingers moving to the beat of her anger. Her eyes fly up from her beer.

The couple at the next table are watching her, pitying, smirking. She glares back. *Fuck you.* Their stares shift from her to each other. They hunch over their drinks, rolling their eyes and raising their eyebrows the way Ian used to, as if she is deranged, dangerous, unfit to bring up her own bloody daughter. She grabs her bag and pushes through the tables to the door.

57

Juliet sees Chris at the bar, sharing a joke with the barman. She checks her watch. She's timed it exactly right. Twelve minutes late. Just long enough for him to down one drink and order another. She approaches slowly, glad of the low lighting, though she's done her best with her hair and makeup and she knows her legs look good in heels.

'Hey, Chris. Sorry I'm late. Did you get my text? Babysitter got held up.'

He leans back a little and runs his eyes quickly from her face to her toes. 'No problem.'

He'd forgotten what I look like, Juliet thinks. She searches his eyes for disappointment. He gives her a lopsided grin and finishes his whisky. 'What are you drinking?'

'Vodka tonic.' She'll make it last. She's not here to get pissed. She perches on the stool beside him, watching his face as he calls to the barman.

'Been to any more children's parties?' she says.

'No, but I got lumbered with the kids of some Saudi prince for a day. Two hours in Harrods and I was praying an armed kidnapper would turn up and put us all out of our misery.'

She laughs. 'That bad?'

'Little sods.'

Juliet finds herself relaxing. He smells of shower gel, the nails of his stubby fingers are clipped and clean and there are more streaks of grey in his hair than she remembered. She clasps her wrist and takes a sip of air as she rotates her hand.

'You all right?'

She smiles stoically. 'I was down in Caxton with Gracie and I fell off a bike. Honestly, can you imagine? Sprained my ankle, cracked my rib and buggered this wrist. Don't know how I'd have managed if Gracie hadn't asked me to stay at Falcon Square.'

There it is. The Gracie effect. The instant shift in the way he's looking at her.

'So the two of you are close?'

'We got friendly through our daughters. They're inseparable. Have you got kids?'

'One. Tanya. She's twelve. Lives with her mother.'

'Do you see much of her?'

'One weekend in three. But it's the day-to-day things I miss. Taking her to school, yelling at her to clean her room, helping her with her homework.'

'My ex couldn't give a damn about that kind of stuff.'

He shrugs. 'As far as I'm concerned it's the whole point of being a dad.'

This isn't the conversation she'd expected to have. She adjusts her skirt so it's not riding quite so high. They sip their drinks and the talk flows so easily she almost forgets why she's here, though she's careful to stick to her limit of one vodka, smiling indulgently when he orders himself a third whisky.

'How long have you been working for Gracie?' she says.

'Couple of years.'

'Did she hire you because of the stalking?'

He nods. 'Tom's idea, though it's just occasional low-key stuff. Mostly driving her around or mingling with the crowd when she's at an event.'

'Do you ever see anything suspicious?'

'All the time. Gracie's so lovely people feel drawn to her and there's always a few who get intrusive.' He trickles a handful of peanuts into his mouth and chews thoughtfully. 'But I'm convinced her primary stalker was someone she knows.'

'*Primary* stalker?'

'These things are infectious. One nutter starts something, it gets picked up in the papers and some other lowlife decides they'll take a pop at the same target.'

Juliet toys nervously with her glass. 'The other night I caught Elsie playing with one of her mum's wigs.'

He seems surprised. 'I never saw her in a wig.'

'I think she kept them for when she went out on her own.'

'It must be hell living with that kind of fear. Like she says, even when it stops she's always on edge, waiting for it to start up again.'

As they move over to their table Juliet finds she's rather enjoying the pressure of his hand against the small of her back. While they wait for their food, he tells her stories about his clients – the money, the drugs, the escort hired by a wealthy Russian who got all hoity-toity about being frisked. 'I said to her, look, I just need to check that you haven't got any weapons concealed about your person. So she sticks her nose in the air, says, "I assure you that won't be necessary", drops her fur coat right in the middle of the lobby and walks stark naked into the lift.'

Juliet is still laughing when their steaks arrive but she hasn't forked out thirty quid for a babysitter to listen to

346

anecdotes about arsey call girls. 'Gracie's barbeque must have seemed pretty tame to you but it's the most glamorous party I've been to for a long time. A real treat.' She watches his face. He's buying every word. 'It's nice how she mixed everyone up. Dreary mums like me rubbing shoulders with the rich and famous.'

He runs his hand lightly over hers. 'I'd never call you dreary.'

She raises her wine glass with a mock coy look. 'Why, thank you.' She takes the tiniest sip and shakes her head when he offers her more. As he pours himself another glass she slips off a shoe and lets her foot brush against his leg.

'That MP, Hugh Dugdale. He always looks so serious on telly but he was really letting his hair down.'

'He's a decent bloke.'

'Was his wife at the party?'

He gives her an odd look. 'She leads her own life.'

Juliet raises an eyebrow.

'They have an *arrangement*.'

Juliet leans closer, exhilarated that her investment in a babysitter is about to pay off. 'Dugdale has . . . affairs?'

'It's more than an affair. Been going on for years.'

'And his wife *knows* about it?'

'It was tricky at first but she's cool with it now. I heard she's got together with her estate manager. Touch of the old Lady Chatterley.'

'How do you know all this?'

'I'm good mates with a couple of government drivers, plus in my job you hear all sorts.'

Keep it casual. 'So why don't they get a divorce?'

'He's chairing some long-drawn-out defence inquiry and the PM doesn't want news of his private life muddying the waters.'

'Makes sense.'

'Dugdale's more worried about his kids. The older girl's got problems. He's not sure how she'll cope.'

'Is divorce such a big deal these days?'

'No, but as soon as he comes out there'll be all kinds of homophobic crap flying round on social media.'

Faintly, from somewhere far away, Juliet hears the clink of cutlery and the sound of laughter. She looks around her at the dark leather seating, the low hanging lamps and the pool of light around the bar and feels hot and stupid, as if she's been the victim of a vicious practical joke. *I don't believe it. I don't fucking believe it. Fuck! Fuck! Fuck!*

'I'm trusting you to keep this to yourself,' he says hurriedly.

She nods. Still speechless.

'Poor bloke's terrified one of the tabloids is going to out him before his eldest gets herself sorted. As far as I can make out it's Gracie and that friend of hers . . . Daphne who are holding him together. They've got some mate of theirs standing by to limit the damage but the news could break any time.'

She goes from hot to cold. It's Daley. He's talking about Daley. Limp and dazed, she murmurs, 'So who . . . who's the boyfriend?'

He laughs. 'I'm pissed but not that pissed. All I'll say is that he's a household name. Hey, you're shivering.'

Juliet is aware of him standing up and slipping his jacket around her shoulders. The silkiness of the lining is cool against her itchy skin, the smell of his cologne clean and citrusy.

'Thanks.'

'You've hardly touched your steak.'

'I haven't had much of an appetite since the accident.' She looks at her watch. 'I have to get back.'

'Juliet.' His hand on her arm. 'I'd like to see you again.'

348

She gazes at him, as if through a haze of smoke and dust. For a minute it clears and what she sees is a nice, middle-aged, lonely guy, with a decent body and a sense of humour. Someone she could learn to trust. 'I . . . I'd like that.'

He grins that lopsided grin and lifts his hand to call for the bill. By the time the waitress comes the dust has closed in again, blanketing Juliet's world in a gritty pall of frustration.

58

Juliet mashes a cigarette into the saucer beside her. She should have known it wouldn't work out. Nothing ever does. Not for her. She lights another cigarette. The infuriating thing is she's still sure that Gracie is lying about Caxton. All right, maybe she's not using the Caxton Arms to meet Dugdale but there's something about that place she's keeping from Tom, some reason she doesn't want him knowing she's been there before. If Juliet can just find out what it is her plan might still work. But what has she got to go on? A fuzzy photo taken in the snow and a six year old bar menu kept in a file that happens to include her own business card. She runs jerky hands up and down her arms. She's obsessing again, she knows that, but she can't help giving in to a new tug of possibility, an undertow of hope that the key to Gracie's secret lies in the link between those four scraps of pasteboard in the 'R' file. She checks her phone. Five missed calls from Gracie and an apologetic text. Let her stew.

She opens her laptop. She'd never heard of the Forward Gallery or the Caxton Arms till she opened the 'R' file, and you'd never catch her watching the sleazy soft porn thinly disguised as reality TV churned out by Laughton's Wink

Productions. Not unless she caught it by mistake and there was nothing else on. She inhales deeply and watches the smoke curl away.

All right. Forget the businesses. What if it was the people *behind* the businesses that Gracie had been interested in? People she checked out with a particular project in mind and for some reason found wanting. She pulls up a publicity shot of Lana Laughton in a slit-fronted shirt and shiny, thigh-length boots. How did *you* fall short, Lana? Too brash? Too cheap? Too indiscreet? And that artist Olga Maswell. What was her problem? Too glum, too old, too bloodless? A quick Google search reveals that she dropped dead six months after her exhibition. No surprises there.

She adds the photo from Olga's obituary to the line-up of faces – a frail old woman in death-defiantly dangly earrings, next to shots of Jess Villiers in her light-up antlers, Lana in her fuck-me boots and the only photo of herself she doesn't hate.

Come on. Four women. What's the link between us? There must be something. She remembers what Gracie said about shuffling bits of paper around to help order her thoughts when she's working on a project. She prints out the pictures, slams open the kitchen drawers in search of scissors and cuts out the photos, then she lays them out face down on the table as if they are cards and she's a fortune teller. One by one she turns them over in search of revelation. Olga, Juliet, Lana, Jess. Come on, Gracie, what project was this? What order? What thoughts?

There's nothing.

'Of course there's nothing.' Ian's mocking voice rings through her head. 'Because *you're* nothing, Juliet. Nothing to Gracie Dwyer. Never were. Never will be. Just a crazy drunk. A lame fucking duck!'

Shut up! Her thoughts flit wildly, trying to gain traction

351

in the cluttered workings of her brain. She gathers up the pictures, shuffles them and deals again. Lana. Jess. Olga. Juliet.

Her hand hovers. Slowly she moves her own photo to sit beside posh frowsy Jess Villiers. What have the two of them got in common? They both know Gracie Dwyer. They've both got a kid. Apart from that? Sod all.

She takes a sip from her glass and pairs trashy Botoxed Lana with wasted white-haired Olga. Not exactly two of a kind. She rummages in her bag for the catalogue of Olga's exhibition and flicks to the biography at the back. The old girl had quite a life – Swiss finishing school, two years as a 'secretary' at Bletchley Park and stints in China, Russia and Paris with the Foreign Office. Never married. Never had kids, and Juliet's pretty damn sure she never appeared on any low-rent reality TV shows. *Okay, so just for a minute let's forget about the dead.* She presses two fingers into Olga's watery eyes and slides her photo to one side. What she's left with is a trio of women aged between thirty-nine and say . . . fifty-five in varying states of preservation, with completely different incomes, lives and outlooks. Her fingers hover and twitch, as if the link she's looking for is rushing at her, whizzing past at breakneck speed, and she just isn't quick enough to grab it.

She pairs her own photo with Lana's – a struggling single PR and a married, millionaire TV presenter. Juliet snorts out loud at the thought of anyone offering her a six-figure advance for the story of her life. Closing her tired itchy eyes, she takes a long drag on her cigarette. The darkness ripples, a shadow passing beneath shadows. She opens her eyes and sits very still. There is one thing that she and Lana have in common. They've both had IVF.

Very slowly she taps the photo of Jess, recalling the way she looks at Jamie, hearing her annoying throaty voice going

352

on about late lambs and little miracles. She slides Jess over to join herself and Lana.

That still leaves ancient, knicker-weaving Olga out in the cold. But it's all she's got. She stubs out her cigarette. First thing tomorrow she'll make a call.

Juliet helps Freya into the back of Heather's car, waves her off to her art workshop and hurries back inside, going over her cover story in her head. It's not perfect but it's good enough. She reaches for her phone and looks up, alert to the thump of the letterbox. She rushes into the shared hallway and kicks through the post on the mat. There it is. Finally. Her delivery from America. Excitement spins her back into her flat, tearing open the packaging as she goes. Her flesh tingles at the touch of the six shiny new keys – perfect duplicates of the ones she photographed on Gracie's keyring. All she needs now is an opportunity to use them. Imagining the satisfying slide and click as they turn in the locks of Gracie's desk, she eases the two smaller ones from the bed of polystyrene and lays them out on the table, where they sit gleaming with promise as she blocks her own number and makes the call. She moves to the window, counting the rings and readying the Scottish burr she uses whenever she needs to disguise her voice.

'Caxton Arms.' The voice is young, off hand, bored.

'Oh, good morning. Could I speak to Mrs Villiers please?'

'Who is it?'

'It's . . . personal.'

The girl yells, 'Jess! Phone!'

Juliet pictures Jess coming through from the back bar, pushing back that frizz of hair as she takes the receiver.

'Hello.'

'Mrs Villiers, I'm sorry to disturb you, I'm calling on behalf of the Selway.'

'The what?'

'The Selway fertility clinic.'

A beat of silence. 'What do you want?'

Juliet is sure she senses something besides confusion. She presses on. 'We've had a request from Durham University. They've got a PhD student who wants to interview women, anonymously of course, who have sought assisted conception in the past twelve years.'

There's a scraping sound, a door being closed. 'How did you get my name?'

'It's in our records, Mrs Villiers.'

'I've never been to the Selway. Why would they have my details?'

'I'm so sorry, I should have explained. Our parent company has recently taken over a number of leading clinics and amalgamated their databases.'

The words are barely out before Jess snaps, 'This is a gross invasion of privacy. I shall make a formal complaint,' and hangs up.

Juliet walks the room, tapping the edge of her phone against her chin, certain now. . . well almost certain, that Jess Villiers had IVF treatment too.

'Oh, God!' She drops into a chair. Even if she did, it's hardly significant. Thousands of women have trouble conceiving – what are the statistics? Something like one in six. Then there's bloody Olga Maswell. What *is* that about? She opens the catalogue, skims the biography again and flips to the introduction by the chair of trustees . . . *The Forward Gallery is honoured* . . . blah blah . . . *discovered her creative ability late in life* . . . *draws on extraordinary personal experience of life and death* . . . *powerful exploration of* . . . Oh my God! Her body goes rigid. Her eyes lose focus, the bold black signature at the bottom of the page blurring and dancing against the white of the paper. *This isn't about Olga Maswell at all.*

The doorbell buzzes. *Not now!* She's tempted to ignore it but it could be the police, with news about Ian's case. They said they'd be in touch. Cursing the broken entry phone she stomps into the shared entrance and flings open the front door. 'Oh!'

Gracie Dwyer is standing on the doorstep. She's got a nervous smile on her face and she's holding out a basket covered in a chequered cloth, looking for all the world like Little Red Riding Hood come to see Grandma.

59

'Juliet. Thank goodness.' She looks panicky and unguarded, Gracie thinks. 'I've been trying to call you.'

'I've been busy.'

Gracie twitches back the cloth on her basket. 'I did some baking with the new apprentices and I know how much Freya loves my polenta cake.' She takes a little step forward. 'Can I . . . come in?'

'I'm on a deadline.'

'Can't you spare me five minutes? Please? I've come to apologise.'

'What for?'

'The way I reacted when you . . . came to the bakery.' She glances back down the street. 'We can't talk about it out here. Can I come in?'

Juliet looks even more uncomfortable, shifty almost. 'I'm working on something confidential. For a client.'

'Please. Just for a minute.'

'Wait here.'

Gracie steps over the threshold and closes the outer door behind her. Whatever it is that Juliet doesn't want her to see, it doesn't take her long to hide it. She's back quickly, but her hands are moving jerkily as she ushers Gracie inside and her voice is stilted as she murmurs, 'Usual mess I'm afraid.'

The place stinks of smoke. Doesn't she care what she's doing to Freya's lungs? 'What happened to your vaporiser?'

'I ran out of liquid.'

Gracie wedges the basket between the dirty breakfast things on the table, shifts a pile of newspapers from a chair and sits down, wondering how best to manage this. Juliet is looking at her with something more than hurt in the set of her jaw.

'I won't keep you,' Gracie says. 'I just want you to know how much I appreciated the offer you made. It was a wonderfully kind and generous thing to do and you deserve to know why I turned you down.'

'It's fine, I—'

'Please.' Gracie looks down and rubs her thumb across her palm, pushing at her wedding ring. 'Tom and I have talked endlessly about the pros and cons of surrogacy and for a long time he was convinced it was the right way for us to go. But he already has a biological child,' she looks up sharply, 'who I totally adore. But sometimes, when he's showing her his old family albums and pointing out great grandparents and cousins that he swears look like her, I feel envious because I can't ever do that. And there's a part of me, probably a totally selfish part, that doesn't want this new child to share any more of a bond with him than it does with me.' She gazes up. 'Does that make any sense?'

Juliet nods, her face softening just a little.

'I've never admitted any of this to Tom, but I know I can trust you to keep it to yourself.'

'Course.'

'It would be such a shame for the girls if there was bad feeling between us.' She draws a long uneven breath.

'Specially with the way things are for Elsie. We found out yesterday that one of the girls in her class is having a big sleepover this weekend and the poor love hasn't been invited. So we're going down to Caxton and it would be great if Freya could come too. Jamie's having a pirate party. Jess says she'd be more than welcome.'

Juliet's head jerks back, as if the invitation has jogged something inside her. 'Oh.' She seems momentarily distracted and her sudden smile has a furtive quality to it. 'Yes. Of course, she'd love to. I. . . I'd better get Jamie a present and . . . I suppose she'll need some kind of costume.'

'Don't worry, I'll get him something from both of them and Heather can sort out a couple of eye patches and neckerchiefs.'

'If you're sure.'

'I'll pick her up on Friday night. About seven, if that's all right, then we can head off early in the morning.'

Juliet's expression is more natural now, she's almost back to her old self. 'Look,' she's saying, 'I totally understand about the surrogacy thing. It was just that . . . after everything you've done for me I was kind of hoping I'd found something I could do for you.'

Gracie lets out a heavy sigh. 'I'm so glad we've sorted it out. But I can see you want to get on.' She gets to her feet and taps the basket. 'Lots of goodies in there. Enjoy!'

Juliet closes the door behind her, her breath coming in jittery bursts. She's still angry at Gracie for doing what Gracie does, reaching out, smacking away, jerking strings. For now though, it suits her to play along.

She retrieves the hastily hidden Olga Maswell catalogue from her bag and turns straight to the introduction. She didn't imagine it. The firm sloping signature at the bottom really is Louise Harper's. Six years ago, when the Forward

Gallery put on 'Images of Old Age', Louise was the chair of their trustees.

She prints out a shot of Louise, cuts it to size and lays it beside the faces of herself, Lana and Jess, looking down at them as she rips the photo of Olga into tiny pieces.

She was totally wrong about Hugh Dugdale.

She could be totally wrong about this. But it has to be possible, doesn't it, that the 'perfect' Louise didn't excel at quite everything? She gazes into Louise's cool green eyes. Poor Tom. *Two* wives with fertility problems – that really would be bad luck.

But if she's right, what the hell was Gracie planning that involved four women who'd all had IVF? A book? An article? A TV documentary? And if she picked Jess Villiers as a potential contributor six years ago, why pretend she first met her this spring? And why make out she was looking for a PR consultant when she approached Juliet at the Hub?

It feels as if she is pointing a telescope at an intriguing patch of night sky, yet can't get the jammed lens to focus. For the image to come clear she needs to know precisely why Gracie picked these particular women. The common denominator has to be something more than just the IVF. Her eyes shift to the box of keys poking from her bag, a thrum of blood in her ears at the thought of what might lie in the locked drawer of Gracie's desk.

Pauline Bryce Diary
September 10th

I track down Mum's address in Cornwall and give her a call to tell her I'm going abroad for a while. She's not interested. She tells me Ron passed away. She's still blaming me for his angina flaring up and somehow she thinks it's my fault she's stuck down there on her own surrounded by strangers. I tell her I'm sorry but none of it would have happened if she'd just lent me the money when I asked her. She goes quiet for a second. Then she tells me not to call again.

'A sloth!' Gracie's laugh is determinedly jolly. 'I know I told Jamie I'd make him any birthday cake he wanted but I'm not sure what a sloth even looks like.' She's been rehearsing this line in the car on the way to collect Freya, a little mum-to-mum joke to ease any residual strain in her conversation with Juliet. She was right to come prepared. There's something decidedly on edge about Juliet's forced smile, a wariness to her look. Gracie drops her hand lightly onto Freya's head. 'You and Elsie will have to find me some pictures of sloths before we start.'

'You can do that, can't you, Freya?' Juliet looks down at Freya, her voice and expression still oddly stilted. 'Go fetch your bag, love. It's on your bed, all packed.'

As soon as she is gone, Juliet lowers her voice. 'Is Heather around this weekend? I thought I might pop over and ask her about the chaperoning thing, you know, have a proper chat about it.'

'They're off to Norfolk I'm afraid. It's Lyall's mum's birthday.'

'What a shame. When's she leaving?'

'Saturday morning, but give her a call. They'll only be sitting on the train.' She darts Juliet a warning look as Freya comes in dragging her overnight bag. Gracie swings it onto her shoulder and stretches out her hand. 'Come on then, we've got some baking to do.'

Juliet seems distracted again and it's not until Gracie and Freya are in the shared hallway that she comes running out, calling for a kiss. Freya turns guiltily as Juliet bends to embrace her and when Freya tries to pull away Juliet holds on as if she's loath to let her go.

'Say bye bye to Mummy,' Gracie says gaily as she opens the front door. 'And when we've done the cake how about you and Elsie draw Jamie a lovely big card?'

When they reach the car Juliet calls, 'Will you bring me

361

a slice of sloth cake, Freya? See if you can save me one of the toes.'

Gracie turns and smiles but Freya, already climbing into the back seat, doesn't seem to hear her.

60

At ten the next morning, Juliet is back in Falcon square, watching the front door of number 17 in the wing mirror of her car. At twelve minutes past eleven Heather comes out with a holdall slung across her shoulder. Juliet drops low in her seat, and gives it another fifteen minutes before she drives off and parks in the street of redbrick terraces around the corner. Returning on foot, she walks briskly up the steps and rings the doorbell, glancing back across the square as she waits. No one comes. Nerving herself, she takes out her duplicate keys, lets herself in and resets the alarm. She breathes in the familiar smells of the house – Gracie's freshness infused with sun-warmed hints of lemon, garlic and coffee and hurries upstairs, eyes darting nervously as she opens the door of Gracie's study. A copy of *Vogue* on the chaise longue. Red leather sandals kicked across the faded Persian rug. The locked drawer of her desk, waiting patiently to give up its secrets.

The small lever key fits snugly into the original brass keyhole; the stubby double-sided one, with a bit of fiddling, slides into the newer cylinder lock. She forces herself to wait, savouring, for one delicious second, the possibility that her shit life is finally about to change. She grips the handle, closes her eyes and pulls. The sweet dusty smell of old paper is inescapable. Her eyes snap open. The drawer is full of old cookbooks. The burn of disappointment feels personal, as if Gracie has set her up for yet another fall.

Even in her frustration she's careful, taking a photo of the layout before she removes the drawer. She tips out the books, checks the underside of the drawer and feels all around the cavity. Nothing. She pulls open the top drawer. The roll of fifties is still there. Who the hell leaves that much cash lying around and locks away a load of old recipes? There has to be something here that Gracie doesn't want the world to see. The room feels alive, predatory, as if it is mocking her, watching her miss something obvious.

She snatches up a yellowing paperback. On the cracked cover, a dapper man in black tie raises a glass to his readers over a crown of lamb topped with a frill of paper holders. She tosses it aside, along with a copy of the *Radiation Cookery Book*, its pages as dry and spotted as Olga Maswell's hands, and shakes open a cook's journal, pouncing on a letter tucked between a messily folded feature about store cupboard suppers and a piece about loaves baked in flowerpots.

Dear Miss Dwyer,

My late wife began collecting these recipes shortly after we were married in 1954. The shortbread was always a particular favourite of mine. As I have no family to pass the book on to I wondered if you might like it for your collection.

Yours sincerely,
Cyril Haskins

She can just imagine Gracie's fawning reply – probably attached to a freshly baked batch of Cyril's favourite sodding shortbread. She ploughs on through more home cookbooks, some sent in by viewers, others, priced in spidery pencil, picked up for a few pence in charity shops. She shakes open a magazine supplement with a photo of an iron-coiffed woman gazing rapturously at a dish of chicken in a sludgy beige sauce decorated with grapes – *Appreciative friends, an admiring husband – that's the joy of being a really good cook!* Juliet flings it down. So that's why she's ended up with neither.

She snaps off the rubber band holding together a water-damaged notebook with *My Recipes* stamped into the warped cover. A screech in her ears. Precious seconds pass before she realises it's the alarm. The front door is opening. Footsteps downstairs. She kicks off her shoes, slipping on the polished floor, tripping, nearly falling in her headlong skid along the landing. She makes for the guest room. She's sinking to the floor of the walk-in closet when she sees through the slats that she's left the bedroom door open. *Damn!* It's hot in the closet, dusty too and she needs to pee. The house creaks. She sees Tom striding down the landing. Why didn't he go to Caxton? How can Gracie stand it down there on her own with two kids?

He's coming back, talking into his phone.

'Heathrow. I need a pick-up at four.'

It's only midday. Four hours cooped up in a space three feet square but she can't risk being found. Imagine the questions, the embarrassment. *Shit!* What if he looks into Gracie's study and sees the open drawer . . . and her phone . . . and her bag. He'll call the police.

The smell of bacon and the chortle of the espresso machine drift up the stairs. Her mouth feels shrivelled, dry as the dust in the closet. She's breathing in sharp breaths and clenching every muscle in her pelvic floor in a desperate bid to stop her bladder from bursting.

Unable to hold it in a moment longer, she drops the notebook, treading on the scattered pages as she pushes open the door, dives across the room and grabs the glass vase from the chest of drawers. It's a big ugly thing, probably worth more than her car. She hobbles back to the closet tugging one-handed at the zip of her jeans. Oh God, will she make it? The release is such bliss she almost doesn't care if Tom hears her pee pounding into the vase's blue glass depths. Afterwards she leans against the wall of the closet, doing up her jeans, her cheek pressing into the wood, a throbbing black roar in her ears.

Time ticks slowly. Will Tom's fucking taxi never come? She looks at her hand. It's trembling. She hasn't eaten since yesterday. She needs nicotine. She slides back to the floor, distracting herself by gathering up the pages of the notebook. The neatly inked lists of ingredients and careful underlinings trip her into a memory of her grandmother's kitchen drawer – a rattle of flimsy tin, tarnished spoons and grease - smeared instructions reverently consulted in the run up to Christmases, birthdays and stodgy Sunday lunches. She turns through water-stained recipes for scotch eggs, stuffed tomatoes and coronation chicken – *boiled chicken meat is so much softer than roast* – and attempts to decipher the messy scrawl she spots on the backs of some of the recipes. She has to squint to make out the narrow writing with its compulsive under-linings and dashes. It's some stroppy teenager, moaning about wanting to leave home, circling her name on the flyleaf with a random pattern of stars, question marks and skulls, cross-hatching the eye sockets and the holes in the *P* of 'Pauline' and the *B* of 'Bryce' with blotchy slashes of biro. Juliet shuffles through the pages, trying to put the jumbled entries into some kind of order. Finding so many missing she gives up and reads them as they come, jumping from Pauline's struggles to get a job in London to some kind of hospital treatment.

October 3rd

I feel sick when I see the size of the syringe but I tell her I can handle it and she says, 'I don't doubt that for a minute, sweetheart. You look like you could handle most things.' Bitch. She's enjoying this, smiling at me when she tells me how much it's going to hurt. I don't care. For this kind of money I can deal with a bit of pain.

October 10th

I can't stick this greasy food. For the last few days, I've been throwing up every five minutes and I've still put on five pounds. If you actually manage to find anyone in this place who understands a word of English and you tell them you're sick of feeling like an over-pumped balloon, they just say you're getting paid so deal with it. If it wasn't for the money I'd walk.

October 17th

This morning they tell me I'm responding so well to the drugs they're going to cut down on the injections! First good news I've had since I got here.

A low murmur of possibility creeps in. Juliet reads on.

November 1st

Today's the big day. They stick me in a hospital gown and put me on a drip – more scary needles – but it isn't till they wheel me into the theatre and start pumping in the anaesthetic that it hits me – these strangers in green masks are going to be slicing me open and rooting around in my insides. I could die!

367

Now the anaesthetic's worn off it feels like they crashed a convoy of trucks in my insides. I should have asked for more money. I will next time.

November 2nd

The clinic is already hassling me to do it again. They want their cut. I've told them I'm upping my price and I won't be giving the whole lot to one client. Why should I? For the first time in my life I've got something to sell that people want to buy and I'm going to make the most of it.

Scrabbling and fumbling she finds the next entry on the back of a recipe for 'Nan's Empress Pudding'. A single word emerges from the scrawl, floating before her like vapour misting on glass. The brassy clang of the doorbell makes her jump. The front door opens and slams shut. Tom has left. She stumbles out of the closet, unable to tear her eyes from the page in front of her.

Where's the rest of it? She races to Gracie's study, shaking open every book, searching every file, desperate for anything written in that tight narrow writing. Finding nothing, she flips back through the pages she has already, going over every reference to the foreign clinic this girl was in.

'Wait,' she says aloud. She closes her eyes and reaches out through the darkness to an image creeping into her brain. A photo, a series of photos. Yes! Yes! She rushes up to Tom's attic and goes straight to Louise's camera box, digging out the snaps of Tom and Louise on that rugged Mediterranean shoreline. The blue-domed church rising above a huddle of whitewashed buildings could be any one of a thousand villages, a hundred islands, but that jut of rock in the distance, the way the bay jags deep into the cliffs feeds the frenzy in

Juliet's head, spinning her back to the time she spent at the Astarte clinic on Kos, the days she spent gazing out at that same bay through the winter drizzle, crying from the pain of the last few injections, the throbbing still so bad she could hardly move. She gazes at the figure of Louise sitting hunched on the rocks, her head tucked into her knees looking down across a sea that turns from grey to a sour vinegary green along the shore, and the shots of Tom, standing by the water, brave-faced, tight-lipped. It's as if the two of them are either praying for good news or digesting bad.

Her thoughts grind in circles. The room is hot but her flesh is cold. For a long time she sits shivering on the floor, with the diary pages spread around her. Uneasy thoughts soar away then veer close, making shapes that tantalise and billow as she reads the final diary entry over and over again.

November 3rd

The nurse comes in this morning with a huge bunch of lilies and two thousand pounds in twenties stuffed in an envelope. She says it's a bonus from my recipients for producing so many eggs. Thirty in one go – she says that's loads. I take the cash and tell her to dump the lilies. I hate that smell.

In the kitchen Juliet knocks back a glass of Tom's single malt. She's still confused, her heart pounding to a new and agitated rhythm, but she's certain of one thing now. She's found the missing link between herself, Lana, Jess and Louise.

61

'Get off!'

'Mum! He's cheating!'

Gracie surveys the choppy sea of yelling, jostling, testosterone-charged boys, all wearing stripy T-shirts and curly eyeliner moustaches, wondering, not for the first time, what it would be like to bring up a son. Pumped up on hot dogs, crisps and fizzy drinks, they're running relays with coins balanced on outstretched rubber swords, trying to get them into the treasure chests lined up by the hedge without dropping them on the way. It's chaos. Freya, after half an hour of timidity, has joined in and now she's speeding ahead, holding out her sword with steady hands, and it looks like she's going to make it to the treasure chest without dropping any of her coins.

'Yes!' Gracie punches the air.

Elsie tugs at her arm. 'I don't like this game, Mummy. Tell Freya she's got to play with me.'

'No, darling. Why don't you run inside and fetch the paper plates for me?'

As Jess wades in to announce the winning team, a fight breaks out over Jamie's new football. To cause a diversion

Gracie whips the cover off the cake and shouts, 'Cake time!' She was up until nearly midnight decorating it and she has to admit she's really rather pleased with the way it's turned out.

The boys come running as she lights the candles. A heart-skip of happiness when Jamie tumbles to a stop beside the table and breaks into a grin. The glow of pleasure lasts all of five seconds before the football arcs across the beer garden and smashes into the sloth's furrily frosted face, hitting it with just enough top spin to take out its carefully crafted toes and leafy, chocolate-coated branch in a hiss of smoking wax.

Juliet pours herself another whisky. With a trembling finger she isolates the shots of herself and Jess Villiers from the four photos in front of her. Gulping the whisky, she flicks through the pictures on her phone of Matt and Jamie in the snow, and moves on to the ones of the dance mums spilling out of Lynda Burton's. With a sick sensation in her gut she picks out her own face in the crowd beneath the Christmas lights. Uncaring of discovery, she logs on to Gracie's computer and reads every email from the US studio she can find, jotting down dates, working backwards in time, her senses firing and misfiring; something, nothing, clarity, doubt, ragged shrieks of insight jerking and dancing to the cries in her head, rising to a screaming crescendo of questions that only Gracie Dwyer can answer.

In a sudden wild fury she snatches up the photos and the diary, grabs her bag and stumbles out into the night.

Her car. Where did she put her car? Not in the square. A fox struts past her unafraid, barely curious. She's almost sure she left it down here, past these dustbins. Yes, she can see it. The sound of running feet. She's not scared. Those hoodies on the corner can fuck right off. She powers on, head held high.

She tumbles into the driver's seat. Her fingers jab 'Caxton' into the sat nav, fumbling and deleting until she gets it right. A voice of calm fills the car, telling her where to go, what to do. Spatters of light in the darkness, shuttered shops, a sliver of moon appearing and disappearing above the high-rises, bitterness on her tongue.

She used to love London at night, the feral restlessness, the dank alleyways brought alive by glimmers of neon, the promise of surprise. Tonight she sees nothing but the road ahead. She hits the motorway: bridges slashed with lines of white, slipways lit dim orange, shudders of air as trucks overtake, an accident on the south-bound carriageway, sweeps of blue and red throwing light through chaos. Light, dark. Doubt, certainty. Fury, calm. Pieces of a picture rising up, taking shape, falling away. She has no idea how long she's been driving – two hours? three? – when the Caxton Arms appears on her right, a single light burning in an upstairs room. She slows for a moment then accelerates on through the village, peering into hedges and down farm tracks looking for the turnoff. A swing of the wheel, a crunch of stones and she's bumping through darkness, ducking instinctively as overhanging branches scrape the roof. She skids to a stop. A light comes on in the caravan. Gracie's face appears at the window. Juliet throws herself out of the car and runs across the grass.

Gracie comes to the door, fastening her dressing gown. 'Juliet! You nearly gave me a heart attack.'

Juliet pushes her way inside, forcing Gracie back. 'I know what you've done.'

'Then you're one up on me.' There's laughter in Gracie's voice.

'Don't laugh at me! Don't you fucking laugh at me!'

'Juliet? What's wrong?'

'You bitch. Everything's got shittier since you came back

into my life. It's *you*, you're doing this to me. Christ, I bet it was you who tampered with your bike. You wanted me to have an accident!'

'What?' Gracie is looking at her open-mouthed with horror. 'Why would I do anything so sick?'

'Because you *are* sick. That's how you get your kicks, controlling people, luring them close then pushing them away.'

'Juliet, what on earth's got into you?'

'Where is she? Where's my daughter?'

'Sleeping. It's gone midnight.'

Juliet thrusts her aside and wrenches open the bedroom door. Gracie hisses from behind her, 'Juliet, please. Keep your voice down. I'm going to make you some black coffee.'

In the watery pink glow from the ballerina lamp Juliet sees Freya sleeping soundly, her head beside Elsie's on the pillow, her hand resting on the rump of the little puppy who stirs and lifts its head as she enters. Juliet sags against the wall, head in her hands, close to tears. She stumbles from the room, furious to see Gracie sneaking an opened bottle of wine into the cupboard above the sink. Gracie turns quickly, a nervous pursing of her lips as she picks up a steaming cup and holds it out.

'I don't want fucking coffee.' Juliet grabs the cup, empties it into the sink and reaches down the bottle from the cupboard, pulling out the cork with her teeth. 'I want answers.'

Gracie watches Juliet slosh the wine into the cup, glances at the door of the children's room and says in the measured voice she uses when Elsie throws a tantrum, 'Why don't we go outside so we don't wake the girls?'

Quickly she lights a jam jar lantern, holding it by a loop of string as she hurries ahead. Cup in one hand, bottle in the other, Juliet stumbles behind her, past the shaggy mesh of willows to the jetty, a finger of black pointing across the moonlit water to the dark serration of the far bank.

Gracie bends to light the other lanterns dotted on the decking. 'All right. Now tell me why you're so upset.'

'You tracked me down. I want to know why.'

Gracie turns in the flickering candlelight and stares at her as if she's mad or dangerous. 'What are you talking about?'

'That's why you turned up at Lynda Burton's.'

Gracie gives a sorrowful shake of her head.

Incensed, Juliet takes out her phone and shoves the picture in her face. 'There!' She stabs the screen with her finger. 'You took this photo of me last winter. Months before you moved to Falcon Square. It was on the flash drive you keep on your keys.'

Gracie blinks, not at the screen but at Juliet.

'You can't deny it.'

The words come out in a shriek, making Gracie jump. She takes the phone, dabbing nervously at the screen to enlarge the picture. 'I . . . I can see that that's Dawn and yes . . . I suppose that could be you. It's hard to see.'

Juliet snatches the phone back, and tosses the hair out of her eyes, her voice erupting. 'You know damn well it's me!'

Gracie glances towards the caravan and steps behind one of the deckchairs. 'Juliet, please. If it is, there's no mystery. Before we moved to Clapton I checked out the local schools and parks and shops, and yes, I took photos. It's how I work. You know that. I had a look at a couple of dance schools and Lynda's seemed to be the friendliest.'

'No!' Juliet lurches forward. 'You moved to Clapton because of me.'

Gracie shrinks back. 'We moved there to be near to the chapel. Ask Tom.' Her eyes dart to the phone in Juliet's

374

hand. 'Why . . . why don't we walk up to where we can get a signal and give him a call?'

'Don't do this! You wangled the move *and* you went to Lynda's looking for me.'

'No,' Gracie's voice grows thin and pleading. '*You* were the one who approached *me*. In Lynda's kitchen.'

'Just like you went to the Hub to find me so you could pretend you wanted us to work together. We both know that was bullshit.'

'I was at the Hub looking for someone to do my PR. I talked to you because I was impressed by your seminar.'

'Bullshit!' Juliet refills her glass and stares at Gracie, triumphant. 'You'd already signed up Daley.'

Gracie shakes her head and draws a long, uneven breath. 'He'd done a couple of jobs for me but we didn't have a formal contract. Not then. My publisher liked what he was doing, so in the end it . . . it was easier to stick with him.'

There's such fear and bewilderment in Gracie's voice that for a moment Juliet's confusion returns. Maybe she *has* got this wrong. She drains the wine in her cup, refills it and drags her hand through her hair. It had all seemed so clear in the car. Now it's getting blurred and distorted.

'No!' Anger, hot and electric, spurs her on. Gracie is a liar. She can prove it. 'You told Tom you first went to Caxton this spring.'

'Yes.'

'So why have you got a Caxton Arms bar menu from *six years ago* in your files? And why were you taking photos of Matt and Jamie Villiers last Christmas?' She's back on her phone searching for the shots, poking and pressing, shoving the screen back into Gracie's face.

Gracie takes the handset, peers at the pictures and says in a small trembling voice, 'That's Tom's brother-in-law, Ben, and his daughter Ellie in their garden in Bristol. We went down there for Christmas.' She drops the phone onto the deckchair and pulls back another couple of steps. 'Juliet, please, you're scaring me.'

Juliet lunges forward, beating at her head with the heel of her hand, air hissing through her teeth. 'I'm giving you a chance to tell me the truth and you, you just go on lying and lying because you think I'm stupid. But I'm not. What about Lana Laughton!'

Gracie swallows, her voice placatory as if she wants to please but isn't sure how. 'The . . . the TV presenter?'

'Why did you go to her book launch?'

'It was years ago, I . . . I think her publicist sent me an invitation.'

'Don't lie!' Juliet's voice rises another octave, shrill and unsteady. 'You went because she had her kid Tybalt with a donor egg.'

'What?' Gracie closes her eyes, her head shaking, as if she's trying desperately to make sense of Juliet's words. 'I . . . I don't think that's what she says in her book.'

'Oh, come on. Two years of failed IVF, then at forty-four she goes off on "holiday" and comes back pregnant. Of course it was with a bloody donor egg.'

'Even if that's true I don't see what—'

'*She* had a baby with a donor egg.' Juliet spits out each word then pauses, never taking her eyes from Gracie's. 'Just like me.'

Gracie raises her hands. 'How could I know that you—?'

'And just like Jess Villiers.'

'Did *Jess* tell you that?'

'It's obvious. Her and her "little miracle".'

Gracie's head goes on shaking. 'Juliet, you're twisting facts, seeing things that aren't there—'

'No!' Juliet can hear Ian's voice now, growling beneath Gracie's. Ian trying to manipulate her. Ian telling her she's mad, deranged, fantasising. She pushes her hands to her ears. 'Don't say that! It's you. You're the liar! You lied to Tom about your US deal.'

'Why *would* I?'

'So he'd have to sell the Wharf House and you could buy this place and cosy up to Jess Villiers.'

'Look. I'll take you to the doctor on Monday. We'll explain that things are getting on top of you. Don't worry. If he thinks you need to rest or to go into hospital, Freya can stay with us for as long as it takes.'

Juliet feels her head emptying, as if the steady rush of the river is sluicing away the strange connections and flashes of certainty. Fear rises in her belly, fear that it's happening again, fear that it will be like last time when they parted her from her baby. But she'd fought it, she'd got well, she'd got Freya back. And this isn't like before. Though it's hard to feel sane when her head is full of dark dirty fragments that won't hold or settle. Her head is floating, she's reaching for a broken memory, trying to connect the pieces. Her voice slides into hysteria, screaming out the words before the thought dissolves. 'It's not "R" for "Rejects". It's "R" for "Recipients"!'

Gracie is still edging away. 'Juliet. Please. I don't know where you're going with this but whatever you think I've done you're making a terrible mistake.'

Gracie takes another step backwards. She looks behind her, sees she's right at the end of the jetty and glances past Juliet, as if hoping for rescue. Juliet, taller and stronger, staggers forward, blocking her escape.

'That's what we are – me, Jess Villiers, Lana Laughton and *Louise Harper*, oh yes let's not forget *Louise*. We all conceived our kids with donor eggs!' The words feel rubbery in her mouth. 'Six years ago you tracked us all down,' she stabs at Gracie with her finger. 'You filled up one of your little files with places you could find us, then you backed off. Now you've come after me and Jess again and I'm not . . .' she takes a teetering step forward '. . . *not* leaving here till you tell me why!'

Gracie's gaze strays into the darkness, fixing on something downriver that Juliet can't see and then, as if she's been struck from behind, she crumples to her knees and pushes her fist to her mouth. 'Oh God.' She's shivering, rocking backwards and forwards, her words coming out in fractured rasps. 'I had to . . . I had to find you.'

Juliet stands gaping, dumbfounded, struggling to process what she's hearing. When she finds the strength to speak, the words erupt in slow disjointed bursts. 'What the fuck is wrong with you?'

'It's not me.' Gracie folds forward, trembling and crying. 'Oh God, I wish it was. It's Elsie. I did it for Elsie. She . . . she's sick.'

'She looks all right to me.' Juliet's tongue feels thick now and dry. She gulps a mouthful of wine from the bottle. 'What's wrong with her?'

'They told us . . . when she was tiny that . . . that by time she was eight or nine she'd need a bone marrow transplant and her best hope of a match was a sibling.' Gracie's voice breaks on the words. 'So I started looking for kids born from the same donor, bribing nurses, clerks, brokers, paying whatever it took to get the recipients' names. I knew it was illegal but I didn't care. I was ready to do anything to find a match. That's when I found you at the Hub.' She lifts her drooping head. Juliet sees the tears glittering in her eyes. 'Then a miracle happened, Elsie's body started fighting back. She was going to be all right. But at the end of last year the fight-back stopped. So I started making contact with you and Jess again, hoping that when the time came you would know Elsie and care enough about her to want to help her.'

Juliet is still blocking Gracie's escape, still trapping her at the end of the jetty. She wants so much to believe this story but there's something not right – something she almost caught that's now slipping from her grasp. Then it comes to her, bobbing up through the dross and confusion. She grabs Gracie's shoulder and jerks her brutally to her feet.

'What about this?' She pulls the battered cook's journal from her jacket, the loose pages spilling out as she waves it in Gracie's face. 'Who the hell is Pauline Bryce?'

There's a terrible moment of silence. Juliet can see Gracie's shock in the jolt of her body, the soundless mouthing of her lips.

'Oh God.' Gracie throws her hands to her head. 'That's what I've been asking myself, every minute of every day since that notebook arrived in the post. I thought it was just old recipes . . . from a viewer and then . . . then I read those horrible diary entries . . . that girl who set out to make as much money as she could from selling her eggs.' Disgust contorts Gracie's face as she eases the book from Juliet's fingers and bends to pick up the pages. 'It's like the stalker is inside my skin, reading my thoughts. Whatever happens in my life, however private or painful, he's in there, poking it, prodding it, twisting it. Maybe this Pauline Bryce is Elsie's biological mother, maybe she isn't, maybe she's the tissue match Elsie needs, or maybe the sick fuck wrote it himself, made it all up just to taunt me.' Her tears fall freely as she tosses the notebook down.

In the guttering light from the lanterns, Juliet feels the click and slide of fragments fitting together. She's not crazy. She's not a fantasist, her instincts were right. Gracie did track her down. Only it was because Gracie needed her, has always needed her. Freya and Elsie are biological half-siblings. Children of the same donor. This time she doesn't hold back.

'Oh, Gracie. I'm so sorry.' She struggles to shape the words. 'Don't worry. We'll sort this out. We'll get Freya tested. We'll see if she's a match.'

'I can't lose her, I can't,' Gracie sobs. Emotion shakes her body. She goes limp, falling forward into Juliet's arms, a fragrant weight of grief, and they weep together. Juliet strokes her hair and feels strong for her. She can stop Gracie's pain, she can save Elsie's life. What deeper bond could there be between two friends?

'Say you forgive me,' Gracie murmurs. 'Please say you forgive me.'

'Of course I do. If it was Freya I'd have done the same.'

Shaken by a fresh wave of sobs, Gracie's body shifts. Juliet totters backwards. Slipping and swaying she reaches for Gracie's arms, grateful for the sudden strength of her grip. For a moment they stagger together, Juliet's sandals slithering on the wet boards and Gracie holding her so close she feels the silky slide of her cheek, the soft warmth of her breath and the sudden twist of a hip that throws Juliet off balance. She braces her toes on the edge of the jetty. Gracie's fingers are loosening. Juliet is tipping backwards towards the water, clutching at air as their bodies slip apart.

She sees Gracie's face as she falls, gazing down at her, sweet and impassive in the flicker of candlelight, then a distortion and a darkening as the icy wet closes over her, a wash of shock and betrayal. She tries to struggle but her body, numb and disconnected, refuses to respond. Water fills her mouth, sucking her down into soupy fronds of billowing black as Gracie's lies and manipulations spin through her head, meshing into the net that reached out, caught her and tugged her in with its slow steady pull. Why? Why did she do it? In a sudden burst of clarity she sees Gracie's name on the amendment to her will. Her hands claw in desperation towards the shimmer of the moon. She bobs and rises but her limbs, heavy as liquid lead, drag her back. Dashed hopes and joys untasted, grudges, rejections and envies explode inside her and then, as the river claims her, the broken pieces wash through her, and out of her, until all that is left is love for her daughter; her baby, her Freya. The last breath she takes is a lungful of regret.

Gracie lifts the jam jar lantern and watches the paleness of Juliet slip away, waiting patiently until the last of her has dropped into darkness and the only sound from the river is the whisper of the current swirling towards the distant weir.

62

Gracie Dwyer Diary
August 2016

*I don't usually underestimate people but boy did I
underestimate Juliet Beecham. Still, given the circum-
stances, I think I rose to the occasion pretty well,
though it was a close-run thing getting the tranquillisers
into that last bottle of wine – her face when she saw
me trying to 'hide' it! And I'm still reliving the nightmare moment when she produced my old diary.*

*She must have been in my drawers, my emails, my
texts, but it still took some pretty sharp deduction
to get quite so near to the truth – even blaming me
for sabotaging my own bike! Considering all the
doctored e-liquid she'd been inhaling, combined with
her anti-depressants and painkillers, plus those delicious 'meals for one' and endless bottles of Sancerre
laced with a little something to keep her twitchy, I'm
amazed her brain was even functioning. I'm just
relieved it made her feel ropey enough to start
worrying about Freya's future. Imagine if I'd had to*

kill her before she'd got round to amending her will! All these months of planning only to have my big picture goal snatched away at the final hurdle. It doesn't bear thinking about.

I know I'm obsessed with timing but tonight I think I got it spot on. I could have cut the whole thing short and gone for the tissue match sob story as soon as she mentioned donor eggs, but that way I'd never have found out just how much she'd pieced together. And there was something utterly fascinating about listening to her circling the facts, coming so close, yet never quite making that final leap of understanding. She'd have got there in the end, though. I'm bloody sure of that.

I'm so careful about identifying potential problems and working out strategies to deal with them it was quite a novelty to be faced with something totally unexpected, but not knowing what the hell Juliet was going to throw at me next definitely upped my game. Maybe Gran was right – maybe I should have gone on the stage. But why go to all the effort of getting into character and giving the kind of performance I gave tonight when the audience knows it's all an act? Though now and again I suppose it would be good to get some feedback – a clap on the back, a bit of recognition or even a chance to chat things over with someone who understands. But that's where the diaries come in – my own private record of all those small steps taken and targets achieved. It still tears me up to see how much damage that burst radiator did to the entries I wrote in Gran's old cookbook. Good thing I'd learned the 'Use What You've Got to Get What You Want' six-point guide to a new life off by heart:

1 – *Fix your 'Big Picture Goal'.*
2 – *Break it down into small targets – the pathway to your dream.*
3 – *Plan small steps to reach each target.*
4 – *Use what you've got to take the first step. (If that doesn't work, take a smaller step.)*
5 – *Plan A might fail. Always have a Plan B standing by.*
6 – *Keep a record of what you're doing. (Use it to keep your plans on track and to remind yourself how far you've come.)*

There! Word-perfect, even after eighteen years!

It was because of point six that I've always kept that first diary within easy reach. Tom's not the only one who needs a bit of validation when things go wrong. If anyone found it I'd always thought I could pass it off as a home cookbook sent in by a viewer. I've learned my lesson on that one! From now on it's staying locked away down here with all the others, safe from prying eyes and household disasters. Otherwise what was the point of paying those Sicilian builders to incorporate a 'hidey hole for my secret ingredients' in the base of my lovely new wood-fired oven?

I'm glad they made the space big enough to take Gran's old cake tin. It's amazing how calming it feels to run my fingers over the familiar scratches, dents and pitted views of Edinburgh castle, specially at moments like this when I'm all het up. I wonder sometimes if I ought to see someone about this need I have to hold on to concrete things. But pulling off the lid, taking out the diaries and little mementos I've collected over the years, feeling the rub of the textures and contours helps me to stay centred. Besides, every time I do it I notice something new. Like the fat blocky letters spelling out 'Pauline Grace Bryce' in the front of Gran's cookbook. Looking at them now I realise I pressed the pen so hard I ripped the paper. Maybe even back then, on some deep subconscious level, I realised that my name was one of the things holding me back. Dropping the 'Pauline', ditching Ron's surname and going back to using my real dad's name was one of the smartest moves I ever made. Gracie Dwyer. It's got a real ring to it – a name you can trust.

But seeing this single coral earring lying in the tin unnerves me even now. OK, so sending myself its twin saw off that slut Alicia Sandelson, but sending myself anonymous packages was always going to be tempting fate. What if it had goaded the real stalker back into action? In my defence I only ever did it three times – twice if you count that business with Brown Bear's eye and the emoticon card as two parts of the same step, and both times were real emergencies. But I'm never EVER going to risk it again. Especially with Jamieson still around – I really didn't like the way he looked at me during our meeting with Elsie's headmistress. But as soon as that social worker . . . what was her name . . . Beverley Mills started banging on about ethnicity and getting all bouncy and eager about fast-track fostering and bumping us up the adoption queue I knew I had to do something to slow things down. Christ, I still break out in a sweat at the thought of being landed with some stranger's kid. And as for Juliet – one of my own recipients – offering to carry Tom's surrogate child and pass herself off as its biological mother. The irony! If I hadn't been so surprised I'd have laughed. And the worst thing is she honestly expected me to be grateful.

I'm leaving my copies of her keys in the tin but I'll take the ones for Ian's flat back to London. If he kicks up trouble over the next few weeks they might come in useful. It's hard to believe that I thought I'd have a problem getting Juliet and Ian at each other's throats but they were both so bitter and mistrustful it hardly took any effort at all. I almost feel sorry for him. For all his faults, that man's no paedophile. But I had to stop him getting custody of Freya somehow. All right, so the way I did it smacked of laziness, a lack of imagination even. But why bother coming up with something new when a fresh twist on a tried and tested method will do the trick?

Sadly I don't have anything to remind me of Jean Jaques Mersaud. I've even deleted his email account – all those messages he sent to Tom, pushing his buttons as only I know how, telling him how much he wanted the Tom Whittaker architectural vision for the amazing old chapel he'd found in Clapton. And all it took was a bit of sobbing and gazing into the distance over a bowl of Stefano's pasta for Daphne to come up trumps convincing Tom we had to move. That woman is so suggestible, so ridiculously easy to manipulate. OH MY GOD! It must have been Juliet who spilled the beans about her affair with Burridge. I don't know why I'm surprised, those two never did see eye to eye. Still, it will be nice to get Daph back into my life, I've really missed her.

And all these lists – the absentee landlords and old dodderers whose identities I used to send in objections to the conversion of the chapel – Juliet really believed she'd found evidence of a stitch-up! But you have to hand it to her, she was damn good at what she did. And this one – the full list of my recipients – thirteen women who bought my eggs and gave birth to a child that was mine. Getting hold of their details was risky but if you target the support staff at these unregulated clinics you can always find a disgruntled admin assistant or a hard-done-by cleaner who's willing – for a price – to dig through the files for a name. And once that bored, flat-eyed doctor had looked up from his notes and told me my chances of producing another viable egg were zero, what choice did I have?

And here – once I'd weeded out the no-hopers and the ones who lived in places I didn't want to go – are the four who made the final shortlist. The four carefully selected names that tripped so shockingly off Juliet's tongue. Lana Laughton was always going to come bottom on account of those teenage twins from her first marriage – who needs that kind of hassle? But it's strange to think that if I hadn't seen Ian's violent outburst at the Hub I might have settled for becoming the second Mrs Murray, loving "step-mum" to baby Freya six years ago. Even stranger to think that back then, before the book and the series took off so spectacularly, I wasn't confident that I had what it took to worm my way into the life of a woman like Louise, let alone become the one to live it.

But there it is, Louise Harper's name, scored through with a stroke of ink. Time to score out Juliet Beecham too. Check!

Poor Juliet. It's Tom's fault she had to die. I was quite content for Elsie to be my one and only until he betrayed me. The way I see it, cheating on your spouse is like taking a life. When you've done it once, you've got far fewer qualms about doing it again. And despite all his whingeing and wailing and protestations of love, there's still nothing to stop him leaving me for some *fucking little whore and taking Elsie with him. But from now on, whatever Tom does, I'll always have Freya. A blood child of my own, to keep and to care for. A daughter who is legally and permanently mine.*

And just in case something goes wrong I've got my Plan B – Jamie Villiers – standing by. But with Juliet dead (granted a little earlier than planned) and Ian out of the running for custody, I don't foresee any last-minute problems with Plan A. Still, when it comes to big picture goals I know better than to get complacent. This little plastic tube that once held a few strands of saffron is a stark reminder of that. When I mentioned it in this diary entry I wrote on another hot summer night five years ago, I never thought I'd have to go through that kind of trouble and trauma ever again. It just goes to show how wrong you can be.

August 4th

I drop in on Louise this morning and manage to steal two more of her sleeping tablets. That makes four. Should be enough. I don't want it looking like she took an overdose. It takes ages to grind them into powder but even with all the seasoning I'm using I'm petrified she'll taste the bitterness. When Tom's away she usually goes to bed around ten so at nine I go down with three extra spicy mini samosas – one spinach, one lentil, one beef – all hot and crispy on a plate. And then I sit with her, encouraging her to finish them up so she can give me a proper verdict. I even bring a pen and paper! The self-obsessed cow actually thinks I give a shit what she thinks about my food.

Instead of going to bed when I leave, she hangs around in the kitchen. I can see her from the roof,

*faffing about folding washing and emptying the dish-
washer. When she does finally go to bed I have to wait
for nearly an hour before she turns off her light and
by that time the wasp is so angry I can actually feel
it buzzing and thumping against the plastic tube in
my pocket. Then I have to give it another half an hour
to make sure she's well and truly under before I shin
down the drainpipe onto their terrace. Jesus, I'm never
doing that again. Half way down I think the whole
gutter's going to come crashing off the wall and take
me with it. So I jump the last bit, trip over, and stub
my toe on some ugly little statue. Thank God Louise
is too zonked out to hear the racket. Luckily she always
sleeps with the window open so no problem getting
into her room, and there she is, totally out of it, her
mouth obligingly open with this little trickle of drool
dribbling down her chin. I must remember that. It'll
cheer me up when everyone starts going on about how
cool and elegant she was. After that it only takes a
couple of seconds to tweezer the wasp into her throat,
close those pink perfect lips and let myself out the
front door. Now all I've got to do is hold my nerve.*

63

It's a year to the day since Juliet died, a year since I last wrote in my diary, nearly two since there's been a peep out of my stalker and exactly three hundred and eighty-four days since my over-hyped brain imagined a threat in the arrival of some perfectly innocuous good luck card, graffitied slogan, garden ornament or piece of road kill. For a while after we moved to Falcon Square I really was getting paranoid. I think it must have been the stress of juggling so many projects, but at times it honestly felt as if Louise was dipping into my darkest dreams and working hand in hand with my stalker, trying to push me over the edge to punish me for selling the Wharf House. Crazy I know, but that's how it felt. And the worst thing was there was absolutely nothing I could do about it and nobody I could tell.

Anyway, that's all over now and I thought I'd mark this new and truly contented phase in my life by starting this brand new diary.

In the end we let Freya decide for herself which room she wanted. She went for the smaller one with the view of the garden. Good choice. We've had a lot of fun decorating it, making it truly hers and she's settling down well at St Mathilda's. She's such a resilient little thing I haven't needed any of those books I bought about helping children to deal with bereavement. In fact she hardly ever mentions her past life at all.

The police were incredibly sympathetic when I told them about Juliet turning up at Caxton drunk in the middle of the night, the struggle I had putting her to bed and the panic I felt when I woke up next morning to find her gone. The coroner returned an open verdict. But what with Juliet's history of depression, the cocktail of drugs and alcohol they found in her bloodstream and her drowning so soon after appointing me Freya's guardian, the police think her death was part of a carefully premeditated plan to kill herself. I've thought about that a lot. OK, so maybe she didn't actually hurl herself off the jetty, but perhaps there's an element of truth in the suicide theory. Let's face it, she wasn't exactly taking care of herself – all that smoking, drinking and pill-popping. In some ways it's a comfort to think that on some deep and selfless level she wanted Freya to have the kind of life that she could never give her.

I could have done with a few more weeks to acclimatise Elsie to the idea of a new sibling but she's getting there, albeit slowly. It's such a help that we'd started talking to her about adoption and that Freya was so much a part of our lives in the weeks leading up to the accident. As for Tom, he adores Freya – loves that she's so sporty. But I'm her sole legal guardian.

*As I explained to him, that's obviously the way Juliet
wanted it, otherwise she'd have named us both in her
will. When I told him I'd had no idea she'd put my
name down he just laughed and said that Juliet had
always been obsessed with me. Which isn't entirely
fair. I saw the way she used to look at him.*

*Today also marks another (and for me even more
important) milestone in the life of our little family.
Stella and Todd are coming to lunch so I'm making
Todd's favourite goat's cheese and fennel tarts and
listening to what has become the soundtrack to this
blissful summer: the whack of bat against ball, the
girls laughing as they run across the garden, Tallulah
barking at their heels and Tom shouting encouragement
– these days we're the stars of the pub rounders team
and he's determined to keep it that way. The sky is
blue, the grass is green and my daughters, my beautiful
healthy, happy daughters, are leaping and tumbling in
the sunshine and just when I think things can't get
any better I hear a little voice calling, 'Mummy! I got
a rounder!'*

*It's Freya! She's grinning at me and waving the bat.
My heart soars. Till now she's been calling me Gracie.
I feel so blessed! That's the doorbell. If I'm lucky it
will be the postman with the proofs of my new book
on wood-fired cookery.*

Gracie locks her diary away and runs downstairs to answer
the door. It *is* the postman and he *does* have the proofs of
her new book. They smile and exchange waves as he heads
off down the path. She tucks the parcel under her arm and
turns back inside, ripping open the official invitation to
Sally's wedding. Elsie and Freya are going to be bridesmaids.
She makes a mental note to call the dressmaker and flicks

through the assorted bills and circulars. There's a postcard. She glances at the picture and falls back like a helpless drunk, crushed by a fear more powerful than any emotion she has ever felt before: passion, envy, rage, grief, terror. It's a photo of the jetty at Caxton.

Unable to breathe she turns it over. There's no message. Just a quotation printed beneath the logo for Wise Words Cards – *Fear is the price that conscience pays to guilt* – and a name and address typed in ten-point Courier New:

```
Pauline Bryce
17, Falcon Square
London
E5
```

'Who?' she whispers aloud. 'Who are you?'

The hallway is too hot, the sunlight too bright, the clink of the latch and the trill of laughter too loud. She lifts her eyes and with a terrible lurch in her gut she sees Stella and Todd, arm in arm, coming up the path.

Acknowledgements

I'd like to thank Sarah Curtis, Beth Holgate, Charlotte Blundy, Maria O'Neill, Richard Skinner and my lovely classmates at the Faber Academy for invaluable thoughts on early drafts. Lily Jones aka Lily Vanilli for lighting a spark, my wonderful editor Sarah Hodgson for her guidance and enthusiasm. Lucy Dauman, Felicity Denham, Finn Cotton and the team at HarperCollins for their tireless support, my brilliant agent Stephanie Thwaites at Curtis Brown who had faith in Gracie from the first. Rebecca Ritchie who did a fantastic job while Stephanie was on maternity leave and my ever patient husband, James who makes everything possible.